## PRAISE FOR
### *DAUGHTER OF THE SWORD*

"A noir modern Tokyo overwhelmed by the shadows of Japanese history . . . a compelling multifaceted vision of a remarkable culture, and a great page-turner."
—Stephen Baxter, author of *Stone Spring*

"*Daughter of the Sword* really captured my imagination. The interweaving of historical Japanese adventure and modern police procedural, Tokyo-style, caught me from two unexpected directions." —Jay Lake, author of *Endurance*

"Effortlessly combines history and legend with a modern procedural . . . will have you staying up late to finish it."
—Diana Rowland, author of *Sins of the Demon*

"An authentic and riveting thrill ride through both ancient and modern Japan. Definitely a winner."
—Kylie Chan, author of *Heaven to Wudang*

"Bein's gripping debut is a meticulously researched, highly detailed blend of urban and historical fantasy set in modern Tokyo. . . . Bein's scrupulous attention to verisimilitude helps bring all the settings to life, respectfully showcasing Japan's distinctive cultures and attitudes."
—*Publishers Weekly* (starred review)

"A great police procedural urban fantasy that deftly rotates between Mariko in present-day Japan and other warriors in past eras." —Genre Go Round Reviews

*continued . . .*

# DAUGHTER
## OF THE
# SWORD

**A NOVEL OF THE FATED BLADES**

# STEVE BEIN

A ROC BOOK

ROC
Published by the Penguin Group
Penguin Group (USA), 375 Hudson Street,
New York, New York 10014, USA

USA | Canada | UK | Ireland | Australia | New Zealand | India | South Africa | China

Penguin Books Ltd., Registered Offices: 80 Strand, London WC2R 0RL, England
For more information about the Penguin Group visit penguin.com.

Published by Roc, an imprint of New American Library, a division of Penguin
Group (USA). Previously published in a Roc trade paperback edition.

First Roc Mass Market Printing, September 2013

ALWAYS LEARNING                                                    **PEARSON**

# BOOK ONE

**HEISEI ERA, THE YEAR 22**

**(2010 CE)**

I

The sword in Fuchida Shūzō's bed was the oldest known of her kind, and he loved listening to her song.

A *tachi* in the *shinogi-zukuri* style, she was forged by the great master Inazuma. She lay now on Fuchida's bed, nestled in his black silk sheets and framed in a rectangle of sunlight. The arch of her back was as graceful as any woman's. Small waves ran the length of her blade, no bigger than clover petals, never wavering more than a centimeter from her razor edge. When he lay this close to her, Fuchida could see the grain of her forging, faint silver lines like wood grain in her *shinogi-ji*, the flat surface between her edge and curving spine. A train rattled by on the Marunouchi Line, distant enough that he could barely hear it, close enough that it drowned out the subtle ring his thumbnail made when he traced it along her ridge. The early evening rush of Tokyo traffic murmured through the open bedroom window, spoiling any chance of hearing her song.

He rose, careful not to disturb her, and walked naked to the window to close it. Beyond the glass stretched the crazed labyrinth of Shinjuku, a werewolf in urban form, biding its time until nightfall to unleash its full madness. Businesses stacked three and four high wallpapered their steel-and-glass faces with signs of neon and animated LEDs: pachinko parlors and noodle shops, nightclubs and strip clubs, Nova language schools and Sumitomo cash machines, shot bars and smartphone dealers. And somewhere beyond all that, there was a second Inazuma. Fuchida had spent fifteen years searching for it, and at last it was within reach. He could go and claim it at any moment. A voice deep within him cried out for it. He needed to get it now.

He silenced the voice through sheer force of will. This was no time to start indulging impatience. He knew where that road would lead. Better to close the window and close off his longing for the second sword.

The air blowing in was cool at this height, twenty-two stories above the street, and the heavy scent of moisture promised evening rain. Fuchida slid the window shut, watching his reflection shift in the glass. In this light he could see only his darkest parts: long black hair, eyes like black coffee, shadows under his pectoral muscles. The blues and blacks and purples of his tattoos traced a random spiderwebbing pattern down to the black triangle of pubic hair. There were darker parts to him, features not visible to those outside the window. Throats sliced open, women beaten, enemies buried in the concrete foundations of high-rises and public schools. Dark desires and darker deeds did not reflect in glass.

He looked down at his tattoos. Dragons and spiders crawled up his arms. A fiery buddha dominated his chest, sword and *vajra* in hand. The dragons and buddhas shed tears, every teardrop marking a kill. There were so many now that he'd lost count. He insisted on the traditional method for every tattoo, grateful for the discipline the hooks and hammers had drilled into him. With the second Inazuma so close, he needed every bit of that discipline not to rush out and grab it. It was said that the Inazuma blades changed the course of history. There was no telling what Fuchida could do with two of them.

For all the years he'd spent hunting the second sword, even Fuchida himself hadn't known exactly how he would use it. Gut instinct had long assured him that with two Inazumas he could carve out his place in history, but it was only a few weeks ago that he finally understood how. It could only be fate: after fifteen years of searching, nothing; then, as soon as he discovered how to make his mark on the world, the second blade suddenly revealed itself to him. He and the swords were meant to be together. It could be no other way.

He slipped back into bed with his beloved. She was beautiful beyond description. If not for that second sword, he felt he could lose hours just trying to put a name to her colors. The gleaming gray of her *shinogi-ji* might be called gunmetal today, but she was already a hundred and fifty years old by the time the Mongols first brought guns to Japanese shores. The pale silver of her tempering had no name at all; it was to be found only in the lining of clouds, and only then when the sun struck at just the right angle. She seemed to glow with her own light. No sonnet had ever described colors so pure; no love song had ever been sung of a woman more beautiful. The thought of lying with two such beauties was enough to make his heart race.

He'd taken to sleeping with her years ago, but couldn't remember how long it had been since they'd started sleeping naked together. He did remember that he'd first done it as another way to test himself. Her blade was so sharp that if he dropped a tissue over her, its own weight would be enough to cut it in two. A bad roll in his sleep would push her deep into his flesh. Even if she did not kill him, there was hardly anywhere she could cut that would not spoil his tattoos. And he had no doubt that she would kill him if he gave her the opportunity. She'd killed men before, dozens of them. Ancient samurai had slain hundreds on her edge, but that was true of any number of swords. The beauty in Fuchida's bed had a will of her own, and a murderous will at that. It was said that she'd killed any who professed to own her. It was said no man could master her. Fuchida Shūzō was the first to prove the legend wrong.

And soon he would forge a legend of his own. Two Inazumas. No one had ever owned two before. Even Master Inazuma himself had never been in the presence of two of his own blades; it was said that he forged but one at a time, devoting himself to it as a priest devoted himself to his god. All Fuchida had to do to claim his place in immortality was to claim the second sword.

And now that sword was so close that it was all Fuchida could do to stay in bed listening to his beautiful singer. With two fingers he caressed the whole length of her, his fingertips drawing a keening note from her as they ran along her tempering. His desire for her was no less for wanting the other sword. It was so close. The woman who owned it was only across town. She was a policewoman, an unlikely owner for such a treasure, and tracking the sword to her had been considerably harder than Fuchida could have imagined. Fifteen years, and now the sword was within his grasp. His breath quickened at the thought.

But he would not indulge that crying voice in his mind. It pleaded with him: he needed to get out of bed, get dressed, get the sword *now*. Fuchida silenced it. He would be disciplined about this. He would spend a final night alone with his blade, one last night with his exquisite beauty before he brought another into their home.

Killing the policewoman could wait until tomorrow.

# 2

It was exactly the opposite of a well-designed sting. Detective Sergeant Oshiro Mariko cursed herself for taking it, cursed Lieutenant Hashimoto for retiring, and cursed the new LT for taking a perfectly good plan and blowing it right to hell.

Mariko would have preferred to stake out the suspect's apartment. There were only so many exits to cover in an apartment building, only so many places a perp could run. That was especially true in the kind of building a low-rent Tokyo pusher could afford to live in, and this Bumps Ryota was definitely low-rent. Mariko could see him now, reflected in the window of the *okonomiyaki* restaurant right in front of her nose. Even from this distance, she thought he walked as if his feet did not touch the ground. He held his arms close to his chest, one palm flat against his cheek as if trying to restrain a nervous tic or muscular spasm.

She should have said no. Hell, she'd tried to say no. She'd wanted to walk away as soon as the good plan hit the toilet. But something had drawn her back to this one, and it wasn't just some vague sense of loyalty to Lieutenant Hashimoto. Her mother would have said that when a person feels compelled, that meant something was meant to be, but Mariko didn't believe in all that destiny crap. She was a detective: she believed what the evidence supported believing. So with all the evidence pointing to a first-class fiasco, why hadn't she said no? What made this case special?

Bumps paced to and fro around a low flower planter centered in one of the main intersections of the open-air mall. Nothing special about him. Nothing special about this place either. A framework of I-beams instead of walls, the beams painted the same pale blue as the bottom of a swimming pool. Mounted above them was a roof of translucent Plexiglas domes, giant versions of those eggs that pantyhose used to come in. Suspended below the huge half eggs were ranks upon ranks of glowing fluorescent tubes, giving everything below not one shadow but a host of thin overlapping ones. Bumps couldn't have chosen a better place to be staked out by the police if he'd tried. No one on Mariko's team would give even a moment's thought to drawing down on him in a public mall. But Bumps's position was better still, smack in the middle of a four-way intersection peppered with shoppers and a million little alleyways between all the shops. Even with a battalion Mariko couldn't have put a man on every possible escape route, and with only two other officers for her sting, she couldn't even cover the four cardinal directions. It was almost as if Bumps Ryota and this new Lieutenant Ko were on the same side.

Mariko's *okonomiyaki* shop was on the southeast corner of the intersection. She smelled hoisin sauce and frying shrimp from within, and saw Bumps's skinny little reflection pacing back and forth in the foreground of her own. Short spikes crowned her image in the plate glass—her hair was still wet from the rain outside—and her eyes looked strained and tired. As well they might, she told herself, given the worst sting operation of all time, but she nipped that thought right in the bud. She already got too little respect from the men on her team; there was no point in undermining her authority further by undermining herself.

She had a patrolman named Mishima about ten meters down the west corridor, sitting on a bench with a couple of shopping bags and looking for all the world like a tired, fat man waiting for his wife. In the north corridor she'd placed Toyoda in a sunglasses shop—a natural fit, since she'd never seen him without a pair of sunglasses propped in his close-cropped hair. Twenty meters past Toyoda the mall opened onto a dark street, traffic hissing by on the wet asphalt.

Mariko had to trust Toyoda's background as a soccer full-back would help him defend that corridor, because if Bumps got to the open street, catching him would become a whole new kind of nightmare. Every neon sign in this mall would linger as sunspots in her officers' eyes, and a half-blind chase in traffic wasn't Mariko's idea of a winning strategy.

Again she cursed Hashimoto for retiring. Why couldn't he have left one week later? She cursed herself too for not sticking with the original plan, even if that meant taking whatever crap Lieutenant Ko might have for her afterward. Better to turn her back on the whole operation than to try to do it half-assed.

Why hadn't she just turned and walked? Her usual answer wouldn't cut it this time. Yes, she had to prove herself to her commander, but she knew that would be true for the rest of her career. Yes, first impressions were important, but that was all the more reason not to take this assignment; it was as if Lieutenant Ko was setting her up for failure. And she'd gone along with it anyway. Why? For the umpteenth time she looked to her reflection for an answer: why did she feel compelled to take this sting?

"Sergeant, this is Two," said Toyoda's deep voice in Mariko's Bluetooth. "I have a possible approaching the suspect now."

Yet another flaw in the operation, Mariko thought. At ten minutes to ten, there were so few shoppers left that you could take a good guess at which ones were looking to score a hit. Bumps, in turn, could guess that the three people who never wandered more than a few paces from their positions might have been, oh, say, cops. And if a buyer didn't come within the next ten minutes, the *only* people left in the mall would be Bumps and Mariko's team.

But Mariko managed to keep a lid on all such lamentations. Instead she said, "Come on, Two. A description might be helpful, don't you think?"

"Tight little number. Orange hair. Fuck-me pumps."

"Oh, I got her," said Mishima. "Yeah, that's real nice."

"I don't suppose I could bother you two to be professional, could I?" Mariko winced as soon as she said it. These guys had been salivating over the air all night, but pissing them off now wouldn't do any good. She needed them sharp.

"Possible has reached the suspect," said Toyoda.

Mariko reached into the purse slung across her torso and withdrew a compact—one she never used except in circumstances like these. Flicking it open with a stubby thumbnail, she used it to look over her shoulder. There was the perp, talking to . . . Oh no. Saori.

Just like that, everything fell into a lower and hotter level of hell. Bumps would be done with his transaction in thirty seconds or less. Pull the trigger on the sting too early and he wouldn't be guilty of anything. Pull it too late and she'd have no choice but to arrest him *and* Saori. Within her thirty-second window, she had another window of one, maybe two seconds where she could nail Bumps Ryota and still let Saori walk.

There was the other option too. She could choose not to pull the trigger at all. Let them go. Tell Ko his plan was a pooch screw from the get-go, then set up a new sting on Bumps and another buyer. Or just let Saori walk and then hit Bumps, hoping he was carrying enough to nail him on intent to distribute.

"On your toes, boys," she said into the Bluetooth. "We go on my signal."

Saori and Bumps were still talking. Saori's hair was longer than Mariko remembered, dyed peroxide orange. Bumps had long hair too, shoulder length, straight pressed, and tawny like a lion's. Both were bone skinny, their clothes hanging off them like sails from a mast in dead air. Their image in Mariko's hand mirror trembled. It was hard to tell if either had passed anything to the other.

"What are we waiting for, Sergeant?"

"Zip it, Three. We don't have a bust if he doesn't sell her anything."

There. Had their hands touched? In the trembling mirror it was hard to tell. Mariko turned around to get a better look. Bumps was definitely putting something into his jacket pocket. What about Saori? Mariko could only see her back. Saori's hands were in front of her belly, her skeletally skinny elbows winging out on either side.

"Hell with it," Mariko muttered. Then full volume, "Move, move, move!"

Bumps Ryota locked eyes with her. They were jumpy, his eyes, but despite the fact that he was amped, he froze in place for one full second before he bolted.

One second was enough time for Mariko to clear the heavy Taser from her belt line, not enough time to close within firing range. Bumps took off like a rabbit on speed.

Toyoda was on an intercept course with him. Mishima bore down on Saori, just on the fringe of Mariko's peripheral vision. Bumps juked right and put a bench between himself and Toyoda. Instead of vaulting it, Toyoda went around. That was all the breakaway Bumps needed.

Mariko bounded over the bench, dashing past Toyoda and not sparing the breath to call him a jackass. She wasn't going to catch Bumps. Five more strides and he'd be out of the dry neon mouth of the mall and into the slick, busy darkness of the streets.

Whether out of inspiration or desperation, Mariko couldn't say, but she chucked the Taser. It wheeled end over end, almost in slow motion, and Mariko was sure she hadn't put enough into the throw. The thing was heavy; it wasn't going to make it. But then it hit Bumps in the base of the neck. He stutter-stepped, stumbled, regained his footing. It was enough.

Like so many others in the Tokyo Metropolitan Police Department, Mariko had taken the department's aikido course. In the heat of the moment, she couldn't remember a single technique. She grabbed a fistful of Bumps's stiff, tawny hair. Bumps kept running. She stopped.

In the next instant Bumps was on his ass. "Stay down," Mariko said, panting, fumbling for her cuffs with her shaky, sweaty left hand.

One of those newer-model Toyotas hissed by, the kind that looked like a pregnant roller skate. A raindrop thwacked heavily on Mariko's scalp. She felt it roll through the forest of her choppy hair, tracing a cold line down the back of her head toward the collar of her blouse. Overhead, the low-hanging clouds glowed white, the way they could only do in a city the size of Tokyo. Every building in sight was the same height, nine or ten stories before disappearing into the haze. The sole exception was the mall, with its roof like rows and rows of mannequin tits, the drumming of fat, heavy raindrops beating against them, loud as a low-flying 747 that wouldn't leave Mariko's airspace.

Bumps was still wheezing, his eyes pinched shut and all his yellow teeth visible, when Mishima and Toyoda approached with a handcuffed Saori. The sunglasses in Toyoda's black hair were off-kilter, and Mishima had his tie undone, his jacket slung over one shoulder. A crowd of bystanders formed a wide semicircle, centered on Mariko as if choreographed that way, their formation stopping at the border between wet and dry pavement.

"Is it true?" said Toyoda. "Is she your sister?"

Mariko looked up at the glowing sky and the domes of Plexiglas. Rain pounded the mall's roof, not half as loud as Mariko's thundering heart. "Give her to me," Mariko said.

"Wait!" Bumps said as Mariko passed him off. "I'm useful to you! I got information!"

"Sure you do," said Mariko, then nodded for Mishima and Toyoda to leave. Both men stood their ground, their gazes flicking between Mariko and Saori. "That guy you're holding is a suspect," Mariko said. "Customarily we take them down to post and book them."

Mishima's chubby face sank, and Toyoda gave Mariko the evil eye, but at last they did as they were told. Mariko shook her head. She didn't know what it would take to earn these boys' respect, but apparently running down a fleeing perp single-handedly wasn't sufficient.

"Miko," Saori said, "you have to get me out of this." Her teeth were like her pusher's, gray where they were not yellow. She'd lost weight since Mariko had seen her last; her cheeks seemed hollow, her lips thin like an old woman's. Her face was flushed, but not with shame; Mariko could only see indignance there.

"I don't know how to help you anymore, Saori."

The sallow face hardened. "Are you kidding? What are you doing, staking me out now? Those guys came out of nowhere."

"Well, that makes one thing that's gone right tonight." Mariko's laugh sounded forced even to her. "Shit, Saori, if you had any idea how bad this thing went down, you'd know how bad you're tweaking."

"I'm not tweaking."

"Uh-huh."

Mariko took Saori by the joint between the cuffs and gave her a gentle shove in the direction the other two had taken Bumps Ryota, toward the pair of squads they had waiting in the mall's shipping dock. She hated being put in this position.

Ever since Saori had started using, all Mariko had ever wanted to do was help. Saori was the reason she'd put in for Narcotics in the first place: to bust the shitheads who would sell to her sister, yes, but also to try to get an understanding of addiction itself. The only understanding she'd gleaned so far was that an addict had to hit rock bottom before recovery. Was getting arrested by her own sister rock bottom enough? Was Mariko helping at all? She couldn't be sure.

As she ushered Saori along, she found the mall had become a breeding ground for shoppers, mostly high school girls still in uniform; their numbers seemed to have tripled in the last minute or so. Text messages had summoned them like a wizard's incantation, exorcising them from every corner of the mall and drawing them all to this one place. Gawking faces passed judgment from every direction, and at least a dozen cell phones had their tiny black bug eyes trained on the fabulous Oshiro sisters. Within the hour every teenager in Tokyo would have received the image from a friend.

Saori fussed at her cuffs, twisting her bone-thin arms. "You know what, Miko? This is bullshit. You want to stake me out, fine. Just don't lie about it. Be the overprotective bitch you've always been; just come right out and say it."

"We were staking out your pusher. It's not my fault you came to buy tonight."

"Whatever. I'm not even carrying."

Mariko stopped. "Is that true?"

"Well, yeah."

"Saori, did the other officers find anything on you?"

"No."

Mariko rolled her eyes. She didn't know why she bothered asking questions anymore; when she was using, Saori would lie to anyone about anything. The only question now was, would she pat Saori down in front of the high schoolers and their phones, or could she find a quieter place?

The quieter place was on the opposite side of a tan steel service door, in a long yellow hallway whose fluorescent tube lights hummed and droned and flickered. As Mariko patted down Saori's ribs and back and belly, the question she really wanted to ask was, Why are you making me do this? Tomorrow's conversation with their mother was sure to be a hoot. Now that conversation would have to include

Big Sister Miko picking on Poor Little Saori by searching her for contraband. No matter how bad things got, Saori always found a way to make them worse.

But this time, thankfully, she was clean. Mariko had to run her fingers over Saori's underwear to make sure, and she wanted to smack Saori for putting her in a position to have to grope her own sister, but Mariko had pulled the trigger just right. They had Bumps and, owing as much to sheer luck as good judgment, they didn't have anything on Saori.

"Do you have any idea how lucky you are?" Mariko said, pushing a brown service door open and ushering Saori through it. A vicious diatribe from Saori echoed throughout the long, narrow hallway, mostly in Japanese but with the choicest words in English. It had always been Saori's favorite language for cursing. Mariko didn't listen to a word of it. She was still thinking about fate. She'd had no way of knowing Saori was buying from Bumps, and yet she'd felt drawn to this case—and now, lo and behold, she was perfectly placed to save her family a lot of shame and grief. Mom would have said it was meant to be. Mariko still didn't buy it, but neither could she deny the compulsion she'd felt.

She walked to the end of the hall, pushing Saori along in front of her. When she reached the door at the far end, she opened it and took Saori into the mall's shipping and receiving room. It was a cavernous space, with undressed lightbulbs dangling from a ceiling high enough to admit a tractor-trailer. Two squads were parked in the loading dock just outside the huge open door. Bumps was already inside the nearest one. Mishima and Toyoda leaned against the driver's-side doors, smoking, the lightbulbs gleaming like a string of stars in the sunglasses atop Toyoda's head.

"Which one of you searched this suspect?" Mariko said.

Mishima and Toyoda looked at each other.

"Damn it, guys, you have to have a *reason* to put handcuffs on somebody." She fished for her key, and with a few clicks Saori was rubbing her red, unshackled wrists together.

"Mishima," Mariko said, pointing at Bumps in the backseat, "take him back to post and process him. Toyoda, go with him. By the time I get there, I want to see a report on my desk explaining why you weren't in position to take down our suspect and why you left me without backup in running him down."

Toyoda scowled at her as if she'd called his mother a whore. "Come on, Oshiro, there were only three of us. I had to leave *somebody* without backup."

"That's Detective Oshiro, and yes, you could have left Mishima without backup. Instead, you chose to help him cuff a woman who wasn't fleeing, a woman who ultimately can't even be charged with anything—"

"A woman who's your sister."

"That's beside the point. You showed bad judgment to-night—all night long, as far as I'm concerned—and I'm giv-ing you a chance to write down your side of it before I talk to Lieutenant Ko about your suspension. So give me a heartfelt 'thank you' and get the hell out of here."

Toyoda's scowl deepened. "What about her?" he said.

Mariko turned to look Saori in the eye. Quietly, som-berly, she said, "I'm taking her to detox. Again. Unless she wants to face charges of conspiracy to traffic narcotics."

The charge would never stick, but Saori didn't have to know that. She looked at Mariko, then at the floor. "Fine," Saori said, "let's go."

Tomorrow's conversation with their mother was looking better and better all the time.

# 3

Fuchida Shūzō rode the train to Hongodai station, leaning against the white wall at the back of the car so that no one would jostle the package slung over his shoulder. At Hongodai, he was last out of the car, and he took his time in joining the stream of passengers as it flowed down the concrete stairs. Elbow to elbow with uniformed schoolgirls and businessmen knocking off early, he followed the herd into a long corridor of off-white ceramic tile, fluorescent light, and posters selling liquor, cigarettes, and the newest cells from SoftBank. The tunnel, cooler than the platform above, smelled of rain and tobacco smoke.

Despite his black suit and white shirt, Fuchida knew he could not be mistaken for the average *sarariman*. There was the lack of a tie, a dead giveaway. Fuchida's hair was longer, slicker, and more stylish than corporate offices would allow, and his trim mustache and short black beard would have been equally unacceptable. And then, instead of a briefcase, there was the package, as long as a rifle and wrapped in dark blue cloth.

That was to say nothing of the tattoos. Only a close observer might have noted the fact that his lips were a bit darker than they should have been, as were the lines rimming his eyes. The fad of men's makeup was still in full swing, but Fuchida's adornment was far subtler than that of the metrosexuals, and far more painful as well. Fuchida knew full well that it gave him a sinister look. His skin was pale, and coupled with the tattoos it looked as if his face were both flushed with anger and as calm as a stalking tiger's. Those few who saw the tattoos for what they were tended to shudder. The very thought of the pain would frighten them, and that was without even guessing at the full extent of his adornment.

Fuchida emerged from the ceramic-tiled tunnel onto a rain-slicked Yokohama intersection, the moon a perfect circle of white behind the gray clouds, the crosswalk signal glowing blue-green and droning its little melody. This kind of place could never feel like home to him. It was too calm, too domesticated. The buildings stood in their ranks and files just like everywhere else, but they were all too short, and there was too little traffic, too few neon lights. Unlike Fuchida's regular haunts, this neighborhood gave the impression that there might be times when it was actually quiet. He crossed the street with the other passengers, and as he did so, a young man hurried past him and knocked Fuchida's parcel with his elbow.

Fuchida caught up to him in two paces and, with a deft and imperceptible sweep, kicked aside the young man's foot just as he was about to weight it. It was the move boys used in junior high schools the world over—and also in judo, where Fuchida had practiced it—and it sent the young man to the sidewalk just as if he had tripped. "Let me help you," Fuchida said, and as he crouched down, he dropped his knee into the nerve cluster at the base of the young man's inner thigh.

He was a college student, Fuchida guessed, his jeans torn across the thighs and his T-shirt so tight that Fuchida could almost see his frightened heart pounding through it. The kid opened his mouth to scream or curse, but a glare from Fuchida stifled him. "You should show some respect," Fuchida said, so softly that only the kid could hear him. "It's expensive, this thing I'm carrying."

The kid clearly had no idea how to respond. His assailant's tone was imperturbably calm, totally incongruous with the piercing pain he was feeling in his thigh. A grimace sealed the kid's lips, and his cigarette breath came quick and shallow with adrenaline and fear.

"Do you know what happened in the old days if you

bumped into a samurai's sword? He'd cut you down right in the middle of the street."

Fuchida gave the kid just long enough to look around, to confirm that he was in fact lying in the middle of the street. He took the kid's hand and twisted it into a wristlock. "Imagine that," he said, "me killing you just for bumping into this parcel of mine."

Keeping the bent wrist too close to his chest for anyone else to see, he pulled it tight, yanking the kid back up to his feet with it. The kid showed enough sense not to yelp. "I'm going to let you go now," Fuchida said. "You so much as turn around and look at me and I'll tear this hand off and feed it to you. Understand?"

The kid nodded as a cornered rabbit might have. Fuchida released his prey and went on his way, eyeing the nearby pedestrians as he went. They all went about their business, blissfully ignorant of what had transpired.

Fuchida spied the apartment building he was looking for, a tall, drab, white building like a stack of balconies. It overlooked a soccer field, and Fuchida found the sight of so much unoccupied land unsettling. Downtown, that much empty space would sell for a trillion yen.

When he reached the building, he found that an electronic security system controlled the front door. But luck was with him; from behind the glass door came the swelling hollow sound of heels clopping down the slatted stairs. Fuchida strode ten paces away from the building, turned, and walked back to the door. He reached it just as the woman descending the stairs did, and when she opened the door enough to pass the locking mechanism, he pulled it the rest of the way open with a chivalrous gesture. He smiled, she returned the smile, and he was inside.

The building was clean but plain, the hallway carpet cheap, the walls painted rather than wallpapered. It was the sort of building he'd expect to find a policewoman living in, and hardly the kind of place a collector of antiquities would choose to keep an Inazuma. The Tokyo Metropolitan Police Department couldn't possibly employ more than a handful of women, and so this one's death would be noticed immediately, but despite all of that, Fuchida would cut this one's heart out if she'd allowed the second Inazuma to rust in this shithole of a building.

The flat he sought was on the second floor. Finding it, he clacked the brass door knocker. He heard unshod footsteps on carpet. Then the homey smell of steaming rice met him as the door drew back the length of his thumb. He saw a narrow band of a woman's face in the crack of the door, bisected by a gleaming brass door chain. She was of an age with Fuchida, mid-forties, a head shorter than he was, with large glasses and a plump frame. He recognized the navy blue skirt and white blouse of her uniform through the door slit and reasoned she couldn't have been home long. "Matsumori-san?" he said.

"It's Kurihara," she said, "but yes, Matsumori was my maiden name. May I help you?"

"Is your husband home?"

"He's still at work. What's this about?"

"If I'm right, you're the granddaughter of General Matsumori Keiichi, of Army Intelligence in the Great World War? Is that so?"

"Yes." She eyed him warily. "Do I know you?"

"I'm looking for your grandfather's sword. I've been looking for it for a long time, in fact. It took me a while to track you down. Do you have the sword here?"

He heard her tighten her grip on the doorknob. "We sold it a long time ago. You won't find any swords here. Go away."

"I'm afraid I can't. As I say, I've spent a long time looking for that sword. I'll need you to tell me who bought it from you."

"I'm calling the police," she said, and her bare feet took her one apprehensive step backward.

Fuchida unshouldered his slender blue bag and withdrew from it his beautiful sword. In one movement he unsheathed the blade and swiped upward. Her song hung on the air. The golden door chain fell into two limp halves. Fuchida entered the apartment, kicked the door shut behind him without looking, and walked toward the fleeing Kurihara-san.

His first slash severed her spinal cord not far above her pelvis.

She collapsed, legs as lifeless as ropes. A dark bloodstain spread across her carpet. It was already as wide as a welcome mat. Fuchida bent down, took the phone from her hand, hit END, and slipped the phone into his pants pocket. "As you can see," he said, "I've already got a sword, but consider me a collector. You're going to have to tell me where I can find your grandfather's weapon."

Kurihara let out a piercing wail. It carried horror and desperation—the twin realizations, perhaps, that she would never walk again and that the same sword that had crippled her would kill her where she lay. Strange to worry about both, Fuchida thought—surely someone about to die needn't be concerned about disability—but her wide eyes darted back and forth from her dead legs to the bloody steel.

Another scream wouldn't do, so Fuchida kicked her in the sternum. "There are other ways to keep you from crying out," he said, crouching on his haunches next to her. "I could run this through one of your lungs. But then you couldn't tell me who bought the sword. I'd need you to write it down or something, and I'd hate to inconvenience you further after all you've been through this evening."

She whimpered through hitched breaths, clutching her midsection. Her face was ashen; her glasses lay at an odd angle because she'd broken one of her arms as she fell.

He did not need to hurt her much to get the name he required. His first thought upon hearing the name was, *That sly bastard. Keeping the sword from me this long—you sly, sly bastard.*

He looked down at Kurihara. She seemed terribly old now, though scarcely a minute ago he'd guessed the two of them were the same age. She was pale, her face wrinkled by fear and pain, her body shrinking into itself.

In the end he wasn't sure whether he killed her out of pity or to keep her from crying out after he left. He supposed it didn't matter. Dead was dead.

# 4

The precinct was a slender two-story core sample bored through the belly of a twelve-story government center. It was an early postwar building, sandy concrete instead of glass and steel, a squat little sand castle compared to the gleaming skyscrapers that surrounded it. Mariko's precinct house occupied about one-fiftieth of the building's square footage. The rest of the complex housed a post office, the ward's finance department, and offices for similar sorts of lethally boring work: construction permits and inspections, parking violations, public works, parks and recreation. The precinct house tunneled exactly through the middle of the bottom two floors, from the hedgerows along the front of the government center right through to the narrow alley separating the complex from the back wall of the abutting office building looming forty stories overhead.

They couldn't do a lot at her precinct, given its limited space, but Mariko felt proud of it anyway. They had only one interrogation room, a holding cell that barely qualified as such—really it was no more than an ordinary cinder block office with a beefed-up door—and the only way they'd managed to acquire any office space at all was to rehab the whole second-floor filing area once the department went digital. The carpet the color of wet cigarette ashes left a lot to be desired, as did the harsh lighting, but with the upstairs renovation Mariko and the rest of the sergeants each got a cubicle of their own. Mariko's had family photos pinned to the fabric wall: skinny Saori at her high school graduation, already showing hints of meth abuse; their mother grinning over a fiftieth birthday cake frosted to look like a Ping-Pong paddle; her dad with his little girls on his knee, all three giving the peace sign. The last one was the only photo in a frame, the only one at the office that had been taken during their time in the States, the only one Mariko had from before he got sick.

The station had one small evidence locker left, on the ground floor next to the arsenal with its little rack of pistols and single box of 9-millimeter rounds. Mariko would have checked her stun gun back in to the arsenal if its allegedly shatterproof plastic hadn't exploded against the concrete after bouncing off the back of Bumps Ryota's head. She didn't know what Tasers cost, but she was sure she'd find out when she saw the deductions on her next paycheck.

Walking past the locked door of the arsenal, Mariko felt her cheeks redden. Even little errors loomed large in her eyes, and she didn't know the range officer well enough to know how big a deal he'd make of the broken Taser. Though she was proud of all her little precinct house could do, and proud of her own accomplishments within it, her feet always seemed heavier here. The pressure for perfection weighed on her like a backpack full of bricks, and that pressure was more intense here than anywhere else. Some days she felt it might sink her into the wet ash carpet.

There were days when she asked herself why she worked here. Not this precinct, not even the TMPD—she wondered why she stayed in Japan at all. Her English was good enough; she could have applied to a department back in the States, or in Canada—hell, anywhere but here. Anywhere she could just worry about being a good cop, and set all the misogynist bullshit aside. The days she entertained thoughts of leaving were the days she had to remind herself of the last promise she'd made to her father. She told him she'd make him proud. Moving halfway around the world, abandoning her mother and sister after they'd already lost so much—it just wasn't the way to earn his pride.

And she had to admit there were days she *was* proud of herself. Even when the pressure made her want to throw her badge out the window, she could look at that badge and see TOKYO METROPOLITAN POLICE DEPARTMENT. It was the most elite police unit in the country, and in that unit she'd made detective sergeant. Of course that was the very source of all the pressure. All she had to do was settle for being a meter maid and she could have made all the stress disappear. There were days she asked herself that question too: Why not go easy on yourself? Why do you always have to pick the hardest road?

Mariko had never been able to answer that question. Even in junior high she'd picked cross-country, not the fifty-meter dash. In high school she made it worse and chose the triathlon. She still ran a tri every summer. There was no reason to it. Nobody *needed* to run a triathlon. Nobody needed to *run* anywhere anymore. The world no longer required it. She told herself that she did it to stay in shape, that so long as she knew she had another race on the horizon, she could not let her body fall into disrepair as so many cops proved all too willing to do. But then the tri only made sense because she was a cop. What if she had taken up chess instead of track and field? What if she'd joined the computer club instead? How much easier would her life have been? She would have been richer, more comfortable, less frequently injured, more *normal*—and bored out of her mind. That was the sole logic of the triathlon, and the sole logic of police work as well: no matter how wearisome it became, the difficult life was her sole inoculation against terminal boredom.

Mariko turned left at the coffeemakers and electric teapots and gave a nod to Mishima, who sat at a desk with the night's paperwork arrayed before him like cards in Solitaire. "Is he in there?" she asked.

"Yep. He's all set."

Mariko opened the white steel door and closed it behind her. Bumps Ryota was pacing, handcuffed, along the back wall, and he gave a startled quiver when she closed the door. He bowed to her, then hurried to the nearest of the two old wooden chairs and half sat, half fell into it. Mariko hadn't noticed earlier, but the man smelled like the bottom of a laundry hamper.

She took her customary seat on the opposite side of the room's lone table, which, like the chairs, was of a vintage that made Mariko think of the wooden furniture in her grade school's library. She was led to believe that furniture like this wouldn't have lasted long in the interrogation rooms of New York's or Chicago's PDs, but this was Tokyo, and perps could be expected to show a certain degree of civility.

All the same, Bumps was amped. His fingers drummed out a hummingbird rhythm against his belt buckle, and while Mariko could have done with a nap, Bumps looked like he was ready for another fifty-meter dash. She slipped her right hand into her purse to wrap around the haft of her Cheetah.

"What have you got for me, Bumps?"

"Huh?"

"You said you're valuable to me," Mariko said. "Right now that's true: you're another arrest I can tell my LT about. Unless you've got something else for me, I'll just book you and call it a night."

"No. I got information. Good information."

"Well?"

Bumps shook his head, his stiff blond hair following a half second behind. "No way. I want a deal first. I don't want to go to jail."

"Neither do I," said Mariko. "That's why I don't walk around with twenty-two grams of crystal methamphetamine on me. That's an intent to distribute charge, Bumps. You've also been selling that shit to my sister, and that makes me want to kick you in the nuts and throw you in the worst prison we've got. So spill this info you say you have before I come to my senses and start kicking."

"Uh," said Bumps. "Okay. Well, word is there's a new mover in town. Not dealing yet—just testing the market, if you know what I mean."

"Not good enough. I can find a dealer under any sewer grate in Tokyo."

"Not like this guy. Says he's going to sell cocaine. Says it's going to hit Japan like Godzilla, and he wants to know who's in line to be his distributors."

Mariko didn't let it show, but for a brief moment she felt gratitude toward Bumps Ryota. Until now he'd only inspired feelings of revulsion and vengeance in her, but this was big. "You got a name for me?"

"No, but I do know he rolls with the Kamaguchi-gumi."

"You're high, Bumps. Yakuzas don't go in for coke."

"Like I said, he's not selling yet. Laying the groundwork, though, I'm telling you."

He looked at her expectantly, the bags under his eyes a curious shade of purple in the light of the ceiling's twin fluorescent tubes. Mariko thought about her service weapon, about how she'd only ever drawn it once in her four years on the force, about how much she'd enjoy drawing it now and giving Bumps a good long look right down the barrel. It was the wrong thing to feel. Not because he didn't deserve it—he did, and so did everyone else in his profession—but she wanted to hurt him because of what he did to Saori, and at the end of the day she knew the one who did it to Saori was Saori. Even if Mariko shot him right here and now, Saori would find another dealer.

Shove her pistol in his face. Cram the Cheetah right in his gray, wasted mouth and pull the trigger. Those were the urges she suppressed as she withdrew her hand from her purse, slipped it into her jacket pocket, and passed Bumps Ryota a thin stack of folded papers held together by the clippy-thing of a ballpoint pen. "These are CI papers. You know what a CI is?"

"Yeah, but—"

"But what? You'd prefer to face charges of possession? Intent to distribute? Evading arrest? I don't think so. I think you and I both win if you sign on as a confidential informant. You're never selling meth again; those days are over. Your choices now are to start selling blowjobs while you're in prison or to start selling information to me."

Bumps's shoulders slumped. He unfolded the sheaf of papers and looked over the cover sheet.

"Better," said Mariko. "Here's the rules. One, you ever sell meth again, we prosecute to the full extent of the law. Okay?"

Bumps sighed. "Okay."

"Two, you provide a steady stream of information leading to arrests. You're going to buy the dope, we're going to set up stings on the guys you buy from. It'll look like it's unrelated to you, so no one's going to put a target on your head. Okay?"

"Okay."

"Three, you ever so much as look at my sister again and you're never going to have the luxury of seeing a prison cell.

I will personally see to it that every arrest we make knows you're the shithead who dimed him out. From there it's just a matter of who gets lucky in the office pool: do we find your body floating in the harbor or splattered all over the subway? Are we clear?"

"Uh-huh."

"Good." Mariko stood in front of the interrogation room's mirror and primped her jacket and hair. "On that coke thing," she said, leaving the room, "have a name for me next time or it's your ass."

"All righty."

Mariko left him looking like a kid who'd just found out he wouldn't be getting a puppy after all. But for her part, she couldn't restrain a smile. Cocaine. From the Kamaguchi-gumi. This was huge—terrible, yes, but huge. The first words her new lieutenant would hear from her would be about what promised to be the biggest drug bust of the year. Perhaps he'd take her more seriously. He might even give this the funding and manpower it deserved. She had two months to close this case—two months before her probation was up and they'd decide whether to accept her application to Narcotics. Two months wasn't a lot of time, but with the right commanding officer and the right backing, Mariko knew she could make it happen.

"Hey, Mishima," she said. "Is Lieutenant Ko in tonight?"

"Nah. I think he pulled a double shift this morning. I wouldn't call him if I were you; I never met an LT yet who wasn't pissy after pulling a double."

"No problem. I'll find him tomorrow."

Mariko left the precinct house with a bounce in her step. Tomorrow was going to be a good day.

# 5

"Come in, Oshiro. Come in."

Lieutenant Ko had an overlarge mouth flanked by deep creases like gills. What hair he had left was graying, and clutching only to the sides of his head. His black eyes were barely visible behind large square glasses, and the word around the precinct was that no one had ever seen him without a cigarette in his mouth. He sat behind his desk, his smoky office oppressively hot and lined with beige steel filing cabinets. Papers were stacked on top of them here and there, with more stacks decorating his desk as well, though there was a clear space in the middle for him to work and to park his ashtray.

It had taken Mariko three days to get an appointment with him—an appointment in the ass end of the morning, no less; the sky was still dark when Mariko's alarm went off. Ko was new to the station and surely had a great deal of catching up to do, but even so, Mariko felt three days was excessive. Her new lead was too important.

"Be a dear," Ko said through his cigarette, "and get me a cup of coffee before we get started, would you?"

"No, sir," said Mariko.

His big fish mouth frowned, cigarette hanging down from his broad lips. "Excuse me?"

"It's not in the job description, sir. I'm a detective, not an OL."

The frown deepened, as did the deep wrinkles framing it. "Close the door, Oshiro."

She did so, then resumed her attention stance, hands clasped behind her back.

"We're new to each other," Ko said, tapping ashes into the glass ashtray. "It's to be expected that we'll all have a breaking-in period around here. That's all right. I just want to make sure everyone understands which way the wind's going to blow."

Mariko nodded. Ko sucked on his cigarette and the end glowed red. "I understand," he said, "that my predecessor cut you a lot of slack. That will cease. I'd cut you from the detective squad if I could, but as you've undoubtedly figured out, I need cause for dismissal to do that. So far you haven't provided it. So far you've been a good little girl."

Mariko felt like a lizard on a rock. Her eyes stung, her skin was so hot she thought it might crackle, and somewhere far overhead there circled a hawk that liked feeding on lizards.

"I see here that you destroyed department property Wednesday night," said Ko. "A stun gun."

"Destroyed and paid for, yes, sir. It's not cause for dismissal."

"Indeed not." Ko sucked on the cigarette and exhaled a thin jet of smoke. "Patrolman Toyoda reports that you were abusive with your power."

"Toyoda's a whiner who doesn't like being outrun by a girl. You saw my request that he be suspended and censured?"

"I did. You'll address me as 'sir' when you're in my office."

Mariko balled two fists behind her back. "Yes, sir."

"You're way off base on this ridiculous cocaine story," he said. "The *bōryokudan* don't sell cocaine. Nor do they stand for anyone else selling it on their turf. Period."

"Until now, sir."

"Excuse me?"

"I have reason to believe one of the yakuzas is looking to change the game. Sir."

Ko snorted. "Why would he do that? They keep the hard stuff out of the country, we go easy when they sling more pedestrian fare. That's the truce. We don't like it but we live with it. You think they want to change that?"

"I'm a detective, sir. I go where the evidence leads me."

"Evidence?" Another snort, this one jetting two cones of smoke from his nostrils. They bloomed up as they hit his desk and made Mariko think of an anime dragon. "All you have is the word of some tweaked-out speed freak."

"With all due respect, sir, the dealers know a lot more about what's happening on the street than we do."

"Hardly a ringing endorsement of your police work. Tell me, have you cultivated any yakuza contacts in all your long years of service?"

"Of course, sir."

"More than I have?"

Mariko hated rhetorical questions. She hated people who asked them, and hated it even more when they sat and stared and waited for an answer. At last she rolled her eyes and said, "No, sir."

"And why not?"

Again with the rhetorical questions. "Because you've been on the force a hell of a lot longer than me. Sir."

Ko gave her a sickening little grin. Despite all her years in the States, Mariko had never quite figured out exactly what they meant by *shit-eating grin*, but she wondered if this was it. In any case, it was the kind of patronizing little grin that made her want to shove Ko's face in a pile of shit.

"These *bōryokudan* contacts of yours," he said, his tone even more belittling than the grin, "have they spoken of an impending expansion into the cocaine trade?"

"Not yet, sir."

"Nor have mine. And, as you say, mine are rather more extensive than yours, *neh*? You'll forgive me if I take their silence more seriously than the word of some desperate junkie you managed to drag in."

"Sir, if a lone yakuza were looking to build himself a bigger empire, the rest of the *bōryokudan* wouldn't know about it—"

Ko gave her a dismissive wave of the hand. "Forget it. The fact that you were even given the chance to apply to Narcotics is just asinine. You ought to know your place. Grow your hair out. You look like a dyke."

"Perps can grab long hair, sir."

He went on as if she didn't have a mouth. "Isn't it enough for you that you made sergeant already? Isn't it enough that you're the only woman detective in Tokyo? Come to that, you're the only woman detective I ever heard of, and I've been wearing the badge twenty-two years. And you're practically *gaijin* to boot. You're lucky you can get a job waiting tables in this country. You're an alien in your own land, Oshiro. You'd think you'd know to be happy with what you've got." He snorted two more jets of smoke at his desk. "Sergeant and detective after only four years on! How you made it that far is beyond my reckoning."

"I'm a good cop, sir. That's how I made it this far."

"It's not proper. Administration, yes, I could see that. Even upper administration. It's not unheard of; I'm sure you can type as well as anybody. But if I had my way, your only role in this station would be to serve the rest of us tea and coffee on demand. Believe me, as soon as you give me cause, I'll have you doing just that."

Now Mariko's face was sweating, not because of the office radiator but out of anger. "Go ahead," Ko said, meeting her glare through a haze of smoke. "Say something. Give me cause to demote you. Or don't. I can be patient. You look at me like I'm a cracked old man, but my ears are sharp. If there's even a whisper that you've broken protocol, I'll hear it. All I need is the allegation. In this department, that's enough."

Mariko's jaw was set, her lips pressed into a thin line. "Don't expect to hear anything," she said. "I'm going to keep on being a good little girl. Sir."

"Perhaps. Perhaps not. What's certain is, you won't be making Narcotics under my command. You'll serve out the remainder of your Narc probation. Then, rest assured, you will be denied your transfer, and I'll have you working low-end property crimes for the rest of your career. And because you could do with some practice with cases like that . . ." He pulled a pale blue folder out from the middle of a stack of papers and dropped it on the front of his desk. The wind it stirred up scattered white ashes from the ashtray. "You'll take the Yamada case. Old guy out near Machida. Says someone tried to steal his sword."

"Sir, like it or not, I've got eight more weeks on Narcotics before you start handing me the shit cases. I've got a right to work legitimate drug busts until then."

There was that shit-eating grin again. "Special request from Machida PD. Entitles me to pick anyone I like. Lucky you."

Mariko said nothing. She picked up the folder and walked out.

# 6

Swords, Mariko thought. *Bōryokudan* violence is swelling, we've got a dead policewoman and no leads on who killed her, cocaine threatens to hit us like a typhoon, and my priority is supposed to be stolen swords.

No, she thought. One sword. An *almost*-stolen sword. A purported attempt at stealing a sword. Not only was this not a narcotics case, but Ko didn't even have her investigating a *crime*. This was an aborted crime, a past possibility of a crime.

She took the train to Yamada's place. She could have commandeered a ride in a squad, but even that might be seen as misappropriation of department resources, and Mariko didn't want to risk it. She could be patient too. There were a lot of cops in the precinct; Ko would only get busier as time went on, and then she'd see if his ears were as sharp as he claimed.

The ride to Machida took almost an hour, the buildings neighboring the train tracks becoming ever shorter, ever smaller as the distance grew between Mariko and the city center. Within the first fifteen minutes the train car had so few people that she could move her elbows away from her ribs, and soon after that she could see from one end of the car to the other. While waiting on the platform for a transfer, she'd had time to make a phone call, during which she learned that Machida's department was tiny, that they'd recently lost their lone detective to retirement, and that as yet they'd found no one to replace him. Even better, Mariko thought. Now I'm playing spare tire to the investigation of an almost-crime.

Not for the first time, she wished to hell Lieutenant Hashimoto hadn't retired. Not that he'd had much choice. Like Mariko, the man had no idea how to do anything halfway. Twenty-six years of eighty-hour workweeks had taken their toll, until finally he'd passed out in his office and woken up to a doctor telling him he was a near case of *karōshi*. As the train clacked along, Mariko thought about how strange that word was. *Karōshi*: death from overwork. What did it mean about Japanese culture that they had a word for that? How could a society survive where so many people worked themselves to death that they had no choice but to come up with a name for it? The Americans had no equivalent—but, then, the existence of the term *drive-by shooting* was every bit as biting a commentary on their culture. Only in a place of unremitting violence could people invent vocabulary to separate *this* kind of shooting each other from *that* kind of shooting each other.

And Mariko had chosen the land of *karōshi* over the land of the drive-by. What did that say about her? There was something so classically Japanese about it, preferring suicide to a random shooting. The samurai once debated whether there was any honor in winning a battle by resorting to firearms. Unlike a sword or an arrow, a musket ball was random, and the true follower of Bushido was honor-bound to kill using only his own talent. Better to die by seppuku, some said, than to claim the empty victory of the gun. Of course, the ones who said that were the ones the musket balls had torn apart by the score.

Now and then people still talked about the samurai spirit. Mariko wondered if she had it, and if it had ever been anything more than sheer stubbornness. No—stubbornness plus a willingness to endure more than the other guy. Mariko was good at that part. It was the only way to beat guys like Ko: she'd outlast him. Even if it killed her, she'd outlast him.

She found she could not enjoy the sunshine, nor the cloudless sky, nor Machida's relative verdure compared to downtown. The pale blue folder in her left hand still smelled of cigarette smoke. She flipped through it for Yamada's address and found the house easily.

Yamada Yasuo, aged eighty-seven, retired, sole resident. No criminal record. Whatever career he'd retired from was lucrative enough for him to afford his own home, a luxury Mariko could never aspire to. Presumably widowed, and an accomplished gardener, for when she reached the house, she found Yamada snipping a huge pink chrysanthemum from its bush beside his front stoop.

"Yamada-san?"

The old man turned around and smiled. His hair was as short as electric clippers could make it, and in the sun it shone like a million tiny points of silver light. He was kneeling—the flower he'd snipped was low on the bush—but even so she could tell his back had a slight but permanent hunch. He wore slacks and a sweater the color of milk tea, and his face was dotted with liver spots. The skin of his hands and face was as wrinkled as any Mariko had ever seen.

"Why, hello," he said.

"I'm Detective Sergeant Oshiro, TMPD. I'm here to ask you some questions about your recent attempted theft. Have you got a minute?"

"Of course. Do come in."

He beckoned her with a wave of the head, and with clippers and chrysanthemum blossom in one hand, he made his way toward his front door. Now that he was standing, she found him to be shorter than she'd expected, not ten centimeters taller than she was herself. His hunch had stolen some of his height. His feet found each step carefully, which surprised Mariko, for he'd stood up from kneeling quickly enough, and he seemed quite fit for his age. When he reached the front door, she discovered why he moved so slowly. He fished in his pocket for his house key, and, finding it, he bent down so that his face was no more than a finger's length from the doorknob. Only then could he fit key to keyhole.

"You're legally blind?" said Mariko.

"None too delicate, are you, Inspector?"

Mariko felt her cheeks warm. "No, sir. Beg your pardon. I've got a grandmother who's almost blind too. She still does *sashiko*, but she has to plot the thread patterns by touch."

"Ah. My doctor says I'd do better to let my fingers do some seeing for me, but I prefer to use my eyes while I still can. Please, come in. Let's sit."

Yamada's home was a sliver of the past. His entryway, which still housed a shallow wooden shoe rack, had a lower floor than the rest of the house. The only furniture in his sitting room was a broad table not even knee-high, surrounded by four gray *zabuton*. The floor was tatami, the walls were lined with books, and the bowl-shaped ceiling light was the only electrical device to be seen. Even the light was a relatively recent addition to the house, if the ceiling plaster was any indication: a straight line, almost exactly the same texture as the rest of the ceiling and yet not quite, led from the lamp to the wall, trace evidence from where they'd run the new wire. There were dead bugs in the light's glass bowl, but the bookshelves were dusted and the gray cushions free of stains. The room smelled of tatami and old paper. A clock ticked loudly on the other side of the room.

Mariko said she would stand, but Yamada insisted, so Mariko slipped out of her shoes, padded into the sitting room, and settled herself on a *zabuton*. Yamada spoke to her from the kitchen as he prepared a pot of tea. "He came for the sword last night," the old man was saying. "In a car, if that's relevant. A smaller one, by the sound of it."

Mariko wrote all of this down, more out of a habit of thoroughness than anything. "What makes you think this person came to steal the sword?"

"I can't think of anything else here worth taking," said Yamada, entering the room now with both hands holding a tray. On the tray were two teacups—traditional, without handles—a steaming pot, and the big pink chrysanthemum. The tea and the blossom blended their perfumes beautifully.

Mariko didn't make a habit of contradicting witnesses or victims as she questioned them, but she couldn't help thinking that a sword was most definitely not worth stealing. What possible use could a person have for a sword in the twenty-first century?

But she voiced none of this aloud. Instead she said, "May I see the sword, sir?"

"Tea first," said Yamada. His hands found cup and pot

handle with ease—could he see them, or had he memorized where he'd set them?—and he poured two small cupfuls of pale green tea.

Mariko sipped hers. As they drank, she asked the usual questions: What time did this car come by the house? What happened next? Did this person actually enter the home, or was it only an attempted entry? Can you describe the person? Was he or she alone?

Yamada answered all of them, though Mariko sensed he was holding something back. She tried varying the questions, repeating them from different angles, but could not get past his reticence. She couldn't decide whether he was deliberately concealing something or whether it was simply a difference in mannerisms between his generation and hers.

At last she concluded that Yamada was a traditionalist. The old-style tea table and cushions, the absence of any stereo system or CD player, the tatami mats in the first room of the house: all of these were reminiscent of an older time. Yamada volunteered nothing that he was not asked, and not everything that he *was* asked, but Mariko thought this had to do with growing up in the last generation that still believed in the sanctity of silence.

As Yamada led her upstairs to his bedroom, where he kept the sword, Mariko noticed there was no television in the house. It was not unusual for the blind to have televisions—her grandmother had one—but Mariko suspected this man hadn't thrown out his TV when his vision faltered. More likely, she thought, that he'd never owned one. There was no obvious place in the house to put one, for one thing, no media cabinet or TV stand now used for some other purpose, and the fact that he still wound that clock ticking so loudly in the sitting room told her he still kept things he couldn't get much use of now that he was nearly blind. But more than this, Mariko thought it impossible that anyone could have read so many books if he spent any time at all in front of the tube.

Yamada didn't even have a computer, which was less surprising—Mariko's grandmother didn't have one either—and yet more jarring, because Mariko couldn't imagine her life without one. Just another generational gap, she supposed.

"Here it is," Yamada said. The bedroom smelled like its tatami floors too. The bed was not, as she'd predicted, an old-style futon, but rather a Western-style mattress on a hip-high frame. Easier to get in and out of, she guessed. Above the bed, on a black lacquered rack on the wall, was the sword.

He went to it, took it down from the wall, and handed it to her. It was surprisingly heavy, and much bigger than she'd expected. But then, she'd never held a real sword before. She'd seen them in museums and castle tours as a girl, of course, and in truth she'd always wanted to open the glass cases and pick them up. It was strange to hold one now, sort of a girlhood fantasy brought to life. A tiny part of her wondered what that meant about her. Saori's girlhood fantasy was to have a pony.

"Unsheathe it," Yamada said.

She obliged him, laying the polished, cord-bound scabbard on the mattress. The sword's naked steel reflected everything in the room, distorting and stretching the images. Mariko could hardly imagine fighting with it, but as soon as that thought entered her mind, she immediately sensed how easy it would be to cut through bone and muscle with a blade this big. And of course the samurai that fought with such weapons were assuredly larger than Mariko's fifty kilos and 165 centimeters. The sword might not have been all that big to them.

"Impressive," she said, hefting it.

"It ought to be. It guides the forces of destiny."

A moment passed before that sunk in. "The forces of destiny?"

"That's right."

"Sir, are you suggesting that this sword is magical?"

"That's one word for it."

Mariko returned it to its sheath. "And that's why the thief came to steal your sword?"

"Why, of course."

"Right." She didn't bother setting the sword back on the wall rack; she just left it on the bed. "And you said you didn't actually see the thief enter the premises?"

"I don't see much anymore, Inspector."

Mariko turned for the stairs. "I think we're all through here, sir. I'll let you know if we turn up anything."

"Oh, Inspector," he called after her, "if it matters to your investigation, the sword is worth a lot of money."

"Because it controls destiny?"

"No. Because it's almost nine hundred years old."

"Uh-huh. We'll get back to you, sir."

She left the old man's apartment clenching and unclenching her fists, reminding herself there was only one way to beat Ko. She'd outlast him. He'd heap shit like this on her, and she'd keep taking it until he had no more shit to shovel.

She sure as hell hoped he'd run out soon.

# BOOK TWO

◆◆◆◆◆◆◆◆◆◆◆◆◆◆◆◆◆◆◆◆◆◆◆◆◆◆◆◆

## KAMAKURA ERA, THE YEAR 124

### (1308 CE)

## 7

Silence fell on the hillside. Orange and gold leaves of autumn drifted lazily to the ground, more of them below than still in the branches. One fell on the face of Lord Kanayama Osamu, his pallor contrasting sharply with the rich redness of the leaf. Most of his blood had already dyed the leaves on the ground in a uniform river of dark crimson. His body was gashed open across the spine, a deep cut from left shoulder to right hip, and his face still bore the crazed snarl he had worn in combat.

"I've never seen anything like it." Saito Toshiro stared down at his fallen commander, lungs still heaving, blood pounding an adrenaline-charged rhythm against his eardrums.

"Neither have I," said Nakadai Minoru, sheathing his *tachi* at his hip. "Not at Kamakura, not at Higashiyama, never." The two men were in many ways the opposite of each other. While Saito was lean and towering in his armor, Nakadai was fully a head shorter and almost as broad as he was tall. Saito had a face of leather, bronzed by the sun and hardened by years of combat. Nakadai had cheeks like red apples and deep, narrow, glinting slits for eyes, like two black marbles pressed into a ball of dough. Both wore the armor and topknot that marked them as samurai, as well as the twin swords, but standing next to each other, Nakadai looked almost like a bull, Saito a weathered tree.

"He fought like a madman," Saito said. "No—like a rabid dog. I don't understand it."

"Yes. By all rights we should be the ones lying here, not him. It's too bad; he deserved a better death than this."

Lord Kanayama had been, among other things, one of the most renowned swordsmen in the Owari territory. He had also been samurai, lord of the castle at Gifu, daimyo of the surrounding fief, and an ally and confidant to Lord Ashikaga Owari-no-kami Jinzaemon, overlord of Owari. Up until a few days ago, Kanayama was one of Lord Ashikaga's generals, and the commanding officer of both Saito and Nakadai. In times of war, Lord Kanayama's counsel was always esteemed, and with a blade in his hands he was unrivaled within a hundred *ri*. But yesterday morning he was to have committed seppuku, his punishment ordered by Lord Ashikaga on charges of treason. And, that morning at dawn, Kanayama had instead taken his swords and his two fastest horses, and fled across the Owari plains.

The first of these horses he rode into the ground. The second, stronger than the first, carried him all the way through the night until it broke a foreleg in his mad dash across the Kiso River. From there Kanayama had fled on foot, where it had taken some thirty hours for Saito, Nakadai, and a dozen warriors to chase him down on Ashikaga's orders. And now, on this isolated hillside, he had doomed himself to suffer a dog's death at the hands of his own retainers.

"I cannot understand it," Saito said as he began to clean the blood from his blade. "If he had simply committed seppuku he could have died with honor. Instead, this! Fleeing like a common thief, hacking at us as if he'd never touched a sword . . . By all gods, when he *kicked* you, I couldn't believe my eyes!"

That kick had sent Nakadai's girth tumbling through a thorny bramble, breaking two ribs and slicing every exposed inch of skin a hundred times over. Nakadai was lucky; anyone who stepped within striking distance of Kanayama Osamu usually met with a swift death. The kick did more than dispatch Nakadai; it also off-balanced Kanayama and allowed Saito to sidestep his next crazed slash. Saito had taken a superficial cut to the forearm on that exchange, but in return Kanayama had exposed his back, and Saito spun and sliced him from shoulder to hip.

"It makes no sense." Nakadai nodded in agreement, looking at the body in disbelief. "I should be a headless corpse, and you should be bleeding to death from the stump of your sword arm, waiting for the lord to cut you down. There was no reason to his attacks, just madness. Perhaps what they say about his sword is true . . . ?"

"Nonsense," Saito said immediately. "He was exhausted. He had been riding for days. He could have been injured when his horse fell at the river."

"That may be, but at Inuyama I saw him slay four men single-handedly, and that was after he took an arrow through the shoulder."

"I cannot explain it," Saito admitted. "Maybe he went mad. Nothing else would explain his turn against Lord Ashikaga."

"Nothing, except the sword."

Saito scoffed. "Put that out of your head. Are you a farmer's woman? Do you also believe goblins will take your children away in the night? It is an Inazuma blade! A sword without equal! Of course there will be legends attached to it."

"Not legends like these," said Nakadai.

"Get a hold of yourself! Legends were spoken of the lord himself. Do you truly believe he killed a hundred men at Kamakura? Neither do I, but that is what the villagers say of him. Choose, my friend, whether you are peasant or samurai. Do you honestly believe spirits can control swords?"

Nakadai's head dropped for a moment. When it rose again, his fat cheeks were split in a smile. "You're right. Of course you're right. Our lord's death must be distracting me." He shook his head as if to throw off the last traces of a bad dream. "I'm sorry. Now, shall we fetch our retainers and return to Lord Ashikaga?"

Saito's eyes fell to the body once more. "You go ahead. Someone has to prepare the head and compose his death poem."

Nakadai nodded and Saito watched him amble up the hillside, on his way to find the dozen *bushi* who had accompanied them on the chase. Saito and Nakadai were the best horsemen among the group and had been able to navigate their mounts deeper through the forest than any of the others. Eventually the trees had become so dense that they too were forced to dismount. The pursuit continued on foot, while the horses stayed obediently where they were left. Saito assumed that wherever Nakadai found their horses, he would also find their retainers.

That didn't leave much time. As soon as Nakadai's round figure plodded out of sight, Saito's gaze fell back on the body of his fallen master. It lay there, legs crossed over each other, the torso twisted in an impossible pose as the spine and rib cage no longer held it to a normal human shape. Kanayama's right hand still gripped the handle of his *tachi*, which was so sharp that it sank half its length into the ground when its wielder fell.

Saito prayed it had not struck a rock when it dropped. He drew the Inazuma blade out of the earth, sighing when he saw that no stone had ground away the perfection of its edge. Inazuma, the weapon's creator, was a sword smith the world would not see the likes of again for generations. Of course he had taken apprentices, but none of them had been able to replicate the genius of the master himself, and after his death the Inazuma school dropped out of existence. That was two hundred years ago, and his legacy only remained in blades such as this, a treasure Saito never believed he would have the honor to wield in his lifetime.

Saito was quite a swordsman himself, even among samurai. Nothing along the lines of Lord Kanayama, but still, he was more skilled than most. In addition to the fencing practice that all samurai made their purpose in life, Saito was also a longtime student of *iaidō*, the art of drawing the sword. He prided himself on the speed of his draw, on how fluidly it flowed into cuts and parries and counterstrikes. A master of *iaidō* could draw, cut, and resheathe his blade before his enemy's corpse hit the ground. Saito was not there yet, but he was trying.

As it happened, this particular blade was forged by the master Inazuma especially for *iaidō*. It was named Beautiful Singer for the whistle of the *tachi*'s edge as it flashed out of its scabbard. An *iaidō* sword had to be lighter than most *tachi* for better speed on the draw; this one felt as if its mass were suspended by muscles of its own, an extension of Saito's arm, weightless.

It was truly a masterpiece. To send it to the afterlife with

Lord Kanayama would have been criminal. It was no dishonor to take the sword. No dishonor at all. If the only way to rescue a masterpiece was to steal it from a dead man, he told himself, then stealing was neither craven nor shameful.

And the rumors surrounding the blade couldn't possibly be true. Saito laughed at the thought as he examined the blade in a beam of sunlight. He wiped its gleaming surface clean, admired the reflection it captured of the leaves above. It is an Inazuma blade, he thought. Of course there will be stories. Men would kill—men *have* killed—to possess a sword such as this. Where such treasures are concerned, the imagination is sure to wander.

Saito gave the sword a final polishing and, withdrawing his own *tachi*, sheathed his late master's weapon in his own scabbard. It fit well enough—not perfectly, but not so loose as to rattle free. Then, removing the inimitable weapon and its sheath from his belt, he sat down and quickly unwound the cord wrappings from both swords' handles. Then he switched them, rebinding the Inazuma with the wrap from his own sword. Though it felt like a violation of Bushido in his gut, in his head he was certain it was not. He tried to convince his gut of that as he switched the braided cords wrapping the scabbards, binding his own around the one carved for Beautiful Singer.

Apprehension gnarled his brow as he eyed the *tsuba*, the round metal hand guards on each sword; switching those would take more time and tools than he had available. The illusion would not be complete. But then, it should not need to be. There would be no reason for anyone to examine the sword Saito wore on the trip home. If the others were loyal at all, their grief over the master's honorless death would overwhelm any other concerns.

Once the handle and scabbard of the Beautiful Singer were bound, Saito hastily rewrapped his own sword with the orange-and-yellow cord taken from Lord Kanayama. With both weapons disguised, he thrust Kanayama's magnificent prize through his own belt and returned his old sword to the late master. It was then that he heard voices approaching over the ridge. With one silent movement, Saito regained his feet and drew the Inazuma sword. The peerless blade glittered as it struck the head from Kanayama's body. The blood was minimal, most of it having already turned the ground to red mud, but Saito cleaned his new weapon anyway. As he whipped it through the air to resheathe it, the blade truly sang, its song high-pitched, nearly inaudible, yet nonetheless unforgettable. Though he could never explain how, Saito was immediately aware that this song had words, and in that moment he knew his fallen master's death poem:

> *The glorious sun,*
> *nigh on reaching its zenith,*
> *shaded by my hand.*

"That's perfect," Nakadai said later when Saito recited the poem to him. "Yes, the lord himself could not have composed better. Too bad that it's all too true."

"What?" Saito looked up at his friend, distantly aware that Nakadai had spoken. The whistling song of the sword still clung to the air, washing over everything else.

"The master's life," Nakadai observed. "Surely you see it. He was the sun, shaded just as he was the coming to the peak of his skills. Or have you written a poem better than you even knew yourself?"

"No . . . the poem wrote itself for me."

Nakadai laughed. "Well, then, perhaps you've attained a glimpse of enlightenment. Maybe you should shave that old topknot and join a monastery." Nakadai chuckled again, but Saito bristled at the thought of retiring his weapons and his station as samurai. He forced a laugh all the same.

They agreed to build a pyre for Kanayama's body just outside the woods, for it was possible that Lord Ashikaga would not allow a proper funeral if they carried the body home. Despite whatever demon had taken hold of the master in his final days, for most of his life Kanayama had been an indomitable warrior and the object of unquestioned loyalty.

The sun had set by the time they'd gathered the mountain of wood they needed, for to burn their lord's very bones to ashes, they needed heat one usually found only in the heart of a forge. At Saito's suggestion, Kanayama's swords were burned along with the body. The lord should die with at least that much honor, he argued. Nakadai quickly agreed: if the ghost stories were true, he said, they would be doing the world a favor by committing the Inazuma blade to the flames. In the blazing light of the late-night fire, no one seemed to notice the *tsuba* on Lord Kanayama's sword, and no one mentioned the hand guard of the late lord's weapon at Saito's hip.

This is no dishonor, Saito told himself. A samurai is to make himself a living sword. Just as the lord does not lightly commit his loyal samurai to battle, a samurai should not lightly let a masterwork sword be destroyed. No, he thought. No dishonor at all.

# 8

Lord Ashikaga Owari-no-kami Jinzaemon was as fearsome as he was powerful. His reign over Owari was unquestioned; by now all his intelligent enemies has simply decided it was easier to wait until the old tyrant died, hoping the Ashikaga heir would not be blessed with the same demonic cunning as the father. The Owari territory was coveted land, to be sure, and every neighboring warlord deeply wished to wrest it from Ashikaga's control. Its long, narrow bay was protected by peninsulas on either side, making it a natural port with geological protection from the all-too-common threat of typhoons. Mountains to the north and west provided further protection against threats of a military nature. The Owari plains were rich rice-yielding bounty, and to make the prize even more tempting, Ashikaga's armies were far smaller than the forces at his enemies' command. But with mountains and the sea protecting his flanks, Ashikaga could devote all his limited manpower to the protection of his eastern front, an easily defensible position for such a masterful general.

Once long ago two rival warlords attacked Owari simultaneously, one with naval power and one by land. Lord Ashikaga routed both of them, devoting only half his forces to each. The first he flanked on both peninsulas as the boats stormed the port, enclosing the enemy in an ever-narrowing V of arrow fire. Flaming arrows did as much damage to ships as steel did to flesh, and the attack was broken off before the first sailor reached the shore. The land invaders were allowed to penetrate deep into the plains before the second half of Ashikaga's troops cut them off from behind and razed their supply lines. The enemy headed south, only to be cut off by archers returning from the sea battle. Turning west, the invaders encountered more archers returning from the opposite peninsula. Surrounded by troops on three sides and mountains on the fourth, the enemy was left to starve for a week in fertile cropland that was unfortunately three months away from the harvest. Both maneuvers were so surprising and so devastatingly fast that the opposing generals had no choice but to believe that Ashikaga's entire army was deployed on the plains and on the sea coast at the same time, and that any general who could simultaneously deploy the same army on two separate fields of battle should be left to die in his own province unmolested, with the hopes that such inhuman skill would not be inherited by his successor.

For all his might and cleverness, Ashikaga was an ugly man. His face was like a skull with leather pulled taut across it, cheekbones cutting the sharp lines one might find in a prisoner's face after two weeks without food. On the left side a razor-straight line ran back from his mouth to a missing earlobe, its path a thick white hairless scar. His topknot and eyebrows were bushy gray, standing in sharp contrast to the ruddy skin permanently bronzed by years of harsh battlefield sun. His body bore the marks of combat as well, but by far the worst of his scars was the sickening twisted knot on his throat. In his youth an archer had put an arrow through Ashikaga's gullet, and only by the grace of some buddha or demon did he survive. It was said he killed two more men that day before stopping to remove the shaft. Some said he even went back and hunted down the man who shot him. Eventually he recovered from the wound, but the healing had twisted the skin of his neck in an eddy of scar tissue, as cloth would twist around the haft of a spear. His vocal cords did not escape the damage. It was more than a year before he could speak again or even turn his head, and ever since, his voice had been more of a growl, gravel under a wagon's wheels, the roll of distant thunder.

To Saito it didn't matter whether the arrow had actually

pierced the lord's throat or only grazed him, whether he really did stalk down that archer or whether his revenge was no more than a tall tale. If a man rose to such stature that people made up legends about him and recited them as if they were true, that was testament enough to his ability. Saito would always refer to the lord as Ashikaga-dono instead of the -*san* used for equals or even the -*sama* he'd used for Lord Kanayama. He would always honor Ashikaga as a warrior and liege lord, regardless of what superstitious foot soldiers whispered in the ranks about hungry ghosts coming back to life.

Saito had been summoned to his general's audience chamber to offer his report on the death of Lord Kanayama. Ashikaga let out a sharp half laugh when Saito recounted the kick that sent his companion through the bramble. "Do you expect me to believe Kanayama Osamu would *strike* a man when he had a sword in his hands?" The wolfish voice was bitter with disbelief. "Why did he not simply cut him down? What are you trying to hide from me?"

"Nothing, Ashikaga-dono. Nothing I have said so far would shield the late lord of any shame. You want the truth from me and that is what I have given you. I cannot explain his actions; he lost all semblance of control. I was loyal to him for many years, but Lord Kanayama died without honor and it was to spare him further dishonor that I took his head. If you still believe I am a liar, please allow me to commit seppuku to protest my innocence."

Ashikaga's black eyes turned down to the lacquered box at the foot of his dais. In the box was a heavy cloth bag, and in the bag was the severed head. "No, Saito-san," he said, brooding. "You will continue your story. Perhaps he truly was insane. Tell me the rest."

Saito related the end of the tale, from the deathblow to the funeral pyre, describing every detail except the swords. He had no fear that Ashikaga would recognize the difference in his *tachi*'s new *tsuba*, for no one entered the lord's audience chamber armed, save the bodyguards and Lord Ashikaga himself. The steward downstairs who had taken Saito's weapon was not of a position to recognize the difference in swords, and so for the present Saito's secret would remain so. But it was with strong reluctance that he surrendered the blade at the door. Even as he thought of it now, the singing whistle he had heard in the forest echoed in the audience chamber, the tip of the sword crying out like a swooping steel falcon. How could the steward not know this was a blade above all others? Just the feel of it was divine, even still in its scabbard. Saito eased his tension in the knowledge that he would be rejoined with his sidearm soon enough.

Ashikaga's rumbling tones brought Saito's attention back to the audience chamber. "You have been honest with me, Saito-san, even at the cost of your lord's honor and your own. You were correct to have burned the traitor's body; had you returned him here, I would not have allowed it. Your judgment is good, and both you and Nakadai-san have demonstrated your loyalty. You will not go as *rōnin*."

Those words released the last uneasiness Saito had been holding, heavy in his gut since he arrived here. A samurai's life consisted of devotion to his master, and without a master that life became purposeless. It was Lord Ashikaga's prerogative to dismiss all of Kanayama's samurai and let them go as *rōnin*, masterless warriors, to further dishonor the Kanayama name. Death would have been preferable; that much was obvious. Now Saito would not have to face such a fate, for Ashikaga had chosen to commandeer Kanayama's samurai and transfer their loyalty to him. The change would be an easy one for Saito; he already revered the old daimyo more than he could express. It had only been a matter of whether Ashikaga would accept such fealty, and now that worry had been swept away.

"Thank you, Ashikaga-dono," Saito said, bowing. "My life and my sword are yours."

"I am sending my third son to Kanayama's castle tomorrow. He will be the new lord there. You will accompany him and introduce him to his new home."

"Yes, lord."

"How large is your current fief?"

"Five hundred *koku*, my lord."

"Now it is a thousand. When you arrive at Gifu with my son, he will select six of Kanayama's finest horses for you to take with you." Ashikaga noted Saito's puzzled look and added, "If you had returned my corpse to my enemy, my spirit would have haunted you for the rest of your life and slit your soul's throat when you died. You chose wisely, Saito-san."

Saito wondered what Nakadai had said when Ashikaga had summoned him to this room, whether he too had received such rewards. *Maybe it was my suggestion to build the pyre,* Saito thought. *No matter. The lord will increase or decrease my holdings as he sees fit, and a good vassal should pay it no mind one way or the other.*

But his new lord's approval assuaged any lingering guilt he felt about taking Kanayama's sword. Ashikaga might have hung Kanayama's body from his doorpost, or fed it to his dogs, or ordered Beautiful Singer to be melted down, reforged into a chamber pot. There was no telling with him. Better to cremate Kanayama as they had, and to rescue Beautiful Singer as he did. It was not as if he'd stolen the sword for profit. A good vassal paid such things no mind.

All the same, when Saito returned home four days later with six new horses and a wide smile, his wife was pleased. Hisami was a beautiful woman, statuesque, not tiny and frail like the courtesans so many women tried to imitate. Of course Saito was long-boned himself, and so Hisami stood only to his shoulder. Among the other ladies, however, she held herself proud and tall like a hunting falcon on the wrist, sleek neck and gleaming eyes, knowing no fear. Today her kimono was pale orange with her underrobe showing the purest white. Her hair was, as ever, immaculate, wide set with two long pins retaining her bun. Saito knew for a fact what anyone else might have guessed: that the pins were actually knives. For Hisami was samurai like her husband, and equally prepared to take up arms and spill her life's blood at her master's command.

She was delighted to see the horses—the late lord's stables were excellent—and even happier at the expanded fief. One *koku* was the amount of rice it took to feed one person for a year, and five hundred additional *koku* would extend the Saito fief to annex the next town as part of its estate. It still wasn't much, comparatively. Kanayama had been collecting taxes from some twelve thousand *koku* before he died, and Ashikaga's domain was at least thirty times that, but a true samurai did not measure his wealth that way. Farmers and filthy merchants had to trouble themselves with such matters; monetary affairs were beneath Saito's notice. He would certainly make use of that wealth in equipping new retainers with swords and armor, but the details would be left to his housemaid. Finances were a concern for moneylenders and women.

As such, Hisami was delighted. "The lord must be very happy with you," she chirped, beaming as he handed over the horses and accompanied her to the tea room. "Doubling your fief, and having you escort his son as well. As a bodyguard, no doubt. I'm sure that's why he sent you."

A mouse-faced maid entered noiselessly, set down a tray with tea and cups, and vanished just as inaudibly as she had come in. "No," Saito said. "Lord Ashikaga needed someone who knew Kanayama's castle. That's why he sent me."

"That may be. But didn't Nakadai-san spend as much time there as you did? And yet you were chosen. Nakadai did not kill Lord Kanayama. Oh, don't look so surprised. The stories got here days ago. Lord Kanayama made a mistake, and it is a shame he had to die without face, but all the same, he was Kanayama Osamu. Ashikaga-dono sent over a dozen to kill him, yet you did it alone."

"I did it with Nakadai. And with regret." He sipped his tea. "Still, there is something to what you say."

Hisami bowed; better to thank her husband for being gracious enough to acknowledge her than to appear the insistent wife. "Our new master is very happy with you indeed. Why, he could have left us to rot as *rōnin*! After all, that . . . Where is your sword?"

Saito's spine bristled with tiny nails of ice. "What?"

"Your *tachi*," she said. "This one is different. The hilt and the *tsuba* have foxes on them."

"Ah. Yes." His stomach twisted; a dull pain shot down into his testicles. Somehow he suppressed any change in his face or voice. "My *tachi* was broken in the battle. I decided to leave it with the master's body when we put him on the pyre." Despite the nausea, the lie came smoothly enough. "It was an excellent blade. Even in dying, Kanayama exacts his price."

Hisami was silent for a pregnant moment, and Saito wondered whether his voice had been as even to her ears as it was to his. Finally she said, "Yes, that is a shame. It was a fine weapon, wasn't it?"

"I suppose this one will do. Lord Ashikaga gave it to me along with the rest."

"Hm. I hadn't heard that part of the story. Surely there is no shame in losing a blade to Kanayama, as good as he was. Strange to omit that part, *neh*? Hm."

Saito forced himself not to swallow. "You know how rumors are. By the time a story gets to the next village, it is hardly recognizable. Surely the details were simply forgotten in the telling, somewhere along the way?"

"Yes, I suppose so. But have I seen those foxes before?"

The throbbing in his abdomen redoubled. This is what had worried him ever since he'd left the funeral pyre. Several years before, Lord Kanayama had visited Saito's home. It happened only once, just after he and Hisami were married. Saito and the lord sat together and Hisami poured tea. But it was the mark of a samurai to notice at all times the weapons carried by anyone around him—or her. A good wife had to have an eye for detail as well, in order to appropriately praise guests and to direct conversation when a lull or an unwelcome topic emerged. Hisami was both a good wife and a good samurai. She would surely have noticed the finely worked foxes resting at Kanayama's hip, and now everything depended on whether her memory had kept what her eye had caught. Saito cut off a curse and waited for the worst.

But today the gods were smiling on him. "I would swear I've seen them before," she said finally, "but I haven't got a clue where. Perhaps it was in another life. No matter. I suppose I've seen a thousand different swords coming through our village; why shouldn't this one look familiar, *neh*?"

Saito nodded, wanting to exhale all the stress in his chest but afraid to do it as long as she sat before him. "You can put these foxes out of your mind. Tomorrow I'm going to have the sword remounted with a new *tsuba*. I think the crest of the house of Saito." He nodded, looking back at the foxes. "Yes, I think my father's crest would be excellent there."

"It certainly will. I'll send someone to the sword smith immediately to make the arrangements."

# 9

Hisami couldn't let her eyes rest on the new *tachi* without rage welling up in her. How could those fools be so useless? Her husband had trekked across forty *ri* to get home, and over all that distance those ignorant, low-born, misbegotten sons of peasants still couldn't manage to forewarn her about the sword. Why on earth did she hire spies in the first place, if not to give her information? They'd told her about the money, and the expanded fief; even the number of horses was correct. But the sword—a sword he would have ridden to the castle *without*, and which would have been gifted to him before he ever received the horses—how could they have failed to notice it?

She was astonished that her husband remained as calm as he'd been, though for every minute their conversation lingered on the weapon he'd looked as if he were going to burst. He had a right to be upset; she should have had the alcove and sword stand already prepared before he ever entered the village. Now she was going to have to sneak a priest in here and have the alcove and stand blessed without her husband's noticing. No, she decided. Better yet, she would do it when she got the new crossguard fitted, and tell him the blessing was for the sword now that it was truly his own. Yes, the family crest would be perfect for that. Certainly he would not be angry then.

In the meantime she was going to have to set some of

those newly acquired *koku* aside for hiring more spies, and more competent ones at that. How was she to be a proper hostess if she didn't know who her unannounced guests would be well before they arrived? Drooling ill-bred mongrels! How she had gotten by this long with such incompetents in her employ was beyond her understanding.

She was so mad at them, she almost didn't notice her husband's tension. Riding usually took that out of him; he was so natural in the saddle. Today, though, he was decidedly on edge. Was it her failure with the sword stand? Somehow his unease didn't seem to be directed at her. Unless . . . yes, of course that was it. It was almost two weeks ago that he'd left, and before he departed, she'd had her monthly bleeding and they hadn't been able to . . . Yes, it was clear to her now. It had simply been too long for him.

An easy problem to solve, she thought, touching her hair. She'd fix it tonight.

# 10

The singing of cicadas woke Saito from his sleep. A sheen of sweat cooled his chest as a breeze blew through the tiny gap in the sliding paper doors. Hisami lay next to him, naked, her nipples lavender in the blue moonlight. She was still sound asleep—but then, she could not hear the haunting sound.

Somehow the melody of the cicadas echoed the whistle of the Inazuma blade slicing through the air. It was as if the two sung in harmony, his memory of the sword's song a soprano to the alto of the chirping cicadas outside. He could not ignore their harmonizing. It seemed impossible, but as he recalled it, the sword's hum through the air was an uncanny match to the chirping in the garden. After a minute or two he found he could repress neither the cicadas' song nor the intrusion of his memories, so he got out of bed. His feet padded silently to the door. Sliding it aside, he stepped through to the next room and closed the door behind him. Hisami stirred slightly as the breeze swelled through the widened gap, but rolled back into her pillow as soon as he pushed the door back home.

Beautiful Singer was sitting in the sword stand in the alcove. A moonbeam shone through one of the paper windows and cast a silky square of luminescence over the weapon. The blade's song echoed in Saito's mind. He walked over to the alcove and picked up the sword.

Its balance could not have been more perfect. Soundlessly he slid the sword from its ill-fitting sheath and spun it through the air. It was a thing of beauty. Inazuma truly was a master among masters; no other sword smith could possibly duplicate the balance of lightness and strength Saito now held in his hand. Still naked, he had nowhere to wear the scabbard, so he laid it aside, then wrapped both hands reverently around the silk-bound sharkskin handle. Beautiful Singer floated in his grasp. He stepped forward and back with it in a ready stance, the Inazuma blade becoming one with him. A silent step off line, and he executed a mock parry and slash. The blade sang again as it fell, and indeed, somehow the cicadas were able to harmonize with it. It was as if Inazuma had taken the pulse of the heart of nature itself and crafted this sword with its rhythm. The gleam of the moon off the blade, the way it hummed in perfect harmony with the cicadas' song—the effect was unmistakable. Saito had never experienced a more perfect human creation in all his life.

Shoving the sword back into that inferior scabbard would almost taint the weapon. Still, he could hardly leave its blade exposed in the sword stand. He glanced outside and saw the moon was still high in the sky. It would be hours before daybreak, hours before a new scabbard could be commissioned. Saito looked at the sheath on the floor indecisively. One of the horses stirred outside. Horses. Of course, he thought. Wasn't the city of Seki just half a day's ride away? And wasn't Seki home to the finest craftsmen in the country when it came to swords? The smiths, the polishers, the men who braided cords for the grips—Seki was home to them all. The finest blades in the world were crafted in Seki, only six or seven hours from here. Saito picked up the scabbard and resheathed the *tachi*. "I'm sorry," he whispered, "but for tonight the Beautiful Singer must wear a shoddy kimono." Then he dressed quietly and prepared for his ride.

I

It was well after noon when Hisami learned her husband was returning. A rider burst into the compound, enveloped in a cloud of dust from the road, and reported that Saito was coming from the west and would arrive within the hour. She cursed the messenger for his lateness and ineptitude—a necessity, since thanking an informant would only make him lazy the next time—and sent another servant into town to fetch the sword smith.

She didn't have the first clue where her husband had been, nor why he'd slipped away in the middle of the night. The sword wasn't resting in the alcove when she awoke, but that meant nothing; a samurai was never without it. For a moment she was afraid she would find his body sprawled in the garden, slain by an assassin or a burglar during the night. She knew it didn't make sense—why would anyone kill him and leave her alive?—but all the same she had searched the grounds that morning and found no trace of him. Nor did she see any signs of a struggle, nor any evidence that a messenger from Lord Ashikaga had come to summon her husband away. Though her network of servants and messengers stretched for twenty *ri* in every direction, not a single one of them could tell her of her husband's whereabouts. Several had heard a single horse galloping hard in the night, but none of the useless dung-eating cretins had identified the rider. Of course it was him, she thought. To think they did not even recognize their own lord! Hisami had relied on imbecilic farmers and craftsmen long enough. With the new wealth Lord Ashikaga had bestowed on the house of Saito, she would hire night watchmen to be her eyes and ears.

The only assumption she was left with was that her husband had gone to one of the pleasure houses. She could accept that, but it didn't explain why he'd been away so long. Perhaps last night hadn't satisfied him. It had pleased her well enough, but somehow he seemed distracted. It was only natural for a man to go to a pleasure house if his wife could not sate him, but why go to one so far from home? How was she supposed to settle the bill if she didn't know which brothel had serviced him?

She masked her frustration as well as she could when Saito finally rode up to the house. She could see the sword smith coming down the road, shuffling in his deep blue robes, and she knew her husband would be happy to have his sword taken to be remounted. There was one problem, however: Saito wasn't wearing his sword.

"By all gods," Hisami exclaimed as he dismounted, "you gave me a fright. Where did you go last night?"

"What concern is it of a wife's where her husband chooses to go?" His voice was gruff, and she could see the sleeplessness under his eyes.

"I do not mean to pry. I was only worried—"

"Stop questioning me, woman! If you want to worry, worry about getting some tea and something to eat. I'm starving."

With an effort she bottled her exasperation. Now she would have to find some excuse to send the sword smith away. Getting him to come back again would be another feat; how could she explain that her samurai husband was without his *tachi*? How could she explain to her husband that to protect his honor, a respected artisan had to be curtly turned away?

Before she could deal with any of that, however, she knew she had to dispel his anger. She sweetened her voice. "Of course. How thoughtless of me. Here, let me help you with your sandals. Haruko!" The name came from her mouth like the crack of a whip. Instantly a servant girl appeared. "Tea for the master! Can't you see he is exhausted from riding? And rice, and fish! Can't you see he is hungry?"

# 1 2

Hisami disappeared out the front door almost as quickly as the serving girl disappeared through the back, leaving Saito alone to wonder what had gotten into his wife. Usually she was properly obedient, but today she was salty. No, he corrected himself. Her tongue always carried an edge. That was one of the things that attracted him to her: she wasn't a meek little rabbit like so many other women. Still, there were times when such a tongue did not befit a woman, and it had already been a long day. The old saying held true: a samurai should allow himself to be wedded only to the sword.

It drove Saito mad to be without his Beautiful Singer. He always felt naked without a blade at his hip, and now that feeling was especially strong. The night ride to Seki was hard and very dangerous in the dark, but with his new weapon bouncing at his side he'd felt no fear. Naturally, he rode back in daylight, and though he was safe from the many dangers of riding by starlight, the trip home left him feeling far more vulnerable. In the dark, pushing a horse to its limit had its thrills: ducking the occasional low-hanging branch, wondering when or if his horse would falter, break a leg, or throw him. Riding unarmed in broad daylight held no such excitement, only the ignominious possibility of being waylaid by bandits.

Saito shook his head and watched Haruko, the serving

maid, quietly set tea before him on a lacquered tray. Wrinkles gnarled his cheeks as he pursed his lips in a self-reprobating frown. It was no band of highwaymen that left him feeling cold this morning. It was the sword, or rather the lack of it, and he knew it. Even without his *tachi*, Saito wasn't completely unarmed. In his waistband he still wore his *wakizashi*, a short sword that no self-respecting samurai was ever without. As fine a sword as it was, a *tachi* could break in battle. That was simple reality. A *wakizashi* was never to be used in combat except in the event that a warrior found himself without his primary weapon. But the true purpose of the *wakizashi* was to be an ever-present reminder of the samurai's mortality. There were only two honorable ways for a true follower of Bushido to die: in battle, or by his own hand in the act of seppuku. Both were the highest act of sacrifice in the service of one's lord. The *wakizashi* was the implement of seppuku, and since honor might demand a samurai's death at any time, he could never be without his short sword. No bandit could face Saito and his *wakizashi* and live. Saito knew that. Even though it was a shorter weapon, he was more than skilled enough to turn that disadvantage against an enemy. It was not the highway thieves that worried him on his ride back from Seki; it could only have been the sword.

What if something happened to her? The craftsmen of Seki were the best in the land, perhaps the best in the world, but, still, none of them was on a level with the immortal master Inazuma. Would they show Beautiful Singer the respect she deserved? Saito grunted and sipped his tea. Of course they would. These were men who devoted their lives to the sword just as Saito had, albeit in a different manner. They would have no choice but to honor her. How could anyone fail to recognize her beauty, her perfection?

And if they did fail? Saito wasn't sure how the question crept back into his thoughts. As he replaced the cup on its tray, a falcon keened outside. The cry swept over the house as the bird continued to circle, and Saito heard a familiar note in it, the song of his Beautiful Singer. What if she was somehow damaged? The question was ineluctable, and with a moment's reflection he knew the answer: anyone who tarnished that sword would die.

It could be no other way. His response was only natural,

he assured himself. Anybody who saw someone destroy a great work of art would be similarly moved. Could a person simply look on as a madman put the sculptures of Unkei to the torch? Could one stand by and allow someone to tear *The Tale of the Heike* to shreds? Never. None of the artisans at Seki would do any harm to his Beautiful Singer, but no one who damaged her could live.

Settled by his decision, Saito began eating his meal. A bowl of steaming rice and a small rectangular plate with slices of raw octopus were sitting on the table before him. Saito realized the serving girl had set them there without his noticing, and the realization shook him. Ordinarily it was impossible for someone to enter a room without his being immediately aware of how they stood, whether they were armed, what defenses there were from where he was seated. That a mere servant could walk in on him unawares was troubling, to say the least. "The ride," he said to himself, taking a mouthful of rice from his chopsticks. It must have been the ride that exhausted him so.

He nodded, satisfied, and dipped a purple-and-white slice of octopus in a shallow dish of soy sauce and wasabi that Haruko had left him. Yes, it *was* the ride. He'd been in the saddle for twelve of the past fourteen hours, more than enough to wear on any man. If it had been left to him, Saito would have stayed the day in Seki, waited to retrieve his sword, and returned home the following afternoon. But no samurai was his own man. Saito was only an instrument of Lord Ashikaga, and Ashikaga did not like his vassals running about without his knowledge. Not even a high-ranking samurai would leave his own village without the lord's consent. Allowing one's warriors to go where they pleased was the surest way to invite insurrection and assassination. Saito was lucky that he fell in the middle ranks among Ashikaga's legions, high enough to wear the twin swords and topknot but low enough to escape scrutiny of his every move. Still, it would not do for him to be absent from home should the lord's messengers come to call. It would also be imprudent to make another unauthorized voyage to Seki; next time he would need permission.

The next time, he knew, would be soon. The craftsmen he'd commissioned in Seki told him that if they rushed, they could finish Saito's new *tsuba* by tomorrow. Saito knew they would have to keep their forges burning day and night to do it; so much the better, he thought. Weren't these tasks what the lower castes were born for? The wooden scabbard he requested would be ready by then as well, and wraps for the grip and sheath were readily available. Very well, he decided as he scooped the last of the rice into his mouth. It would be tomorrow.

He sent for Haruko again and ordered her to tell the house's head messenger to prepare a carrier pigeon. Soon enough the messenger came to the porch, and Saito dictated a request to make the trek to Seki. Satisfied, Saito went to the bath already prepared for him and drifted off to sleep.

# 13

n the morning a new pigeon was waiting in the coop of the Saito clan compound. A tiny cylinder of hollowed bone was tied to its leg, and the case found its way to Saito's breakfast table. He slid the translucent scroll of paper from the little tube and read it silently.

Hisami's curiosity was obvious. "Lord Ashikaga sends word?"

"Yes," Saito replied. "He says the taxes are late in Iwatani. I am to go immediately to investigate." It was only a lie of omission. The tiny note did in fact say all of that. It also said that Saito's voyage to Seki was approved, but that in the future he would not be so vague in his requests of the lord. This last part was not stated directly but rather by nuance. Not that Ashikaga himself had ever shied away from being blunt. Quite the opposite: the man had no talent whatsoever as a diplomat. Subtlety was beyond him, perhaps even beneath him. But a pigeon could only bear so much weight in flight, and there was only so much room to write on such a tiny scroll. The note's actual text read, "Iwatani taxes late. Investigate and report. Seki approved; kill your pigeon keeper."

Though unstated, the true message was clear. Saito's communiqué was deemed curt, presumptuous, and wholly improper for a vassal of his lowly status. He had committed an act of gross misjudgment in making his vacuous request to go to Seki without informing the lord of his purposes, but this time the lord would choose to interpret this as the messenger's mistake. Saito would have to find himself a new pigeon master, a man of greater discretion. This essentially meant Ashikaga would never grant Saito this sort of reprieve again. One warning was more than the lord was wont to give, and though the note made Saito's face redden, he knew he was lucky.

Saito didn't bother to mention any of this to Hisami. He barked to one of the house retainers to prepare his horse. Hisami reached out and touched his hand. She swallowed dryly before she spoke. "What's troubling you?"

He grunted noncommittally. "Nothing. It's just that Iwatani is so far from here. Our fief has expanded, but it hardly stretches that far. This should be none of my concern."

This was also a lie, but only partially. Iwatani was his concern by way of sheer coincidence. The town lay a mere thirty *ri* from Seki, on the periphery of Lord Ashikaga's domain. Its nonstrategic location and small population made it unworthy of a permanent garrison. Thus, if Saito rode to Seki, he would conveniently become Ashikaga's closest samurai to the area. If Saito hadn't sent his request, he wouldn't have been dispatched to Iwatani. Saito wondered whether the errand had been given as a minor form of punishment.

Again he chose not to voice any of this to his wife. She would be suspicious enough of where he'd gone the night before last, and all this time she'd been holding her tongue about his sword. He knew she'd noticed it was gone. She was samurai, after all. That she hadn't made mention of its absence yet was only a testament to her good sense. If she didn't ask, he wouldn't have to answer, so he wouldn't have to lie and thus would not be caught in a lie. Her silence preserved honor for both of them. Now if only he could get out of the house and into his saddle before she decided to say something.

"Don't worry so much," was her only advice. "The lord has already widened your fief, *neh*? Perhaps he has plans to extend it further. Perhaps he will grant you everything between here and Iwatani! That would be grand, wouldn't it?"

Saito smiled despite himself. "You are a good woman, Hisami. Buy yourself a new kimono while I'm gone."

She beamed. "Oh! Thank you! You're too good to me. Tell me when you'll be back so I can have it on for you when you return. And then I'll take it off for you, *neh*?"

He smiled again, but this time it was hollow. Somehow the thought of lying with her made his stomach turn. He was anxious to get on the road and return his Beautiful Singer to his side. "Yes. When I return."

"When will that be?"

He made some quick calculations in his head and said, "Tomorrow." On a map Iwatani was farther than Seki, but the road to Seki followed the wide curves of a valley, making that journey the longer one. Getting from Seki to Iwatani involved backtracking along that valley, and he knew he couldn't retrieve his sword and finish his business in a single day. "There may be a great deal to settle in Iwatani," he said, stretching the truth again. "I can't promise I'll make it home tonight."

She nodded, smiled, and helped him prepare for his journey. Saito only took a moment to locate the man in charge of his pigeon coops and tell him to start looking for his own replacement. Then he went back to readying himself for the journey to Iwatani. He packed only what he would require for the road, leaving behind everything he knew he might need should he be delayed in Seki and be forced to camp between there and Iwatani. A man didn't carry a bedroll unless he planned to sleep on it, and as far as Hisami was concerned, Saito would spend tonight at home or at an Iwatani inn. Even as he chose to leave the bedroll stored where it was, he wondered why he was deceiving Hisami yet again this morning. In the seven years they had been married, he couldn't recall one instance of lying to her before yesterday.

# 14

"It is an exceptional blade, my lord," the sword smith stammered. Saito looked at the man quizzically. He was young, not yet thirty, but hardly a boy to be frightened into stammering by the presence of a samurai. He was clad in the white robes of a Shinto priest, a black cap atop his head. All the smiths of Seki were priests, and their swords were fashioned with religious ritualism. It was their reverence and dedication that made them the best. "I have never seen the like."

"No, you have not." Saito expected relief to wash over him upon seeing his Beautiful Singer again, but instead his heart plunged into his bowels. The priest's nervous tone was enough to sicken him, and over the white-robed shoulder he saw his beloved sword lying stripped on the tatami mat behind the priest. The handle was removed from the weapon, and the blade lay naked on a silk cloth. "What have you done to her?" he demanded.

The priest-smith's eyebrows rose momentarily at the accusation. "N-nothing. The *tachi* is fine; we simply have not remounted the handle yet."

"Why not?"

"The, um"—the sword smith faltered—"the inscription. You have seen it?"

"No, though you are an insolent one for asking." The smith might have been an ordained priest, but he still ranked below a man of samurai lineage. "I know what it says. It is an Inazuma."

"More than Inazuma, lord. It is the Beautiful Singer."

Saito's brow gnarled. "And?"

The priest-smith's eyebrows jumped again. "I dare not offend you, but it is best that you know: the blade is cursed."

"Is said to be cursed," Saito corrected him.

"But the legend—"

"Is nothing but a legend. I've faced scores of men on the battlefield; do you expect me to be afraid of mere words?"

The young priest swallowed. "Begging my lord's forgiveness, 'mere' is not a word I would use in connection with this blade."

"Quite to the point—she is anything but ordinary. I assume the work you have done for me is equally exceptional?"

The priest knew he had already overstepped his bounds and hastily turned to pick up the new *tsuba*. "I sincerely hope it pleases you."

Saito took the metal disc in his hand. It was black-lacquered steel with the Saito family crest gilded in the center. The crest was a double-diamond motif, one layered atop the other. A hole the shape of an elongated teardrop would allow the *tachi*'s blade to be inserted right through the center of the diamonds. The double diamonds gleamed in gold against the black, and Saito inevitably thought of his deceased father. The Saito clan had long been samurai, but it was Saito's father who rode into battle under the flag of those diamonds and made them worthy of Ashikaga's notice. The house of Saito had been a minor one until then, but his father's victories pushed the family's star high into the sky, making Saito proud to bear his name. Saito hoped he could accomplish as much himself one day.

Next the priest offered Saito the new scabbard, while two other acolyte-smiths carefully fitted the Inazuma blade with her new grip and *tsuba*. The scabbard was oak, lacquered to a flawless black sheen with the Saito crest once again in gold leaf. The craftsmanship was unsurpassable, the final product a masterpiece, but Saito paid it no mind. His eyes glossed over the scabbard, but his thoughts remained locked on the sword itself. When the sword smiths finally bowed and presented her to him, it was all he could do not to snatch her out of their hands, and to thank them instead.

Once she was back in his grasp, he felt like a whole man again. Abruptly he realized his earlier haste and tried to cover it. "You have done well," he said, sheathing the sword. He bowed to the three smiths and they to him; then he was off to Iwatani.

# 15

The sight of a samurai on horseback was more than enough to terrify the average farmer. In the saddle, any warrior was fearsome—a thousand pounds of galloping muscle were threatening enough—but when that warrior wore the topknot of a samurai, his riding inspired fear and reverence in any commoner. So it was that Saito entered the village of Iwatani. Roads cleared for him, and crowds hushed as he passed. By the time he reached the town square, all eyes were fixed on him.

"Who is your headman?" he bellowed.

A reed of a man scampered out from the encircling crowd and fell to his knees, dust rising around him. "I am, lord." The village headman was old, nearing sixty, and Saito could see almost every bone and tendon in his body. Few commoners were overweight, but this man looked as if the skin had been pulled tight against his frame by some goblin sitting inside his chest. He was browned by long hours in the rice paddies and wore no more than a loincloth and straw sandals.

Saito looked down at the top of the man's head. "Your name?"

"You may call me Ojiya if it pleases you, lord."

Saito urged his horse to retreat a few steps, then dismounted. "Rise, Ojiya. Look at me."

The frail little man obeyed. He met Saito's gaze with awe, as if staring at the very face of Buddha himself. Then, with the same reverence, he dropped his eyes again to Saito's chin. "My lord?"

"Taxes," Saito said, seeming to project his height over the man into his voice. It was no wonder the villagers were struck by him. A samurai ate fish and vegetables with every meal; these people were lucky to get more than a bowlful of rice gruel a day. They were also lucky to be drawing breath, Saito reminded himself. Without Ashikaga's protection, bandits or other warlords would steal even their gruel from them. That protection demanded a price. "Taxes," he intoned again.

"We have paid ten *koku*, my lord."

"The tax is forty."

Ojiya bowed again, trembling with nervousness. "My lord, we have paid what we can. You can see for yourself we have no more."

Saito's eyes roamed the surroundings. "I see perhaps a hundred of you standing here. Why are these people not in the fields?"

"My lord, it has not rained in twenty days. Lord Ashikaga must understand—"

"Lord Ashikaga understands what he wishes to understand; you are in no position to tell him what he *must* do." Saito's tone earned him a new fit of bowing, heads all around the square bobbing with renewed vigor. "Now, then," he said after Ojiya returned to his feet, "you will tell me when the remaining thirty *koku* will be paid."

"Lord, we cannot—"

"You must have something stashed away. How else do all these people get food? I can see for myself that they aren't farming it themselves."

"But the rain—"

"Rain does not concern me," Saito barked. "Lord Ashikaga protects you even through typhoons and earthquakes! If the elements cannot stop him, why should you allow them to stop you?"

Ojiya trembled where he stood. Those around the two could not pull themselves away. "My lord, if we pay even a bowlful of rice more, some of us will starve."

"I did not come for one bowlful. I came for thirty *koku*."

"We cannot do it," the headman stuttered. "Lord Ashikaga asks the impossible."

"The impossible?" Saito bellowed. "Do you call the lord an imbecile?"

"No!" Ojiya protested. "No, not at all!"

"But everyone knows the impossible cannot be done."

"Yes, but—"

"So only a true imbecile would demand something no one could possibly satisfy?"

"My lord, I only—"

"Then choose your crime, headman! Have you called the lord a fool, or have you slandered him by telling me of an order he never gave?"

"My lord—"

It was too late. The Inazuma blade hung in the sky just long enough to catch the gleam of the sun, then fell like a diving hawk. The old man's head bounced next to his feet. A moment later, his body dropped next to it.

Saito whirled the sword in a fast silvery arc that whipped most of the gore from the blade. Bringing it back around, he cleaned the remaining blood between his thumb and forefinger and resheathed the blade without ever looking down to find the scabbard.

"Now, then," he said grimly to the crowd. "Who is your headman after Ojiya?"


That night Saito lowered himself into a steaming cauldron of water, the bath heated by a volcanic vent. Minerals from deep in the earth scented the spring with flavors of copper and jasmine. Hot water turned his skin red, and fragrant steam misted on the mirrored edge of Beautiful Singer. The steam would permeate the wood of her scabbard and warp it, so he brought her here naked, like himself. How beautiful she was, he thought. Even now she hummed to him.

How enchanting her voice was, never louder than when she sang through the headman's neck on the town square. It was as perfect a cut as Saito had ever delivered. Ordinarily an *iaidō* sword was not used to behead; such a thin blade was likely to lose its edge on hard bone. Better to slice the front half of the throat, cutting only the soft tissues. That was how Saito had intended to take Ojiya, but at the last moment some impulse made him extend his strike a hand's breadth further. It was almost as if Beautiful Singer wanted to prove herself to him—or perhaps he wanted to prove himself to her. In either case they were a worthy pair. His draw was flawless, his cut precise, and the Inazuma blade severed the spinal cord without so much as a nick.

He could still feel her song resonating through his hand as he tilted her steel to catch the dim light. He let his shoulders relax against the stone rim of the bath and sunk deeper into the water. The relaxation was well deserved; he'd made a fine showing today. After Ojiya's execution, the villagers were prompt to produce a large golden Buddha worth almost a *koku* by itself. They promised another nine *koku* by the end of the harvest, thereby doubling the tax they'd already paid. Saito said he would accept the statue and would take their offer before the lord to determine their fate. Every last one of them scattered afterward, save the owner of the inn in which Saito now bathed. The innkeeper was so anxious to avoid the samurai's wrath that he charged nothing for the room, and proffered a meal such as no one in this village had seen in years.

A heavy meal and a hot bath normally made a man tired, but Saito was feeling energized now that Beautiful Singer was back at his side. His mind was on the future, on the arrangements he would complete here tomorrow, on what would come to pass after that. Success here might warrant further rewards from Lord Ashikaga. He decided not to go home and report to the lord by messenger or pigeon. He would ride to the castle himself.

# 16

"Fool!" barked Ashikaga. "You killed him for that?"

"Of course," Saito said defensively. "He insulted you."

"He did nothing of the kind. Of course I ask the impossible! Ask these lazy peasants for three *koku* and the most you can possibly hope for is one. But if I want one *koku* and that is all I demand, I will never see half of it. They never do the least bit of work unless you ask the impossible. Making them strive hopelessly is the only way to meet the least of your expectations."

Saito's face reddened under the barrage of Ashikaga's words. He bowed his head, not out of deference but to hide his shame and rage. "My lord," he stammered with all the control he could muster, "I—"

"Silence. You only harm yourself by speaking."

It was all Saito could do to stay in place on the floor. Never before had he wished he were armed in the presence of his master. Now he yearned to hear the familiar song ringing in this chamber.

"Look up," Ashikaga's bear-voice said. Saito swallowed his anger and looked the old warlord in the eye. "I am too harsh with you," Ashikaga rumbled. "You are no politician; it is not your place to understand such things as taxes."

Saito was astonished. An apology from Ashikaga was

unheard of. Still, in this case, Saito thought, it was certainly warranted. "You did well in bringing this statue to me," Ashikaga went on. "As for the nine *koku*, I doubt they will produce more than two. Even then, I hope it does not kill too many of them to give it up. You do understand, dead farmers pay no taxes."

"No, Ashikaga-dono," Saito muttered, bristling at the insult, "they do not."

"I must instruct my samurai better in the ways of politics. Or else I must send better-educated men to perform my errands."

This too made Saito grit his teeth. He said nothing in response.

"I can see you wish to take your leave," the lord's gravelly voice intoned. "You are dismissed."

Saito bowed low, then stalked out of the room. Only when the door slid shut behind him did he release a growl of frustration. The audacity of that man! A samurai's existence was truly thankless, Saito thought. Even in apology, the lord found room to ridicule. He stormed down the stairs and into the weapon steward's chamber, where Beautiful Singer awaited him on a tall black stand against the far wall. Six other *tachi* were racked above her.

"Which one is yours, sir?" asked the sword steward, a boy of about twenty.

"Only the finest weapon in this room. How dare you place her below those others?"

The steward started at Saito's tone and dashed to retrieve his sword. "My apologies, sir, and please pardon me for not recognizing it as yours. It is a different blade from the one you last left with me, is it not?"

"Certainly not," Saito snapped, his hands hungry to hold her again. "And for one who does nothing but handle swords all day, you should remember quality of this caliber by feel alone!" He snatched back the sword like a wild dog tearing meat.

"My apologies again," the steward said, faltering. "I only meant that the scabbard and the *tsuba*, they are new, are they not? And quite beautiful, if I may say so."

Saito's hackles rose. "New scabbard?" Why should this boy notice something like that? He thinks I have something to hide, Saito thought. A new sheath means a new sword, and that means he knows about Beautiful Singer. "Insolent cur! What makes you think I have something to hide?"

The steward's eyes went wide with bewilderment. "You wouldn't, sir! By all gods and buddhas, I never thought anything like that!"

Saito lunged into the room, kicking the table aside and sending the steward back on his heels. The boy tripped backward and tumbled to the ground, his head striking the sword rack.

"Do you dare to draw a weapon on me, boy?"

"No!"

"Then why move for the swords?" Saito took another menacing step forward and the steward scrambled from the room on all fours. He regained his footing and dashed for the hall. Stumbling, he landed face-first against the wall outside. He turned in terror as his aggressor emerged from the room. Saito wrapped his fingers around Beautiful Singer's grip; he could already hear her song in the air.

*"Stop!"*

The command rumbled like thunder. Saito's gaze shot up the stairs and saw Ashikaga towering there, livid. His scars and his glare were more fearsome than his sword, though that too now hung at his hip. "Explain yourself, Saito!"

"This boy insulted me," he said angrily. "He insulted me and my sword. I would reclaim my honor."

"Swords do not feel insults," the lord said, glowering, "and since you are my sword, neither should you."

"My lord, his impudence—"

"Stands. At my pleasure. He is a trusted man, and there are not many so trustworthy as to guard the weapons at my very door. Takagi!"

Takagi, the steward, was stunned to speechlessness, but he acknowledged his master's summons with a hasty, trembling bow. "Apologize to this man," Ashikaga growled, "for any offense you have paid him."

It took a moment for Takagi's tongue to function. "Ap-apologies, sir. A thousand apologies."

"There," the old warlord said. "Does that satisfy your honor?"

It was not a question. "It will have to," Saito replied, his voice hollow. In equally hollow words he added, "A thousand apologies to you as well, Ashikaga-san, for the disturbance."

# 17

At last these spies are doing me some good, Hisami told herself. Her new hires were working out better than anticipated. Of course she knew her husband was at Lord Ashikaga's stronghold; even the most incompetent of her informants could have told her that. What was new came from Seki. One of the informers she had just put on salary hailed from that region, and he was able to tell his mistress where her husband had gone on last week's midnight ride. What business the lord had in Seki, he couldn't say, but Hisami realized immediately what his only purpose there could have been. He'd left with his sword and come back without it; he could only have paid a visit to the sword smiths.

But why go in the dead of night? And why ride there and back at such a furious pace? Hisami was puzzled. Surely Lord Ashikaga would not have taken offense to such a simple errand had Saito only made the request. Strange indeed, she thought. What on earth could have been so urgent in Seki?

There was only one way to find out. She called a stable hand to prepare her favorite horse. When she told him to pack her things for an overnight stay, the servant shot her a conspiratorial look; it was untoward behavior for a woman to leave the house without her husband, and downright scandalous for her to sleep elsewhere. No matter, she thought. Saito need not learn of it. It was one day's leisurely ride to Seki, and a hard two days' ride to Ashikaga's castle. Even if her husband still had a mind to run his horse into the ground, she should still be able to beat him home.

She pushed her steed harder than usual nonetheless, in order to reach Seki before sundown. Mountain roads were more dangerous for a lone woman than they were for a man, and while she knew she could handle any brigands foolish enough to cross a samurai's path, it was pointless to invite trouble. Her course of action was reckless enough as it was.

The sun was just dipping below the treetops when her horse trotted through Seki's main gate. She presumed the priests would have retired from their forges by now, so she paid for a room at the inn and had a dinner there of tofu and abalone. The next morning, she set out to find a sword smith.

"I am Saito Hisami," she told the black-robed youth who answered the door at the foundry. "I wish to speak to the man who met my husband."

The acolyte ran off and soon returned, accompanied by a surprisingly young man wearing white robes and a black hat. "Saito-sama," the priest said nervously. "Please, come in."

"Don't be afraid," she said, following him to a sitting room. "I do not come to express dissatisfaction with your work."

"Understood, madam, but I fear what you have come to talk about is far worse."

"Oh?" The two of them sat, and the boy disappeared. The air was thick with the smell of steel and smoke, and noticeably hotter than it should have been. The priest was sweating, though Hisami could not tell whether it was from nervousness or the heat from the forges.

"You are the wife of the Saito who came to have his hand guard and scabbard replaced?"

"Yes."

"Then you know your husband carries an Inazuma blade."

"Hardly! He could never afford—"

She stopped herself in midthought. Inazuma's works were priceless; not even by selling the entire Saito fief could she acquire one. Indeed, she'd only ever seen one in her life, and that one belonged to ... Kanayama Osamu. The memory instantly resurfaced in her mind. The twin foxes! That was House Kanayama's symbol, and now it was on her husband's weapon. That was why he had come here so quickly: to have the late lord's crest removed before she could remember where she'd seen it. The shame of it was unbearable; her husband was a thief. There could be no other explanation. Kanayama could have bequeathed the blade to Saito before his death, but that would have been a thing of honor, not something to ride off in the dead of night to conceal.

"Thank you," she told the priest uneasily. "I believe I understand the situation now."

"I'm afraid you do not," he cautioned. "Whether or not the sword is your husband's, you must know the truth of it. It is cursed."

"Cursed? Rubbish!"

"It is true, my lady. Master Inazuma crafted that sword especially for Motoyori Hidetada, the famous warlord of Echizen. Motoyori was renowned for his swordsmanship and also for his passions. He never married, but he was known to have regular beds in pleasure houses throughout the north. One of his consorts was a geisha whose beauty was said to be unmatched. Her voice was also without equal, and it is said she used to sing him to sleep.

"The story goes that this geisha fell in love with Motoyori and wanted to marry him. Of course a high-ranking samurai like Motoyori could never marry a woman of her profession, so instead she begged him to give up all other women but her."

"And did he?"

"A man cannot deny any request from such a beautiful woman. He said he would be hers alone, but as I said, he was a man of great passions. Inevitably he became unfaithful to her, and when she learned of it, she tried to kill him. No mere geisha could best a swordsman of his caliber, of course, but she caught him unawares. Ordinarily he would have tried to restrain her, but he reacted unthinkingly to her surprise attack and killed her.

"Motoyori was so distraught by her death that he brought the blade that killed her back to Master Inazuma. He composed a death poem for his lover such as befits the passing of a samurai, not a lowly prostitute. Inazuma inscribed the poem on the tang of the blade. I have seen it myself:

> *The glorious sun,*
> *nigh on reaching its zenith,*
> *shaded by my hand.*

"She was the sun, you see, glorious in her beauty and becoming ever more so until his hand put out her light. The sword became known as the Beautiful Singer thereafter."

Hisami's forehead furrowed. "A sad story, to be sure, but hardly a curse."

"Motoyori only shaded the sun; he did not extinguish it forever. It is said her spirit followed the weapon, and when her death poem was inscribed, she entered the blade as well. Since his passions betrayed her, she would make them become his downfall as well. The sword performed better than ever after her death, a fact only to be explained by her spirit's strength guiding it. It is said to be lighter and faster than any other blade, and truly, madam, it is so. My own hands have held it. But her will exerts itself from within the sword. She drove Motoyori mad with rage and jealousy until finally he could no longer control himself. The urges within him took over, and he died senselessly in a duel. He drunkenly accused another man of sleeping with one of his favorite prostitutes and was cut down in the street, too blind with jealousy for his sword to find its mark."

Hisami let out a long breath. It was evident in the priest's manner that he earnestly believed every word of his tale to be true. Indeed, he was so serious that Hisami was almost inclined to believe him.

She shook her head, and better sense took over. "What does this have to do with my husband? He never knew this woman; she would have died hundreds of years ago."

"The sword remains possessed to this day, madam. All who have owned it have died. Some men fall quickly to its spell, others last longer, but every man succumbs. If I may ask, my lady, is your husband a passionate man or a temperate one?"

"How dare you even ask? Every samurai controls his emotions when needed." She surprised herself with her harsh tone, and immediately she wondered why she'd snapped at him like she did. After a pensive moment she understood. "My husband is . . . well, in certain company he can be quick to laugh. And quick to anger."

"Then I fear the Beautiful Singer will make short work of him. You must get the sword from him and have her spirit exorcised."

"How am I supposed to do that? The sword's scarcely left his side since he brought it home."

"All the more evidence that it is still possessed, my lady."

The priest had a point, she thought. Why else would a man leave his bed, his wife, in the middle of the night for the sake of a sword? "Why didn't you exorcise it when you had it here?"

"We had no time," the smith-priest pleaded earnestly. "It was all we could do just to complete the work he'd commissioned in the time he allowed. We only knew the name of the sword after we removed the handle, and by that time he was already on his way here to retrieve it."

"And you told him what you told me?"

"Only that it was cursed, madam. He refused to listen to anything else."

Hisami considered the priest's tale. Possession? She thought only farmers scared each other with legends like that. Still, the story went a long way to explain her husband's behavior. He had always been "passionate," to use the priest's term, but never impulsive. Rashness was not a good quality in a samurai. The past five days were different, though. Riding off like that, then returning in a huff, leaving again the next morning: it wasn't normal.

Her mind turned to the late Lord Kanayama. That one was like a stone. Emotionally stoic, unflappable even in the midst of combat. Hisami never met him more than briefly, but in all her contacts with him she had never seen him laugh, never a frown or a grin. Yet he was as wild as a tiger when he died. Could the sword have turned him? And if so, how much more quickly would it bewitch her husband?

She thanked the priest and took her leave. She would have to hurry now. Nothing about her husband was predictable anymore, and the consequences would be deadly if she was not home when he returned.

# 18

Saito's mare galloped through the gate, dust billowing in her wake. She was breathing heavily, lungs pumping like bellows, and Saito was panting too. He'd ridden her hard, and the wind from the ride was a cool relief on his sweaty brow. It was good to ride a horse like that from time to time. It spoke to the condition of the animal, and also made it clear who the master was. He felt the need to assert his mastery this evening.

Swinging off the saddle, he handed the reins to his stable hand and gave the horse a pat on her flank. On his way out he patted his wife's favorite horse as well, feeling energized from the ride. As he wiped the coarse brown hairs from his palm, his mood suddenly soured.

Hisami, dressed in gold and black, bowed deferentially as he slid open the door. "Welcome back," she said sweetly. "Allow me to take your sandals and put up your swords. I'll have the maid bring some tea."

"No."

"No tea?" she asked, proffering her hands for the sword.

"No," he said again, walking past her and taking his customary seat.

Hisami eyed the sword nervously. "Is something wrong?"

"No. Don't get so upset."

"Shouldn't a wife be upset when her husband goes armed in the house?"

"A wife should not be meddlesome," he grunted angrily. "Nor should she go out without her husband's permission."

She arched an eyebrow. "Go out?"

"Your horse is drinking deeply outside. It sweats."

Hisami swallowed. "It is a hot day."

"No," he snapped. "It's been riding. Hard. Where did you go?"

Hisami struggled not to blush. "I did go riding earlier," she admitted hesitantly, "but only on business. To see that all our family affairs are in order." Her eyes fell to his weapon again.

"Meaning what?" he demanded.

"Meaning only that your behavior has been somewhat irregular for the past few days. I wanted to ensure that everything was well with you."

"I don't need a doctor," he grumbled.

"No, you don't."

His eyebrows knotted in a suspicious glare. "What do you mean, then?"

She blinked quickly and padded over to her cushion, across from his. "You know," she said, sitting, "I was thinking we still haven't had a priest come to have the house blessed. Why don't I summon one? Then we can have your father's emblem anointed as well, to bless your newly adorned sword."

"Again with the sword! Why can't you just let me be?"

"I'm not talking about the sword," she protested, her face a mask of false innocence. "A house blessing is only natural—"

"No priests! Our house is blessed enough." His eyes transfixed hers with a murderous glare.

"I went to Seki," she blurted out. "I know about your Beautiful Singer. And its curse."

"Nonsense!"

"It isn't nonsense. It's what killed Lord Kanayama. It's what brought you into ill favor with Lord Ashikaga as well."

"Meddlesome wench! You and your damned spies!"

Saito's face was red with fury. "It is a wife's duty to know the affairs of the house," she retorted.

"It is also her duty not to let her ears stray in places they should not go!"

"Please," she implored, "let me summon a priest."

He jumped to his feet. "Never! This idiotic superstition is trying my patience. I won't hear another word of it."

"Then you won't hear another word from me."

Saito grunted, thinking the matter settled. It took another moment for her implication to set in. "What do you mean?"

Hisami rose to her feet. "I cannot stay under the same roof as the spirit of that woman. It is obvious to me now that you are bewitched. Allow me to summon a priest for an exorcism, or allow me to leave."

"What?" The muscles in his arms tensed as if he were about to strike her. "This is ridiculous! Have you become some peasant now? What you speak of is pure fairy tale!"

"Then why does my husband shout and threaten me—*armed*—in his own house?"

"I shout because you've lost your mind!"

"Someone in this room has," she swore bitterly, her voice losing its implacable calm for the first time. "Let us find out who! Choose! Choose one of us, me or your spirit whore, and let your choice speak for your sanity!"

Hisami's voice was an eagle's, piercing. Saito didn't hear it; his ears were filled with an all-too-familiar tune. The keening note sprang from his hip and trailed a silver arc through the air. The Beautiful Singer whirled and returned to her scabbard. Then the first drops of Hisami's blood hit the ground.

Pale, she raised a finger to her throat. Her trachea hung open, a crimson waterfall flooding over her breast and dyeing her silken robes. It was a perfect cut, as long as a finger and half as deep. Her hand rose higher; she stumbled forward. Saito took a step back and watched her draw a hidden blade from her hairpin. She looked up at him, already dead on her feet, and made a final lunge. Then she fell to the floor.

Saito touched his cheek. Surprised, he rubbed blood between his fingertips. It was only a scratch, fine as a hair. A slash of red traced below his eye, as finely as an artist could paint one. A lake of the same red pooled on the floor. Saito looked down at his dead wife, at the spattered red flecks on her beautiful white cheek. Then he drew Beautiful Singer from her sheath and made sure she was clean of stains.

# 19

Saito fell to his knees under Lord Ashikaga's withering glare. He had been ordered to Ashikaga's chambers the moment the news of Hisami's death reached the castle. Saito had never seen that gruesome face so angry. Rage flushed the skin but the scars remained white, adorning the lord's scowl with strokes of war paint. "Explain yourself!" he roared.

"My lord, she stepped out of line."

"No! You're the one who is out of line!" Fury swelled in Ashikaga's face, even his scars turning red. "How dare you kill one of my own without my permission?"

"She was only a woman."

"She was samurai!"

"But lord, she was my wife. It is my prerogative to—"

"She was *my* samurai! And you dare speak to me of your prerogative?" Ashikaga rose to his feet, dark as a thundercloud. "You cut down one of my samurai without so much as consulting me? Without considering my honor? She questioned you on a matter that should well have been questioned, and you killed her for it. In this, she was more loyal than you."

"But lord!"

"Enough! You will commit seppuku tomorrow at dawn. Get your affairs together and choose your second."

Ashikaga stormed off the dais and out of the room, the echoes of his words still vibrating in the air. The silence that followed was heavier still, leaving Saito alone in the emptiness to contemplate his fate.

# 2O

The first ray of morning crested the tree line and limned the paper walls with rose. The gathering was set. Ashikaga sat on a broad cushion, twenty armed samurai flanking him in attendance. A platform lay before them, upon it a miniature table bearing a dagger folded in a sheet of paper. Nakadai Minoru stood on the left side of the stage, near the door. Outside the door, Saito was held firmly by the wrists, a pair of samurai watching over him. He was dressed head to toe in white, the color of death.

Beautiful Singer lay in the grasp of one of his guards. They would not let him touch her, lest he kill himself prematurely on her edge. They had even stripped him of his *wakizashi*. He'd spent the previous night in a cell, denied any means whatsoever to bring about his death. The lord wanted him to die only on his orders.

Yet Saito had not a single thought for suicide, and he found his mind strangely clear. No doubt Hisami would have said this was because his haunted sword no longer plagued him, but Saito scoffed at the thought. It could only be his own imminent demise that had left him so oddly serene.

Lying all night on the dark floor of his prison, he'd had a long time to contemplate his two last wishes. The first was for vengeance. Someone had betrayed him. At first it was not clear who, but after long consideration he concluded it could only have been Nakadai. Only Nakadai could have told Hisami of the Inazuma blade. He was obsessed with the curse. Nakadai could have seen his master's *tachi* on Saito's hip and secretly reported it to Hisami. He could even have pressured her into riding to Seki to snoop. Saito had underestimated him; he never would have thought the fat man could be so observant, so traitorous, so bold.

Yet Nakadai was the obvious choice to be Saito's second. In seppuku, the second was responsible for beheading the condemned after his self-disembowelment. For a samurai to die with honor, his second must also conduct himself with honor, and so it was a position of the greatest trust. Hisami herself could have been his second, were she still alive. Without her, it would be either Nakadai or Ashikaga's official executioner. The executioner was generally reserved for common criminals, not samurai, and up until Nakadai's treachery, he and Saito had been lifelong friends. Besides, by choosing Nakadai, at least Saito could vocalize his hatred, even if he could not act on it.

Revenge being unrealizable, Saito's second dying wish was to hear Beautiful Singer's song one last time. Lamentably, that too would be impossible. The guard whose hands now sullied her sheath was under the strictest orders not to hand over the sword until Saito was kneeling before the sacrificial knife. It was customary for a samurai to die with his weapons, but many a man tried to hack his way out of a death sentence, and it seemed Ashikaga feared Saito would do the same. That Saito suffered the dishonor of being suspected of such cowardice would also please the lord. Saito wondered why he had become the object of such contempt. He also wondered whether, with Beautiful Singer in his hands, he could cut deep enough through the surrounding warriors to make a bid for Ashikaga's own neck. Perhaps that was why he was denied his sword. The possibility that Ashikaga feared him made Saito smile.

But such dreams were not to be. He would be without his weapon until he was seated with the knife in front of him and with Nakadai behind, ready to behead him once he committed the ultimate act of sacrifice. He would die with Beautiful Singer resting asleep in her scabbard, and he would never hear her enchanting voice again.

And now, standing at the very doorstep of the place

where he would die, he was overcome with sudden realization. If he longed to hear her voice, then her voice had a hold on him. Could Hisami have been right all along? Had he killed her for nothing?

The thought was too terrible to bear. Even if it was true, there was no way to undo what he'd done. His only remaining recourse was to avenge her. It was right, then, that he should die by his own hand, for he himself was to blame—but only partially. Nakadai was a coconspirator. It was Nakadai who had whispered rumors of the curse in her ear. How else could she have heard of it? Yes, it was Nakadai who had pushed her to the point of obsession. Even if Saito admitted that he himself was also obsessed, it was Nakadai who made their two obsessions collide.

Saito's need to hear his Beautiful Singer one last time was no less intense. But now his desire to exact vengeance on Nakadai burned hotter and brighter than ever before.

Saito smiled, and smiled triumphantly because suddenly he knew how to realize both of his wishes at once. When the door slid open in front of him, he felt no fear. When his guards shoved him forward, he walked confidently to the center of the dais. He saw Nakadai there, his narrow eyes sorrowful. Saito bowed to him proudly and knelt before the knife.

"A request," he said serenely as he took his place. He kept his voice so low that Nakadai had to step forward to hear him. "Would you do me the honor," Saito asked, "of carrying out your duty with my sword?"

Nakadai looked down at the *tachi* and Saito saw he did not recognize it. Then the big man looked up at Ashikaga and repeated Saito's last wish. The lord considered the request, conceded it with a gruff nod of the head. Saito took the sword by the sheath from one of his guards and carefully set it at his right side, where it could not easily be drawn. Still Nakadai approached it cautiously. The other samurai tensed, all of them expecting trickery. Saito watched as Nakadai crouched behind him, grasped the scabbard, and lifted the sword. An *iaidō* master could have drawn and cut even with his sword in another man's hands, but Saito remained still. He closed his eyes and offered a prayer to Buddha.

Ashikaga nodded again, and with this permission Saito

took up the knife and ritualistically cleaned it with the paper. He stripped the white robes from his shoulders, baring himself to the waist. Then, with great resolve and immeasurable self-control, he picked up the blade and thrust it into his abdomen.

Sensation vanished in a wash of pain that left him in an icy shock. The room went white. His body was numb as the knife bit into him and then across. The last thing he heard was an ethereal song in the air, just before his head separated from his neck. His last thought was that his were not the only ears that heard it.

# BOOK THREE

HEISEI ERA, THE YEAR 22

(2010 CE)

# 21

As he crossed the waiting room, Fuchida Shūzō wondered what everyone else there was thinking about. All the faces were impassive, downcast. It was dinnertime for these people. Fuchida had only just woken a few hours earlier—like all of nature's deadliest predators, he was a nocturnal creature—but most of the visitors in the waiting room were accustomed to being home at this hour or else still at work, enslaved by the impossible hours of the *sarariman*. It was not an especially active time for acute care, and only a dozen or so sat on the powder-blue pleather couches. All of these people waited on a loved one, or else waited to receive attention themselves. Which ones were thinking about death? Which ones chided themselves for their own stupidity? Dog bites, falls from ladders, unexpected allergic reactions—most of the injuries here were foreseeable, avoidable, and nonlethal. Stupidity. But then there were the ones that required paperwork to release remains to the morgue. Which ones were they?

Fuchida could not tell, nor was he certain why he could not tell. Was it the unflappable demeanor the Japanese were famous for the world over? Or had he so little compassion that he could not tell the mildly irritated from the panic-stricken?

Fuchida felt neither irritation nor panic. He'd felt both in the past, when the diagnosis had first come through, but now coming here was scarcely different from going to the post office or collecting protection money. It was just something he did.

His only feeling was a vague sense of something missing. It bothered him like a song stuck in his head that he couldn't place and couldn't shake. He felt this way often when he was without his beautiful singer, but even a yakuza couldn't get away with carrying a sword through the halls of a hospital. Now that he thought about it, he did feel a niggling irritation too, not at having to come to the hospital but at being deterred from hunting down the Inazuma blade he'd been seeking for all these years. Time was growing short. It had never been in the cards for him to hold on to the second Inazuma for long. He hadn't understood that before, but it was clear to him now. For fifteen years he'd thought to make himself the first man in history to own two Inazumas, but now he understood that he could parlay the second sword into something greater, something too valuable for him to consider keeping the weapon for himself. Yes, he would be the first to hold two Inazumas, but only briefly — just long enough to seize the reins of his own destiny. But if he did not acquire the second blade soon, the only option left to him would be to sell his beautiful singer, and that he could not abide. Better to be a mere courier for the second Inazuma than to part with his beloved.

Fuchida walked across the faded blue carpet of the waiting room, his path already worn gray by thousands of prior patients, and jabbed the elevator button with his thumb. When the elevator came, he pressed the button for the tenth floor, then spent the ride examining his distorted reflection in the polished steel walls. He wore his black suit and white shirt again, a bolo tie today, his hair tied back in a tail. Would someone say he looked sad? Anxious? Bored? Fuchida couldn't tell. He just looked like himself.

He got out on the hospice care floor and went to the room he always went to. His father was watching television. The volume was low — whatever else might be afflicting him, the old man's hearing was still as sharp as a wolf's — and Fuchida didn't recognize the program. Some show about movie stars. His father lay under a dark blue blanket and pale blue sheets. His hospital gown was also light blue, and he huddled in an extra blanket wrapped about his shoulders and chest.

A thin clear plastic tube was taped under his nose to supply oxygen.

"Hello, Dad."

"Shūzō. Come on in. Sit."

His father muted the television, and they talked about the usual. "You ought to come by for breakfast sometime," the elder Fuchida said. "The morning shift's got a nurse with an ass like a ripe peach."

"She should let you chew on it. They're not feeding you enough, Dad."

"They feed me plenty. I just can't keep anything down. How's business?"

Fuchida bunched his lips, nodding. "Fine. Looking better all the time."

"You move those DVD players we talked about?"

"There's no money in electronics, Dad."

His father coughed, a hacking cough wet with phlegm and displeasure. "Plenty of money in it," he said, raising a fist to his lips. There was another plastic tube running down his forearm, its end concealed by the white tape that held it to the back of his hand. "Plenty. Thought I taught you better than to get greedy like that."

"The market's different now. The way you used to run things isn't enough anymore."

Another cough from the old man. "Then you ought to rethink what you mean by 'enough.'"

Fuchida closed his eyes for a moment, the better to keep himself from rolling them.

"You think I'm out of touch," his father said. "Obsolete, *neh*? Well, I think you're acting like some woman's got you by the short-and-curlies. Making you spend money you don't have. Making you take risks you know you shouldn't take. The old way's the old way for a reason, son. Your grandfather made his name with it and so did I."

Fuchida looked at the floor this time to keep his father from seeing his face. They'd made the Fuchida name known, all right. Every cop and every yakuza knew the Fuchidas served the Kamaguchi-gumi. Street muscle. Movers of anything stolen. Hirelings, not leaders. The Fuchidas had territory, even good territory, but they didn't have an empire.

"Dad, I've got everything under control. Honestly."

"I'll bet. You want to make a big name for yourself in the

*ninkyō dantai,* you do it my way. Otherwise you just get to be a big name with the police."

"Is this something you want to talk about so openly?"

His father laughed, coughed, laughed again. "See? These risks you're taking, whatever they are, they've got you looking over your shoulder. That ought to tell you something, son." Another cough. "We've done things our way for a long, long time. Cops know it, business knows it, and we do our thing anyway. Because we have a code and we stick by it."

A cough from deep in the diaphragm left the old man breathless for a moment. A fleck of spittle on his lip drew attention to the fact that his skin had become as dry as paper. At last he said, "You young bucks today, you watch too many movies. You think the real money's in drugs. But the code, it's not just ours; the cops hold by it too. We don't sell the hard shit, and they look the other way if we sell a little speed. And why shouldn't they? Those damn dopeheads end up killing themselves. Look at the Americans, son: shooting each other day and night over that shit."

"Dad, speed's half the business these days."

"*Neh?* And look where it got us. In my day shakedown money was enough. You wanted extra money, you'd steal something and sell it. Did I ever tell you about the time I sold that fire department their own trucks?"

"Yes, Dad."

He laughed a rasping laugh. "They even thanked me for cutting them a good price. That was the power we had. But these days . . ." He snorted. "You kids. I never met a one who could sell speed without using it himself. You start using, now you've got the bosses looking in on you. Maybe they start wondering if you're worth the risk. Then one day you wake up wondering why you can't breathe with all this concrete filling your lungs. Listen to me, son. Break the code, people start paying attention. Stick to it, you make as much money as you want to make."

Not as much as *I* want to make, Fuchida thought. His father was right: he was breaking the rules; he was taking risks. But there was a new order now. The old guard lived in a world defined by Japan's borders. Now the borders were found only at the edges of cell phone coverage. The corporate world had been the first to see that, and the result was record profits. There was no reason the *ninkyō dantai* couldn't follow. There was a new virtue, one the old guard never thought to honor: ambition. They lived with limits on how much a person could make without taking from everyone else. Now the sky was the limit.

"You're thinking it's a new age, *neh*? You're thinking a man can aspire to higher things these days."

Fuchida looked up at his father. The old man's ability to read people was uncanny—it bordered on telepathy, in fact, and Fuchida wondered how he did it. Was that the real cause behind his rise to power? His ability to read people and then to steer them, cajole them, get from them what he wanted—it was an awe-inspiring gift.

And his father wasn't through using it. "Let me tell you something about aspiration, Shūzō. For those ordinary folks, it'll get them anywhere. For a yakuza, it'll only get you killed. See, the ones up top, they don't see aspirations; they see insurrections. Don't aim for the moon, son. Aim for a nice condo in Akihabara and regular pussy."

It's not up to me, Fuchida wanted to say. My sights are set higher than yours. I'm hardwired that way. You're not, and that's all there is to it. But instead he said, "You're right."

"Ahh, you don't buy that. You're saying that to shut me up."

Again with the mind reading. Fuchida could lie to anyone, even to a polygraph, but he'd never been able to lie to his father. "All right, Dad. I'll try to see it your way. I will."

"*Neh*? There's a good boy." A wrinkled hand with yellow nails found the TV remote and turned the sound back on. "This here's a good show. You ought to see the girls they bring out on this one."

Fuchida stayed until dinner came around, and after he'd seen his father eat enough, he excused himself.

Walking down the sterile corridor, antiseptic smells assaulting his nose, he wondered: A man can't help his ambitions, can he? Controlling desire was one thing. Controlling fear was another. Fuchida had mastered both of those. But ambition was not the same as desire, was it? Ambition governed the upper limits of desire. It called for planning, not gluttony. And in Fuchida's experience, ambition was inborn. Some people sought to lead. Most did not. Some people sought to star on television, or show in art museums, or become prime minister. Everyone *said* they wanted such things, but only a few were born with the ambition to accomplish them. And how could anyone change what was innate?

Besides, Fuchida wasn't looking to upset the balance of power. Usurping leadership of the Kamaguchi-gumi was the farthest thing from his mind. He only wanted to follow his own path, not a path chosen by some *kaichō* from a more powerful clan. Taking the second Inazuma would be his first step on the road to creating a new power, an empire all his own.

All the pieces were already in place. He needed only to kill the old man and claim the sword. He could do it now, without his beautiful singer—just drive over there, break in, take the sword. But even blind, the old man was dangerous with a blade, and ever since Fuchida had started sleeping with his beautiful singer, he had no taste for carrying a pistol or a knife. That old house was full of swords, and the blind old man would have the advantage in the dark.

And there was the other thing too: there was a time when they'd been friends, he and the old man. Fuchida had been forced to kill a friend before. Endo, the kid's name was. Fuchida had been little more than a kid himself. The order had come from Kamaguchi Ryusuke himself, no more than a piss-ant *wakashū* at the time, but he was a Kamaguchi all the same, and a Fuchida had to obey. Endo had stolen from the family, and Fuchida strangled him for it. He remembered how surprised he'd been to learn how long it took to kill someone that way. He didn't get the same high from killing Endo as he did from a stranger, and ever since, Fuchida had been careful about getting too close to people.

No, it was too risky to go kill the old man himself. Fuchida looked at his watch. Too late to set up a hit tonight. All the guys he would have called would be halfway drunk by now, and he wanted them sharp. Fuchida felt a spike of irritation and willed it away. He wanted the sword, but he could be patient. A day wasn't too much to wait. Out of respect for the friendship, he thought, and gave himself an approving nod. A day wasn't too long to wait to murder a former friend.

# 22

Standing on the sidewalk in front of her mother's apartment building, Mariko felt she was preparing to enter a boxing ring. No one else would have seen signs of an impending altercation. The building was as clean as if the developer had just cut the ribbon that morning. So was every other building on the block. Even the streets and sidewalks were immaculate. There was nothing ominous about the spotless glass or polished steel of the building's revolving door. Everything Mariko could see was as clean and sterile as a scalpel.

She knew these buildings concealed darker truths. In her first year on the force she had worked the midnight-to-eight shift, the hours when a cop only deals with bad people doing bad things. She had knocked on hundreds of doors in buildings like this, called on scene not by the victim but by her neighbors when the violence got loud enough that they had no choice but to call. In Japan it took a lot to cross that line.

Back when her father got his promotion and moved the family to Illinois, they'd lived in a big house on a big lot, and the man next door used to beat the hell out of his wife every two weeks. Every payday he'd get shitfaced and come home surly, and all the neighbors would pretend not to hear the doors slamming and the coffee cups being hurled against the walls. They wouldn't call the police until the sounds were human. It got so bad that even the Oshiros would call, but that had taken some getting used to. Interfering in other people's private lives wasn't in keeping with the Japanese spirit. The flinch response to sue, to call a cop—that was an American thing, and that too had taken getting used to.

The Americans had a saying: "Silence is golden." Mariko used to wonder why there was no equivalent in Japanese. It was only when the family moved back to Tokyo that she understood. There was no need for such a saying in Japan. Japanese people didn't bellow into their cell phones. They didn't shout across a train car to each other, or laugh so loud that everyone else in the room could hear. Grocery store managers didn't announce their business over loudspeakers; they found their employees themselves, and even that they did only rarely, because the employees were so well trained that they didn't need to be told to open another register or to clean up aisle five. Americans would have thought it bizarre to devote that much time to training a grocery store clerk, and yet they were more than happy to complain loudly whenever lines got too long or a clerk gave incorrect change.

Japanese shoppers weren't like that. Japanese housewives weren't like that. They tended to keep their suffering silent, and their neighbors tended to do a more thorough job of pretending they didn't hear what was going on next door. So Mariko had been in a hundred buildings like this one when it should have been a thousand. Every time she had followed protocol, keeping her voice soft and diplomatic when she asked the abusive asshole if there was a problem. Illinois cops were different: they hammered on doors even in the dead of night, and they weren't afraid to pick a fight with the husband if the wife wouldn't press charges. At any given hour of any given day, Mariko preferred Japanese silence to American rowdiness, but whenever she worked a domestic she wanted to bash the door down like a good old American cowboy.

It had been nearly a year since she'd been called to a domestic, because ten months ago she'd started her probationary assignment with Narcotics. Domestics were her least favorite calls, and so she sure as hell didn't miss them, but now she felt guilty upon returning to the boxing ring. For a lot of her mother's neighbors it was almost literally that: it was a place they'd go to get in a fight. It wasn't that way for her mother, who lived alone now and whose husband had been a good, kind man when he was still alive, but Mariko couldn't help thinking about what happened behind some of the other doors.

That guilt would have to wait for another time, because today had worries of its own. She didn't know what to anticipate with Saori. They hadn't spoken to each other since Mariko dropped her off at detox eight days before, and though Mariko always hoped rehab would bring her sister some emotional stability, in her heart of hearts she didn't know whether she'd be having dinner with the twenty-two-year-old her sister really was or the petulant teenager her sister preferred to act like all too often.

In any case, Saori was due to be at her meeting at five o'clock, and so Mariko had deliberately timed her arrival at her mother's place for five minutes after five, rather than coming straight over when her shift ended at four o'clock. She hadn't spoken to their mother face-to-face since Saori's most recent drug bust, and she hoped that with a little one-on-one time she might talk their mother into maintaining a unified front. Too often their mother made excuses for Saori's addiction, but maybe this time Mariko could convince her to stand strong.

Even that was likely to create a quarrel if it wasn't handled right, and Mariko knew full well how bad she was at handling this sort of thing. She'd spent her formative years in the States, and that had deprived her of the peacemaker mentality that defined so many Japanese women. She was a foreigner in her own country. That was why men like Lieutenant Ko didn't like her: Mariko had no sense of how to be conciliatory. That, plus the fact that she actually had ambitions toward a career, made her more than a foreigner; by her culture's standards she was clinically insane. That was certainly how men like Ko saw her, and how her mother saw her too. How could she explain to her mother that for an addict like Saori, all the diplomacy and peacemaking and refusal to confront simply amounted to enabling?

Mariko had no interest in quarreling with her mother, especially not on this of all days. But this was not the day to avoid seeing her mother either, so she pushed the revolving door and entered the lobby, leaving a handprint on the otherwise unblemished steel.

She found her mother exactly where she expected to find her, in the gym on the fifteenth floor. The building wasn't posh, but it did have its comforts, and the gym with its Ping-Pong tables had been the reason her mother had moved there. Whenever Mariko came to visit, she inevitably found her either kicking a neighbor's ass in Ping-Pong or else smoking a cigarette on the terrace outside the gym with the person whose ass she'd just kicked.

Today it was at the tables. Her mother was dressed as if the game were being televised: navy-blue tennis shorts, white socks pulled high, and a matching polo shirt with the Killerspin logo embroidered on the left breast pocket. Mariko opened the door just as her mother returned a serve almost too fast for Mariko to see. The ball dipped left, cut right as soon as it hit the table, and her mother's opponent dropped her paddle on the table with a defeated thwack that indicated match point.

Her mother pirouetted on her heel, smiling a victor's smile. "Miko-chan," she said, double-taking halfway through her spin. "You're here."

"Wouldn't miss it."

Her mother excused herself from her vanquished foe and retrieved her gear bag. "Mom," Mariko said, "why do you need a whole bag for this game? An extra ball or two I can see, but why the extra paddles?"

"They're *rackets*, Miko, and anyone who calls them paddles has a lot to learn about table tennis. I'm sure I never questioned you on why you would pay so much for those bike shorts of yours. Or why you own so many pairs. Or why you don't just bike in your swimsuit."

"Because—" Mariko cut herself short. There were perfectly good explanations. Triathlon shorts shed water better than cycling shorts, and if there was a swimsuit out there with enough padding for thirty or forty kilometers on the bike, Mariko hadn't found it yet. But she swallowed all of that and laughed. "All right, good point. Do you want to catch a smoke first or should we go downstairs?"

"No, we can go right down." Lowering her voice, her mother said, "To tell you the truth, Maeda-san isn't much competition. I hardly worked up a sweat."

Mariko waited until they were alone in the elevator before she brought up the obvious. "How's Saori?"

"Oh, she's staying with me," their mother said. "Staying out of trouble. I'm afraid she's still a little mad at you for arresting her last week."

"Is that what she's saying now? I didn't arrest her, Mom. I got her out of being arrested. And anyway, it's hardly my fault—"

"I know." She patted Mariko's forearm. "She twists things. I know. It's not her, honey—it's the addiction talking."

Mariko did her best to keep the exasperation from her voice. "You're making excuses for her. Again."

"I'm taking care of my daughter in the best way I know how. Is it so bad to try to keep you two from fighting?"

Not exactly a boxing ring, Mariko thought, but not friendly territory either. She had never been able to understand why their mother took Saori's side. "I'm not fighting her, Mom. I'm doing my job."

"And who says you need to have that job? What was so wrong with wanting to be a reporter? Nobody stabs reporters."

She was talking about the Kurihara murder. A meter maid in Yokohama, killed by a large knife according to the ME's report. It was already a cold case. More than a week old, no motive, no suspects. Mariko and her mother had both taken an interest, each for her own reasons. Mariko's mother watched too many *Law & Order* reruns, and her imagination tortured her with wild speculations about what might happen to her daughter; an actual attack against a policewoman was impossible for her to ignore. Mariko would have been interested in the case out of sheer solidarity—you just didn't fuck with cops—but she also couldn't let go of the fact that the victim had been crippled before she was killed, and that there was no sign of rape, robbery, or any other motive for the homicide. She didn't like cases she couldn't understand, and something told her this woman wasn't tortured and murdered for giving someone a parking ticket.

But tonight Mariko was distracted from trying to figure out the killer's motive. The reporter comment had arrested her normal stream of thought. She'd almost forgotten she had wanted to do that. She'd entered college only a few months after her father's death, and declared a journalism major because she wanted to get to the bottom of what had happened to him. Liver cancer at forty-three was weird, weird enough that it drew attention when he was not just the sixth engineer at his plant to die of it but the one who lived the *longest*.

In good American fashion, it was the suit against the TPC plant in Teutopolis that finally broke the story. Takemata Plastec had moved a number of its Tokyo engineers over there, Mariko's dad included, and one of them had gone native enough to file a lawsuit. It was his case that revealed the connections between the '89 earthquake, the microfractures, the vinyl chloride monomer leak, and the angiosarcoma of the liver that cropped up like the plague among TPC employees over the years to follow.

The engineer who had sued paid the price for it. The Americans had a saying for stories like his: *The squeaky wheel gets the grease.* The Takemata Plastec Corporation subscribed to the Japanese counterpart to that saying: *The nail that sticks up gets hammered down.* Once TPC showed it was the Tokyo plant, not the Teutopolis plant, that suffered the leak, the lawsuit in Illinois yielded nothing. Those employees who stayed silent were rewarded for their loyalty. They lived with just as much pain and died just as miserably, but TPC took good care of their families. Mariko's mother would never have to work again, provided she never raised a fuss.

As a budding journalist, Mariko scooped none of those stories. Everything came out through the American lawsuit, and Mariko had made it all of three months beyond graduation before her editor told her she just wasn't a writer. It was a crushing blow at the time, but now Mariko understood she had a greater taste for justice than discovery. She had a talent for research and investigation but was only interested in exercising it in order to nail somebody. Even the best reporter couldn't uncover corporate scandals on a weekly basis, nor even on a yearly basis. But police investigators spent *every day* unearthing scandal and betrayal and wrongdoing, and better yet, they actually got to do something about it.

"Mom," Mariko said, "come to think of it, weren't *you* the one who said I was destined to become a detective?"

"I never said that."

"You did. As soon as I graduated the academy. You said,

'What does a reporter need with all that cardio training you do? They don't chase anybody.' You said a detective is really an investigative journalist with a badge."

"Did I?"

"Yes. I said I felt like my whole life had been leading up to this, and you said it was my destiny."

"No, no. I said it was your fate. Or karma, maybe."

"I stand corrected," Mariko said. Her mother observed Buddhist and Christian and Shinto holidays with equal fervor, and she invoked fate, destiny, God's will, and karmic repercussions interchangeably. Mariko didn't believe in any of those things. She believed in evidence, and in making the most of opportunity when it presented itself. She was more like her father that way.

The elevator opened onto a dim and warmly lit hallway, and right away Mariko caught the scent of potatoes au gratin wafting from her mother's door. She knew the smell came from her mother's kitchen, because her mother always cooked potatoes au gratin on this day. It had been her father's favorite, and today marked nine years since he lost his battle with cancer. Mariko wished she had been there, to know for certain whether he'd suffered to the end as she feared, or whether he'd passed in peace as her mother had always told her. She had no appetite for sugarcoated truths, no patience for pretending a hard fact was something other than what it was. There too she was more like her father than her mother.

"I'm trying something new with the potatoes," her mother said as she opened the apartment door. Clapping her hands and grinning, she said, "Fennel."

"Yum." Mariko couldn't help but smile; her mom announced new recipes with the same fervor with which other women her age announced new grandchildren. "Sounds great, Mom. I can't wait to— Oh! Saori."

Her sister was leaning against the oven, the bones of her arms almost as skinny as the oven's door handle. "Hey," she said, not looking up from whatever she was texting.

"I thought you'd be at your meeting," Mariko said.

Saori shrugged, still not looking up. "I went to the three o'clock over in Meguro instead. There's a cute guy there."

"Well, good. I'm glad you went. How are they going? Your meetings, I mean."

Saori always called it a meeting, never naming the organization. That was all right. She didn't need to broadcast it. Mariko just found it interesting that Saori, and indeed everyone she'd ever met in the program, referred only to meetings. And when they said it, all of them knew what kind of meeting it was. Mariko wondered what word they'd use for meetings at work, or a board meeting, or a shareholders' meeting.

Again Saori shrugged. "More my business than yours, *neh*? *Anonymous* and all that."

"I just wanted to know how you're doing, Saori."

"Yeah. Always being the big sister. Always taking care of the poor little baby."

"Now girls," their mother said, and that was that.

Dinner was superficially pleasant. It never had a shot at being joyous, given the occasion, and given the circumstances of the most recent drug bust, Mariko supposed superficial pleasantry was the best they could have hoped for. As always, the food was delicious—better than their father had ever eaten with them, Mariko thought ruefully; their mother watched cooking shows religiously, and the cooking fad hadn't really been a presence on cable when Mariko and Saori's father was still alive.

Mariko didn't care to speculate on whether exceptional food made up for the constant efforts at steering conversation away from the uncomfortable. Their mother missed no opportunity to comment on the absence of men at family dinners. Of all the things to be worried about in Saori's life, Mariko found it stupefying that their mother should focus on Saori's lack of a boyfriend. So Mariko tried to talk about the batty old guy out in Machida, and somehow the conversation boomeranged back to men, and how Mariko might get one if only she'd let her hair grow out a bit, or at least stop cutting her fingernails down to the nub, and would it be so bad to lighten up a bit on all the running and biking and scaring off all the men at the gym? She told her daughters how men liked a bit of softness in a woman, sharing this information as if she'd won it dearly after scaling the mountain of wisdom.

That was enough for Saori. Resorting to English—always the favorite language for cursing—she said, "I'm in fucking *rehab*, mom. You think I *want* to be this skinny?"

"Saori—"

"No, fuck this. I'm going to have a smoke."

Mariko quickly excused herself, promising to talk Saori down. "I'll take her down the street to the Lawson," she said. "Maybe get us a pint of ice cream for dessert."

She caught up to Saori halfway to the elevator. They walked down the dimly lit corridor side by side, the Oshiro girls together again. Mariko wondered how much of her life she'd spent that way, the two of them side by side. Twelve years, Mariko thought. For twelve years they were all but joined at the hip, from the day Saori was born until Mariko reached her seventeenth birthday. Then their father's illness finally came to an end, and the two sisters reacted so differently—differently, and yet so much the same. Mariko hid from the pain by submerging herself in college entrance exams. Saori hid by submerging herself in booze. Then came college for Mariko, then police academy, and high school and hard drugs for Saori. Mariko had told herself it was just Saori's way of grieving. She would outgrow it, get past it, but they'd already started to drift apart, and even then Mariko could no longer get the truth from her as she once could.

Sometimes Mariko wondered why she'd thrown herself headlong into the academy. She knew it was for Saori; she just didn't know why. Was it a warning, a way of telling Saori to straighten up before a cop was a permanent presence in her life? Or was it to be a better role model for her little sister? Or—and Mariko feared this was most likely—was her heedless dedication really an escape, healthier but otherwise not so different from Saori's? Whichever it was, it didn't work. By the time Mariko got her badge, she was the good daughter, the successful daughter, and there was nothing she could do for Saori without being seen that way. The fuckup daughter just couldn't hear what the good daughter had to say, and afterward they'd never been able to rebuild their sisterhood as it once was.

"Christ," Saori said, still in English, "can you believe her?" She lit up a Mild Seven before they even made it to the elevator.

"I don't think you're supposed to smoke in here."

"So arrest me. I mean, Jesus fucking Christ, Miko, what's her deal?"

"That's Mom for you."

"Such a fucking hypocrite. She's not married and she's fifty-two. What the hell is she riding our asses for?"

"Probably not the best day to tell her to find another husband," Mariko said.

Saori laughed. "Can you imagine? I know I can be a little shit sometimes, but that would be bad even for me."

At least she was speaking Japanese again. That meant she was feeling calmer. And feeling pensive too, Mariko thought. Knowing it was risky, she said, "How's everything going? With the rehab, I mean."

"Eight days sober. But it feels different this time, you know? Like maybe I've finally found the right path."

It was exactly what Mariko wanted to hear, and for that reason it sounded suspicious. She hated mistrusting her sister that way, but by now Mariko knew more than she'd ever wanted to about addicts and deception. Saori had been her teacher and had taught her well.

They crossed the lobby; the revolving door cut a cloud of cigarette smoke in half as they escaped onto the street. Mariko nodded toward the blue-and-white Lawson sign on the corner. "Ice cream?"

"Sure. But that's not why you followed me down here."

Mariko swallowed. Saori met her gaze and studied her as carefully as Mariko would study the scene of a homicide. "Come on, Miko, you've been counting the days just like I have. So, seriously, what's up?"

A breeze swept the street, cool now that the sun had all but set. There were street noises: a distant train, the electric buzz from the floodlights warming up in the hedgerow surrounding their mother's building, the wind whistling as it cut between buildings. On every side the high-rises towered over the Oshiro sisters, each building so close to the next that it seemed they huddled together for warmth against the biting wind.

"What do you know about cocaine?" Mariko asked.

Saori shrugged. "Tony Montana does a lot of it in *Scarface*."

"Be serious."

"I am. Nobody around here does that stuff. I mean, I know a few who have, but the yakuzas beat the hell out of anyone who tries to sell it. You pick it up on vacations in Hawai'i, stuff like that. In Japan it's too hard to come by."

"That's about to change," Mariko said. "Someone's going to try to change it, anyway, and my lieutenant won't let me take the case. He won't put anyone on it, actually, and I'm worried about you."

Saori took a step back, her shoulders stiff, her head cocked. "Why? You think I'm going to start snorting coke?"

"No. It's just that . . . well, you and stimulants have a bit of a history."

"Yeah," Saori said, glaring now. "A history. As in past. As in mind your own business."

"Saori—"

"No. For the first time in my life I feel like I have this thing under control, and now you come here to undermine me? No, Miko. I'm not the baby sister anymore."

"Fine," Mariko shot back. She felt the steam rising in her. Saori's jaw was set, her breath coming audibly through her nose. No point in talking to her when she's like this, Mariko thought. And here I thought she'd get *less* moody when she got sober.

"Thanks so much for taking a little walk with your little baby sister," Saori said. Good, Mariko thought, add sarcasm to the mix. That always helps. As soon as she thought it, she convicted herself of the same crime, but it was too late to try a different approach. Saori flicked her cigarette hard against the plate glass storefront of the Lawson, turned on her heel, and stormed back toward their mother's building.

Mariko's eyes were on the cigarette, not her sister. It flared red in flight, sparked on impact, and trailed a looping ribbon of smoke as it fell to the sidewalk. Mariko ground it under her toe.

Her hand found the cell in her purse and dialed automatically. "Mom? Sorry, dessert's off. I'll talk to you tomorrow."

She closed a fist around the phone, crushing it more than folding it, still squeezing it even after it was closed. Not for the first time, she wished she was back at academy. She wanted a target to beat on and a baton to beat it with. Damn Saori, damn her cynicism and her selfishness, and damn her ability to wheedle her way under Mariko's skin. It made Mariko's blood boil just to think of her. This wasn't the kind of frustration she could just run out of her system. She wanted to break something.

Behind the Lawson, on her way toward the train station, she found two banks of vending machines. The first was typical fare: coffee, soft drinks, snacks. The second bank included one machine selling porn *manga* and another selling used high school girls' panties.

She kicked the disgusting machine. The glass didn't even crack, but Mariko damn near sprained her ankle. She wanted to rip the thing down, slam it on its face, kick it while it was down. Even that wouldn't have been enough. She thought of that sword in the old man's house out in Machida, remembered the heft of it, imagined stabbing the goddamn panty machine through the heart. Chopping it into little pieces. Now *that* would have set her mind at ease.

She spent the whole train ride home torn between berating herself for her loss of self-control and wondering where she could get a great big sword like that, what it would cost her, and where she could buy a few lengths of bamboo to hack up until there was nothing left.

# 23

When the newest details on the Kurihara murder came out in the morning's briefing, the first person Mariko thought of was Yamada Yasuo.

Like everyone else in her precinct, Mariko couldn't stop thinking about the case. One of their own had been killed. She wasn't TMPD, and it was hard to even call a meter maid a real cop, but Kurihara Yuko had worn the uniform and taken a department paycheck the same as everyone else, and that made her one of the family. So far the husband had been unequivocally dismissed as a suspect and no other suspects were forthcoming. The investigators on her case were no closer to establishing a motive than they were on day one, but the newest forensic report prompted Mariko to take another trip to see Dr. Yamada.

It was a busy day, though—Mariko had old paperwork to file, hours' and hours' worth, all of it pertaining to the drug cases she actually cared about—and it was easy to put off Yamada and his magic sword nonsense until later. So the sky was dark by the time she got out to Machida, the moon not yet risen, the stars far more plentiful than Mariko had ever seen from her apartment window downtown. The houses here were so cute, like little cottages, each one snuggled behind its high garden wall. She realized that was the American side of her brain talking; even the smallest of these places was five times the size of her tiny apartment, yet even the biggest would have been too small to sell back in Illinois.

Lights were turning off here and there in Yamada's neighborhood. She smelled the cool breeze coming to her from his chrysanthemums. There was a shuffling within the house; then the heavy wooden door creaked open.

"You're back," Yamada said. The air from inside his house smelled like tea. "I trust you haven't found anything about my would-be thief."

Mariko wondered what made him say that—his tone bespoke more familiarity with the case than any civilian had a right to—but she had more pressing things on her mind. "I need your input," she said. "That is, I'd very much like to have your input, if you're willing, sir. Yokohama PD's investigating the murder of a woman who worked in their parking patrol. The victim's name was Kurihara Yuko."

"Oh my."

His response gave Mariko pause. There was sincere sympathy in his voice, almost as if he'd known the victim. Once again he seemed too familiar with the case. Or was he just a sweet old man who would have reacted that way to anyone's murder? Mariko couldn't be sure.

Those questions could wait; she had more pressing mysteries to solve. "Dr. Yamada, I think our medical examiner has us looking for the wrong murder weapon. I think you can help me prove it."

"How? What do I know about murder weapons?"

"This one cut through a steel door chain, probably without even leaving a nick on the blade. Forensics was only able to recover a few tiny filaments from the weapon. Only the first of their test results is in, but their best guess so far is that the weapon is between five hundred and a thousand years old."

"Aha. Like the sword I showed you last week."

"Don't worry," Mariko said. "I'm not going to charge an eighty-seven-year-old with taking the train across town to murder a policewoman during her dinner. But I think the ME's initial report was wrong. The murder weapon wasn't a large knife. Sounds more like a sword, *neh*?"

"It certainly does."

"If so, this is the second ancient sword I've run across in the space of a week. What's going on here?"

"Sounds like fate to me. Do come in, Inspector."

She followed him into the house, closing the heavy oak door behind her. "I'm afraid I've just finished my evening tea," Yamada said, "but I can brew more if you'd like."

Mariko slipped out of her shoes. "Thank you, no," she said. "I wouldn't want to put you out."

He filled his teapot anyway and put it on the stove. His kitchen floor was hardwood, not tatami, his sock-clad feet susurrous as they crossed it. "Now then," he said, "what makes you come to me?"

"I did some research on you," she said. He took her by the elbow in an avuncular way, and she allowed him to escort her into the sitting room. "Doctorate in medieval history," she said. "Professor emeritus from Tōdai. Ninth *dan* in *kendō*, ninth *dan* in *kenjutsu*, eighth *dan* in *iaidō*, with a few more black belts here and there. Your biographer called you 'Japan's elder statesman of swordsmanship.'"

Yamada smiled, a warm, toothy smile that deepened the laugh lines in his face. "You've been reading Mizubayashi. He was gunning for tenure when he wrote that."

"He's not the only one to voice his respect," Mariko said. "I'm ashamed of myself for not connecting the dots before. When I was last in this room, I noticed something similar about all the books in that bookcase behind you. Every last one of them is about swords."

Yamada sat at the low tea table, but Mariko went to the bookshelf. "*Smithing Methods of the Kamakura Period*," she read aloud. "*Muromachi Era Sword Smithing. The Evolution of Sword Combat: A History*." Her eyes roved across the spines. "Wait a minute. This whole shelf . . . you wrote these? All of these?"

"What can I say? I'm an old man."

Mariko scanned the rest of the books in disbelief. The bookcase in front of her housed only works on medieval history. The one to its left, the history of swordsmanship in the martial arts. To the right, history from the Heian period and earlier. And on each bookcase the middle shelf held only volumes authored by Yamada.

"I can't believe it," she said. "You must have thirty books here."

"Forty," said Yamada. "Well, forty-some, anyway. My publisher says the complete works will span twenty-five volumes." He laughed. "Can you believe the gall? Complete works! You'd think they'd wait until a fellow was dead before they called it that. Suppose I feel like writing another one?"

Mariko looked at the man with new eyes. Had he lost his sight from all the writing? She reassessed his gnarled knuckles, the hunch in his back. A pen in hand, hunching over paper—was that how these books were born? Somehow she was certain Yamada had penned all those pages with his own hand, never resorting to a computer.

And why would he? By the time computers were advanced enough to help him, most of these books would have already gone in and out of print. She pulled a yellowed volume off the shelf, opened it, checked the publication date. Shōwa 31. She did the math in her head: 1956. Her parents weren't even born yet.

"Take one," Yamada said, grunting a bit as he got up from his knees. "Keep it. These old eyes have trouble reading anymore. I certainly won't waste them reading my own work."

As he walked to the kitchen, Mariko heard the first chortling of the teapot preparing to whistle. Yamada had sharp ears, sharper than Mariko's, and she prided herself on her attentiveness to her surroundings. This old man was an enigma. A keen intellect, an alert mind, and yet he'd spoken of magic swords with all sincerity. One might as well put stock in ghost stories. Mariko was a person who relied on evidence—who prided herself on that, in fact—and yet she found herself feeling respect for this man, a man who had spoken of fate and destiny as if they lived next door to him, as if he could see them and hold a conversation with them.

"So you've come to talk swords," he said from around the corner. "What about?"

"Well, I thought to myself, how many swords can there be in greater Tokyo between five hundred and a thousand years old? Then I did a little digging, and what I turned up told me you're the man to ask. So? How many?"

"Maybe ten," said Yamada, "but that's not the question you should ask."

"Oh?"

"What you should be asking is, how many of those swords are . . . well, how would you police officers put it? 'At large'? What I mean is, how many of those are swords a man could use to commit a murder?"

Ten was a much higher number than Mariko had expected. Now that she heard Yamada's question, though, she put two and two together. "They're in museums," she said. "These ancient swords, I mean. They're under glass in castles and history exhibits and such. So how many are in private hands?"

"Three that I know of, but only two that count. Of those, one is upstairs. I should think it was the other that killed your murder victim."

Mariko had heard this tone from the old man before. He spoke with more assurance than he should have. His voice was heavy with familiarity, as if he knew all about the circumstances of the murder. Only the investigators on the case had that kind of knowledge. No, Mariko thought. The murderer knew all the details too.

"Dr. Yamada, may I go upstairs and look at your sword again?"

"Of course," he said, reentering the room, a cup in either hand issuing steam. "I'll go up with you."

He smiled with a nod and handed her a cup. She did not drink from it. "Smells good," she said.

She made a point of walking behind Yamada. Mariko had ruled him out as a subject as soon as she'd learned of the Kurihara murder — it was his demeanor, not just his age, that had eliminated him — but now she questioned her judgment. His first comment about the would-be thief was too intimate, and now he spoke of the murder in the same intimate way. He was connected to both crimes. Mariko was sure of it. She just couldn't figure out how.

For a brief moment she was lost in her ruminations, and, coming back to herself, she saw Yamada was much faster than expected. He climbed the stairs with none of the hesitation she'd have guessed from someone so nearly blind, but she'd forgotten: this was his home. He lived within a perfect memory of it. And he was already at the bedroom door, just a few paces from the sword.

Mariko dashed up the stairs, hot tea splashing onto her hand. The teacup hit the carpeted stair. She reached the doorway to the bedroom just as Yamada turned to face her, his right hand holding the scabbard, his left hand supporting the tip. Her hand darted into her purse to find the Chee-tah.

"Here you are," Yamada said, moving toward her slowly, the sword held out to her in his right hand. "Inspect away, Inspector."

"Put the weapon down," she said. "On the bed."

"As you like," said Yamada, doing as he was told. He took a step back from it. "Have I given you a fright?"

With her eyes fixed on his hands, Mariko reached down, found the sword with groping fingers, and picked it up.

"Do forgive me. I didn't realize a man my age could still frighten anybody." He sat on the bed, hands on his thighs. "You should know, a sword is only dangerous when held in the left hand. The right must be free to draw and cut."

Mariko pulled the blade from its sheath and held it to the light. Again the sheer size of it impressed her. "I didn't know that."

"Oh, yes. Proper *kenjutsu* is always taught right-handed."

Her heart was slowing. She'd misjudged him. There was no sign of blood on this blade—none less than a hundred years old, anyway—nor any sign that he'd bleached it to remove trace evidence. This was not a man who would cover up a killing anyway; not only was he not the type to wantonly murder, but he would probably rather spend his life in prison than douse an ancient masterpiece in bleach. And now the back of her hand was starting to sting from where she'd spilled the tea.

Yamada smiled at her, his eyes unfocused; at this distance she was sure she'd blend into the wall for him. "I'm sorry I startled you," he said. "I should have known better than to approach a policewoman with a weapon in hand. Still, I'll have to teach you more about swordsmanship. You have a lot to learn."

Mariko looked at him curiously, then at the blade in her hands. All of a sudden she felt self-conscious about how she held it. Yamada was a lot stronger than he looked; Mariko needed two hands to hold the sword steady, yet Yamada needed just one. It was embarrassing not to be able to match the strength of his one wizened hand. And she was certain her grip was wrong too, but she had no idea how to properly hold a sword.

Self-consciousness was not something Mariko felt often.

Shame was all right with her. When a person did something wrong, she ought to feel shame. But self-consciousness—being ashamed having done nothing wrong, feeling shame just for being there—was not an ordinary part of her experience. Even as she thought about it, she found it quickly replaced by resentment.

"What makes you think I have any interest in sword fighting?" she said. "And even if I did, what makes you think I'm suddenly going to ask to be your student?"

"There's nothing sudden about it. I've been waiting for this for a long time."

Mariko sheathed the sword, immediately aware that there was a correct way to do it, and feeling equally sure that she hadn't sheathed it properly. There was that damnable self-consciousness again. She felt her cheeks flush, and she willed the embarrassment and resentment away. Somehow this man made her feel like a pupil. She could not pinpoint why.

"Sir," she said, her frustration threatening to boil over, "I never met you until a week ago. You haven't been waiting for me. You can't have been."

"Right," said Yamada. "I forgot. There's no such thing as destiny. Please, forgive an old man. Go on about your life."

Mariko dropped the sword on the bed. Back to the magic swords again, was it? Then that was enough for Mariko. The Kurihara murder wasn't her case. It wasn't even in her jurisdiction. She just wanted to help. But not if the price was putting up with all this nonsense about sorcery and fate. She had hoped to be able to give Yokohama PD a lead on their murder weapon, but she wasn't about to call in and tell them to look for a magic sword. She was done.

"Sorry to bother you," she said, the blood pounding in her temples. "I'll be on my—"

Yamada held a callused palm in front of her face and a wrinkled finger to his lips. Mariko could have screamed at him for silencing her like that, but then she heard the noise.

The front door was opening.

And then it was open. There were footsteps. Many steps: three people, maybe four. Whoever they were, none of them spoke.

Someone entered the kitchen. She imagined shoe heels

tearing the tatami floor in the sitting room. Mariko's hand went to her purse. Yamada picked up his sword.

She was going to tell him to stay here, to call the police, but he was already out the door. Swift and sure, he swept down the stairs. For half a second Mariko wished her pistol was tucked into her waistband, not tucked into a locked drawer at work. She followed Yamada quietly, the Cheetah's haft cold in her hand. She could see no one downstairs.

Then came a shout. Yamada drew his blade and slashed. Somehow, somewhere along the way down the stairs, he'd thrust the sword's scabbard through his brown leather belt without Mariko seeing him do it. And now the draw, the step, the cut, it was all one smooth motion. Someone screamed in the kitchen. Mariko could not see who it was; she only saw blood spatter the far wall.

A shadow moved below. Someone was approaching Yamada from behind. Mariko did not think; she just jumped the balustrade and landed in the sitting room.

The man rushing Yamada's back was tall, powerfully built, the tail ends of tattoos winding up the back of his neck from beneath the collar of his white shirt. He heard Mariko and whirled, too late.

Mariko thrust the head of the Cheetah into his breastbone and pulled the trigger. Nigh on a million volts crackled into the man's body. He gritted his teeth and groaned, the tendons in his neck standing out like high-tension lines, the Cheetah still buzzing. The man recoiled, reeling, his face a snarl of surprise, pain, and fury.

Yamada's sword took him, a deft stab through the throat.

Then Mariko was on the ground, a hundred and fifty kilos crushing her. It was another intruder. He was on top of her before she saw him, and now all she knew of him was his balding head and his smell like the inside of a *gyoza* restaurant. Her right hand, the Cheetah with it, was pinned to the floor. She felt the man's weight shift; his right arm was moving, reaching for a weapon.

Mariko tried to pull the trigger on the Cheetah and couldn't. Her hand, smashed under her attacker's bulk, could not budge its trigger finger. She brought her face close to the fat man's cheek and bit his ear.

He shrieked, shifted, punched her in the ribs. All the air left her lungs. She saw stars. But he had moved enough.

The Cheetah sent 850,000 volts into the giant's belly. He recoiled a bit but it wasn't a clean contact. He punched her again. Her ribs turned into a thousand little knives. Again the Cheetah crackled. He flinched away.

At last Mariko could breathe again. Through the stars she saw her attacker regaining his feet. She stabbed out, swinging hard for the groin. The fat man seized her wrist with his huge left hand. Steel flashed in his right, probably a knife. She flicked up with the Cheetah and zapped the arm that held her.

He released her, slashed, missed. She chopped at his knife hand. ABS plastic made hard contact with bone. Mariko didn't stop swinging. The throat, the temple, the base of the neck—then the fat man lay still.

Adrenaline cleared the stars from her eyes and she saw Yamada. Two men faced him, both wary, one with tattoos like barbed wire bracelets. Mariko rose to help him but a thousand tiny teeth bit into the left side of her rib cage. The pain felled her like a tree. Yamada stood, one foot on the first stair, the other on the floor.

The men before him both held knives, huge ones, the sort a Stallone character would carry. The one with the bracelets withdrew, and with a sudden flick he hurled his blade at Yamada.

Yamada's sword knocked the weapon from the air. In the same movement, the old man stepped toward his second attacker. The attacker's knife came in, then fell to the ground, a hand and forearm still attached to it. The one with the bracelets dashed for the front door. Yamada's sword slashed the back of his thigh, drawing a scream, and the intruder fled from sight.

Then it was over. Yamada was as still as a statue. His blank gaze fell on the bodies before him. Only Mariko's fat man was likely to live. One had trailed a river of blood through the gaping front door, one sprawled facedown in the kitchen, and a third was bleeding out with his forearm lying next to him.

Mariko's training took over. Her first priority was the one she'd knocked out; if he got back up, there was no guarantee she could put him down again. The handcuffs in her purse couldn't come close to fitting him—he had wrists like Christmas hams—but she carried zip ties too. As she cinched them around his thumbs, she hoped to hell two would be enough.

Next was the guy bleeding out. She snapped a handcuff around his stump, clamping it down as tight as she could get it. Even as she called 110, she knew he didn't have a chance. The thought of him dying made her sick, and she wondered if Yamada shared her nausea. On the job she had seen traffic fatalities, suicides on skyscraper sidewalks, but never had she seen anything so coldly gory as this.

Yamada seemed a different man. His shoulders were rounded with the weight of the sword; his face was like a wooden mask. Senseless, she thought. This was senseless bloodshed, and yet necessary. Inevitable. The coppery smell of blood gave the room a slaughterhouse smell.

It dawned on her then: Yamada could see none of it. The stink of blood would reach him, and the fast, shallow gasps of the dying man whose maimed right arm twitched in her grasp, but none of the rest. "I can't believe it," she said. "Your sword *is* magical."

Yamada's blank eyes turned in her direction. "What's that?"

"Your sword. It's magical after all. It lets you see?"

Yamada grunted. "No. What you saw there was no magic at all, just years of practice."

Mariko felt a sheath of ice envelop her heart. "You . . . you've *practiced* killing people?"

"Of course."

Mariko shuddered. Yamada was silent for a while, his head craned oddly toward the door. Then, as if understanding her meaning for the first time, he gave a wolfish laugh. "You've got a lot to learn about swordsmanship," he said. "The practice is mostly with wooden swords, Sergeant Oshiro. It takes an expert to train with live steel. I suppose I'm reckoned an expert, but don't worry; I'm not like the men who led the Bataan Death March. I don't cut people down just to test the edge of my blade."

Mariko blushed and shook her head, then realized Yamada could see neither. "No," she said, "I didn't mean to suggest you were a butcher."

"Yes, you did. You believed it, if only for a moment. That's all right. What's more important is that you believed in the power of the sword. Magical, you called it. You're a believer now."

"No," she said. "Magic isn't real."

"Then call it something else. The blades of Master Inazuma are works of art, and like any great art, they have the power to sway men's souls. No finer masterpiece was ever crafted in steel; thus no steel can match the power of an Inazuma blade. I call it the flow of destiny. You may call it what you like."

How could this man lecture so calmly about art? The stink of blood enveloped them. Mariko squeezed her eyes shut, and images of Yamada wielding the sword flashed in her mind. Poise, balance, and power—there was nothing supernatural there. Why had she leaped to the conclusion that the sword had done it? She was a detective. She gathered evidence and drew inferences from it. How had she let herself stray so far from reality?

Not for the first time, she felt embarrassed in Yamada's presence. It maddened her that he could elicit such shame so readily. "I don't know what I was thinking," she said. "It's the adrenaline. The fight. It's got me confused."

Yamada shrugged. It was an odd gesture coming from a man wielding a huge, bloody sword. "Combat has a way of letting us see the truth of the world," he said. "Come close to death, and your food tastes better. In truth it always tastes that way, but day by day we let ourselves grow blind to it."

Strange thing to hear from a blind man, Mariko thought, but Yamada wasn't finished. "You haven't lost your mind, Sergeant Oshiro. You've only opened it. Why not leave it open for a spell?"

Mariko closed her eyes again. "No. This destiny stuff, it's all nonsense. The universe doesn't get to pick what I do next."

"Indeed not. Or at least not often. But consider the evidence, Inspector. Tonight of all nights, you come to speak to me about the murder in Kamakura. She was killed for a sword, a sword that was not there, and killed by a sword as well. The blade that killed her is of similar vintage to mine, hence your coming to see me. And when do you come? On the very night that men break in to take my sword."

"Coincidence."

"Is it? I told you already: there are only three swords of this kind in private hands. One is in a place no one can steal it. I am holding the second. The third slew a woman in Kamakura, and the man who killed with that one intends to own this one as well."

Mariko frowned. "This is the third time you've spoken of these crimes that way. You're much too familiar with what's going on to be an innocent bystander. Tell me how you know so much about the Kurihara murder."

"You're dodging the issue, Sergeant Oshiro. Only three swords of their kind, and your work has led you across the paths of two of them. What you call coincidence is indistinguishable from destiny. And what's more, you believe in the power of the sword now. Destiny brought you to me just as it brought the sword to me. It's brought you and the sword together."

No, Mariko thought. It was a fluke, a random convergence. But even as she thought it, she could not deny that for that one moment she truly believed there was more to Yamada's blade than molecules. Even if only for a moment, she was certain it gave him the power of second sight.

Even now she found the thought as unsettling as an earthquake. What did she have if not a rational mind that relied on logic and data? What would be left of her if she let those go? Her father died because Takemata Plastec was willing to cover up the facts of its gas leak and sugarcoat the truth about its effects. Mariko's career as a detective was born out of a desire to uncover the facts and expose the truth. There was no room for magic in her worldview. To change that now would be to change who she was.

As much to change the subject as to get an answer, she said, "I just figured it out. You keep talking about the one who wants to steal your sword as if he's not here. None of these guys are the one. There's somebody else, isn't there?"

"I wonder when your colleagues will get here," Yamada said. "Would they consider it tampering with evidence if I clean my blade?"

"Now who's dodging the issue? You know who he is, don't you?"

Yamada shuffled, sword in hand, back to the staircase, his feet feeling their way around the dead body whose blood had irreparably stained his tatami floor. Once his hand found the banister he said, "My cleaning kit is up-stairs. Will you excuse me?"

"Don't. It *is* tampering with evidence, to answer your earlier question. Now answer one of mine. Tell me who he is, Doctor."

Yamada's feet went on, finding one step after the next.

"This conversation isn't over," Mariko said. But she had a feeling it was.

# 24

The moment he saw Mariko, Lieutenant Ko asked, "What are you doing in my station? Aren't you supposed to be off tonight?"

"Yes, sir," she said, already bristling at his tone. Most cops would be praised for coming in on an off night, but for Mariko there was only abuse. She watched her fingers tighten on the armrest of her plastic office chair, then channeled her frustration into that hand so it would not take residence in her voice. "I'm here to offer testimony, sir."

Ko brightened at that. "Done something wrong, have you?"

"No, sir. I witnessed a break-in and an attempted murder."

"Really? Just watched it happen? Didn't try to stop it?"

Mariko offered a thin smile. "Actually, I fought like hell to stay alive, sir. Maybe I forgot to mention: I was in the victim's house at the time of the break-in. And I brought in that great big son of a bitch, if that's worth anything."

She nodded toward the giant who had jumped her in Yamada's sitting room. She would have pointed, but every time she moved her left arm she received riotous complaint from her ribs. Sooner or later she'd have to get them X-rayed.

The perp was sitting, thumbs still zip-tied behind his back, on the edge of a steel desk. None of the office chairs would accommodate him. He reminded her of Konishiki, the famed sumo wrestler, but with a thinning buzz cut instead of a topknot, and a policeman taking photos of the tattoos on his massive arms. In truth the perp was probably only half Konishiki's size, but even at half size he was still a beast. Gamera had fought smaller monsters. Mariko could see already that Ko had no intention of believing she'd collared him.

"We'll see about this," he said, frowning. "I want an incident report on my desk in twenty minutes."

Mariko closed her eyes and told herself not to call him a slimy son of a bitch. Done right, the report would take the better part of an hour. If she didn't do it right, he'd be justified in accusing her of a slapdash job. There was no winning with him.

She pulled the report and went to work anyway. Now and then she glanced up to see Ko speaking quietly with her giant tattooed *rikishi*. Getting his side of the story, no doubt, and gathering ammunition to shoot her down.

Nineteen and a half minutes later, he was still talking to her perp when she handed him the best she could do with the report. She wanted to dare him to find any cop in the department who could have done better. She also wanted to ask what he and a yakuza hit man had so much to talk about, but that shit-eating grin of his shut her up. Her blood was at a full boil, and she was afraid that if she opened her mouth, she'd get herself fired.

Ko lit a new cigarette and smirked. "Sloppy police work, Oshiro." He hadn't even started reading the damn thing.

"Your officer does you great credit," said a reedy voice behind her.

She turned to see Professor Yamada exiting an interview room, escorted by one of the few officers in the station at this time of night, a tall cop she didn't know by name. "Had she not been there," Yamada said, "I should surely be dead now."

The tall policeman nodded appreciatively. At first Mariko could not understand why; she knew she had the respect of a lot of her coworkers, but almost none of them were willing to show it publicly. Then she realized the giant with the tattooed arms was behind her, directly in the tall cop's line of sight, and that the tall cop was not half as im-

pressed with saving Yamada's life as he was with the fact
that Mariko had kayoed a suspect three times her size.

That was good, she supposed, since she certainly hadn't
rescued Yamada. If anything, it had been the reverse. Had
four assailants caught her alone in that house, she didn't
foresee it ending well for her.

Ko, his cigarette dangling loosely from overlarge lips,
nodded at the officer escorting Yamada. "Let's see the difference between a job done right and Oshiro's way of doing
things." His beckoning finger gestured at the manila folder
in the tall cop's folded fingers. A lanky arm handed it over
and, as Ko leafed through it, the taller officer thanked Yamada for his time and excused himself.

Lieutenant Ko frowned at the papers reflecting in his
glasses. Mariko considered explaining the difference between
interviewing a witness and filing a complete and detailed incident report, but thought better of it.

As soon as Ko opened his mouth, she regretted her decision. "Three DOAs? One arrest? That's not the way we do
things, Oshiro. Perhaps you'd feel more at home if I trans-
ferred you to Chicago or Detroit."

The *at home* comment was a deliberate dig; he might just
as well have called her a *gaijin*. "With all due respect," she
began, telling herself the man wasn't due any respect at all,
"I had nothing to do with those deaths. Professor Yamada
killed two in self-defense. The third died because he was
stupid."

"Is that so?"

"A man with a deep leg wound shouldn't try driving a
car. If he hadn't fled, maybe I could have got him to an ambulance. But he drove off, and my best guess is that he
passed out behind the wheel. I didn't put his car through
that woman's concrete garden wall, sir. That was his own
fault."

Ko didn't bother looking up from the crime report. "And
whose fault was the dead man's deep leg wound?"

"Mine," said Yamada. "Or it would be, if I should be held
at fault for it. In any case, I'm the one that cut him."

"With a sword, it says here." At last the dots connected
in Ko's mind. "You're the Yamada that reported an attempted break-in last week. I assigned Oshiro to your case.
Oshiro, what were you doing there on your night off?"

Mariko couldn't answer. She certainly couldn't admit she'd been looking into the Kurihara murder. That was none of her business, a matter for Yokohama PD to worry about. And Ko was looking for any breach of protocol to pin on her, anything at all. As Ko had happily told her himself, even an allegation would be enough. She could find nothing to say.

"She gave me her card," Yamada said. "I was told I should call if I remembered anything else about the case. I'm afraid I didn't know Sergeant Oshiro's work schedule. It's all right that I called, isn't it?"

Lieutenant Ko looked at her, then at Dr. Yamada. "Yes," he said at length, his jaw tight. "We're always happy to serve."

A frown beset Ko's face; his wide lips, large glasses, and the lines around his mouth made Mariko think of a carp. "So you've got a good handle on this case, have you, Oshiro?"

"Yes, sir."

"Good. Then we won't be hearing any more of this Narcotics nonsense, will we?"

He gave her a triumphant smile, or as close to one as his fish lips could manage. Then he stubbed out his cigarette in a nearby ashtray, lit a new one, and closed himself in his office.

"Well," Mariko told Yamada, "I guess I'm stuck with you now."

Yamada winked. "Destiny."

"Uh-huh. How about you tell me what you know about these people who tried to steal your sword? These guys tonight seem like hired hands, and not just to me. You know who sent them. Tell me his name."

Yamada held his wristwatch a thumb's length from his eye. "It's late," he said. "We'll talk tomorrow."

"I can book you for obstructing justice, you know."

"I suppose that's true."

"I'm trying to help you, Dr. Yamada, and I don't appreciate you interfering with how I do my job. Why won't you give me his name?"

Yamada's face darkened, as if a shadow passed over him. "Fuchida," he said at last. "Fuchida Shūzō."

Mariko felt a thrill run up her spine. At last a real lead. "There," she said, "was that so hard?"

Yamada's face grew darker. "Harder than you know."

"He lives here in Tokyo?"

"I don't know."

"What does he do? Does he have a day job? Has he got a record?"

"I don't know."

"Come on, you've got to give me something."

Frown lines deepened in Yamada's face. "I've given all I can give you tonight. Please, Inspector, let me go home."

Mariko felt her face flush. The thrill of the hunt had overwhelmed her; only now did she notice how much this conversation had hurt Yamada. "I'm sorry," she said. "I'll do a little looking into this Fuchida. We'll talk later, all right?"

Yamada nodded, his usual vitality completely drained. "Until then, Inspector. Good night."

# 2 5

Throbbing bass quivered the bones in Fuchida's chest. It was American rap music, the lyrics much too fast for Fuchida to make them out, but he'd heard the song before. A lot of the girls requested it. They liked to dance to it.

They were dancing now, eight of them, the others being either on break, drinking with customers, or up in the champagne room. The eight on stage danced in cones of color, the light from the spots seemingly solid with all the cigarette smoke suspended in it. The club was warm with the heat of the Friday night crowd, but not so warm for the girls; Fuchida could see the erect nipples crowning the shadows of their breasts, swaying in the semisolid light.

The bartender nodded to Fuchida as he walked in, already reaching for a bottle of Maker's Mark. Fuchida threaded through the crowd and up the stairs to the club's upper deck, where customers rarely came except on their way to the champagne room. The second floor overlooked the first, but it was too far from the stage for most customers' liking, and the first floor was more than roomy enough.

Naoko, one of the dancers, brought Fuchida his drink. She wore low heels, an electric-blue thong, and a baby-doll T-shirt that read "Nice Claup" in *romaji*. She sat on his lap as he sipped at the whiskey, but only briefly. "I can't stay," she said, her lips close to his ear so as not to shout. "My set's up next."

He sipped again from his Maker's Mark and watched the men gawk at her as she made her way through them. They knew better than to touch her. That happened a lot at the Kabukichō clubs, but not here, not even the drunks.

The black faux leather creaked under him as he settled into the booth to watch the clientele. He recognized a group of them. Friday night regulars. They were stockbrokers, he thought, or something like that, anyway. He wasn't a hundred percent sure what the difference was between a stockbroker and a trader and an investment banker, but whatever these guys were, they were the kind of useless that needed to pay to see a naked pair of tits. They'd be here until the trains started running again at five or six in the morning, laughing at their boss's jokes, drinking themselves legless just because he said so.

If there was a worse fate for a man, Fuchida didn't know what it was.

Downstairs, a boy came in from the street. He was skinny as a bamboo pole, maybe twenty or twenty-one. He wore his hair the way they did these days, an hour spent carefully arranging it to look the same as it would right after a good postshower toweling. The kid's grandfather was tight with Fuchida's dad, and so the family had made sure the kid had a job. For now he was Fuchida's errand boy, but the kid was smart, and Fuchida predicted he'd make his way up the ladder.

The boy scanned the club, his eyes probably still adjusting to the dark, and when he spotted Fuchida he scurried up to the upstairs booth. "Boss," the kid said, "the cops nailed Kaneda."

Fuchida looked the boy in the eye. "They have him now?"

"Yeah. I hear it was a lady cop who brought him in."

"You're kidding."

"Nope."

Stupid fat fucker. "Begging for help, is he?"

"He wants a lawyer, yeah."

"All right." Fuchida returned his gaze to the dance floor. "Go home; get a good night's sleep. When you wake up, find yourself a good suit. Tone your hair down; make yourself look like a lawyer. Then go see Kaneda and tell him he gets a real attorney when he manages to actually win a fight against an eighty-seven-year-old cripple. Until then, tell him he can put his fat ass on the cot in his cell and sit there until he's skinny enough to slide between the bars."

"You got it."

"Get out of here."

One of the drunk stockbrokers was waggling his nose in Naoko's muff. Fuchida had a mind to walk down there and smash a shot glass or two with the guy's forehead. It wasn't a matter of being territorial; he just wanted to break something. Four men. Four men against a blind man old enough to remember when Fuji was just a molehill. How could so much have gone so wrong?

Twice now he'd made an attempt on the sword. The first time he'd gone himself, and he would have broken in too if it hadn't been for the song. It was his beautiful singer with her high, crooning cry, serenading him to fight, to kill, to prove himself to her. He knew better than to indulge her. Give in to her now and only madness could follow— madness, and then death. So he'd sent Kaneda and the others instead. And now this.

He was poised to carve out his place in history, and now the universe conspired to delay him. Becoming the first to own two Inazuma blades was just the first step in creating his legacy. Even that would pale when he parlayed the old man's sword into the creation of his new empire. He would not compete with the bosses of the Kamaguchi-gumi, but neither would he settle for leading his father's life. Fuchida had no interest in being the underworld equivalent of those useless drunk stockbrokers. He would not live in thrall. He would take the reins of his own destiny, and to do that all he needed was to get his hands on that sly old bastard's sword.

His phone rumbled in his pocket. He knew who it was without looking; only one person would call this number at two thirty in the morning. He walked quickly for the door to the manager's office and let himself in. The bass still thumped through the door behind him, but quiet was a relative thing in a strip club.

"Mr. Travis," Fuchida said in English, the *v* giving him trouble. Differentiating *v* from *b* had always eluded him. "How are things in California?"

"I'm sorry?"

The reply came in Japanese, and from a woman. Fuchida looked at the phone. The caller ID said HOSPITAL WEST, followed by a number Fuchida didn't recognize. "Who is this?" he said.

"My name is Ichikawa Junko," the woman said. "I am the night nurse in palliative care at St. Luke's International. Begging your pardon, but I was given this number as an emergency contact for a Fuchida Tatsuya-sama. Have I misdialed?"

Fuchida blinked hard. He wished he'd brought his drink with him. "No. You called the right number."

"I'm so sorry, sir, but Fuchida-sama has taken a turn for the worse. The file we have for him instructs me to call should anything change in his condition. I'm terribly sorry to be calling so late."

"Just get to the point, will you?" Fuchida opened one drawer after the next in the manager's black sheet-steel desk, looking for a tumbler and something to fill it with. "What's going on with my dad?"

"I'm so sorry, sir, but his breathing has become quite irregular. His oncologist fears he may not survive the night."

A double beep overrode the nurse's next obsequious apology. Fuchida looked at the phone's little screen again. PRIVATE NAME, the caller ID said, and below it, PRIVATE NUMBER. He looked at the phone, almost said something into it, looked at it again. Then he hit the green CALL button and switched to the other line.

"Mr. Travis," he said.

"Fuchida-san," the American said, his voice booming and friendly. To Fuchida he sounded like an overeager car salesman. "What's up? You got my sword?"

Imagined visions flashed in Fuchida's mind. Kaneda, that useless whale, sitting on a cot in a holding cell. Mas, Tiger, Takeshi—probably all dead. He envisioned them as he would have killed them: Mas with a puncture wound through the center of his enormous forehead; Tiger's belly fat oozing from a stab wound right through the navel; a slash across the side of Takeshi's skinny neck, just above the collarbone. "Yeah," he said in his best American English. "I have it. We can do business now, yes?"

"Hell, yeah. Pretty soon you won't be the only badass samurai in the biz, huh?"

"You will be badass samurai too. When do you come?"

"The ship's already en route. You're sure we got no trouble with the cops?"

"No trouble," said Fuchida, still searching the manager's desk. Americans never seemed to be able to understand the role of yakuzas in Japan. All those mafia movies swimming around in their heads gave them weird ideas about police and their ability to interfere with organized crime. Somehow *gaijin* just couldn't get their heads around the idea that for all intents and purposes yakuzas *were* cops. The *ninkyō dantai* were police departments for those who couldn't go to the police. It was the same as in *The Godfather* and *Goodfellas*, Fuchida thought, so for the life of him he couldn't get why Americans had such a hard time understanding that policemen were the farthest thing from the average yakuza's mind. It would take a death wish *and* a wish for career suicide to make a cop interfere with the clans that kept his whole country from going to shit.

Still the American droned on in his ear. "You're going need a big crew to handle five million dollars' worth of merchandise. You know that, right?"

Finally, a fifth of Wild Turkey, the good imported stuff, in a drawer meant for those hanging green file folders. And a set of four glasses nestled in there with it, only a little dusty. He blew one out and filled it. "Do not worry, Mr. Travis."

"I'm not the one who needs to be worried. All I have to do is plan what I'm going to do with my layover in Hawai'i. It's all on you after I jet over there to get my sword. I'll call you later with the when and where."

The American hung up, and Fuchida reflexively closed the phone and dropped it into his pocket. It buzzed immediately. Right. The hospital. He drained his glass, pulled the phone out again, and flipped it open. "Yes?"

"Sir, your father," the night nurse said. "Did you hear what I said? He's taken a turn—"

"Yes," Fuchida said. "A turn for the worse. I heard."

"I think you should come now, sir." Her tone was equal parts compassion and reprobation.

"I think you should mind your own business," said Fuchida. "Don't tell me what I should and shouldn't do."

"Begging your pardon, sir. It's just—"

"I know. A turn for the worse. I'll be there."

# 26

For two days straight Mariko had been in a panic.

Panic didn't come naturally to Mariko. Her little apartment was orderly, as was her cubicle at the precinct, as was her mind. Usually. Panic made a mess of everything, and Mariko's coping strategy had always been to arrange everything in order so that panic could never get a toehold.

Because of that, once panic got a grip on her, Mariko didn't know how to shake it. She felt it like a tight bear hug around the chest. It made her ribs hurt. It made her breath come in short little gasps. And it had been locking down like a boa constrictor for two days running.

She'd filed the missing-persons report. She'd followed up on every unidentified case in every last hospital in greater Tokyo, then in greater Yokohama, asking specifically about unidentified patients with drug-related symptoms. She'd abandoned the hunt for Fuchida Shūzō entirely, choosing instead to read reports on every drug-related arrest or evidence seizure in the prefecture. Doing so violated no small number of departmental regulations. Those reports were none of her business, and she knew that son of a bitch Ko would have her ass in a sling if he ever caught word of it. But she did it anyway. She had to know what happened to Saori.

The triathlete in her wanted to jump in the ocean and

swim until she could feel nothing but exhaustion. The cop in her told her that would kill her; she'd never certified as an EMT, but she'd picked up enough to know that her battered ribs would see her drown if she tried to swim across anything wider than a bathtub. That left the sister in her screaming like a madwoman. She had half a mind to run out to Yamada's place, grab that sword of his, and start hacking. She wanted to swing the goddamn thing until there was nothing left to chop and no strength left in her arms to chop with.

It drove her crazy, not knowing where Saori was. No one had seen her since she stormed off that night, and now she wasn't returning calls—not from Mariko, not from their mother, nothing. Mariko felt the way she felt when she couldn't find her keys, the kind of obsession that wouldn't let her pay attention to anything else. But this was amplified a hundredfold, leaving her perpetually on the verge of nausea.

And then Bumps called, and Mariko kicked herself for not thinking of him beforehand. Again she risked drawing Ko's attention when she did a quick search for the Narc guys who were using Bumps to bait other dealers. Then she hitched a ride with the nearest squad and went screaming downtown to the stakeout.

She called the lead on the case along the way, using the cell number she'd lifted from the computer. He arranged to meet her in a sushi bar across the street from the panel truck he was using to stage his surveillance. They didn't bother exchanging descriptions; every cop in the precinct recognized Tokyo's only female detective.

As such, Mariko was surprised to see a familiar face in the sushi bar. "Well, if it isn't the giant-slayer," said the tall cop she'd crossed paths with on the night of the attack at Yamada's house. "Name's Ino. Nice work the other night hauling in that beached whale."

"Thanks."

"No, seriously. I've never seen a perp so big that you couldn't cuff him. Me and the guys were wondering how you even got him into a squad car."

"Thanks. Where's Bumps?"

Ino nodded toward the window, which overlooked a sort of urban caldera. A small plaza stood surrounded by steep walls of steel and glass, concrete and neon, as if the city had erupted all around it and left this one little lowland behind. A one-way street cut through the plaza, though even with no traffic this could never have been a quiet place; the first few floors of every building were jammed full of Starbucks and McDonald's, Mos Burger and CoCo Ichibanya, kara-oke bars and Hello Kitty stores. But even with its thousand shoppers milling around like ants, this place was as serene as Tokyo got. In the center of the plaza there were even trees, short, fat palms sprouting out of a short, fat planter, surrounded by benches and looking like the spiky green hair of a creature from Dr. Seuss.

Mariko saw Bumps Ryota marching back and forth past the palms like a caged animal. He paced in that strange jittery meth-head way, looking as if he might blow away at any minute. "He's alone," said Ino. "The buyer isn't supposed to be here for another hour, but still, I'd appreciate it if you'd make it fast."

"No problem. I don't relish being near that smelly bastard anyway."

Mariko stormed across the street, Ino's long striding footfalls right behind her. Bumps gave her a glazed-over look, then stiffened up when he finally figured out who she was.

"Uh . . . hi, Officer," he said. "I'm so glad to see you."

He wasn't. He looked nervous enough to wet himself, in fact, and Mariko was upset enough to punch him in the bladder just to see if it would happen.

Instead she grabbed him by the sleeve, dragged him to the panel truck, and shoved him inside. Her ribs bit her like a pissed-off Doberman as she hauled herself up into the truck. Ino closed the door behind her, leaving Mariko and Bumps alone in the van.

Bumps Ryota blinked hard, maybe trying to shake off sunspots. He took two steps and collided with a small aluminum table jutting out from the right-hand wall. He bounced from that to a stool, which he caught with his shins and tripped over. "Hey," he said, palms flat on the floor, "this isn't like the movies."

"You're a movie star now?"

"No. The truck. I figured you guys had video and phone

taps and all that. Isn't this a surveillance van? Only thing in here is a microwave."

Surveillance, she could have told him, was mostly eating, drinking, and watching nothing happen. She could have told him that in circumstances like that, the only thing more important than a microwave was a toilet. Instead she said, "Nothing in a cop's life is like the movies, Bumps. Now where is she?"

"Who?"

"Saori. She's missing. Where is she?"

Bumps slid from his prone position to sit upright in the corner. "How should I know anything about her? You told me to get something on that coke dealer of yours."

"You were her pusher, Bumps. Did she come to you? Is she using again?"

He blinked hard at her. "How did I get on the floor?"

"Is she using, Bumps?"

"You think I'm an idiot? We got a deal, Officer. I sell your sister so much as a Tylenol, you rat me out to the guys I get my shit from. Why would I have anything to do with her?"

Mariko blew her breath out through her nose. She had a pounding headache, and Bumps Ryota's dirty-laundry smell wasn't helping one bit. "Addicts are creatures of habit," she said. "If she's using again, she'll go to people she knows."

"Well, not me."

He was telling the truth. Mariko listened to a lot of people's lies in her line of work, enough of them that she wasn't often wrong about them. She pressed her fingers to her temples to relieve pressure.

"So," Bumps said, "did you, you know, want me to tell you what I found out about your coke dealer?"

"Frankly, I don't give a shit," Mariko said, not even meaning to say it aloud. She didn't have time to think about the cocaine trail. Saori was the sole priority.

No. Mariko wanted that to be true—at the moment she wished more than anything that it could be true—but reality was harder and colder than that. Pushing any harder on the search for Saori would only serve to draw Ko's attention, and even if Mariko found her, she couldn't help Saori anyway. Saori had made it all of eight days into rehab before falling off the wagon. Even if Mariko got lucky and found her again, all she could do was take her back to a detox program that didn't work.

"Fine, Bumps, go ahead. Tell me about your dealer."

She heard herself say the words, and heard Bumps blather on too, but she didn't even bother getting out her notepad. As soon as he said, "I don't have a name for you yet," Mariko tuned out the rest. "Tall guy" and "ponytail" and "tattoos" did her little good without a name. Mariko felt powerless. The only two things she could muster the energy to care about were her sister and the cocaine threat, and she had no leads on either of them. Yamada's sword case had grown interesting, but she had no leads there either. She was sure Dr. Yamada knew more about the would-be thief than he was letting on, but he was strangely reticent about revealing details.

"Detective Oshiro?"

"Huh?"

Bumps was staring at her. "Are you listening to me? I'm telling you, this is one dangerous son of a bitch. Gives you the feeling he could snap at any moment, you know what I mean?"

"Uh-huh. This from the guy who needs a minute or two to realize he's tripped and fallen on the floor. I'm sure your instincts about him are spot-on, Bumps."

"I'm telling you—"

"What? What are you telling me? That life as a CI isn't as safe and comfy as you thought? Bumps, you're a drug dealer. Did you think the biggest risk in your profession was not having a pension?"

"You can't blow me off like this. You're supposed to protect me."

"So help me protect you. You got a name for me?"

"Uh. No. But—"

"Don't bother calling until you do. Unless you can tell me who your coke dealer is or where my sister is, as far as I'm concerned all you hoppers and dealers can swindle each other and kill each other all you like."

Then something clicked for her. Scum associated with scum. Dealers with dealers. Cops with cops. Everyone associated with their own kind.

She pulled her cell from her pocket, cycled through the recent calls, and rang one of them back. If she couldn't make any headway on Saori or the coke case, at least she could make progress on the other thing. "Dr. Yamada?" she said. "We need to talk. I'll be at your place in half an hour."

# 27

Yamada's front door was unlocked. Strange, Mariko thought, given the attack the other night. It was a remnant of a more peaceful era. She opened the door to be greeted by the familiar scent of green tea. Yamada was in the sitting room, kneeling beside his low table and facing her.

"It's me, Dr. Yamada. Detective Oshiro. You really shouldn't leave your door unlocked. You just had a break-in, you know."

"As polite as ever," Yamada said. His wrinkled hand gestured at the table, where two steaming teacups were waiting. The tatami mats were still stained brown where his assailants had bled on them, though it appeared he'd taken pains to clean up what he could. "Do come in, won't you?"

"I'm sorry," Mariko said. "I shouldn't tell you how to run your own house."

She stepped out of her shoes, bowed curtly to the professor, and sat across the table from him. The battered left side of her rib cage protested every step of the way. "My sister's missing, so I've been rude with everybody. I was looking into her case when I had an insight into yours. Well, not so much into your case as into you, sir. This Fuchida Shūzō, the one who's trying to steal your sword, you've met him personally, *neh*?"

"Of course."

There it was again: that maddening capacity of his to make her feel like a twelve-year-old version of herself. How could that possibly be an "of course" kind of question?

She forced herself to take a deep breath. Then another. "Why didn't you tell me that before?"

He shrugged. "It didn't seem relevant."

"How could it not be—?" This time it took two deep breaths to keep herself from screaming. "Dr. Yamada, you could have told me his name the first day I came out here. What took you so long?"

"All things in due time. Come now, Inspector, you've done some research on him by now. What have you learned?"

"Nothing." Mariko didn't appreciate the fact that he just assumed he knew how she'd go about doing her job, and she liked it even less that he was dead right. She'd pulled up files from every police database she could find, and filed a dozen warrants to search the files of mortgage lenders, car dealerships, banks, and governmental services for any records on a Fuchida Shūzō. The warrants had yet to yield any fruit, and just when she'd started delving into the police records, Saori had disappeared, and it seemed she'd taken Mariko's ability to concentrate with her.

"Now, now," said Yamada, "you're brighter than that. I think you've already deduced rather more about him than the fact that he and I have met. Why don't you tell me what you know?"

Mariko felt the bile burning in her stomach. Her ribs pained her too, and neither was as painful as the effort it took to restrain her frustration. "All right. He's involved with the *bōryokudan*, isn't he?"

"I don't know. What makes you ask?"

"Tattoos. The fat man had them. The others who broke in the other night, they had them too. A lot of yakuzas do. If this Fuchida sent those four the other night, he's probably a yakuza himself. Hm. I can't say I ever spent much time cultivating contacts in the *bōryokudan*, but I'll ask the yakuzas I know and see if they've heard of him."

A look of shock spread across Yamada's face. "You know yakuzas personally?"

"Sure."

"And you *speak* to these people?"

Mariko laughed. "Of course. I'm a cop, Dr. Yamada; it's almost impossible *not* to get to know a yakuza or two. Besides, they're handy; they know what's happening on the streets long before we do, and there's nothing they love more than showing off to cops. I'll ask my guys. If they know him, believe me, they'll brag about it."

Yamada's eyebrows slowly sank back to their customary place; his mouth relaxed its O shape as the stunned look evaporated from his face. "I'm sorry, Inspector. It never occurred to me that police officers and criminals would be so . . . so . . . well, so *friendly*."

"'Friendly' isn't the word for it. Call it professional courtesy. Let's hope they can come up with something better than I can get through official channels, because so far our databases don't have shit."

"Are all young ladies of your generation so well mannered?"

"Sorry."

"Forget your databases. What have *you* discovered about him?"

Yet again she found herself feeling shortsighted and immature. Somehow he adopted the roles of grandfather, schoolteacher, and commanding officer in her mind. But now that he asked the question, in the simple way that he'd asked it, she found herself making connections she hadn't consciously drawn.

"He's an expert too, isn't he? On swords, I mean. He'd have to be. You can't break into houses at random in hope of stealing medieval weapons. Only an authority on the subject would know which ones to steal and where they were."

"Keep going," said Yamada.

"How many authorities on medieval swords can there be?" Now the connections were flashing like lightning, so fast Mariko could barely keep up with them. "You're an academic. You go to conferences and such, *neh*? That's it. You know him because he's an academic like you. Is he another history professor?"

"No."

"Then one of your students. A grad student? No. Not a lot of criminal types there. It's one of your martial arts students, isn't it?"

Yamada bowed deeply, his short silver hair shining like

a million stars as it caught the light. "Very good, Inspector. In fact I did meet him at the university. That was before he started training in my dojo. You don't see a fighter the likes of him more than once or twice in a lifetime."

"What can you tell me about him?"

Yamada shrugged. "We met when he took my class in Heian era history. A bright young man. Driven. We spoke about sword combat quite a bit, and then he started training under me. I can't recall anyone making *shodan* so quickly."

"Why didn't you tell me who he was the first time I came out here? I could have made a lot of progress on your case by now."

"Destiny works at its own pace."

"Oh, no. I'm not letting you off that easy. Look, what happened here the other night, the night of the break-in . . . well, I'll grant you, that was weird. But whatever you think about destiny bringing us together that night, you can't have known that was coming the first time we met."

Yamada gave her an impish grin, his eyes twinkling. "You know a lot about destiny for someone who just started believing in it, Inspector."

Mariko couldn't decide whether to grin back or strangle him. He was cute in that sweet old man sort of way, but all his fate crap was wearing thin. "Come on," she said, "you're telling me you've been waiting for ages for a policewoman to come to your door?"

"A swordswoman, actually."

"I'm not—" An exasperated laugh escaped Mariko's lips. "You drive me nuts—you know that?"

"As polite as ever, Oshiro-san."

"Listen, suppose you're right. Suppose I really was destined to come here, and somehow you're going to talk me into learning how to sword-fight, and . . . assume all that stuff. If that's really what destiny has in store for us, what difference would it have made if you'd told me Fuchida's name from the beginning? We'd have ended up right here anyway, right?"

"Oh ho," said Yamada. He raised his wrinkled hands as if she were holding a gun on him. "Not bad, Inspector. I think you've got me with my own logic."

"Damn right I do. So answer the question. Why didn't you tell me his name on day one?"

Yamada rubbed his face with his hands, then pressed his palms together, his forefingers resting against his lips. He looked like he might be about to pray. At last, peering over his steepled fingertips, he said, "Haven't you deduced that already, Inspector? Why, it's embarrassing. Fuchida-san was my *student*. What does it mean about a professor if his own student comes back to rob him?"

Mariko nodded, ashamed that she'd made him spell it out. Any properly Japanese person would have seen the connection. But Mariko had spent most of her childhood in the States, and she didn't think of relationships in the way most Japanese did.

Mariko's father had moved his family back to Tokyo so that his daughters could get into a good Japanese university, which they could never do without going to a good Japanese high school. When Mariko had asked him why, he'd explained *gakubatsu* to her. She'd tried to understand the word in English, her primary language in those days, but "school clique" didn't come close to translating *gakubatsu*. The closest American equivalent was a Marine Corps tattoo: *gakubatsu* was a badge, a unifying force, a marker of something awfully close to family. It was out of *gakubatsu* that alumni from the same school hired each other, promoted each other, ran whole corporations and universities and political parties together. And because of *gakubatsu*, if one person tarnished the good name of the school, everyone else in the school's family suffered.

"I'm sorry," Mariko said. "I should have understood. Police work is a bit like university work that way: if I step out of line, I embarrass everyone who wears the badge—especially my CO." She gave a rueful snicker. "Of course that last part only matters if you *respect* your CO. I have the luxury of not giving a shit, because my CO's a total pain in the ass."

Yamada sipped his tea. "And yet you seem less than liberated, Inspector."

Mariko sighed. "It's Saori. You think having your student come back to steal from you is an embarrassment? Try being a narc with a junkie for a sister."

"Would you care to talk about your sister?"

She didn't. She wasn't a fan of having emotional talks with strangers, much less with civilians whose cases she was investigating. But something about Yamada made her open up. It was that damned grandfatherly disposition of his, and even as Mariko wished she could stop herself, she found herself talking. "There's nothing I can do about her. I keep acting like there is, but I should have learned my lesson by now."

"And that is?"

"That nothing I can do can stop Saori from using. That she's going to kill herself one of these days and there's not a damn thing I can do to stop it."

Mariko sniffed. Thin ribbons of steam spiraled up from her pale orange cup of pale green tea. She watched them, then gave a light exhalation and watched how they wheeled and whirled in response. If only she had as much influence over Saori.

"You wish to surrender my case and look for your sister?"

"No. Well, yes, of course I do, but I can't. My CO's a jackass, and cops don't usually spare much time for missing junkies anyway. Besides, those hooks are in deep on her. They pull her down, out of sight, to places I don't even know about."

She gave a sighing, hopeless laugh. "I've had this straitlaced, prim and proper life," she said, "all the way until I became a cop. You know, I never even saw meth before I went to academy? They lit a joint for us too, to recognize the smell, and all these smiles lit up around the room. Memories from their partying days, you know? And it was the first time I ever smelled it. I don't know how she got so mixed up in that shit when I was always so far away from it." Mariko looked up—she'd been watching the steam all this time—and she saw a compassionate smile on Yamada's face. "Why are you smiling?"

"Because the only alternative is to cry," he said. "Let me tell you a story. Something to take your mind off things, but also a story like yours. This one is about something that gets its hooks in too, something that goes on to destroy families. Would you like to hear it?"

Mariko sighed and drank her tea.

"It begins with a famed samurai from Echizen," Yamada said, "a man called Motoyori Hidetada. He had a sword named Beautiful Singer. This was about eight hundred years ago, though by then his sword was already nearly a hundred years old. His house fell to ruin when he should have been at his prime. Beautiful Singer is passed down to his sister's eldest son, a warlord by the name of Nagafusa. The Nagafusas, a powerful clan, are destroyed within a decade.

"The sword passes out of history for a while, reappearing about a century later in the hands of one Kanayama Osamu. Lord Kanayama's house falls to shame and infamy when he flees like a common criminal rather than committing seppuku. Immediately after the fall of Kanayama, another esteemed house, the Saitos, suffers a similar fate. Not twenty years later, the house of Nakadai is laid to waste. The Saitos and the Nakadais were closely allied with House Kanayama. Historical records cannot confirm that they possessed the sword, but nor do they offer any concrete reason for the ruin of any of those houses.

"The sword does not appear again until the Meiji Restoration, when it is mistakenly called Glorious Sun. Again, its wielder falls ingloriously. It appears again in the Second World War, in the hands of an officer named Iwasaki. Iwasaki goes on to take a command role in the butchery that the world now calls the Bataan Death March. Before that he brought the sword to Nanking, China. The butchery there was worse."

"Nice bedtime story," said Mariko.

Yamada winced. "Iwasaki was killed too, by the way—shot by his own men. It took a lot of work to connect Glorious Sun to Beautiful Singer, and even more work to piece its story together. I devoted twenty years of my life to discovering the truth of it and never wrote a book about it."

"Why's that?"

"Because Beautiful Singer was crafted by Master Inazuma. You must understand, Inspector: no one in academia believes Inazuma ever existed. I see him as the first of the great sword smiths, but no one else will believe me."

"Why not?"

"He used tempering techniques we don't see again for over a century. You cannot underestimate his genius. The two most celebrated sword smiths in history are Masamune and Muramasa, but Inazuma perfected Masamune's high-heat forging style more than a hundred years before Masamune was born. The oldest *shinogi-zukuri*-style sword we have is a Yukimasa from the late Heian period. I date Beautiful Singer fully twenty-five years earlier than the Yukimasa."

Mariko blinked. "I'm not stupid, Dr. Yamada, but you're going to have to run that by me again."

Yamada nodded, his blind eyes twinkling. She smiled despite herself; she'd never seen him this excited. "All right," he said, "imagine how historians would react if I claimed Henry Ford based his design for the Model T on a car built by Galileo in 1600."

"They'd flip their lids."

"Exactly. Now imagine if you'd never heard of Galileo because the historians all think he's a fairy tale. If I were to publish a book on Inazuma, it would discredit all the rest of my work."

"Even if what your book said was true?"

"The nail that sticks up gets hammered down, Inspector."

"But you're not basing this on nothing. You're a historian. You have evidence."

"Why, there's evidence and then there's what's publishable. Even if I could find a publisher, I question the wisdom of drawing attention to Beautiful Singer. That sword should be destroyed and then forgotten." He refilled Mariko's teacup, then topped off his own. "But this is too grim a subject for a night like this. Would you like to hear another story?"

"Is it a good one?" Mariko said.

"This one also stars a sword. Tiger on the Mountain, it's called. It's said that so long as this blade is within a castle, that castle can never fall."

"Let me guess: there's nothing in the history books about it?"

"No, indeed. But now and then you can find records of an entire village burned to the ground, save one house only. An earthquake topples candles onto spilled oil, drops roofs into fireplaces, even brings the local castle down, but not that one house. One fisherman's house stands, and a castle falls."

"This is Japan, Professor. Earthquakes and weird coincidences go together like rice and shoyu."

"Of course. So naturally you will think it mere coincidence that here and there a tsunami will strike, erasing every hut but one. Or a bombing raid in the Great War: again, it levels every house in the neighborhood but one. Wherever you find the lone standing building, there you find some connection to the Tiger on the Mountain." He smiled and winked. "Coincidence, I'm sure."

Mariko smiled back at him. "Which sword is upstairs?"

"Neither. Would you like to hear that story too?"

"Is it another cursed sword?"

Yamada let out a wry laugh. "Hard to say. But there is another story, the most stunning of all, for the tales of all three swords are interwoven. All three were made by the same master sword smith, a man whose story has fallen out of the histories altogether. I am the only scholar left who even believes he existed."

"Master Inazuma," Mariko said.

"Precisely."

Mariko nodded. "I'm sure you've got a good story for him too. But I'm more impressed by the way you tell your stories. I make a point of knowing when people lie to me. But you—you really believe every word, don't you?"

"I can prove every word. Dates, families, wills bequeathing this and the other swords from generation to generation. It was my life's work to find them."

"And no mention of this in any of your books?"

"Not a word. You must understand: even when I first discovered the existence of Master Inazuma, there were already serious doubts about his very existence—and that was nigh on seventy years ago. We fought and lost a war since then. We've redefined ourselves as a nation several times over. No one takes the time to study the old ways anymore. Most react as you did: with scorn. There's no such thing as magic, *neh*?"

Mariko felt ashamed. *Scorn* was a harsh word, though she didn't have a ready replacement. But she also noted that he'd spoken of her scorn in the past tense. He regarded her as she was increasingly regarding herself: as a woman who believed in magic. Or if not magic, then whatever the right name was for the powers of fate expressing themselves through a sharpened length of steel.

"Fuchida Shūzō," she said, her voice distant even to herself. "You told him about the swords?"

"Of course."

"Why?"

"I thought he could help me destroy Beautiful Singer." Yamada's shoulders sagged a bit, and his unseeing gaze fell to the tabletop. "He's a man of remarkable focus. As diligent a martial artist as any I've seen. When I first met him, he was already in the habit of inuring himself to pain. He collects tattoos, you see. Always by the traditional method, and usually on sensitive areas: pressure points, soft tissues, *neh*? I wonder now why I couldn't see the dark side in that, but at the time he impressed me. Only a man of focus and resilience could subjugate the will of Beautiful Singer. Or at least that's what I thought back then."

"And now?"

Yamada sucked at his teeth. "Now?" he said, his tone heavy with resignation. "Now I don't believe there's ever been a man alive who could overcome the sword. Nevertheless, it's been my life's work to destroy it. You must help me with that, Sergeant Oshiro."

Mariko's palms dropped heavily to the table, shuddering the last few drops of tea in their cups. "Well, if no one on earth could pull that off, I don't see how I'm supposed to help. But I guess we could start by figuring out where this Beautiful Singer is."

Yamada gave her a nod, lips bunched, eyes slightly narrowed, the kind of expression she would have received from her father on the day she graduated from the academy. "Good. Good. Now, if you want to find the sword, you only need to find Fuchida Shūzō."

"That part shouldn't be hard. He seems to want to come to you, or at least to keep sending his men your way. We'll get someone to talk. But how do you know he's got the sword?"

Yamada shrugged. "He used it to kill that woman in Kamakura, didn't he?"

"I hate when you do that," Mariko said, slapping the tabletop again. "You talk about all these things you couldn't possibly know as if you were standing in the room when they happened. How the hell did you get to be a better detective than me?"

Yamada gave her a grandfatherly smile. "I beg your pardon. Perhaps I should explain. That woman in Kamakura, what did you say her name was?"

"Kurihara Yuko."

"When I met her, her name was Matsumori Yuko. The sword I have upstairs is an Inazuma, and an erstwhile heirloom in her family. I bought it from her some years ago to keep it safe. Fuchida killed her to get the sword, no doubt, not knowing she'd sold it. It seems he wants to expand his collection."

"But that doesn't explain anything. How do you know Fuchida has Beautiful Singer?"

"Oh, that's easy. He stole it for me twenty years ago."

Mariko gawked. She couldn't help herself. "He what?"

Yamada gave that shrug of his, the one that made the most obscure of facts seem as plain as the table in front of her. "I told you," he said, "I trained Fuchida because I thought he could help me destroy the sword. He did the first part admirably: he stole it from a private collector—a man who is still alive today, I might add, probably because he no longer owns Beautiful Singer. It was the second half of his task that Fuchida failed: he never delivered the sword to me. In fact, I haven't seen him since."

"But you said he embarrassed you by trying to steal your sword. You were in on the Beautiful Singer theft from the beginning!"

"You misunderstand, Inspector."

"I think I understand just fine. The Americans have a saying for this, you know: 'No honor among thieves.' How can you be shocked if you trained Fuchida to steal swords and now he wants to steal one from you?"

Yamada closed his eyes and sighed. "It is not the theft that wounds me, Inspector. It is the betrayal." Now he looked at her, and though she was certain she was too far away for him to see her, he seemed to look directly into her eyes. "You must understand, I only involved Fuchida-san in my plot to destroy Beautiful Singer because I thought he was a friend. When he disappeared, it was like a knife in the heart."

Mariko knew the feeling. Saori's disappearance stabbed her through the heart too. Once again she felt clumsy in front of this man—this kind old man, whose wounded heart she'd just kicked around because she had all the tact of a drunken baboon.

"I'm sorry," said Mariko. She could hear crickets chirping in the garden, and she realized it was well past sundown. "Look, I'm . . . I'm an emotional klutz, okay? But I think we've finally gotten to something I can start investigating. You taught at Tōdai, *neh*? They'll have some record of Fuchida being a student there, and maybe through that I can find a connection to his finances."

Yamada's forehead wrinkled. "Why should you care about his finances?"

"You really are old-fashioned, aren't you?"

"Polite as ever, Inspector."

"Sorry." Once again Mariko found herself blushing in Yamada's company. His ability to make her feel self-conscious was extraordinary, but no less so than her own ability to put her foot in her mouth when she was around him.

"Let me start over," she said. "These days, if you buy something expensive, it's probably in a computer record somewhere. Find that and sometimes you can find other big purchases: cars, down payments on apartments, that kind of thing. It's not hard to find suspects that way."

"Ah. This modern world."

"The *bōryokudan* guys ought to have something for me by now too. I'll be in touch. Until then, keep your doors and windows locked, and call 110 next time before you go drawing your sword on anyone, *neh*?"

Yamada chuckled. "I'll do that."

As she slipped back into her shoes, Mariko said, "Thank you, Dr. Yamada."

"What for?"

"Distracting me. With your sword stories, I mean. It doesn't do me any good to get all worked up over things I can't do anything about, but sometimes I can't help it."

"Impulse control, my dear. Study swordsmanship with me. You'll learn something of it."

# BOOK FOUR

AZUCHI-MOMOYAMA ERA,

THE YEAR 20

(1587 CE)

# 28

The Okuma compound commanded a sweeping view of the east coast of the Izu peninsula, so Okuma Daigoro saw the rival swordsman's company approaching many *ri* before it reached him. He watched as the horses rounded the curve beneath Kattō-ji, the temple on the mountaintop overlooking the road. The challenger rode under banners the color of dry moss. There were a dozen riders in all, and as the column drew nearer, Daigoro could make out long white centipedes snaking up the fluttering fields of green. It was the Yasuda clan, then. Daigoro had not expected a challenger to come from his family's closest ally.

He limped out of his study, which overlooked the eastern coastal road, and made his way ponderously to the main gate. As he stepped off the veranda onto the sand of the courtyard, his right knee buckled and he collapsed. He gripped his skinny leg through his wide, flowing *hakama* pants to ensure it was not injured. His knee was only as wide as his elbow, and ever since birth the nerve endings had been sluggish at best. His fingers were a better judge of whether it had dislocated.

Finding no serious injury, Daigoro shifted his weight off his scrawny right leg and onto his left, and from there he pushed himself to his feet. He could hear hooves approaching, louder now than the ever-present chorus of waves beating the black rocks of the coastline. It would not do for his clan's visitors to find him a dusty mess; he made a quick but thorough job of brushing himself off, then hobbled toward the gate.

"I come to challenge the sword of Okuma," called the young man on the roan mare. "I come to challenge Okuma Tetsurō!"

He was young, not yet twenty, Daigoro supposed, with a meager beard that invited associations with mangy dogs or half-plucked hens. His forearms, however, were like stout twisted ropes, and his hands were thickly callused, sure signs of long sword training. He rode at the head of a column of ten samurai, and beside a smaller man whose hair was as white as wisps of cloud. The older man clucked his tongue and said, "Manners, Eijun."

Turning his gaze to Daigoro, the older man said, "I am Yasuda Jinbei of Shimoda. Good day to you, young Master Okuma."

"I haven't forgotten you, Yasuda-san," said Daigoro, "nor the *mochi* cakes you used to bring me on the New Year when I was a little boy. What brings you here?"

Lord Yasuda dismounted his horse—spryly, Daigoro noted, in defiance of the many years the old man had spent in the service of the Okumas; Daigoro wondered whether he had ever looked so graceful himself. Once on the ground, Lord Yasuda was of equal height with Daigoro, which marked him as unusually small. Yasuda's belly was rounder, his skin darker and etched with wrinkles. He bowed to Daigoro, and Daigoro returned it.

"Begging your pardon," Yasuda whispered, "but my grandnephew Eijun insisted on riding here to announce his challenge. I told him it would be the height of rudeness, to say nothing of pridefulness. I told him also that he stands no chance of victory, but still he persists."

"I'm sorry to announce that my father is not here," Daigoro said, loudly enough for all in the company to hear. "He rode north more than a week ago, to negotiate a treaty with the great Lord Toyotomi. I regret that my elder brother Ichirō is also away. If you wish to challenge the sword of Okuma, I'm afraid the only one for you to face is me."

"You!" said Eijun, still in his saddle. "You can't be more than fifteen years old!"

"I turn sixteen this winter. As I say, I am the only one here for you to duel."

"Please, Okuma-sama," whispered Lord Yasuda, and his eyes flicked down to Daigoro's right leg. The *hakama* were wide and billowy enough to conceal his legs and feet entirely, but Yasuda had known of the disfigurement since Daigoro's birth. "There's no need for you to face him. The boy is slow, my lord. He nearly drowned as a child—held his breath too long and was never the same since. I accompanied him here only to humor him."

But Daigoro only winked to the old man.

"Fifteen!" barked Eijun. "Not even of age yet, and undersized to boot! No, I'll wait here to test my steel against Glorious Victory."

"You may be waiting a long time," said Daigoro. "That's my father's sword, and I don't know when he plans to return."

"Is there no one here I can fight? Are all of you cowards?"

"Eijun!" barked Lord Yasuda, but Daigoro brushed off the insult with a wave of his hand.

"It's no matter of cowardice, but simply a matter of time. If you wait until my birthday, I'll come of age and we can fight in the snow."

Eijun scoffed, but Lord Yasuda smiled and bowed to Daigoro. "As excellent a judge of character as your father," he whispered. Then, louder, he said, "Shall we be on our way, Eijun?"

"We rode all morning for nothing!"

"I seem to recall telling you as much before we left." Lord Yasuda stepped up into the saddle, nodded deeply to Daigoro, and bid him farewell.

Only when the last of the Yasuda samurai turned his horse down the road did Daigoro release his breath. Challengers came regularly, as often to test themselves against Glorious Victory as against the swordsmanship of the Okuma clan. Both were famous, both as yet undefeated. For the past thirty years and more, Daigoro's father had defended the clan's honor, and that duty would never pass to Daigoro. His brother Ichirō would be the next champion—Ichirō, whose limbs were whole, whose body was as big and strong as their father's. Daigoro had trained as hard as anyone in the samurai arts, but the mark his father had set had always seemed unattainable.

Thus it relieved him to see the dust settle on the road. With luck, he thought, he would not have to be the one to answer the door when the next rival came to call.

# 29

The following morning was hot. The sun reflected furiously from an unusually calm sea, and there was no breeze to speak of. Daigoro immediately thought it strange, then, when he saw the lone horseman dashing up the coastal road at a gallop. It was no way to treat a horse in such weather. When he saw the moss-green banner, he had no doubt it would be Yasuda Eijun. Once again he made his way to the main gate of the compound, and this time he loosened his *katana* in its scabbard.

The younger Yasuda's mount was foaming and panting as it clattered to a halt before the gate. "Your father!" Eijun shouted, panting as heavily as his horse.

"He's still not here, Yasuda-san."

"No," said Eijun. "He's dead."

The body of Okuma Tetsurō returned home via the eastern road, in a palanquin fit for the mightiest daimyo. Over a hundred red Okuma banners marched ahead of it, a hundred green Yasuda banners behind. Behind the Yasudas were the Nagatomos, the Ushidas, the Soras, the Inoues. In all, some six hundred men and a hundred cavalry escorted the body home. Many would ride all through the night to return home, for the Okuma compound could never house so many; only the lords and their immediate retainers could stay.

His father's body. It lay before Daigoro, swathed in a white kimono, wooden sandals on the feet so his spirit would be able to walk comfortably in the afterlife. There was an unnatural depression above the breastbone where the musket ball had struck. His black hair was without a touch of gray; the mustache and beard were trimmed, the lips pursed. Shaded by the roof of the simple shrine built for the occasion, his face did not have the pallor Daigoro had seen when the body was first removed from the palanquin. Six copper coins lay with him, and his best pair of chopsticks. He would leave this world with nothing that would not burn away.

Sandalwood incense, the cries of the wailers, the weight of his father's sword at his hip: these were what comprised Daigoro's experience in the moment. Not grief. Not his mother's shoulders quivering in his embrace. It was his brother who cradled their weeping mother in his arms. As for grief, Daigoro could not find it. He loved his father dearly, wanted very much to cry for him, but each time he grasped at grief, it slipped away like a rabbit through the trees of a forest.

The forest, he supposed, was shock. It surrounded him, so dense as to leave him no lingering sense of direction. His father was only fifty-three. Every samurai expected an early death, but Okuma Tetsurō was strong and crafty. If ever a frontline warrior was to die of old age, everyone thought Okuma Tetsurō would have been the one.

Daigoro bowed to the visiting lords one by one as they offered their condolences. He felt distant from them, still deep in the forest, their voices so faint he could not make out the words. Each time he bowed, Glorious Victory pulled at his waist. It was heavy, surprisingly so, heavy enough that Daigoro could not imagine wielding it in one hand. A vision of his father sprang to mind, seated on his galloping horse, the huge ōdachi flashing in his right hand. He had been so strong.

Even lost in the forest as he was, Daigoro noticed the eyes of those who had come to pay their respects; those that took note of the sword inevitably widened with surprise. Daigoro was the second son. Now that their father was gone, Ichirō was the head of the clan. By all rights the sword was his. Or rather, by all rights save one.

Drawing himself out of his reflections, Daigoro found the area around the shrine was nearly empty. The shrine was enclosed on four sides by walls of white cloth hanging from lines suspended from tall posts. The long curtains flapped in the faint breeze, and within them, all that remained were Daigoro, his mother and brother, the body, and the first cords of wood to be used in the cremation. An enormous pile of logs lay just outside the cloth barrier; Daigoro had seen it as he entered and was astonished by how much wood was needed to cremate a corpse.

"Come," Ichirō said softly to their mother, "we should go inside."

Daigoro limped to the white curtain, the huge sword unbalancing him as he went, and parted a gap to allow his family through. As Ichirō ushered their mother to the house, his eyes strayed to the sword. Daigoro could not help but notice. "I'll be in shortly," Daigoro told him, and gestured for the Zen abbot and his priests to come in and begin the cremation. Even the abbot's gaze lingered on the blade; was there anyone who did not think ill of him for bearing it?

As he watched the first flames lick the logs under the body, Daigoro wished he had one last chance to ask about his father's decision. Why did you bequeath it to me? Why not to your firstborn? I have never been a swordsman. You should have left it to him, Father. At the very least you should have told us why you chose me.

The first wave of heat struck his face as the center of the pyre flared up. He smelled pine smoke at first, then a sickening, greasy smell like roast pork. Over the crackling of the fire and the chanting of the priests he could hear the sizzle of fat on meat. Holding back a retch, he limped as quickly as he could for the house.

His leg betrayed him; he stumbled and fell as soon as he passed through the curtain. He landed on his right side, instinctively protecting Glorious Victory from harm. Two Okuma samurai ambling about the compound came immediately to help him stand up. He waved them off and with effort pushed himself to his feet. He'd done it a thousand times, but this time was harder. Was it because of all the eyes on him, or was it the weight of the sword?

"Would my lord prefer an escort indoors?" asked a voice. At first Daigoro thought it was one of the samurai, but looking up he saw it was Lord Yasuda. His white robes bore a curled green centipede, and his silver topknot shone in the sun.

"I can manage," said Daigoro. "I've lived with this leg all my life."

"Of course," said Lord Yasuda. "I assumed it was your grief on this tragic day, and not your leg at all, that led to your fall. Any one of us might be thankful for support on such a day."

Something deep inside Daigoro relaxed. "You have my thanks. Support I'll decline, but I'd happily accept your company, Yasuda-san."

Daigoro dusted himself off, made sure the ōdachi and scabbard were clean, and limped alongside Lord Yasuda toward the house.

"How fares the Lady Yumiko?" asked Yasuda.

"Mother is as well as can be expected. Thank you."

"Good." After a moment, Yasuda added, "I am happy to see you wearing your father's weapon."

Daigoro gave him a sharp glance. "Are you always so forthcoming? I thought we might bandy about for a while before coming to the inevitable. The weather, the state of the war, perhaps your grandnephew, *neh*?"

"I am an old man, my lord, at a younger man's funeral. What little time I have left will not be spent wastefully."

"So be it," Daigoro said, wanting to smile but refusing to indulge that inclination. If he could not feel grief, at a minimum he would not be seen grinning like a fool even as his father's body burned. "If we are speaking candidly, tell me, Yasuda-san, why are you pleased that the famous Glorious Victory should rest at the hip of a cripple rather than in the able hands of his brother, a warrior of some repute? Why does it please you that, contrary to tradition, the younger brother should inherit the sword, and not the new head of the clan?"

"Since when has it been contrary to tradition to uphold a father's dying wish? It seemed possible, my young lord, that your brother would claim the sword as his birthright, even in defiance of the late Lord Okuma. It was made by the great master Inazuma, after all; wars have been waged over the possession of such a blade. Hence it pleases me to see it with you because the late lord's request was so earnest and so specific. He had clear reasons for bequeathing it as he did, even if those reasons were clear only to himself."

Daigoro felt his heart quiver and his throat stiffen. Something was stirring within him: perhaps at last it was grief, but now it was mixed with anger. It was impure, so he suppressed it. "How," he said with some effort, "do you come to know so much about my father's dying wish, when his own sons and wife received it just yesterday, and only in writing?"

Lord Yasuda bowed his head. "It was my hand that wrote it, Okuma-sama. It was I that tended to him at the last."

Daigoro stopped in midstride. Until now he'd assumed his father had written his last will himself, and Daigoro had taken comfort in the idea that even in dying his father had maintained such a steady hand. Nor was Daigoro the only one; his mother had been the first to suggest that the graceful handwriting indicated their father had not been in significant pain.

He shuffled half a step closer to Lord Yasuda and whispered, "How many know you wrote his last letter?"

"My young lord and myself," said the aging daimyo. "There were serving women as well, two of them, ministering to your father. Shall I have them dispatched?"

"No. There has been enough blood already. But they will say nothing of his death. To anyone."

"It goes without saying, my lord."

Daigoro nodded. At least his mother would be spared that much grief. He turned, and Yasuda turned with him, to face the column of gray smoke ascending from within the square of billowing white curtains. "He suffered much, then, before he died?"

"The ball pierced his breastplate and smashed his spine. The bleeding was bad, but worst was that his arms and legs were like a dead man's. He could not move them at all. But if his body was like a dead man's, I do not think it pained him."

"But he could not move his hand to write."

"No, my lord."

With a curt nod from Daigoro, they continued toward the main house and climbed the wide, shallow stairs to the broad veranda surrounding the building. But instead of heading left, toward the main gathering, Daigoro led the two of them slowly around the right side of the house. "The gunman," he said. "You saw him?"

"No, my lord. Your father came to us in the middle of the night. How he managed to stay on his horse that long, I'll never know. I gather he rode all the way from Edo, and half that distance with a musket ball in his chest. The men that rode with him were too weary to stand, and they were uninjured."

"What did they tell you of the—the assassin?" It was the right word. *Assassin.* His father was dead. An assassin had killed his father.

"Very little," said Lord Yasuda, and Daigoro had to struggle to remember what this was in answer to. "His bodyguards said they saw blue smoke after the shot, a cloud of it in a tumble of rocks near the water. They fired arrows at it, and saw the back of a man as he made a dash for the sea cliff. This was just south of Odawara castle." Yasuda closed his eyes, took a breath, and opened his eyes again. His gaze was fixed on Daigoro's feet. "My lord, the gunman escaped. Your father's bodyguard told me he put an arrow through the man's thigh, but the assassin was still able to leap into the sea. One of them searched the shoreline to kill him or collect the corpse, while the others brought your father to me. As soon as I heard, I sent my fastest riders to assist in finding the killer, but his body never resurfaced."

"Never mind," said Daigoro. "He is dead."

"He may be," Yasuda said with a bow, "but my men still scour the coastline in case he is not."

"Leave them there if it will ease your mind, Yasuda-san, but any assassin who would use one of these southern barbarian guns is no man of magic. A *shinobi* would have used an arrow; there's no telling where a musket ball will fly. No, it was a lucky shot that killed my father. No assassin worth paying would rely on the southern barbarians' weapons. I would not be surprised if it was a disgraced rival, resorting to the musket since he could not win with the sword."

Lord Yasuda shook his head. "I am ashamed I did not think of it myself, young lord. Perhaps your servant has

grown too old to be useful. Please allow me to commit seppuku to atone for my oversight."

"You will do nothing of the kind."

"Then allow me to shave my topknot and retire my
swords. I am not fit to serve."

Daigoro looked at him sternly, but Yasuda did not meet
his gaze. "The Yasuda clan has protected our northern flank
for generations," said Daigoro. "Even an aging tiger is still
a tiger. We would have you remain where you are."

Even as he said it, Daigoro wondered to what extent his
advice applied to himself. How many times had he considered shaving his head and joining the monastery on the
hill? Swordsmanship demanded great strength from the
right leg in particular, the right being the leading foot, and
to fight from the saddle one needed to control a horse with
one's legs. Daigoro's right leg was no bigger than his right
arm. He had learned what he could of archery to compensate, but his brother was the finest marksman in the Okuma
clan, maybe the best on the whole Izu peninsula; what could
Daigoro offer in light of that? No, better to save his family
the disgrace of a crippled son. Better to join the monks before he had to join battle in defense of the clan.

How many times had those thoughts plagued him in the
quietest hours of the night? And now his father was dead,
and Ichirō would need to call on him as he learned to lead
the clan. Even if their father were still alive, Daigoro could
not have it be said of the finest cavalryman in the region
that his crippled son was too afraid to take up arms. If Yasuda was an aging tiger, Daigoro was the runt of a tiger's
litter. A kitten with a lame leg. Was that still a tiger?

# 30

The evening's silence was hard earned; there had been so much to do. The wailers required payment, having done their job of sending off Ōkuma Tetsurō with the pronounced grief befitting a man of his station. The guests needed feeding and *sake* and time to speak individually with the family. There was the matter of removing the bones from the ashes, seeing the ashes into the urn, setting the throat bone atop the ashes before the urn was sealed. The abbot and priests wanted payment, as did the Shinto priest who had come afterward to see to it that no evil spirits beset the compound or the ghost of Daigoro's father.

But at long last it was quiet, and Daigoro and Ichirō sat with their mother in the main hall of the house. Embers crackled faintly and filled the room with fragrance and warmth. Daigoro could hear waves in the distance, beating their never-ending rhythm against the rocky coast.

At length Daigoro chose to break the silence, to share some of what Lord Yasuda had told him. He said nothing about how the musket ball struck, but he did tell them that by now the assassin had either drowned or died of his wounds.

"Father's bodyguards were fools," said Ichirō. "They should have placed outriders; they should have foreseen the ambush."

"They would have been searching the hills, not the sea-coast," said Daigoro. "The assassin was the fool, to position himself without an escape route. He was no brave man, using a coward's weapon as he did. Our men could not have predicted an ambush so bold and yet so craven as this."

"You make excuses for them," said Ichirō. "We should send a messenger in the morning to tell Yasuda to have those guards killed."

"They died before Father did," said Daigoro. "Believe it."

"You spoke to him about this?"

"I didn't need to. How could they have done otherwise? I have no doubt those men slit their own bellies as soon as they had escorted Father to a place of refuge. And if they did not, we can be sure Lord Yasuda has seen to it that they died most painfully. He takes any offense against Father as an offense against himself."

Ichirō snorted. "He should have told us that, then."

There was no need, Daigoro wanted to say, nothing to have been gained by speaking of more bloodshed during a funeral. But nor was there anything to be gained by saying as much. Daigoro held his peace.

But Ichiro did not. "Did you command Yasuda-san to commit seppuku for his failure?"

"He offered. I refused him."

"Why?"

"Because Father would not have wanted it."

Ichirō gave a laugh. "Does his spirit speak to you already? How do you know what he wanted?"

Daigoro bowed low. He had no desire for a protracted disagreement with his elder brother, least of all on a funeral day. "I only remember what he taught us about tactics. 'Those who make their home on the end of a peninsula do well to ally themselves with their neighbors.' We are vulnerable."

"Vulnerable? Whose swordsmanship can rival House Okuma's? Let anyone come at us! We can take them."

"*If* they come at us, I'll never disagree," said Daigoro. "But it takes rice to feed a strong sword arm, and if we turn our northern allies against us, we are cut off. Father always counseled peace over war, especially with our neighbors. Lord Yasuda gave no offense. His men failed to find a dead assassin; that is all."

"That is all!" Ichirō scoffed. "A vassal failed, and 'that is all'? Father is dead, and 'that is all'? I should demand his sword from you right now!"

Daigoro bowed, stood up, and made for the door. He didn't need to turn around to hear his brother fuming. He imagined he could feel the heat from Ichirō's reddening face—or was it his own blood flushing his neck and ears?

"How dare you turn your back on me?" demanded Ichirō.

Daigoro stepped out of the room onto the veranda, turned, kneeled, and bowed again. "I must respect my brother and I must respect my father. When my brother asks that I disrespect my father, I have no choice but to take my leave. Begging your pardon, I wish you good night."

Daigoro lay atop his layers of futon and gazed at the squares on his ceiling, and after stubbornly doing so for an hour he conceded that he would not fall asleep. With a grunt he rolled to his knees and slid open one of the exterior walls to admit more moonlight. He could smell the tatami mats under his shins, and the promise of rain on the wind. He donned a thin robe decorated with a bear-paw motif and tied its belt around his waist. Then he went to the alcove on the north wall of his sleeping chamber and removed Glorious Victory from its place on his sword stand.

Through the wood and paper of the shoji door to his left, Daigoro could hear one of his bodyguards shifting in his sandals. Daigoro thrust Glorious Victory's scabbard under his belt and into position at his left hip. The sword was too long to wear as he usually wore his *katana*; he had to shift it forward across the front of his hip, almost onto his lap, lest the end of its wooden sheath touch the tatami behind him. Glorious Victory was small as *ōdachi* went, which meant it stood to Daigoro's chin, not over his head. Its handgrip, wrapped in ruddy, sweat-stained cord, was fully a hand's length longer than that of his own *katana*, the better to manage the huge blade.

Daigoro knew the sword well, knew it better than he knew either of the samurai watching his door tonight. It was born in the fires of Master Inazuma almost five hundred years ago, the last weapon the great sword smith ever created. Glorious Victory was a horseman's weapon, long enough to hamstring a foot soldier from the saddle, and also long enough for someone caught afoot to slay a mounted opponent. The steel was strong and pure, with a blood groove running from the base of the blade almost to its tip. Daigoro's father once plunged it into the heart of a charging warhorse, and the blade had emerged as straight and true as it was when it went in.

Its cording and lacquered scabbard were russet in color, to match the armor and helmet of its former bearer. The enemies of House Okuma had dubbed Daigoro's father the Red Bear of Izu, a name he liked well enough to make the bear paw his personal crest. "Slow to anger, bears," he'd once told Daigoro. "I've seen them in the east country. Left alone, they won't bother you. Once disturbed, nothing I know of can hold them back. A young samurai would do well to take bears as his teachers."

And thus had Daigoro counseled his brother. Now, looking at the sword in his hands, he wondered whether that truly was the way of Bushido. Did the true warrior avoid combat? Seek to be left alone? What did that imply of a sword like this, one that had drawn so much blood? What did it imply of the battlefield exploits of so many samurai, Daigoro's father not the least among them? *Show me the way of the warrior,* Daigoro thought. *I will follow it if only I can find it. Tell me, Father, why the path is so difficult to find.*

# 32

The next morning was hot almost from the moment the sun dawned on the compound. By the hour of the dragon, the laborers hired from Shimoda to build a permanent shrine on the site of the previous day's cremation were spending as much time fetching water as they were digging post holes for the roof supports. By noon even the sentries had taken positions in the shade of trees or under the eaves of buildings, and these were samurai, men for whom physical discomfort was a passing trifle.

It was in the hour of the horse, the midday hour, that Ichirō approached Daigoro's study, a serving girl in tow bearing tea. "May I interrupt, brother?"

"Of course," said Daigoro, setting aside his brush. He cleared his low writing desk and Ichirō knelt beside it.

As the girl served their tea, Ichirō said, "I hope I haven't disturbed anything important."

"Not at all. I was writing letters to some of the lords who attended yesterday, to thank them for their respects."

"Lord Yasuda among them, I suppose."

Daigoro braced himself for a fight. "Yes."

"Good," said Ichirō. "Express my thanks as well, if you would." After a moment he added, "I was in the wrong last night. Please forgive me."

"Grief," said Daigoro. "It does strange things to us all. No forgiveness is necessary."

The two of them sipped tea, and Daigoro watched the hot air shimmer over the sand of the courtyard outside. Grief remained as elusive as the waves of heat: try as he might to grasp it, it escaped him. He looked away from the sand, fixing his gaze instead on Ichirō's white overrobe. Better, he thought, to focus on relief than grief. It was good to be sitting in the shade without animosity.

"I've got an idea," said Ichirō. "We should have an archery competition, as we did when we were boys. What do you say?"

"I haven't been serious competition for you since I was ten and you were twelve. I'm not even sure I held my own with you then. I always wondered whether you were holding back to keep me in the race."

"We were just boys then," said Ichirō. "Two years is too great an advantage to be overcome by a ten-year-old. Now we're grown; it's not so much anymore. Come, let's go out to the orchard. I'll have some targets brought out."

"If you wish," said Daigoro.

The targets were nearly as wide as Daigoro was tall, covered in deer hide and propped against the outside wall of the family compound. Daigoro and Ichirō stood by as one of their samurai measured thirty-three bow lengths from the target and marked a firing line among the camphor trees. Having the firing line in the shade would make for more comfortable shooting, but more difficult as well; arcing shots through the canopy would be troublesome.

Ichirō and Daigoro both wore white, and both wore the swords they were never without. The three samurai attending them wore their rusty-red house uniforms, with white sashes instead of the usual brown. There was only the faintest of breezes coming off the ocean, its salty smell melding nicely with the camphor leaves crushed underfoot. Daigoro felt a bead of sweat roll down his spine and soak into his waistband.

"Will you take the first shot?" said Ichirō.

"I suppose so." Daigoro hobbled up to the line, took his bow from an attending samurai, and set an arrow to the string. His right leg made archery difficult because it was hard for him to find a stable stance. He had to weight his left leg heavily, draw the arrow to his ear, and then settle on his right foot as he could. The process required holding his arrow at full draw for a long time while finding his stable stance. It had always been difficult for him, and today the Inazuma blade hanging from his left hip offset his balance further. The wrist and fingers of his right hand strained as he tried to stabilize himself.

At last he loosed his shot and heard it rip through the overhanging leaves. It sank into the target about halfway between the center and the outer rim.

Ichirō's landed just inside of Daigoro's, closer to the center by a finger's length. His delivery was smooth, his posture elegant. Somehow he managed to release his shot without disturbing a single leaf overhead.

"It seems I got the better of you that time," he said. "Let's have another go."

They fired three more shafts apiece. Each time, despite the pulling of the sword, Daigoro managed to put his arrow closer to the center than the previous shot. Each time Ichirō's landed right next to Daigoro's, and just inside of it, closer to the center by less than a thumb's breadth. "Now I know you're toying with me," said Daigoro. "You can hit the center anytime you like."

"Perhaps. But what's the fun of a competition if I don't keep you in the running?"

Daigoro shrugged. "As you say. Put one in the center, then. Let me see how close I can get."

Ichirō pursed his lips, drew a fifth arrow, and plunged it in the very heart of the target. "There. If competition bores you so much, why did you bother to agree?"

"To watch my brother excel."

"Take your last shot and let's have done with it."

Daigoro became aware of the sweat on his neck, and he knew it was not born of the summer heat. His every effort at peacemaking seemed doomed to failure. He limped up to the line, nocked an arrow, and drew. His father's sword pulled heavily at his belt, but this time he did not bother to compensate for it. What would be the point? Ichirō wanted his victory. Teetering off balance because of the sword, he loosed his arrow.

It split Ichirō's arrow down the middle.

One of the attending samurai gasped. Another stifled his astonishment by trapping his mouth shut. The third showed the least restraint of all, laughing and saying, "Excellent shot, my lord!"

"It was," said Ichirō, glowering. Though Daigoro managed to keep the emotion from his face, he was as angry as Ichirō, for different reasons. The samurai's blurted praise was an unofficial announcement that Daigoro had won the competition; no shot of Ichirō's had earned similar accolades. Wholly accidentally, Daigoro had managed to show up his brother in the skill Ichirō excelled in most.

"It was nothing," said Daigoro, knowing it was too late. "A lucky shot."

"Then you have the luck of the seven gods of good fortune," said Ichirō. "It's not often a man gets to see the work of the gods. Let's do it again."

He snatched an arrow from the samurai who'd managed to keep his mouth shut and fired it at the target. It struck just a finger's breadth higher than Daigoro's last shot, so close as to make the feathers quiver. "Come," he said, stiff-jawed. "Test your luck again."

Daigoro stepped up to the line and drew back another arrow. For a moment he considered drawing less than full strength and letting his arrow fall short of the target. But that would not do; it would be too obviously a deliberate miss. Instead he tried to fire as he normally did, centering his weight as best he could at full draw, then releasing his shot when he was stable. He aimed for the upper half of the target, far from Ichirō's most recent shot. But again he found the counterweight of the sword difficult to manage, and just as he thought he was stable enough to fire, his balance shifted to his left. His shot was already airborne, and Daigoro watched with a mixture of horror and awe as another one of his shafts splintered his brother's arrow.

This time all were hushed. At least their attendants were reading Ichirō's emotions rightly, Daigoro thought. He would have all three of them sweating with the shrine laborers before the day was out. But the immediate problem was Ichirō. Daigoro could think of nothing to say that would appease him, yet saying nothing and letting him find his own peace was no solution either. Ichirō was in no mood to seek peace; he was unsettled and savoring it.

*His father is dead too,* Daigoro reminded himself. *He's found grief before you have; maybe this is how he is letting it run its course.*

"Swords," said Ichirō. "We can stage a duel."

Daigoro's heart sank. This was not about grief, he realized. It was about revenge. About jealousy. In short, it was about the Inazuma.

"No, Ichirō. I won't fight you."

"No? You'll let the fickle habits of the wind carry your arrows, and let everyone believe you're the better archer?"

"No one here believes I'm better than you. As I hear it, I could sail two days in any direction and still not find a better archer than you."

Ichirō's left hand gripped his scabbard just behind the *tsuba*. His right hand stabbed a finger at Daigoro's chest. "If those were lucky shots, then you need to bring that kind of luck to the battlefield. With lucky arrows like those on your back, who could stand against us the next time we go to war?"

"I have no interest in going to war."

"Ha!" Ichirō spat on the ground near Daigoro's feet. "Listen to the son of Okuma Tetsurō, wielder of Glorious Victory! A samurai who will not make war!"

Daigoro took a deep breath and let it out, hoping his brother might do the same. "I did not say I would not make war. I said I would not go to war. If war comes to us, I will kill as many men as the enemy can line up in front of me. I'll keep fighting until death finds me or the last of our foes is lying headless at my feet. But Father said war is bad enough without going looking for it. I will not seek out enemies for the clan, and I will not have you as my enemy."

"You'll die of old age, then. You'll sit here and let that sword rust in its scabbard."

"If I am that lucky, yes."

Ichirō barked a scornful laugh. "Well, you've got no shortage of luck, *neh*? Look forward to your senility, little brother. For my part, I look forward to spilling my blood to make Okuma a greater name."

With that he stormed away, alone, leaving Daigoro with the sea breeze at his back.

# 33

Returning to the compound, Daigoro brushed the dust from his feet, entered his study, and drew Glorious Victory. It was slow on the draw, so long that even when he pulled the scabbard back with his left hand he could scarcely clear the tip of the blade. Once again Daigoro had to imagine what strength his father must have had to wield the sword one-handed.

Was it possible the blade was cursed? He'd heard legends of cursed swords, even of cursed Inazuma swords, but he'd never heard anyone speak ill of Glorious Victory. On the contrary, he'd heard countless stories of his father's sword, and all of them sung its praises. But Daigoro knew almost nothing of how the sword had come to be in his father's possession. At one time his father had had two brothers, but they had both died in war when Daigoro was still in swaddling clothes. Had the sword caused enmity between them? When Daigoro's grandfather died, did he pass the sword directly to his son Tetsurō, or did the three brothers fight over it first? Daigoro had never heard those stories. Had this weapon stirred animosity in his house before?

Or was it just Ichirō's nature to covet the sword? If so, why was it not bequeathed to him? Daigoro had no desire for it; he wanted only to fulfill his father's will, and to follow the path of Bushido. As Daigoro understood them, these two were one and the same. Why could Ichirō not see that?

Daigoro felt his heart racing, felt the heat creeping into his skin even in the cool shade of his study. Better to put his mind somewhere else, he decided. He wrapped his left hand around the base of the pommel, settled his right foot, and experimentally attacked the air in front of him.

He slashed a ceiling tile, nearly burying the blade in one of the rafters. The sword was too long for indoor use, at least for overhead swings. Red faced, Daigoro resheathed it and limped outside.

He found a quiet place near the *sake* stores where he could practice unobserved. With each thrust and parry, his feeble right knee threatened to give out. His wrists and forearms lacked the strength to stop the blade with any precision. As it sliced through the hot afternoon air it hissed, and the pitch of the hiss told him this was the sharpest blade he'd ever encountered. That was no surprise: Inazuma steel was said to hold an edge better than any other. But this sword would demand more of him than any other. He needed strength to complement its power, balance to make the most of its reach. Lacking these, he tried shorter swings, tighter movements. The sword sang in the air; he could almost hear it asking him for more. More speed, more ferocity, longer cuts, wider arcs. Still he could not manage it, and now he felt he was disappointing not only his father but also his father's sword.

When at last he allowed himself to relax, he found his body covered in sweat and the sun drawing close to the treetops beyond the compound wall. Sand shifted underfoot behind him, and he turned to see the Zen abbot who had presided over his father's funeral. The abbot had been watching him, Daigoro guessed; Daigoro had been too focused on his exercises to notice. Now the abbot walked away, a preternatural grace to his movements that Daigoro found both admirable and mysterious. Where did it come from? Was it enlightenment made visible in the body's movements? Daigoro didn't think so. If anything, the abbot actually reminded him of his father. There was balance, strength, and sureness in the old man's steps; he moved like an expert swordsman facing an opponent.

But he was only there for a moment, disappearing behind the *sake* storehouse on whatever errand had brought him here. Now Daigoro could hear voices on the far side of the storehouse. Shuffling toward the commotion, he saw the Okuma samurai arrayed in the courtyard for sword practice and, on the opposite end of the courtyard, the abbot exiting the main gates of the compound.

Tired as he was, Daigoro limped forward to join the last rank of warriors. His father would have asked no less of him. Usually Daigoro and Ichirō did not take part in swordsmanship exercises with the common troops. Theirs was the family that headed the Okuma clan, and Okuma the clan that led so many others. They were not royalty, but they were as close to it as anyone in the region, and so they had always trained under their own sword master. But their father had always told them they were not too good to train with the men. Better, he said, to train beside them from time to time, to be certain their swordsmanship was all it should be.

As the nearest samurai noticed Daigoro among them, they bowed deeply, then resumed their attention stance as if he were no more than a passing shadow. Daigoro stood likewise, and did his best to keep up with them as they began their exercises.

No sooner had they started than Daigoro was dripping with sweat. His burning muscles begged for release. At fifteen, Daigoro had already been practicing swordsmanship for eleven years, but the samurai around him had been training for longer than he'd been alive. Most were battle hardened, and none had spent the afternoon training with a sword too big for him. It was not long before Daigoro noticed he had stopped sweating entirely. Soon after that, tingling white spots came to dance before his eyes.

Still he pushed himself. His feeble right leg wobbled and threatened to buckle. His forearms were so fatigued that he could hardly make a fist. Still he trained on.

"Stop!"

All motion ceased on the courtyard; then, as one, Daigoro and all the other Okuma samurai sheathed their swords and bowed. Daigoro thanked the gods the exercise was over. He was on the verge of vomiting; his eyes tingled and his ears rang; he could scarcely see the man in front of him for all the dancing spots.

"Your exercises will continue," barked the sword master at the head of the throng, "under Lord Okuma Ichirō. The lord has honored us by offering to train us today. You will listen carefully to what he has to say, and you will thank him for honoring us with his presence."

With one voice the battalion shouted, "Thank you, Okuma-dono!"

Daigoro could not see his brother, but he imagined the sword master bowing to Ichirō and Ichirō returning the courtesy. Daigoro heard the footfalls of wooden sandals on the veranda some thirty paces ahead, and in his mind's eye he envisioned Ichirō standing before the throng. "You are also honored by my brother's presence today," he heard Ichirō say. "Lord Okuma Daigoro stands at the rear. He deserves your gratitude as well."

Again the samurai shouted their thanks, and though he could not even see most of them Daigoro offered them a slight bow. He followed along as Ichirō ordered all of them to form a circle and be at ease. Wordlessly the samurai obeyed, kneeling in a ring around empty sand. "Today we spar," said Ichirō. "Your targets will be the torso, the arms, and the head." He called two names to be the first to fight.

The man seated next to Daigoro had been named, and a boy dashed over to him and delivered a *bokken*, a stout wooden sword the same size as a *katana*. The samurai accepted it, tied back his sleeves, and entered the circle in a ready stance. The tingling spots had thinned enough for Daigoro to see another warrior enter from the opposite side of the ring. Ichirō marched over to sit at Daigoro's right.

"You look sick, little brother. Have you been training too hard in this heat?"

"It's no more than Father would expect of me," said Daigoro.

"Indeed."

Ichirō nodded, and the *bokken* clacked loudly with the first exchange of blows. The match was over as soon as it had begun: an attack, a parry and counterattack, and one man hit the sand clutching his ribs.

The second match lasted longer: the *bokken* clashed three times before the loser dropped. Succeeding bouts varied in length, and in each case the previous winner faced the next man to enter the circle. Five or six duels had passed when Ichirō whispered, "What do you say, Daigoro? Have you recovered enough to fight?"

He hadn't. Only now was his breath coming without labor. He'd not yet begun sweating again; his body wanted water. "The enemy does not wait for recovery," he said. "I'll fight whenever my name is called."

"Okuma Daigoro!" Ichirō shouted, even as the samurai who'd lost the last bout picked himself off the ground. The samurai bowed to Daigoro, offered him the grip of the *bokken*, and went to take his place in the circle, nursing a badly bruised forearm.

The *bokken* was light compared to Glorious Victory, its weight very close to that of the average steel *katana*. Daigoro made a mental note to have a new *bokken* fashioned, one as long and as heavy as his father's *ōdachi*. He closed his aching hands around the polished wood and nodded to Takeyama, the samurai who had won the last two bouts.

Takeyama circled him, and Daigoro shifted awkwardly on his right foot to compensate. There was a sudden lunge, a sword smashed aside, and Daigoro's blade crashed down on Takeyama's collarbone. Takeyama fell, gripping his shoulder, and Daigoro nearly fell with him. He hopped on his left foot and willed the white spots away.

The next opponent circled him a long while, then crumpled when Daigoro landed a thrust to his breastbone. "Do not go lightly when fighting your lords," Ichirō called to the circle. "We face the same enemies you do; if you will not attack us in earnest, how can you expect us to fight well?"

Daigoro blinked hard and took a deep breath. Had the last two gone easy on him? Had they noticed he was barely standing, and slackened their attacks accordingly? If they had, Daigoro hadn't noticed. Exhausted as he was, though, he knew such details could easily have passed him by.

"Let me show you how to face a lord of your clan," said Ichirō, and he tied back his sleeves. Wrapping his fingers around the *bokken*, he rose from his knees into a fighting posture and advanced on Daigoro.

Daigoro positioned himself for defense and fought back a wave of nausea. His brother's sword slashed at him through a field of fluttering white specks. He flicked his weapon to parry, but Ichirō's blade swooped low and smashed his right knee. Daigoro went down in a heap.

"I'm sorry," Ichirō said immediately, offering Daigoro a hand. "I shouldn't have struck at the leg during sparring. I saw the opening and I took it. I was too eager to show these men proper aggression. Please, I beg your pardon."

Daigoro regained his footing without his brother's assistance. The act of standing upright was enough to bring on a surge of nausea. He was so light-headed he feared fainting. Summoning all his attention to the grip of his sword, he fought back the sickening swell in his throat and ground his toes in the sand.

Ichirō came at him again. Daigoro stabbed at his belly, but Ichirō batted the *bokken* aside, battered Daigoro's forearms with a downward blow, then chopped him in the ear.

Again Daigoro crumpled to the ground. His breath came desperately. The courtyard had disappeared behind a cloud of tingling white. His brother's voice came only faintly, though he was certain Ichirō stood close enough to reach out and touch him. Ichirō was saying something about aggressiveness in fighting. Daigoro could make little sense of it. He cared only for water, and getting out of the sun, and water again.

It seemed odd to need so much effort to stand, for he was so faint that his body seemed weightless. Nevertheless his right leg struggled with the task of carrying him to a place of shade, where he ordered the nearest soldier to fetch him a water bucket. It was the better part of an hour before he could pay attention to the sparring. Even when his wits finally returned to him, the same questions flitted back and forth through his mind, as distracting as a cloud of mosquitoes that would not leave him be: Was his father's sword cursed? Did it have a hold on Ichirō? And if so, what would it take to break the curse?

# 34

"He was an embarrassment, Mother," Ichirō was saying. "He fell twice before the entire garrison, and hobbled off like a wizened old man."

"Your brother is infirm," their mother replied. It was evening, the air was still and humid, and their mother wore white under pale yellow. Her shimmering black hair was drawn back in a long tail, and she knelt behind a short red-lacquered table, where a cup of tea gave gave birth to thin, rising ribbons of steam. She and her two sons knelt on broad cushions in the same wide hall where the guests of the funeral had gathered. The last light of sundown painted the rice paper windows orange.

"Infirm since birth," she said after sipping her tea, "and two and a half years younger than you, *neh*? As I heard the story, you beat him mercilessly, and in front of a host of our own samurai, no less. Don't you tell me *he's* the embarrassment."

Ichirō bowed low, a wisp of his black hair touching the tatami. "Begging your pardon, Mother, I meant only to demonstrate the truth."

"And what truth is that?"

"That he cannot defend Father's sword. He ought not to be the one carrying it."

Their mother's eyes shifted from Ichirō to Daigoro. "And

you?" she said. "You've been silent so far. What do you have to say for yourself?"

I was exhausted, Daigoro thought. Beyond exhausted; scarcely able to stand. He declared the leg an illegal hit, then struck me in the leg—my weak leg, in fact. Daigoro could have said any of these things, but instead he wondered how his father would have replied. What response did the code of Bushido demand?

"Infirmity is no excuse for a samurai," he said finally.

"There," said Ichirō, "you see? I should be the one to bear the sword."

"Begging your pardon, but I think you misunderstand," said Daigoro. "Infirmity is no excuse, but Father knew as much when he bequeathed me Glorious Victory. Please, Mother, do not ask me to relinquish the sword. If you do, I cannot obey you. Infirm or no, I will uphold my father's wishes as best I can."

Their mother nodded, a pensive look on her face, but Ichirō bristled. "I am the head of your clan. She is your mother. Are you suggesting you won't give up the sword even under direct commands from both of us?"

"I will retain it until death takes me," said Daigoro, "and even then I hope the one who takes the sword has to cut my fingers from it one by one. Father would expect no less."

"Mother, do you see? He's become impudent! Please, try to talk some sense into him."

Her first response was to take a sip of tea. Her second was to touch a finger to her already immaculate hair. "There is no question," she said at last, "that of the two of you, Ichirō is the better swordsman."

Ichirō nodded at this, his eyes all but glowing with triumphant light.

"There is also no question," she added, "that the sword was left to Daigoro."

Ichirō sank back on his heels, looking as though he'd been kicked in the ribs and was trying not to show pain. Daigoro did his best to retain equanimity; an untamed urge in the back of his mind wanted to ask why his brother could not do the same.

"It is my wish," their mother said, "that my husband's

sword remain with the most worthy Okuma samurai. It is beyond me to choose which one of you that may be. I find both of my sons worthy, and a mother cannot be asked to choose between them. I am sorry, but I'm afraid you must work this out between yourselves."

# 35

At last the heat wave abated, but to Daigoro the atmosphere of the compound was no less stifling. Ichirō said nothing to him, but his silence was blaring to the point of distraction. Daigoro donned his swords, fitted his chestnut horse with a saddle specially made to accommodate his shriveled right leg, and rode off for Kattō-ji.

The temple sat atop a craggy pyramid of black rock. Kudzu and other windswept shrubs draped the jagged black in a carpet of emerald. Not for the first time, Daigoro wondered which came first, the kudzu or the name Kattō-ji, Temple of the Twining Vines. Both were ancient, but was the temple named Kattō-ji because of the vines already growing there, or did the monks cultivate the vines because their temple was called Kattō-ji? He'd asked one of the monks once; his answer was, "Vines are vines, temples are temples."

Halfway to the temple, Daigoro gingerly lowered himself from his saddle and tethered his mare to a weathered yew. He stood on the edge of one of the few flat, open places on the little mountain, and the wind buffeted the leaves and whipped at his clothing. He drew Glorious Victory and held it in a ready stance.

Between the wind and the weight of the sword, he could not have asked for a better way to test his balance and footwork. With the wind off the ocean as his only companion, he advanced and withdrew, parried and struck and counter-struck. Now and then he would attempt the mighty one-armed slashes his father used to execute so easily, and after each one Daigoro fought to retain his balance and his grip on the sword.

For all of that, he could feel Glorious Victory's power. His every muscle was needed to control it, and as such, the strength of every muscle was behind each movement. Already he felt stronger than he'd been the day before. Could it be that it was not the man who made the sword powerful, but the sword that forged the man?

"That is a fine blade."

The voice came from behind him; Daigoro's heart jumped like a hooked fish. He whirled and raised his sword to face—

The abbot. The old man wore priest's robes of the deepest blue, and his bald head glistened in the light filtering through the leaves of the yew tree. "I thought you were a horse thief," said Daigoro.

"Oh, no," said the abbot, "just a thief of silence today. I beg your pardon; I should not have interrupted."

"Where are you going?"

The aging priest extended a finger toward the hilltop. "Back home." His eyes fell on the sword again. "More than fine," he said. "A masterpiece. Are an old man's eyes going blind, or could that be an Inazuma?"

"Yes," Daigoro said hesitantly. "You know a lot about swords for a man who will not shed blood even to eat. How?"

"I know about single-mindedness. That sword was crafted with the utmost concentration. I should think anyone could see that. It is a work of art. But too big for you, I think."

"Then you understand not only swords but swordsmanship. Tell me how."

"I know you struggle to retain your footing when you swing it," said the abbot. His hand, oddly smooth for a man his age, stroked the chestnut flank of Daigoro's mare. "I am only observing what anyone could see."

"You see more than most, or else my balance is worse than I'd thought." After a moment, Daigoro added, "I suppose it would be too much to think it's the former and not the latter."

"Ah, well," said the abbot, giving the mare a final pat before turning to march up the hill. "It's the best kind of problem to have."

"Why?" Daigoro limped after the old man, but he knew from the beginning that he could not keep pace with him, especially not uphill. "Wait! What do you mean?"

"Your problem is the best kind," the abbot called over his shoulder, "because it contains its own solution. Farewell."

Daigoro spent the rest of the morning puzzling over what that might have meant. His initial instinct was that some lesson in Buddhism was hidden in the abbot's advice, but the more he thought about it, the more he convinced himself it really was a lesson in sword fighting. The uncanny grace in the abbot's steps, even the fact that he must have observed Daigoro for some time before announcing his presence: it bespoke a man well versed in swordsmanship. It made no sense—every Zen monk took a vow of nonviolence—but for all of that Daigoro was no less certain.

This certainty did nothing toward solving the riddle, though. Daigoro could only see how his problem contained other problems. An off-balance swing could expose his vitals to the enemy, and once dead he'd no longer have the problem of managing so heavy a sword, but that hardly constituted a *solution* in Daigoro's eyes.

But he'd run out of time to figure it out. From the mountain of Kattō-ji a green ridge concealed the coastal road approaching the Okuma compound, but Daigoro could make out dust rising above the ridge. Someone was riding toward his home, and riding fast. Daigoro had a sneaking suspicion who it might be.

# 36

When Daigoro reached the main gate, he saw a familiar horse, its tack dyed a familiar green like dry moss. Daigoro rode into the courtyard just in time to see his brother chop Yasuda Eijun in the throat with his own *bokken*.

Eijun collapsed, weaponless, in a cloud of sandy dust. Ichirō stood above him with a *bokken* in either hand; the one in his right hand was spattered with blood.

Daigoro muscled his horse between the two fighters. Cursing his right leg for slowing him, he dropped to Eijun's side and looked for signs of life. Eijun was barely breathing. His face was a gritty red mask of sand glued in place by blood. The nose was broken, both lips bleeding, at least four teeth hanging loosely in their sockets.

Daigoro glared up at his brother. "He was a simpleton! There was no need to fight!"

"He asked for a duel. I gave it to him."

"Gods and demons, Ichirō, did you break his wrists?"

"I had to disarm him somehow."

"Had to? And then you *had to* bash him in the throat? How many times did you *have to* hit him in the face?"

Daigoro probed Eijun's throat with light fingers, hoping to find the airway intact. With some effort he stood up. "He'll live. At least we can be thankful for that. By the gods, he's a Yasuda, Ichirō. Could you not beat him without embarrassing the whole clan?"

Ichirō let the *bokken* fall from his left hand. It bounced listlessly and settled among the red tears dripping from his other weapon. "Maybe you should have been here," he said. "He said he came to challenge the sword of Okuma."

"I wish I *had* been here! I could have talked him out of it, as I did before. Do you understand nothing about alliances, Ichirō?"

"I understand more than you," Ichirō replied, advancing a step and glaring down into Daigoro's eyes. "This is a time of war, little brother. Toyotomi is defeating everyone who faces him, and we should be fighting alongside him!"

"There is no need for fighting. Father's last act was to treat with Toyotomi."

"Yes," said Ichirō, "but now Father is gone, and a new treaty must be made. We can negotiate our way to the highest levels of power, but not by avoiding every fight that comes our way. Your method is weak, Daigoro. We should be taking all comers, and fighting our way to supremacy!"

"Would you fight Toyotomi as well, then? The man who conquered all of Shikoku in a matter of weeks? The man who stands to bring every last warlord to heel? We are a small clan. If we are to survive this war and retain our lands, it will be by remembering who our friends are and making more powerful friends where we can."

"Gah!" Ichirō stepped back and threw his bloody *bokken* at Eijun's softly rising chest. "I draw more blood with a wooden sword than you do with an Inazuma! Go back up to your monastery and shave your head. Just leave the sword here before you go."


Daigoro accompanied Eijun back to the house of Yasuda Jinbei, the two of them riding in the same palanquin that had borne his father's body home. The Okuma clan's best healers had done what they could for Eijun, binding his wrists to help the bones mend and removing the broken teeth as painlessly as they could. The young man could only speak awkwardly and hoarsely, the combined effect of a broken nose, missing teeth, and a throat so bruised it was black in places. As such, he could hardly pronounce his granduncle's name when they reached their destination, and he seemed more slow-witted than ever.

Lord Yasuda did an admirable job of masking what could only have been furious anger. The samurai lining the hall in attendance were less successful; Daigoro could feel them behind him as a hare might feel the unseen presence of foxes stalking in a dark wood. He did not presume to relate what had happened; he left that to Eijun, whose recollection favored himself rather more than the actual events.

"And why have you come, then, young Master Okuma?" Lord Yasuda's voice betrayed only the slightest tremor of his wrath.

"Twice Eijun-san rode a long way to challenge Glorious Victory. I thought he deserved the honor of seeing it."

Daigoro withdrew the sheathed sword from his belt, all too aware of the swordsmen shifting in their armor behind him. Apart from the palanquin bearers, he'd come without escort, knowing in advance that his safe departure was in no way guaranteed. Now he moved with slow, careful precision as he laid the long, heavy weapon before Lord Yasuda. "I thought it should not be an Okuma who drew the blade before him," said Daigoro, "lest he take it for another attack. With all respect, Yasuda-san, I hoped you might be the one to draw it and present it to him."

Daigoro heard the intake of breath behind him, gasps cut short by the attending samurai. Glorious Victory was an heirloom worthy of greater respect than anything in the Yasudas' possession. To allow a bested opponent to handle it showed him the highest honor.

Lord Yasuda inclined his silver-haired head, drew the Inazuma blade, and could not help but examine it for himself. After a long moment he bowed to Daigoro and then to his grandnephew. Eijun was unable to hold Glorious Victory himself—Ichirō had seen to that when he broke both of Eijun's wrists—but he knelt before the weapon with the same reverence one might have shown in approaching the emperor's newborn son. He studied it so closely that he seemed to be bowing before it. His breath misted on the ancient steel, momentarily clouding over the cloverleaf temper line that ran the length of the blade. Daigoro found himself wondering whether Eijun truly was the lackwit everyone thought him to be. Fools weren't known to appreciate great artistry.

After Eijun was finished, Lord Yasuda called for a square of white paper to clean the blade, then returned it to its scabbard. "You have done us a great honor," the old samurai told Daigoro. "Moreover, you have done it at no small risk to your own honor, and to your life as well. Whatever wounds existed between our families, all of us will consider them healed."

Daigoro bowed, but the old man was not finished. "My grandnephew was not ready to challenge the house of Okuma, and he has paid the price for his impatience. I fear the price your brother pays will be worse, Okuma-sama. But that is not a price for you to pay. I shall send an escort of riders home with you, as a token of our esteem. Thank you for coming here."

Daigoro bowed deeply, reclaimed Glorious Victory, and took his leave.

# 37

Yasuda Eijun was by no means the last of the challengers. Okuma Tetsurō's renown as a swordsman was spoken of in every port in the islands, and of course some men would have come just to face one of the few remaining Inazumas.

The next to arrive had walked all the way from Kyoto. He was too poor to afford the passage by boat, and as he'd left some months before, he was surprised and dismayed to learn the man he'd come to duel was dead. His name was Katsushima Goemon, and he shook his bowed head when he heard the news. "What a shame," he said. "A man like that, to die from such a cowardly attack. May the southern barbarians and all their muskets fall into the sea."

Daigoro guessed Katsushima was fifty years old, or close to it. He wore wide, wooly sideburns and his topknot was unkempt, perhaps the result of so long a trek. His brown clothes were faded, his sandals worn. Daigoro's immediate instinct was to like the man; he had an air of grace about him that the dust of the road did nothing to tarnish. He arrived with his sleeves tied back and his pants bound about the knees; in short, he came ready to fight. He would not be taken by surprise, and clearly he was not overly concerned with appearance or comfort. Daigoro suspected the man had more than a few insights to share about the Bushido path.

"Yes, he's dead," Ichirō told Katsushima. "If you've come to fight an Okuma, you'll fight me."

"I came to challenge Okuma Tetsurō," said Katsushima. "Now it sounds as if I'm the one being challenged."

"All right," said Ichirō. "I challenge you here and now. I would have you face my father's sword, but sadly my brother would have it otherwise."

"Wood or steel," said Katsushima, "it makes no difference to me."

"It makes a difference to me," said Ichirō. "I would prefer the truest test, the test of steel on steel, but my brother refuses to let our illustrious weapon see the light of day. With *bokken*, then, and the first to fall loses."

Katsushima shrugged, bowed, and set aside his *katana*. Ichirō did the same, and Daigoro braced himself for another embarrassment.

It went better than the fight with Yasuda Eijun, but not by much. Katsushima was a patient fighter, and smashed Ichirō's hands twice as Ichirō lunged to land a solid blow. Ichirō feinted and chopped at Katsushima's wrists much as he had in the last duel, but Katsushima neither cried out nor dropped his weapon. At last Ichirō proved the faster, slashing Katsushima's knee out from under him. When his challenger hit the ground, Ichirō followed the blow with a vicious chop to the spine.

Katsushima conceded defeat and left without a word. Daigoro called after him, offering a meal and a bed for the night after such a long journey, but Katsushima would not even turn around to acknowledge the invitation.

"Let him go," said Ichirō. "Obviously he doesn't want our hospitality."

"Can you blame him?" asked Daigoro. "You said to the fall, and then struck him after he'd fallen. Where is the honor in that?"

"Where is the honor in fighting with children's toys? You should have let me face him with Glorious Victory."

"You complain of fighting with a child's toy, and then you conduct yourself like a little boy! That man was willing to fight you because you are the son of Okuma Tetsurō! Do you suppose Katsushima thinks Father only taught you swordsmanship? No! A man learns manners from his father, and virtue, and honor, and you've shown none of these!"

"Be careful, little brother—"

Daigoro scarcely heard him. "You've sent an honorable man to speak ill of our father all across the countryside! He'll say the son of Okuma Tetsurō is an ill-mannered spoilsport who breaks his own rules and hits a man when he's down."

"I should slap your face, *little brother*. You'll watch your mouth."

With a deep breath, Daigoro clapped his mouth shut and took a shuffling step back. He'd lost his composure, and in doing so he'd behaved no better than Ichirō. Now both of them had disgraced their father's memory. "I will watch my mouth," he said through gritted teeth. "But Katsushima Goemon won't. He's going to walk all the way back to Kyoto, and in every village along the way, rumors will spread of what shameful conduct he saw here. The Tokaidō Road will be overrun with swordsmen looking to best you."

Ichirō smirked. "Let them come."

# 38

"Daigoro," his mother implored, "please reconsider."
They stood alone outside Daigoro's bedchamber, with moonlight making the floorboards seem black with a sheen of blue. A cool breeze raised chicken skin on the backs of Daigoro's forearms and carried with it the smells of seaweed, salt, and camphor leaves. Their respective bodyguards watched them from across the courtyard, dark topknotted shadows in the blue light.

"I cannot, Mother."

"What am I to do? Your brother asks me to intercede on his behalf, and you ask for nothing. How must you look to everyone else, if you will not even ask for my support? Why will you not speak to me about the sword?"

Because I will not draw my own mother into a quarrel during her time of mourning. Because there should be no quarrel in the first place. Because Father's will was clear, even if the reason behind it remains a mystery to all of us. Daigoro wanted to say all of these things, and he encapsulated them as best he could: "Because Bushido demands it."

"Are you so sure? Is the path so clearly laid before your feet?"

Yes, Daigoro wanted to say. A true samurai would not bring discord into his home over a mere possession, not even if it was his sword. A samurai would uphold the will of his father, especially if his father had been the living embodiment of the code. But in truth he was not sure and might never be sure. Was it better to fulfill the wishes of a dead father or a living mother? Whom was it better to disappoint? Was there no way to satisfy both at once?

And why could Ichirō not follow the code as Daigoro sought to? Was the code like the moon, ever changing in its appearance yet always the selfsame moon? Could it appear differently to every samurai? Father, Daigoro thought, if ever I needed you, now is the time. Your sword is too big for me. Why could you not leave me guidance instead of the sword?

"Daigoro," his mother said, and for a brief moment he feared she had mistaken pensive silence for petulance. "If you will say nothing, you leave me little choice. Do not force me to side with your brother. The whole clan will turn against you."

"What else can I do, Mother? Do you remember what Father said about what to do when in a quandary?"

A smile touched her careworn face, and she nodded. "'When torn between two choices, see which one is easier, then choose the other.'"

"This," Daigoro said, touching her shoulder, "*this* is what I want: for you to *smile* when we speak of him. I want an end to the quarreling. But how many times did he give us that advice? Bushido admits of few laws that can never be broken, but when in doubt, the harder road is almost always Bushido's road. I cannot invite you to join one side or the other in what stands between Ichirō and me. Nor can I give Ichirō the sword. Those are the easier roads. Please don't make my road harder by making me disobey you too."

# 39

By the time the moon waxed full again, a steady stream of challengers had begun to call at the Okuma compound gate. Though Daigoro had predicted as much, Ichirō refused to credit him for his foresight. Yet again Daigoro wondered whether Glorious Victory carried some kind of curse that estranged one brother from another.

The duels had only increased in rancor since the defeat of Katsushima Goemon. If a clan champion came to fight using steel, Ichirō would insist loudly that he could not, then toy with the challenger before trouncing him. If the challenger came to duel with the *bokken*, Ichirō would mock him for not facing him with a live blade. Once goaded into a fight with steel, Ichirō would maim his opponent and then refuse to kill him. The opponent's right arm was his favored target; more than once the house servants had to strew fresh sand after disposing of severed fingers or forearms. It seemed Ichirō had acquired a taste for blood, and no reasoned argument against it could get through to him.

For his part, Daigoro could only keep on training with Glorious Victory. He continued to struggle with the weight of it, with its extraordinary length and what that meant for wide cuts with the sword. He'd even begun to study the fighting styles of the rivals who came to challenge Ichirō, hoping for some insight on how to manage Glorious Victory's great size. Daigoro hadn't yet found a way to maintain his balance, but his ability to recover his balance was improving quickly, and he thought even his right leg might have been getting stronger.

One day just after sundown the gate guard announced a visitor. Ichirō took what was now his customary place in the courtyard, *bokken* in hand, with his now-customary glare at Daigoro and the huge sword at his hip. Daigoro limped to the gate, looked outside, and was shocked by what he saw.

The gleaming black palanquin was difficult to make out behind the ranks of horses and spearmen. Daigoro could not see the crest embossed on the palanquin itself, but he did not need to, for it was well displayed on the armor of the forty-odd samurai surrounding it and on the red banners hanging from their spears. The crest of the *kiri* flower was well-known, for it belonged to none other than Toyotomi Hideyoshi, the warlord poised to dominate all the Japanese islands.

Daigoro ordered the gates opened at once, and ordered an honor guard with his next breath. He, Ichirō, and their mother bowed deeply as the bearers set down the palanquin in the center of the courtyard. A small man emerged from it, his robes golden, his gray hair marked with a few lingering wisps of black. His topknot was immaculately kept and his pate closely shaved. "I am Shiramatsu Shōzaemon," he said, "emissary of his eminence, the lord regent General Toyotomi. We shall sit in a cool place and we shall talk."

Daigoro's mother hastily arranged for tea to be served in the largest hall in the compound. Shiramatsu sat on the dais at the end of the hall, a spot Daigoro had only seen occupied by his father. The emissary was so slight, and Daigoro's father had been so large, that Daigoro felt the room had somehow grown much longer, or that his seat was somehow farther away than usual. Daigoro and his family knelt in a row before the dais, their honor guard arrayed behind them, a select few Toyotomi men kneeling behind the emissary. The walls were open to admit the warm evening breeze, yet the air was preternaturally still.

"The great lord general sends his displeasure," Shiramatsu began, showing none of the tact Daigoro would have expected from a diplomat. Briefly he wondered whether diplomacy was no longer required when one rose to the heights Toyotomi had achieved. But then the emissary was speaking again and Daigoro focused on his words. "His eminence pacified this region so that he could put it out of his mind and devote his attention to other fronts. To speak more precisely, he treated with Lord Okuma Izu-no-kami Tetsurō, because Lord Okuma was said to speak for all the clans of Izu. Was this a lie?"

Daigoro heard Ichirō exhale a brooding breath, could almost feel him bristle at the implication that their father was a liar. To Daigoro's great relief, it was their mother who was the first to speak. "It was no lie, sir."

"And do the Okumas still speak for Izu?"

"Yes, sir."

"So there is an allegiance here after all. Why, then, his eminence wonders, are there so many reports of the region's best swordsmen being slashed to ribbons in petty conflicts?"

"Sir, they come to challenge my house," said Ichirō. "Would you have us ignore our honor?"

"As I hear it, the challengers are not the ones who have besmirched your honor. But what I would have you do is irrelevant." The emissary smoothed his mustache, then his beard. "His eminence the great lord general would not have the best men of these islands reduced to cripples. Do you not understand that your challengers come from far and wide? Do you not understand that some of them come from lands his eminence has already brought under his reign? These men are *his* samurai, to call upon as *he* sees fit. And you too will be his one day soon, when the great lord general unites Izu and the Kantō and all the eastern lands under one rule. You are not to waste his samurai needlessly, and you are certainly not to create a military disturbance among clans the lord treated with as a single entity. His eminence would retain Izu as a region united. Is that understood?"

Everyone on Daigoro's side of the room bowed deeply. "Now then," the little man said, "I have heard that these challengers come to face the sword of the late Okuma Tetsurō. It is said to be a weapon of the highest quality — an Inazuma, I am told. I am also told that they are routinely denied this honor. Is this so?"

"Yes, sir," Ichirō said with a bow.

"I am sure I will not have to ask why."

Before Ichirō could answer, Daigoro said, "Because, sir, it was not my father's desire that my brother wield the sword, and it is my brother who faces the challengers."

"Ah." The emissary's thin black eyes fixed on Daigoro. "You are the second son of the late Okuma Tetsurō, are you not? A cripple, I am told."

"Correct, sir, on both counts."

"Do you lack the will to face these challengers?"

"No, sir, I am willing."

"But you would prefer that your brother does it?"

"No, sir." Daigoro paused a moment. "Sir, I do not have a preference, except to be of service to my father's house. My brother is the better swordsman, hence he faces the challengers instead of me."

Shiramatsu stroked his mustache. "I see," he said with a nod. "Henceforth, if a man comes here to duel, the great lord general Toyotomi would have the duel take place with *bokken*. If the challenger insists on fighting with steel, only the Inazuma sword will meet the challenge, and the duel will be fought to the death. The lord general will not have his samurai crippled, nor will he have them dying for nothing; you are to give them what they come for. Is this understood?"

Again everyone on Daigoro's side of the room touched their foreheads to the floor. Then, as unexpectedly as he had arrived, Lord Toyotomi's emissary marched off into the night.

A stunned silence hung over the compound in the wake of the emissary's departure. Ichirō went to bed, leaving Daigoro and his mother alone to watch the moon rise through the silhouettes of the trees. They stood for a long time before Daigoro broke the silence.

"Did Father get along with his brothers?"

She pursed her lips. "Not especially, I suppose. I almost never saw them."

"Why not?"

"Your grandfather was a very important man. His sons performed important tasks for him in every corner of Izu. Then, after your grandfather passed on, there was much more work to do. Your father and his brothers had all become important men."

"But when you did see them," Daigoro said, "when you saw Father and his brothers together, was there tension between them?"

"Oh, I don't think so," she said. "But then, they only came here when we married, and when you and your brother were born. It would have been most improper for them to spoil our home's harmony."

"So they never came here except for special occasions?"

His mother searched her memory for a moment. "I suppose not, now that I think of it. Daigoro, why do you ask all these questions?"

"Is it possible," he asked, "that they begrudged Father because he was the one to get grandfather's sword?"

"Of course they begrudged him, but I don't think it had anything to do with the sword. Your father was named head of the clan. In effect, your grandfather bequeathed him all of Izu. Who wouldn't begrudge that?"

A good samurai wouldn't, Daigoro thought. He was in no position to judge whether or not they had been good samurai; he knew so little of his uncles. But if he assumed the best of them, if he assumed they followed the path as surely as his father had, then it wasn't the rulership of the clan that they resented, nor even the mastery of Izu. Despite what his mother had said, Daigoro still suspected the sword.

# BOOK FIVE

◆◆◆◆◆◆◆◆◆◆◆◆◆◆◆◆◆◆◆◆◆◆◆◆◆◆◆◆◆◆◆◆◆◆◆◆◆◆◆

## HEISEI ERA, THE YEAR 22

### (2010 CE)

# 40

Fuchida sat on a chair of golden aluminum and beige cushioning, the fanciest kind of chair that could still be stacked by the dozen and stowed in a closet. Had this been a traditional *wa-shiki* funeral, there would be no chairs; people would either stand or kneel. There would be hardwood underfoot, or perhaps even dirt, but certainly not carpet. But this was a Western-style funeral parlor. The Fuchida family was nominally Buddhist, but as their temple refused to perform cremation services for an infamous gangster, stackable chairs and maroon carpeting were the order of the day. Not two steps in front of Fuchida's chair, sitting on the burgundy Berber, was the green plastic box that stored his father's ashes.

The box surprised him, though now he wasn't sure what he'd been expecting. An urn? There was hardly any point; after today no one would ever see the urn, for his father was to be interred in the family mausoleum. Fuchida didn't know what else human ashes came in. Surely not a sack from the grocery store, but he'd never envisioned a green plastic box. It looked like something one might use to house electrical sockets in a garden or public park; the box was the color of plastic army men, the color hose reels and garden caddies came in. It seemed industrial somehow. It was small too, much smaller than he'd thought it would be. His father died at half the size he was in his prime, but still, a human body was pretty big; Fuchida had imagined the ash pile left behind to be a lot bigger than the box in front of him.

Most of the guests had gone, as had those who had come to pay their respects but couldn't be called guests, as had most of the funeral home people, and the caterers, and the Shinto priest. Fuchida sat, the small of his back pressed flat against the chair, his hands resting limply on his belt buckle as he looked at the box. He could hear voices behind him, muted, and the sigh of the air-conditioning passing through a vent somewhere above and behind him. Its breath was cold on his neck, but he didn't have the energy to go sit elsewhere.

Footfalls against padded carpet approached, and Fuchida saw movement over his right shoulder. "Shūzō-kun. My condolences for your loss."

It was Kamaguchi Ryusuke, then. His lisp was unmistakable. They said someone had bisected his tongue in a knife fight once—stabbed him right through the cheek to do it. That was in his youth; now Kamaguchi had a watermelon of a belly and had to dye his hair black. One of the chairs creaked softly as he settled his weight into it.

Fuchida did not look up from the green plastic box. "My family thanks you," he said.

"There is not so much of your family left," said Kamaguchi. "Your uncles are all gone. You have inherited leadership of the Fuchidas."

It was an obvious statement, and yet it only became fact when Kamaguchi Ryusuke pronounced it. The Fuchidas were beholden to the Kamaguchi-gumi, and their right of succession had always been defined by the parent clan. "I thank you," said Fuchida, "and I will see to it the family prospers as never before."

"And now we come to that," said the old, fat man. "I hear rumors of a new mover in town."

"Oh?"

"Yes. Pushing drugs I have not authorized. A fatal mistake—one I am sure you are not stupid enough to make. And yet I hear your name connected to these rumors. What do you know about it? Is there new activity in your territory?"

Fuchida shrugged. "Nothing. The usual guys slinging speed in neighborhoods where my people collect, but that's nothing I'd call 'new.'"

"Look at me," Kamaguchi said. "Tell me you have no involvement."

Fuchida looked away from the little green box for the first time in their conversation. He turned his head and looked Kamaguchi in the eye. Kamaguchi's black hair was punch-permed. A hairless scar the shape of a bullet stared out of the middle of his left cheek. His eyes seemed too small; his lower jaw seemed too long, his lower teeth just visible as they touched his upper lip. He wore a blue-gray suit with a blue tie and a pair of big gold-rimmed sunglasses hanging from the left breast pocket. Fuchida thought of a boar wearing the same suit.

"I have no involvement with selling drugs." The lie flowed easily; Fuchida's heart did not quicken. It never quickened, not even when he lied right to the face of an underboss from the Kamaguchi-gumi. The only man he could never lie to was now reduced to ashes in a green plastic box. "Not in any of my neighborhoods. Not anywhere else either."

Kamaguchi nodded, making the fat of his neck fold around his shirt collar. "That's good. This is no time to be changing our arrangement with the police, Shūzō-kun. That business a couple of years back with the Takahashi-kai still has the cops on edge. They won't tolerate another gunfight in the streets. And believe me, drugs bring shooting."

In other company, Fuchida would have disagreed. The ruckus with the Takahashis was old news, and even then it hadn't been much of a gunfight; more like an assassination. Only one side did the shooting, and if it happened over people's lunch hour, so be it; let the people of Tokyo remember why they once feared the *ninkyō dantai*. The last time Fuchida visited an *onsen*, no one had even taken the trouble to clear out of the bath.

They would have if he'd had the sword with him. He wished he had her now. Even Kamaguchi Ryusuke would think twice about telling him what to do if there were a blade near at hand. But the sword was at home—Fuchida's mother would have been embarrassed by it, so he'd left it behind—and here was Kamaguchi telling him what to do. The same man who had ordered him to kill his childhood friend, Endo, so many years before; the same man whose commands Fuchida's father had followed all his life. Once again a Kamaguchi was telling a Fuchida what to do. Fuchida bowed with his head only, and did not bother to get up from his chair.

"So we are in agreement," Kamaguchi lisped. "Your father was a good earner, Shūzō-kun, and I would like to believe he has passed that on to you. But if I hear one more word of you disrupting the status quo, you'll have a little green plastic box just like your father's. You will see to it that no more rumors reach me of your drug peddling."

"I certainly will," said Fuchida, and he meant it sincerely. Heads would roll for this.

## 41

Mariko looked at the medical examiner's reports with a growing sense of dread. The first of the homicides was a familiar face. Sagamihara Kintarō usually went by "Saga," and he had been Mariko's first narcotics arrest. On her first weekend with the Narc guys she'd busted him for possession, a charge that should have stuck on anyone with Saga's drug priors but one that Saga wriggled out from because he had a baby's face and an unusually incompetent prosecutor. Now Saga was dead at nineteen, his throat slashed in the garden below Tokyo Tower, with three missing fingers that suggested he'd raised his arms in defense against an edged weapon.

The next homicide, a man named Hitoshi, was probably Saga's supplier. They seemed to have been killed in the middle of a deal. Murders during drug deals weren't unheard of, but this one was weird. Usually it was one pusher making a move against another, but this time the evidence suggested the two vics were accosted by an unrelated assailant with a large edged weapon. Homicide's initial notes said Hitoshi, a chubby little toad of a man, bled out from a pair of stab wounds, one through the belly button and one puncturing the left lung from behind. That didn't feel right to Mariko, so she called the ME and asked him to see if it was a through-and-through. Her desk phone rang even as she studied the crime scene photos.

"Oshiro."

"Detective Oshiro, this is Saigō, the medical examiner. We spoke earlier?"

"Yeah."

"Just wanted to tell you thanks for the beer."

"Huh?"

"Okada from Homicide happened to be down here when you called about your through-and-through. He's the lead on the Sagamihara/Hitoshi murders? Well, he's also the one who said it was multiple stab wounds that killed this fatso, and he bet me a case of Kirin that there was no way in hell this was a through-and-through. Said the murder weapon would have to be a meter long to go all the way through him. I told him he was probably right but I'd take him up on it anyway. So now he's out buying me a case of Kirin."

"Really?"

"Yep." Dr. Saigō sounded quite pleased with himself. "Single wound channel, probably entered through the abdomen. Hell of a nice catch, by the way. What made you think to even ask about it?"

"I don't know," Mariko said, cagy about mentioning Fuchida. Ko wouldn't even approve of this phone call, much less her interest in the murders. "Isn't it sort of standard procedure? You know, investigating every possibility and all that?"

"Yeah, maybe, but Okada and his partner have both been on Homicide for, like, ten years, and neither of them thought of it. So, you know, thanks for the beer."

Mariko laughed. "You're welcome. Set aside a couple for me."

"Oh. Uh . . . I'll have them in the cooler when they get here."

"So?"

"Uh. The cooler's where we keep, you know, dead people."

"Right. I'll take a rain check. Thanks, Dr. Saigō."

Mariko hung up the phone, not knowing how to feel. Outdoing the Homicide guys was thrilling; knowing word of it might get back to Ko made her gut freeze solid. Ko would insist these murders had nothing to do with the attempted sword theft he'd assigned her, and Mariko had nothing in the way of a counterargument. Why would Fuchida stage a random assault against a pair of drug dealers? If there was any connection to Yamada's sword, Mariko couldn't see it. Her best hope was that the newest homicides were the aftermath of a turf war. If so, then at least she'd know Tokyo Tower was within Fuchida's territory. That would be her first hint as to his whereabouts, and Mariko had logged too many hours looking for this shithead to remain empty-handed.

Her lack of progress on Fuchida frustrated her to no end. His wanton violence made her want to redouble her efforts, but she had so damned little to go on. Everything Tokyo's *bōryokudan* unit had on Fuchida was dated and petty; the man hadn't seen face time with a cop for almost ten years. Fuchida made no appearance in Yokohama's police records, nor in the files of any nearby city whose records she could get a warrant to search.

She did find a few cases connected to Fuchida's father— none related to narcotics, but it seemed the Fuchida family had been selling stolen merchandise for the Kamaguchi-gumi since at least the 1960s, and carrying out executions when Kamaguchis didn't care to send their own muscle. The elder Fuchida seemed to share his son's knack for lying low: he hadn't set foot in a courtroom in over thirty years, and even back then he managed to outmaneuver his prosecutors. He'd collected four acquittals in four years, and in each case a key witness disappeared just before giving testimony. After that the old man vanished from the justice system entirely.

Mariko cursed her luck when she read about the elder Fuchida's death. She couldn't have asked for an easier opportunity to catch her lead suspect than at his own father's funeral, but she only learned of the funeral after the fact. There hadn't been an obituary; she'd only got word of the old man's passing because someone with the National Health Insurance mistakenly forwarded her his death certificate. The fact that she'd missed the funeral made her feel guilty. Fuchida didn't commemorate his father by going out and getting blitzed that night like the rest of his gangster buddies. Instead, he murdered two pushers for no apparent reason. Without any hard evidence, Mariko couldn't have done anything at the funeral except take photos, but still the guilt gnawed at her, and more than once she'd racked her brain trying to figure out a way she could have saved poor, baby-faced Saga from having his throat slashed open at the age of nineteen.

Fuchida Shūzō was nonexistent on Google. He didn't pay taxes or claim health insurance benefits. He'd paid his tuition to Tōdai in cash. No car had ever been purchased in his name; ditto with airfare; ditto with houses, apartments, condos, storefronts, retail spaces, or empty lots. He had no bank accounts, no post office boxes, no landlines or cell phones under his name. Apart from a few dated police records, she hadn't produced so much as a single receipt with his name on it.

Mariko knew she'd never get back to Narcotics until she put Dr. Yamada's sword case behind her, which of course was exactly the reason Lieutenant Ko had given her the case in the first place. He couldn't have guessed that Fuchida was an electronic ninja, master of the art of bureaucratic invisibility, but he'd known full well that property crimes like this were damn near impossible to solve. The clock was ticking: her probationary period on Narcotics was dwindling away day by day, and if at the end of the year her arrest record wasn't impressive enough, Ko would be well within his rights to deny her transfer.

If there were any justice in the world, then if she couldn't hunt down Fuchida, at least she could have found Saori. But there was no justice, and no luck either, because Saori was still a phantom. Their mother was a nervous wreck, and as she had no one else to call, Mariko was the one to absorb all the fallout. Dealing with her mother's stress left Mariko no energy to cope with her own.

Not for the first time, Mariko wished she were back at academy, for that was the one time in her life where bashing something with a stick had been a regular part of her day. She remembered it fondly, that satisfying shudder moving up the baton and into the bones of her arm. She was all too aware that all she had to do was pop by Dr. Yamada's and she could start a brand-new phase of combat training. But that would expose her to another talk about magic and destiny and all that crap, and she liked Yamada too much to tell him to shut the hell up.

It was ultimately the little things that broke her. Three

minutes after she hung up the·phone with Dr. Saigō, the computer in her cubicle crashed. It was annoying but manageable: leaving the baby-faced photos of Saga on her desk, she tried calling the *bōryokudan* unit across town to talk about which yakuzas controlled the territory around Tokyo Tower. No sooner did they pick up than her line went dead. Then she remembered the morning's briefing: an IT crew was finally upgrading the precinct's DSL service to fiber, so lines would be cutting in and out all day.

Again, annoying but manageable. She figured a good walk might get the stress out her system anyway, so she went to take a train across town to the *bōryokudan* unit. It took two trains to get there, and both times she sprinted up to the platform only to watch the doors slide shut right in front of her face. She felt her blood pressure rising as she called her contact in the *bōryokudan* unit to tell him she'd be late—to beg him, in fact, to stay on a little while after his shift ended. But an automated message answered instead, telling her that her own phone number was no longer in service.

"Great," she said to herself. It was a computer snafu, easy enough to fix if only she could give Docomo a call. But this was her only phone, and she couldn't just head back to the precinct to take care of it. Even if the IT guys had finished, Ko forbade personal calls at work. Leave it to a damn cell phone company to highlight yet one more way her CO could piss her off.

She didn't have the patience to go all the way to the *bōryokudan* unit just to find out her contact there had already left for the day, nor did she have the patience to go back and try to deal with a tetchy office computer and its spotty Internet access. "Fuck it," she said to herself in English. She resolved to get on the next train, wherever the hell it was heading, and just sit on it for a few minutes and try to get her heart rate to simmer down.

The next train in the station was bound for Machida. Yamada's neighborhood. Destiny.

So it was that she found herself breathing the cool air of Yamada's backyard, trying to enjoy it, trying to leave the rest of the world outside. Her fingers wrapped tightly around the haft of the heavy Inazuma sword, feeling oddly natural there. Her toes dug into the cold grass. A high slat fence surrounded her on three sides, with the back of the house on the fourth. The fence was the color of milk tea, overgrown in places with clematis and climbing fern. A wooden lattice arched behind her, all but invisible beneath the luxurious wisteria that hung from it like white clouds in a perfect summer sky. Her forearms ached with the weight of the blade, and she'd only been holding it for a few minutes.

"Shoulders over your hips," Yamada said. He was sitting on a stone bench settled within a species of chrysanthemum different from the one growing along the front of the house. Those were pink; these were white. "Settle your weight."

"If you say so," Mariko said. She didn't see how her weight could be anything but settled. What else was it supposed to do, float?

"The correct response is, 'Yes, Sensei.' If you want to train, do it seriously."

But I don't want to train, some part of Mariko's mind responded. But here you are training, another part said; do as you're told.

"Better," Yamada said. He stood, unsheathed the sword he'd had lying across his lap—the old man had a small arsenal in the house—and stood in front of her. She mirrored his stance, then aped his movements as he led her through the first drill. Stepping and striking, stepping and striking, back and forth, over and over. In ten minutes her bruised ribs felt like coals in a fire—the idea of stopping in for an X-ray seemed better and better by the minute—and her thighs burned hotter still.

"This sword is too big for me," she said, eyeing the smaller blade Yamada held so easily.

"That sword is too big for everyone."

"Then let me use yours."

Yamada clicked his tongue.

"Sensei," she added hastily.

"Swords are not like shoes; one does not break them in. You must accustom yourself to the weapon. Again." And he led her through the exercise once more.

"Sloppy," Yamada said, watching her.

My arms are tired, Mariko thought. What do you expect? But she said nothing.

"Getting sloppier," he said. "You're just swinging it now."

This time she almost spoke her mind. She caught herself with her mouth open, took a panting breath instead, and consciously avoided his gaze. If she looked at him, she thought the next chop might come down on his stubbly head.

"Where is your concentration? If you're just going to waste time here, I'd rather see you out on the streets looking for your sister."

Mariko stopped the sword in midair, her fists clenched tight with anger. She wanted to stab a hole in the fence. She wanted to chop down the lattice archway and hack at its remains.

"Perfect!"

Mariko shot a sidelong glare at Yamada. "Perfect!" he said again. "That is the energy you need. Without the rage, though. Power, but with focus. Do you understand?"

She scoffed. "I don't even understand *why* I'm doing this, much less *how*." Her shoulders slumped; the sword was heavy again in her trembling, aching hands.

Yamada walked close enough that he could set his fingertips on her shoulder. "Do you know what you just did? You controlled the weight of Glorious Victory Unsought. You arrested it in midswing, and in doing so you were still ready to attack. You did think about attacking me, didn't you?"

Mariko was sure her cheeks would have flushed, if only they weren't already red under the sheen of sweat. "Actually," she said, "*that* time I thought about killing your lattice archway. I was thinking about killing you earlier."

Yamada laughed, and Mariko did too. "Good," he said. "You're releasing that tension of yours. You've got a lot of it, you know."

"Work. Saori. The usual."

"It feels good to let it go, *neh*?"

Mariko let her mind rove over her body. Everywhere it touched down—her shins, her thighs, her elbows, her neck—it found pain, but not in a painful way. It was like a tongue exploring the gap left by a missing tooth, odd but satisfying. The idea of a satisfying pain didn't make much sense to her, but there it was. Even the soreness from running a triathlon wasn't the same: she enjoyed the endorphins, and even the feeling of rubbery, totally exhausted muscles, but the hurting itself was still something she'd rather avoid. But in any case Yamada was right: the tension caused by Saori's disappearance had vanished, if only for the moment.

Mariko went to the bench where her weapon's scabbard was lying and sheathed the blade. Yamada joined her as she eased herself to a seated position. "The sword has a name," she said. "Glorious Victory Unsought. Does it have a story too?"

"Yes."

"I like the way you tell stories. And I could use a story to keep my mind off of everything else."

Yamada squinted and frowned. "It's too early for you to look to swordsmanship for distraction. I want focus from you first. I promise to tell you its story, but only after the blade has broken you in."

"What I'm wondering is. . . . Oh, I can't believe I'm going to even ask this. Sensei, do you believe this sword is cursed?"

"Hm. Not an easy question to answer. What makes you ask it?"

"Because it sure as hell looks to me like it behaves differently depending on who wields it."

Yamada's white eyebrows arched at that. "Now, that's an interesting observation. How on earth did you deduce that already?"

"When I watched you fight with this sword, you held it as easily as I hold a TV tray. But when I pick it up, it's everything I can do just to keep it pointed at your throat like you taught me. I'm not a weakling, Sensei. I keep myself in shape. And besides that, I'm sixty years younger than you."

"Ever the polite one, Sergeant Oshiro."

Mariko swallowed. "Sorry. But you see what I'm saying, neh? Why is this so hard for me and so easy for you?"

"Because I'm sixty years older than you. Your body is stronger than mine, but my muscles know nothing but swordsmanship. It's in my bones. But take heart. You show promise."

"Well, that makes one thing that's going right."

Yamada clucked his tongue. "I take it you have not yet found Fuchida-san."

Mariko shrugged. The motion pushed fingers of pain through her shoulder muscles. "No address, no phone. A criminal record but no known associates. The guy lies low even by yakuza standards."

"I see. And what of your criminal friends? You've spoken with them?"

"Yeah. They know the name Fuchida, but they've never heard of any Fuchida Shūzō. The thing is, to me that's all the more reason to believe he's a yakuza."

"Oh?"

"Definitely. For one thing, it's the kind of job that tends to run in the family. But more than that, it's in the way these guys talk about him. They'd brag about knowing his every move if they could, but since they can't, they brag about how they're too big to pay him any notice. That tells me he's one of them."

"So where does that leave you?"

"With an idiot of a commanding officer. We know what Fuchida wants and where it is. The least we can do is put a stakeout on your house and wait for him. But if my LT had any brains at all, he'd launch a massive manhunt. This city has more security cameras than stoplights. We need eyes on every last one of them. And we need beat cops pounding the pavement, looking in all the dark corners where the cameras can't see."

"And you think Fuchida-san would fall into your dragnet?"

"We're a lot more likely to nab him my way than by hoping he turns himself in." Mariko punched her palm, causing stabbing pain to shoot through her ribs. It was just one more frustration in her life. Unable to keep the heat from her voice, she said, "I swear, Sensei, the last thing in the world I want to be is a paper pusher, but sometimes I wish I could make lieutenant just for a day so I could show everyone else how it's done. I can catch this guy, you know? I just need my damn CO to get the hell out of my way."

Yamada pressed his wrinkled lips together, making the frown lines deepen in his cheeks. "There's an old soldier's saying: Commanders can always be relied upon to do the obvious, once all the alternatives have been exhausted."

Mariko laughed and laughed hard. Her ribs bit back at her with every chuckle—she really was going to have to get them X-rayed sometime soon—and even that made her giggle. Little grunts of pain accompanied each laugh, but the grunting was funny too. None of it was funny enough to warrant such a belly laugh, but she was exhausted and her sister was missing and the world was hopeless, and there wasn't anything else to do but laugh.

She was still chuckling, doubled at the waist with her hair brushing her knees, when she heard Yamada speak again. "You'll make a fine swordswoman, Sergeant Oshiro. We'll see what we can do about that commander of yours."

## 42

Mariko was entering data into the Yamada case file when she got the call. "Oshiro," Lieutenant Ko's voice said through the speakerphone on her desk, "get in here."

She clicked SAVE and abandoned her work. A tension headache was already setting in and she hadn't even set foot in Ko's office yet. This was the second day in a row that she'd come down to the precinct to find that Fuchida had killed again. It was eerie being the only one who knew Fuchida's handiwork for what it was. She felt like he was watching her, like he was killing just so she would find a new set of photos on her desk in the morning.

"What were you doing?" Ko asked when she opened his door.

"Reading up on another drug-related homicide, sir. Last night someone gutted a dealer behind Shinjuku station, and not with a knife. Looks like another sword killing."

"You're in Forensics now, are you?"

"No, sir. But the slash wound was a single cut, and it opened the vic's belly like a piñata. ME says the cut came within a few millimeters of the spine. No way you cut a grown man nearly in half with something the size of a kitchen knife. Not in one slash you don't."

Ko frowned, then lit a cigarette off the butt end of the

one he was finishing. "And this is related to your Yamada case? How?"

"How many sword killers can there be, sir, even in a city this size? I've got evidence that the Yamada case is linked to a murder two weeks ago in Yokohama, and—"

"Enough." Ko stabbed the cigarette to death in his ashtray. "This has gone too far. First you want me to put you on Narcotics, then you start tying your theft case to every murder within a hundred kilometers. And now—now a requisition comes across my desk for a province-wide manhunt? You want me to divert half the department's manpower for a simple B and E?"

"With all due respect," Mariko said, "this case is hardly simple. Tokyo usually sees about a hundred and twenty murders a year, *neh*? Two or three a week? In the last two nights we've had three dealers killed by the same MO—the same MO you'll find in the Kurihara murder, by the way—not to mention the three bodies we've got from the break-in at Dr. Yamada's place. That's six fatalities, sir, six in one case—"

"*If*, Oshiro. One case, *if* this can't all be chalked up to delusions of grandeur on your part. What's the alleged link between the Yamada case and these drug dealers?"

"I haven't figured that out yet, sir. But if you bothered reading my reports, you'd see the Kurihara-Yamada connection. You sent me out to Yamada's place to follow up on the attempted sword theft, *neh*? Well, Kurihara-san was the one who sold that sword to Yamada in the first place. And now she turns up dead, killed just like these dealers were killed, by a sword of all things. Come on, sir, you've got to see the connection."

"I see circumstantial evidence at best," Ko said through a cloud of smoke. "Conspiracy theory at worst. And I *have* read your reports, by the way. Please tell me you're not serious about this yakuza nonsense."

"Sir, I saw you talking to Fuchida's soldier the night I brought the guy in. The big fat one? You want to tell me that guy wasn't a yakuza?"

Ko adjusted his overlarge glasses and took a pull from his cigarette. "I don't know what he is. What I do know is that getting a few tattoos doesn't make him a yakuza, and I also know he was sitting in custody during the murders of the three drug dealers you seem so concerned about. That means the fat man's not a suspect."

"I never said he was, sir. It's Fuchida—"

"Oshiro, I'm ordering you to put a stop to all this conspiracy-theorist bullshit this instant. Is that clear?"

Mariko's eyes burned with cigarette smoke. She knew her jacket and blouse would stink of if later, and she hated the thought of carrying traces of Ko with her for the rest of the day.

Ko's frown lines deepened. "Well, Oshiro? Is that clear?"

"Sir," she said as calmly as she could manage, "am I to understand you're giving me a direct order *not* to investigate possible *bōryokudan* activity?"

Ko grinned. It was a ghoulish expression, but Mariko couldn't decide whether it was his fat lips and beady eyes that made it so gruesome, or whether someone had to know his shriveled, black heart to get the same chills she did. "Why, Oshiro," he said, his tone every bit as sweet and as ghoulish as his grin, "I think at last we understand each other."

"I'm not sure we do, sir. Isn't it illegal to order me to overlook organized crime?"

Ko crushed his cigarette like a bug. Still forcing a smile, he said, "You wouldn't be questioning my orders, would you, Oshiro? That would be cause for disciplinary action."

Through clenched teeth Mariko said, "No, sir."

"Good. It would be a shame to douse any hopes of your transfer to Narcotics before you even finished your probationary period. That sort of thing doesn't reflect well on an officer's record. We do understand each other now, don't we?"

Mariko suppressed a growl. "Yes. Sir."

"How nice. Then I'm sure you'll be forgetting any aspirations of commanding a citywide manhunt for this suspect of yours. I don't expect to hear any more wild fantasies of yakuza involvement either. The next time you come in here with nothing but circumstantial evidence—"

His phone interrupted him. It was his cell, not his desk phone—the ringtone, oddly, was a Thee Michelle Gun Elephant riff, something she'd have expected to hear from Saori's phone—and Ko's own policy placed an absolute ban on personal calls during official meetings. He flipped the phone open anyway. "Speak," he said.

Mariko watched his eyebrows jump as high as they could toward his hairline. He looked at the phone; whether he was verifying the caller's ID or the existence of the phone itself, Mariko couldn't tell. Ko's face went slack. He dragged on his cigarette, then cut off his drag midway, as if the speaker on the other end of the line had scolded him for smoking.

"Yes, sir," he said. Then, "I understand, sir." Then, "I will, sir, right away." Then he folded the phone shut and slid it into his pants pocket.

"You should know," Lieutenant Ko told her, "generally it's not considered a wise move to go over your superior's head with a request. Politically, that is. A record of that sort of thing tends to hold a person back from promotion, if you know what I mean."

"Sir, I have no idea what you mean," said Mariko, sincerely in the dark.

"Really?" Ko frowned; his eyes narrowed at her. "Well, then, let's say I've had a change of heart. This Yamada case you're on—how much did you say that sword is worth?"

"I didn't. But Dr. Yamada says it could fetch upwards of five million dollars at international auction."

Ko blinked at her.

"Sir," she added.

"Indeed. My change of heart tells me that a national treasure of this ilk deserves greater attention from the department. I'm authorized to devote as many resources as you need to catch your thief, Oshiro."

Mariko looked at him, gobsmacked. At last she said, "You're . . . you're making *me* lead on the manhunt?"

"Don't get ahead of yourself. Your manhunt's an overreaction. You'll live with a stakeout. Yamada's house, your suspect's usual haunts, whatever you need to do."

It wasn't enough, Mariko thought, but it was still ten times more than she expected from him. "And this is to be my command, sir?"

Ko fumed. The cigarette smoke seemed to rise from him as if he were a brooding volcano. "Do you expect me to do your job for you? See this case to a close, Oshiro, and do it soon."

Mariko couldn't have been more surprised if Lieutenant Ko had sprouted wings and flown out the window. He couldn't bring himself to say the words aloud, but Mariko didn't care; he'd actually given her command of a major operation.

She even considered thanking him, but then she got hold of her senses: this was not Ko's doing. Someone had bullied him into this. She wished she could take his cell from him and see who had called.

Then she realized she didn't need to check the cell. She knew the one she could ask. "I'll get right on it, sir," she said, and left the smoky room with purpose in her stride.

# 43

Mariko heard the sledgehammer long before she reached Dr. Yamada's house. Her feet were sore—she wouldn't ever wear these shoes on duty again—and the hammering was an oddly pleasant distraction.

When she rounded the corner onto Yamada's street, she saw the construction crew and the concrete wall they were working on. The last time she'd seen the wall, there had been a toothy maw in it the width of a car—precisely the width, in fact, of the Mercedes that had punched the hole. That was where Yamada's assailant had died, probably seeing spots well before impact, sitting in a warm pool of his own blood. Now the gap in the wall was half again as wide, and getting wider as a man went to work on it with the sledgehammer.

Mariko couldn't tell which one of the construction workers was the cop. That was good. It wouldn't be the hammering one; he was too distracted by his work to keep an eye on the house. There were four men in the crew, three of them idle at the moment, one of whom would never do any work apart from watching Yamada's house. All four of them had explicit instructions to make the job take as long as possible. Mariko could not have asked for a better opportunity to put an invisible officer in plain view of the house. She had every intention of leaving him there for as long as the crew could drag out the work.

There was another, she knew, in the Toyota Grand Saloon she passed two doors before reaching Yamada's, though the officer inside was doing well at his job too, for the van seemed empty. These narrow residential streets were no place for something as conspicuous as a panel truck; even the parked Grand Saloon straitened the lane for through traffic. Neighbors might complain about that; she'd have to look into another place to put that pair of eyes.

It was strange, not having room for a van on a modern city street, but after the firebombing Tokyo had been reconstructed right onto its former footprint. She remembered finding that strange even when she'd learned it in high school history class. Chicago had burned to the ground once too, but there they'd remapped before they rebuilt. The whole city was built on a grid, but the streets of Tokyo's neighborhoods looked like nests of tangled snakes.

In effect, the people in this neighborhood lived in a three-dimensional representation of Japan's attachment to the past. There were days when Mariko loved that brand of traditionalism and days when she despised it. The cultural forces that allowed Lieutenant Ko to be a sexist prick were the same forces that allowed a martial art based on the sword to endure into the twenty-first century, hundreds of years after the sword lost any real battlefield relevance.

No matter how she was feeling about traditionalism, Mariko knew she was going to have to find a better solution than that van. Even so, Mariko explained the van to Dr. Yamada as soon as they exchanged hellos. She also explained why she'd be replacing it, and why the construction crew across the way was going to take forever with a fairly straightforward repair job. "I see," Yamada said. "And you've come to relieve your comrades?"

"Not quite. The officer at your neighbor's wall will leave in a few minutes. The one in the van just got here at five. He'll stay until midnight, and then he gets relieved. And across the street we have at least one officer around the clock."

"Across the street? In Aihara-san's house?"

Mariko nodded. "Your neighbor's getting twenty thousand yen a week to lodge a surveillance team in her second bedroom. We've trained hidden cameras on every window and door in your house."

Yamada nodded thoughtfully. "You seem to have everything covered," he said. "So why are you here?"

"Sword practice," she said with a smile. "And to ask you a question."

"Practice first," he said. Then he led her to his backyard.

Her bare feet were thankful for the cool grass of Yamada's small lawn. She wondered how he kept it so neatly trimmed. Not a single blade strayed out of the lawn's boundaries and into the flower beds. For a man who couldn't see more than a hand's breadth beyond his nose, managing that must have been a chore.

He was teaching her footwork this evening. The sword was heavy, and she had to hold it in the same position for the first hour. Her shoulders and triceps blazed. She felt like he could cut her at will, despite the fact that his blade was two-thirds the length of hers. His was of WWII vintage—a relic in Mariko's eyes, a mere zygote in comparison to the Inazuma.

"Remember your ready stance," he scolded. "This is an art, not a quiz show; what you learned yesterday matters today."

"It's hard," Mariko said. It sounded stupid as soon as it came out of her mouth.

"My sensei must be rolling over in his grave," Yamada said. "It's breaking tradition, you know, teaching a woman these things. *Naginata* fighting was always the way for women. In the old days they would have stripped me of my belt for such an offense."

Mariko wanted to say it wasn't because she was a woman that it was hard; it was hard because in her entire life she'd spent all of three or four hours with a sword in her hands. "I told you already," she said, "this sword is too heavy for me."

"And I've told you: that sword is too heavy for anyone. It carries within it the full weight of Bushido itself."

"Then why make me use it? Why not give me a different weapon?"

"What other sword would suffice? You are steel in a forge, Inspector. This weapon is your blacksmith. It will forge you into a weapon as no other weapon can."

Mariko opened her eyes. "What about Fuchida's?" she said. "Beautiful Singer. It transforms people too, *neh*?"

"That it does. But it does not strengthen. Fuchida-san will be brittle steel before the end."

With some effort, Mariko stood. A light breeze cooled the sweat on her neck. The evening was getting cooler. "We should just sit back and let the sword destroy him," she said. "It'd save us a lot of trouble; he'll be easier to find once he's dead."

Yamada clicked his tongue. "And how many would die while we waited?"

"I know." Mariko took her ready stance, firmed her grip on Glorious Victory Unsought, and practiced the footwork he'd taught her. It seemed stupid to her, stepping forward and backward over and over. She wanted to learn how to fight, not how to walk. She wondered how much time the ancient samurai ever spent just walking backward and forward in straight lines, holding their swords instead of actually striking and counterstriking.

As if he'd read her mind, Yamada assumed his ready stance and stepped toward her. Mariko had to jump sideways or else be cut. His sword might have been older than he was, but he kept it razor sharp.

He stepped toward her again and again she jumped away. This time she landed badly, stumbling to one knee. She stiff-armed the ground with her left hand so she would not fall, and with a disdainful slap he knocked her weapon from her grip.

"Why did you retreat?"

"You were going to cut me," she said, instantly regretting the defensive tone in her voice. She realized now that she'd been at no risk. Despite his blindness, he'd disarmed her with ease. Somehow he knew exactly where her sword was. In fact, he seemed to have more control of it than she did; his control over his own blade was not something she'd question again.

"What attack did I use?"

"I don't know."

"Oh, come now," he said. "A thrust? An overhead strike? You're the one who dodged it. Tell me."

"You didn't attack. You just stepped forward."

"So why did you retreat?"

"Because—" "You were going to cut me, she was about to say, but that was the answer she'd given last time, and Yamada wasn't the type to ask the same question twice. He was pushing for something else.

It only took her a moment to understand. "You stepped toward me because I wasn't holding my sword right."

"Very good. Pick it up."

She did as she was told. This time she held it exactly as he'd taught her, with the tip of her weapon pointed right at the notch between his collarbones. He trained his own weapon on her throat too. She stepped forward, and this time he had no choice but to retreat. Hers was the longer reach.

"Better now," he said. "Understand this, Oshiro-san: in sword combat, everything is attacking. Standing still, you threaten my throat. Stepping forward, you aggress me. If you learn nothing else but to stand still and step forward, you are already dangerous."

Mariko thought of the photos from the ME's report: Saga's baby face splattered with red, severed fingers lying in the grass, spilled intestines, pools of blood pink with oxygen. Drug dealing being a dangerous profession, most of Fuchida's victims had been armed; even so, they never stood a chance. Maybe in the States, where there were more guns than people, he wouldn't have been such a terror, but in Japan pistols were hard to come by, and even then most people couldn't hit a target beyond six or seven meters. At that range Fuchida would only need a step or two to be in striking distance.

"He's a nightmare, isn't he?" she said. "Fuchida, I mean. You say I'm dangerous just from holding my sword the right way. He's an expert. If I ever get in the same room with him, he'll cut me apart."

"Yes."

"Well, that sucks."

Mariko made a mental note not to even look for Fuchida without a Taser and a pistol handy. She made another note to tell everyone on her stakeout team the same thing. Then she renewed her concentration on her footwork. With every step forward she envisioned stabbing an opponent through the gullet. It was a horrific image in her mind, but it did wonders for her focus.

"There is a grim air about you, Inspector," said Yamada. "Has he killed again?"

"Three times. A drug dealer last night, and two more the night before that. The medical examiner says all three were killed with an edged weapon at least half a meter long."

"Why do you suspect Fuchida?"

"Who else? I don't see why he'd target pushers, though. They haven't got anything to do with ancient swords."

"I can see no connection either. Fuchida-san would have no interest in them. When I knew him, he did not even drink alcohol. He said being drunk made him feel paranoid. I've known many in the martial arts to say the same: when you are accustomed to being in control of your body, losing that control leaves you feeling unsafe."

Mariko's breath came heavily, but the sword was moving smoothly. Control was coming for her too, albeit slowly. She concentrated on her footwork as her blade cut the garden air. "Maybe there's another connection between the victims," she said. "Something I'm not seeing."

"I hope there is, Inspector, and I hope you find it quickly. The sword has a hold on him now. Even brittle steel can cut to the quick."

"I know." Mariko reined in the heavy blade, turned to face Yamada, and took her ready stance. "Show me what I should have done before instead of almost falling on my ass."

Yamada grinned a warrior's grin, the kind Mariko had seen the Special Assault Team guys get when they practiced kicking down doors. He took his ready stance and said, "Come."

She trained her weapon on his throat and stepped in. He stepped in too. Their swords crossed, and somehow it was hers that turned aside. She stopped short with his blade a centimeter from her skin.

"Do it again," she said.

"'*Please* do it again, *Sensei*,'" he chided, and they repeated the exchange. Again Mariko's longer, heavier blade was turned aside.

"I don't get it," she said.

"Again," he told her.

So they did it once more, and Mariko tried to study him with her hands as well as with her eyes. She could feel him turn her blade aside, but the how of it eluded her. Three times, ten times more, and Mariko lost every one.

At last her forearms could not take any more; her sword was simply too heavy. This time when he advanced, she stepped back, keeping him at bay. "Yes!" he said. "You've got it."

"Huh? I retreated."

"Yes, but you didn't lose your balance this time. That's progress."

"I failed. I'm trying to learn to do it the way you did it."

Yamada laughed. "I've got seventy years' more experience than you have. What makes you think you can do this the way I do it?"

Mariko grunted. She saw his point, but she couldn't sort out how to apply it so long as her mind boggled over the other thing: *Seventy years?* That meant he'd been practicing swordsmanship for twenty-odd years before Mariko's parents were born. Mariko didn't know anyone who'd been doing *anything* for seventy years, except maybe breathing.

Overhead the stars had begun to come out, and Mariko took a moment to enjoy them. This was the second time sword training had caused her to forget life's tensions. It felt good. Even with the pain wracking her arms and shoulders, it felt good. She wondered what her mom would say about that—or a psychiatrist, for that matter. She wondered what they would say about the fact that this eighty-seven-year-old man was quickly becoming the person she most enjoyed spending time with.

Yamada snapped her mind back to the present. "You came here to ask me a question, *neh*? What was it?"

Mariko sheathed her weapon as Yamada lowered himself onto a bench of white stone, a heavy-looking slab held up by two statues of Kwannon. "You know," she said, "a funny thing happened at work today. I was talking to my CO, and out of the blue he authorized all the surveillance on your house. Made me primary on the case, in fact. I don't suppose you know why he had a sudden change of heart?"

Yamada's face was pure innocence, the sort of look Mariko had seen on her grandfather's face during her childhood when he'd conspired with Mariko or Saori to break their grandmother's rules about sweets before dinner. "Why ask me?" he said.

"Because you said you'd see what we can do about Lieutenant Ko, and then Ko got a phone call. Took him down a few notches, that did. He looked like a fish who'd forgotten how to swim."

Still the mask of innocence. "That made you happy, I should think."

"It did. I know you weren't the one who called him; when you came down to the precinct, it was clear he'd never seen you before. So whoever you know in the TMPD out-ranks Ko. Who is it?"

"You're the only police officer I know, Oshiro-san."

"Come on. This was your doing. I just want to know how you did it."

"Does it matter?"

"Don't get me wrong: whatever you did, I'm grateful for it. But I don't like owing people favors, and I like it even less if I don't know who I owe the favor to. So out with it: who do you know in the TMPD?"

"You don't owe anyone any favors, Inspector."

Mariko blew a breath out her nose. "But you called *someone* in my department."

"No."

"Fine. The mayor's office, maybe?"

"No."

"You know the answer I'm looking for. I'm just not ask-ing the right questions."

Yamada nodded. "You're a good detective, Oshiro-san."

"And you better get in the mood to tell me how high up the ladder this goes." Mariko felt her shoulders stiffen and her jaws clench. "You're enjoying this, aren't you, Sensei?"

"A very good detective indeed, Oshiro-san."

"Come on. This isn't fair."

"You'd rather not know. You'd look at me differently."

"I won't," she said. "I swear I won't."

"You're not the type to make promises you can't keep, Oshiro-san. Don't start now."

Mariko sighed. "You're really not going to tell me, are you?"

Yamada laughed. "Good night, Inspector."

# 44

Fuchida watched as a small, slender woman walked down Yamada's front stairs. Her hair was short, cropped even shorter on the back of her head, and there the hair stood in dark, sweat-slicked spikes. The sweat gave fuel to doubts in Fuchida's mind. When he'd seen the woman enter, he figured her for the Oshiro woman, the one who had arrested Kaneda. (It seemed improbable—Kaneda was three times her size—but the biggest man and the smallest man had the same response to pepper spray.) But now the sweat was throwing him off. Had she given the old codger a fuck? No, not while the house was under surveillance. But if she wasn't a whore, who was she? What other sort of woman would go in there for two hours and come out sweating? A masseuse would have brought her tools of the trade, as would an in-home nurse. Yamada had always been meticulously neat; no way this could be a maid. But if it was the lady cop, what could explain the sweat?

He shifted his position in the bucket seat of his rented Nissan Versa, which was parked a block and a half from the old man's house. Staking out a stakeout was boring, joint-stiffening work, and risky besides. The Versa was parked facing away from the house, the better to make a quick departure, its dashboard monitor wired to a Sony Handycam poised on a GorillaPod to face out the back window on maximum zoom. Without the camera Fuchida could never have got close enough to see the woman's sweat, nor even to clearly see her face. With the camera, Fuchida ran the risk of someone spying the dashboard display, and therefore had to maintain constant vigilance over every passerby.

Even so, he was glad he'd thought to call his man in the TMPD about the surveillance. If running surveillance on a police sting was risky, at least it was better than walking blindly into one. Fuchida had almost done it too. Whenever he had his beautiful singer in his hands, he wanted nothing more than to put her to use. Even now she called to him; he'd had no choice but to lock her in the back, or else drive himself mad listing all the reasons why he shouldn't go right up the street and show all those cops why stun guns and batons and even their puny pistols were no match for a sword.

His phone buzzed in his pocket like a cicada. Fuchida cursed the distraction. Then he saw the caller ID. "Hello, Mr. Travis."

"My favorite samurai. How's it hanging?"

Fuchida didn't understand the question. That was hardly a problem, since the American left him no time to answer it. "Listen," he said, "I want to see my sword. Send me a picture of it."

Fuchida glanced in the rearview mirror, to the damnable house of the damnable man who still had the damnable sword. "So sorry," said Fuchida. "I do not have picture."

"So make one. You're in the birthplace of the camera phone, right?"

"So sorry, Mr. Travis. I do not have camera phone."

"So buy one."

Fuchida held his thumb over the receiver for a moment, the better to mask a sigh of frustration. "It is not advisable, Mr. Travis. The flash is bad for . . . *nan to iu ka na?* The paint. On the wood."

"The lacquer," said the American. "On the scabbard. And I don't give a fuck. It's my sword now, and *I'll* tell *you* what's good and bad for it. Right now what's good for it is me showing it to my girlfriend. She wants to know what I'm flying all the way to Japan to get."

Fuchida switched the phone to his left hand, then started the car. He didn't know how seriously the police were taking this stakeout, but it was possible they might monitor cellular traffic.

"Hello?" said the American.

"I am here, Mr. Travis."

"So when are you sending me my picture?"

"Terribly sorry, Mr. Travis. I cannot access the sword just now."

"What'd you do, lose it? No, don't even answer that. Just listen. You get your hands on my sword, and you do it pronto, or else your whole world is going to turn to shit. You do not want to stand between me and what I want."

Fuchida smiled. "Do you threaten me?"

"You bet your ass I'm threatening you."

Fuchida wished he had better command of this language. "Bet your ass" was one of those phrases that would never come naturally to him, utterly inexpressible as it was in his own tongue. Someday, when he was rich enough to command his own destiny, he would arrange to live in the U.S. for a year and master as many of their offensive sayings as he could.

For the present, his English would have to do as it was. "You are a stockbroker, Mr. Travis. You cannot hurt me."

"I'm a commodities trader, you ignorant fuck. And I don't need to hurt you. All I need is Ryusuke Kamaguchi's phone number. Surprise, motherfucker. Didn't think I knew about him, did you?"

There followed a torrent of words too fast for Fuchida to follow. Then, slower, "I know all about your rules against pushing coke. I make one call to your *oyabun* and you end up in bowls of shark fin soup all over your shit-ass little country."

"Shark fin soup is Chinese, not Japanese, Mr. Travis."

"Good for the Chinamen."

"Your ship, it will arrive here shortly, yes? Much too late to turn it around. I think you should not threaten me, Mr. Travis. I think now you have no choice but to deal with me."

"Maybe. Or maybe I sell all the shit to the Koreans and let them infiltrate it into your market. Then you don't see a penny, do you? One way or another, I'm getting paid. I'd tell you I don't give a fuck how, but the fact is I want that sword. When the ship gets there, you're going to be standing on the dock to meet it, sword in hand. My boys don't see it, they give me a phone call—and then Kamaguchi's getting a phone call. *Wakaru?*"

"I understand, Mr. Travis."

Fuchida folded the phone shut and dropped it in the seat beside him. He tucked the Nissan into the next parking spot he saw, then took his BlackBerry from his jacket pocket and waited as it pulled up his calendar. He could not help but feel that, if only his English were better, he could have properly asserted himself over the American. He could not understand how they had managed to permeate every corner of his country with their language and still leave the possibility that he could not speak it. The BlackBerry with its impossible distinction between *r*'s and *l*'s, the Versa with its unpronounceable *v*; he lived in a world that defied speech.

The *burakuberi* showed him what he'd memorized already, what he double-checked now only out of frustration. The American's ship would arrive on Wednesday. A week from yesterday. To walk into Yamada's house, take the sword, and walk out again might take as long as two minutes. He had six days to accomplish it. He wondered how he could manage it given so little time.

# 45

Mariko hated to admit it, but Lieutenant Ko was actually good at police work. Yes, he was sexist; yes, he was a horrid, ugly, evil little troll; but damn him, he had been right on the money when he'd accused her of collecting nothing but circumstantial evidence. Fuchida had left no fingerprints at any of his murder scenes, and as he'd committed all but the Kurihara homicide in public places, there was no point in trying to collect fiber evidence. Even if some go-getter in Violent Crimes had wanted to look for any trace fibers Fuchida might have left behind, Mariko couldn't have told him what her perp was wearing, how long his hair was, or any other detail. Neither she nor a single member of her team had even laid eyes on their suspect.

Mariko had nine cops working under her in round-the-clock shifts, and so far all she had was hours and hours of unremarkable footage. Her stakeout team knew Yamada's mailman on sight. That was all.

No record of Fuchida connected him to any of the slain drug offenders. Nor did he appear in connection to any known drug offender in Tokyo. A search in the opposite direction generated hordes of drug offenders with *bōryokudan* connections, but none of interest: all of them were pushing pedestrian stuff, few were ever prosecuted, and none of them had any known association with Fuchida. Here and there she found cases of rogue coke and heroin dealers, most of whom had been chopped up by yakuzas before they ever showed up on a police department's radar. The *bōryokudan* were brutally efficient at maintaining their end of the tacit agreement; all the cops had to do was look the other way at the softer narc crimes they allowed yakuzas to commit with impunity.

Everything Mariko discovered made it all the more reasonable to think Fuchida had nothing to do with the drug scene. So why was the morgue cooling off three dead pushers with sword wounds? Surely Tokyo couldn't have more than one sword killer at large. Mariko was certain that Fuchida was responsible, but the evidence that was good enough to confirm a hunch wasn't evidence enough to convict.

And from there she could only conclude that she'd never find Fuchida unless he walked right into her sting. The thought hardly inspired hope. It seemed as likely as Saori popping back up, and it had been eight days since anyone had seen her. In fact, the last person to see her was Mariko, who had watched her storm away from the Lawson just down the street from her mother's apartment. Saori had been sober for eight days then, and in all likelihood she'd been high for the eight days since.

Their mother was worried sick, of course. Mariko found it odd that she wasn't feeling the same worry herself. A family having its youngest daughter go missing for more than a week should have been worrisome, shouldn't it? Yet unlike her mother, Mariko had been able to overcome her initial panic. Maybe her *kenjutsu* training had already instilled some self-control in her, or maybe it was just that after a few days her brain had gone into survival mode. Maybe she'd taken all the panic she could take, and now she just shoved the rest into some deep, dark corner of her mind. Every time she thought about Saori, she felt her stomach do backflips, but the cold, hard truth was that she didn't have to think about Saori every minute. Most of the time she found a way to go about her day: work, sword training, going into the Docomo store to get her phone contract sorted out.

It was while waiting for the Docomo guy to fix the computer glitch that Mariko figured it out. If she were the big sister in any normal family, the panic she'd felt at first would probably have grown worse with every passing day. But Mariko was the sister of an addict. Their mom was the mother of an addict. And that came with certain facts, one of which was that until Saori got sober, she was apt to disappear into some deep, dark hole now and again.

Once she figured that out, Mariko got a better understanding of her mother too. Her mom thought of their family as normal. She'd always thought of them that way, despite having a husband die of cancer at forty-three and despite having two daughters react to his death in the most incongruous ways possible. And because their mom thought of the family as normal, Saori's absence was the biggest thing in the world. It had replaced the sun: everything revolved around it, and everything took on a different color in its light.

It was only when her mother stopped playing Ping-Pong that Mariko understood how bad things were for her. Mariko had been sleeping at her mom's ever since, though the combination of sleeping on the sofa conspired with Yamada's relentless *kenjutsu* drills to put a crick in Mariko's neck that just wouldn't quit. For the past few days she'd eaten breakfast and dinner with her mother every day, but even so, when Mariko finally got her phone back and working, she checked her messages hoping for something from Saori and found thirty-eight messages from their mother instead.

So instead of looking for Fuchida, and instead of looking for Saori, Mariko went looking for a quiet place where she could sit and call her mom. Worry was one thing, but they'd have to have a chat about why thirty-eight messages was a little much for someone she was going to see for dinner every night.

As it happened, Mariko was right across the street from the shopping mall where she'd arrested Bumps. She went in and sat on the same bench where she'd stationed Mishima on the night of the sting. The mall was dead, and a listless gray light shone down through the roof of translucent plastic half eggs.

Mariko called home to talk her mother off the ledge. That phrase, *talk her off the ledge*, struck her even as the phone was ringing. Saori had first coined the phrase, back when Mariko was still in academy. Their mother had always been the hysterical sort, overprotective of her children yet more than willing to bully them with guilt. It was a New Year's party, and over a secretly shared glass of *shōchū* Saori had asked whether Mariko got to learn any supersecret police negotiation skills, the better to talk their mother off the ledge when she inevitably flew off the handle about Saori's drinking underage.

Those were the days before Mariko knew that Saori had a problem, days when a little sister drinking with her friends in the park was no cause for alarm. Mariko had done her share of partying too—or if not her share, a little bit, anyway. Everyone had. After her twentieth birthday, Mariko bought for her sister just as a friend's elder brother had bought for Mariko. How could she call herself a good elder sister and do otherwise?

"Hello?" her mother's voice said through the cell. "Mariko? What are you giggling about?"

"Nothing, Mom. Sorry. Just wanted to tell you my phone's working again."

"Oh."

"You okay?"

"I just thought . . ." Her tone was as lifeless as the dull gray Plexiglas mannequin breasts overhead. "Since you were laughing, I was hoping maybe you'd heard from your sister."

"Nope. Sorry, Mom. I was only thinking of something funny she said."

"Oh. What was it?"

"Something naughty." Mariko sighed. "Why is it that when she's gone, it's easier to remember her being bad than being good?"

It was strange to be having this conversation *here*, where memories of handling Saori with handcuffs flared so vividly. Mariko thought about fate, about that night, about how, of all the junkies in the city, it had been Saori to walk into her bust. If only she could get so lucky with Fuchida.

"Miko," her mother said, "do you remember the time your sister walked right through the rock garden at Ginkakuji?"

"Sort of," Mariko said, which was a lie. The sight of Saori's pretty pink hat catching the wind just so, and of Saori's little footprints leaving all those craters across the concentric rings so carefully raked into the pebbles—they were among the clearest memories of Mariko's childhood. The story was old and worn, but she knew how much her mom enjoyed telling it. Mariko laughed at all the right parts, and in the meantime she wondered whether Saori had any choice but to be an abuser. What had pushed her over the edge? Was it Mariko, implicitly condoning her habits by buying her booze while Saori was still wearing her uniform skirt as short as their high school teachers would allow? Was Mariko's culpability deeper because she'd been a police academy recruit at the time? Or was the cause something so deep-seated that even Saori couldn't say what it was? Some genetic factor? Or could the whole problem be chalked up as Saori's response to their father's death?

Mariko blinked hard. These were the questions that would run like a bullet train, taking untold kilometers to stop if she let them build any momentum. She tuned in to her mother again, laughing sincerely at the part in the story where the big *gaijin* tourist got so mad that a little girl had ruined his photo opportunity of the rock garden. "I was *so* embarrassed, Miko-chan. There aren't even words to describe it." But her mother was laughing all the same.

"She's always been a troublemaker," Mariko said. "Mom, listen, I should get back to work, okay?"

"I thought today was your day off."

"It is, but I'm running this stakeout, remember? I'm not really going to have a day off until it's done."

"All right. You'll be home for dinner?"

"You bet."

Mariko folded her phone shut and used it as a paperweight, preventing the crosswind blowing through the mall from claiming the folder she set down on the bench beside her. She slid the top page of the report from the folder and skimmed it. It was the latest status report from her stakeout. It had half a ruddy brown thumbprint on one corner—barbecue sauce, Mariko guessed—and nothing else unusual. The comings and goings of the neighbors. An argument between a boyfriend and girlfriend, loud enough to get the surveillance officers' attention, neither protracted enough nor violent enough to believe it was meant as a distraction. Fuchida remained a ghost.

Mariko jumped in her skin when a pigeon burst forth

from under her seat, startled by something only another pigeon could guess. Her pulse pounded hard and fast in her temples, but Mariko realized it wasn't because of the pigeon. She would find no peace and quiet here, nor would she find it at work, nor at her mother's apartment. There was only one place she could go to find a little serenity.

"Why, Inspector," Yamada said when he opened his door. "Have you come to update me on my many observers?"

"I was hoping we might do some sword training, actually."

Her sensei smiled. "That's the spirit. I'd just as soon not hear about your stakeout anyhow. It's strange knowing they're out there watching. I never know how much they can see."

"Pretty much everything," Mariko said, and she told him how the thermal imaging worked.

"Then I was right after all," Yamada said, sighing. "I've been feeling self-conscious all day. Even when I brush my teeth, it occurs to me to wonder whether they think I'm doing it right."

"I wouldn't worry about that. Some of those guys haven't discovered toothpaste yet."

Yamada laughed. "Oh, I bet the boys just love working with you."

"I'd love working with them too if they would just treat me like one of the boys."

They made their way through the house to the backyard, with a quick stop at the sword rack in the study on the way. Mariko loved the fact that Yamada had a sword rack in his study, and the fact that he had another one in the bedroom made his house the best place in the world. It was like standing on an island in time: everything progressed normally all around it, but here on the island time stood still. Cooking was done on a stove, not in a microwave. Writing to a friend meant pen and paper, not an e-mail, certainly not a text message.

And yet despite Yamada's uncanny ability to stand apart from the forces of modernization, there was one respect in which he made the rest of the country seem positively medieval. "Thank you," she said as they walked down the back stairs. "For treating me like a student and not a girl student. I wish the guys at work would learn a thing or two about that."

"Oh, what do they know? I hear some of them haven't even discovered toothpaste yet."

They practiced for two hours straight. After stance and footwork came overhead strikes, then diagonal strikes, until Mariko's shoulders were so sore she could hardly lift her arms, much less her sword.

Sweating and panting, she said, "Sensei, maybe we can take a little break."

"Oh ho. Think you've learned enough, eh?"

"Not enough, but maybe enough for now. After all, you said this sword is called Glorious Victory Unsought, *neh*?"

"Ah. So you were paying attention."

"Of course. I'm glued to your every word, Sensei." Mariko smirked. "And since I've already got Glorious Victory well in hand, why push so hard on the training? With a name like that, how can I lose?"

Yamada narrowed his unseeing eyes. "This is the sword that will kill you the moment you drop your vigilance against that very thought. You weren't paying attention at all, little girl."

"Don't call me that."

"If you want to joke around with that sword in your hands, I'll call you whatever I like. I'm the sensei here, little girl."

"Don't," she said, and she stepped in to press the attack. He turned her sword aside, just as he'd done a hundred times before.

Mariko anticipated the move. She slipped to the side too, evading his *katana*. Now she had him. His whole right flank was exposed. Little girl, my ass, she thought, and she raised her sword to strike.

Yamada didn't bother raising his weapon. He just stepped aside. Mariko didn't even see it when he kicked her foot out from under her. She hit the grass, careful to land on her left shoulder, holding the sword high and clear of the ground in her right. But in protecting the sword, she forgot about protecting herself. The ground hit her like a truck—a truck with a big, sharp hood ornament to stab her in the ribs.

She looked at Yamada's blade, hanging easily in his wrinkled hand, its razor-sharp tip close enough to tickle her under the chin. The tip of her own weapon brushed the close-cropped lawn. He didn't need to speak the lesson aloud; had it been a real fight, the price for her imbalance would have been her life.

At last the weight of the sword overcame her, and she flopped to her back so that she could rest the blade on her chest. An ache throbbed deep inside her right shoulder, as if it still strained to hold the sword off the ground. On any other day, she would have found the back of the heavy blade painful across her breasts. Today she let the narrow line of pain sit there, the better to rest her shoulders.

"Do you know how I felled you?"

"Temper." Mariko spoke with her eyes shut. "You called me a little girl and I lost it."

"No. You wanted to show me that you were not a little girl. You wanted to show me what you had learned. Then the sword betrayed you."

With her eyes closed, Mariko could smell her own sweat, overpowering even the fresh scent of the grass. "What do you mean *it* betrayed me?"

"Had your posture been balanced, I could not have swept your foot. You know full well I cannot see even as far as my own toes. I stepped where I guessed you might step; it was your imbalance that took you over my foot. I did not sweep you so much as you did—or, properly speaking, as your weapon did."

It was impossible. Steel couldn't betray anyone. And yet his explanation matched the facts exactly.

Mariko surprised herself with how quickly she came to accept the impossible. But in the end she was a detective; she believed what the evidence told her, and that was that.

She got to her feet, her ribs and aching shoulders protesting the whole time. "Sensei, will you show me what you did to me before? That foot thing?"

"'That foot thing' is called a sweep," Yamada said, settling easily into a ready stance of his own. He seemed bigger, instantly threatening; images sprang to mind of a panther perched on a branch above unsuspecting quarry. "Come," he said.

She lunged to the attack. He sidestepped. Her foot

struck his; she felt her weight lurch forward; she only barely saved herself from falling.

"Well done!" said Yamada, practically in her ear. His naked blade was mere centimeters away from her. The big Inazuma was too long for such close quarters; if he wanted to counterattack, she would be dead.

Mariko gave a noncommittal grunt. "You would have killed me."

Yamada laughed. "But not the way I would have last time. You did not fall prey to the same sweep twice. You're improving."

"Ehh. Not quickly enough."

"You demand too much of yourself, Inspector. Not even Musashi learned all his swordsmanship in an afternoon."

Mariko knew all about demanding too much of herself. It was why she needed to win triathlons, not just finish. It was why she'd made sergeant, why she'd made detective, why she wanted to command a manhunt instead of a stakeout. It was why she hadn't given up on her sister yet. Leaving Saori to reap the consequences she'd sown for herself wasn't just the easier choice; it was the *reasonable* choice, much more sensible than trying to save an addict from herself. But Mariko couldn't do that any more than she could let Beautiful Singer run its course with Fuchida.

And yet that too seemed so easy, so tempting. The sword might well kill him. Mariko didn't understand how inert steel could betray a freely choosing human being, but now that she'd experienced that phenomenon herself, she could not deny the possibility that Fuchida's sword had the same power. If Yamada was right, Fuchida's body would turn up soon enough, and it seemed the only collateral damage would be a few dead pushers.

Mariko wished she could be content with that. Stakeout work was easy. Mariko didn't have the disposition to just sit and watch the monitors like some of the guys did, but she was lead on the case. She could commandeer the Aihara house, and during the hours she had the place to herself, she could do sword drills all day. The thought of Ko *paying* her to practice her *kenjutsu* brought a smile to her face. The smug bastard deserved it. She'd taken enough shit from him. She deserved her day of rest.

On top of that, half the cops on the force would have

said whoever was next on Fuchida's hit list probably deserved to die. Wages of sin and all that. But they were wrong. Mariko knew it. Even drug dealers had rights, and Mariko had taken an oath to uphold those rights. Even if the sentence for trafficking were death, it should have been a judge that pronounced it, not a crazed yakuza butcher.

And that butcher was out there somewhere. Mariko sheathed Glorious Victory and handed the sword respectfully to Yamada. Bowing, she said, "I'm sorry, Sensei, I've got to go home and look over my case notes again. There's got to be some hint in there of how to nail Fuchida. I just have to see it."

"Good luck, Inspector."

Mariko replied with a wry laugh. "This isn't another one of those things where you know all the answers in advance, is it? Because that was annoying as hell the last few times around."

Yamada chuckled. "I'm afraid not."

"It's just . . . I've got this feeling, you know, like I'm right on the cusp of figuring something out, but by the time I figure it out, it'll be too late. You ever get that feeling?"

"Once."

"What happened?"

Yamada frowned. A dark shadow fell over his face, and he cast his unseeing gaze to the ground. At length he said, "People died."

Mariko frowned too. "That's what I was afraid of."

# BOOK SIX

## AZUCHI-MOMOYAMA ERA,

## THE YEAR 20

## (1587 CE)

## 46

"My name is Ōda Yoshitomo," the challenger said when Daigoro and Ichirō greeted him at the gate. "I come to test the skill of the Okumas."

His entourage was just four horsemen: two retainers and an older samurai with thick eyebrows that made him look vaguely owl-like. The older man, Daigoro soon learned, was Ōda Tomonosuke, head of the Ōda clan. Yoshitomo, champion of the Ōdas, had eyes that flicked to and fro like startled minnows. He was lanky, a bit shorter than Ichirō, and thus almost a head taller than Daigoro. He wore faded gray with black *hakama*, and his sword grip was well-worn.

"What will you fight with," Ichirō asked, "wood or steel?"

Lord Ōda's forehead furrowed, and his champion said, "Lord Toyotomi has decreed that duels should be fought using *bokken*."

"Ah, that he has," said Ichirō. "If the house of Ōda has no will of its own, I suppose we can follow the will of a greater house."

All of the Ōdas immediately tensed, and Yoshitomo was out of the saddle with his hand on his sword before Daigoro could get a word in. "Lord Ōda," Daigoro said, inserting himself in front of his brother, "please, let us take some tea and discuss the terms of the duel."

"No," said Yoshitomo. "He has insulted me! I demand satisfaction."

The elder Ōda looked at his champion, then at Ichirō, then at Daigoro. At last he said, "First we will have tea."

Negotiations lasted as long as it took the sun to set. First Daigoro introduced his mother. They spoke about the weather and conditions on the road and news of the war in the west. Daigoro complimented Lord Ōda on his horses, and on the fitness and fiery zeal of his challenger. Ōda revealed that Yoshitomo was his son—his fourth of six—and complimented Daigoro and his mother on the beauty of the family compound. At last they came to the matter at hand. Daigoro argued for a battle of *bokken*, and his terms were granted at last—on the condition that he be the one to fight.

Daigoro and Ōda Tomonosuke emerged from the tea house, paid their respects to the shrine of Daigoro's father, and found their respective champions glowering at each other, kneeling in ready positions just two paces apart. "You shall duel with *bokken*," Lord Ōda announced, "and you shall face young Master Daigoro."

Lord Ōda's son tightened his fists, ground his knuckles in the sand, and bowed stiffly to Ichirō. Then he stood, his body tense as if Ichirō were a venomous snake whose reach he was unsure of, and bowed to Daigoro. Daigoro noticed the bow to him was deeper than that to his brother. He was thankful that Ichirō failed to notice the fact, but Ichirō could not have seen it, for he had shifted his glare to Daigoro. "Coward," he muttered.

Ōda Yoshitomo whirled, unsheathing his *katana*. He came within a hand's breadth of cutting Ichirō's head from his shoulders when his father bellowed, "Stop!"

"He called me a coward!" said Yoshitomo. "You heard him!"

Daigoro tried to intervene, tried to explain the true target of the insult, but his leg was too slow to carry him into the courtyard and Ichirō's voice drowned out his own. "It seems our rival would prefer a battle of steel on steel," said Ichirō. "Give me the sword, Daigoro."

"I won't," Daigoro said. "Why are you doing this?"

"I'm only giving him what he wants. Now give me Glorious Victory."

Daigoro now stood between his brother and the armed Yoshitomo, who had sunk into a combative stance and trained the tip of his sword on Ichirō's throat. "You know I won't," said Daigoro.

"You would deny the will of Toyotomi himself, the man who may well become shogun?" There was no need for Daigoro to answer. "Then get out of my way, little brother." Ichirō drew his own sword. "The duel begins now."

Daigoro stood his ground, and Yoshitomo circled around to his left. Ichirō shot Daigoro a final glare, then shifted to match Yoshitomo's movement. Daigoro hobbled backward toward Ōda Tomonosuke, preparing his abject apologies.

Before he reached him, the duel was over. There was the ring of clashing steel, then a garbled cry from Ichirō. Yoshitomo stood back as Ichirō fell to his knees. His back was drenched with blood, torrents of it cascading from the base of his neck. His head hung forward, unattached on one side. He fell face-first to the sand.

Yoshitomo whipped his sword in a gory arc, cleaning it of blood before resheathing it. He bowed to Ichirō's bleeding form, then to Daigoro, then to their mother, who stood aghast beside Lord Ōda. As servants and healers flocked to Ichirō's side, the Ōdas took their leave.

# 47

The wound was as grave as any Daigoro had heard of. According to the family's chief healer, who had once exchanged medical techniques with a southern barbarian doctor and had even spent some years learning his trade in China, Ōda's sword had cut one of Ichirō's neck bones. The spine was still intact, but only barely. Had healers not been standing mere paces away from the fight, Ichirō surely would have died where he lay.

But they had managed to stitch his neck back together, and then the question became how to get tissue and bone to mend. Old Yagyū, House Okuma's chief healer, called for timber, a carpenter, and as much rice as could be found.

While the carpenter followed old Yagyū's instructions, three servants dug a pit in the courtyard deeper than Daigoro was tall. Yagyū and the carpenter tied a rope around Ichirō's head and bound it to a beam. Under Yagyū's supervision, the healers lowered Ichirō into the pit, holding him erect, trying at the same time to shoo away the flies congregating on the jagged, bloody black line of stitches on his neck. Then the healers filled the pit with rice and affixed the beam on Ichirō's head to bamboo poles thrust vertically into the rice. When the work was finished, Ichirō was buried up to his chin, his head fixed so that he could not move it at all. Yagyū rubbed a mixture of oil and pine resin over the stitched wound just before the last layer of rice was shoveled on. Ichirō could not move, but he might live.

A month later Ichirō was still alive and no more duels had been fought. At times Ichirō's stagnant muscles would pain him so badly that he would cry out, moaning through his lips since his jaws were tied tightly shut. Other times he was beset by madness; the itching was so bad. Servants sat with him constantly, fanning the horse flies away by day and the mosquitoes by night. Drinking was a laborious chore; eating was even harder. More than once Ichirō asked his attending servants to kill him. He never asked Daigoro, for Daigoro made the asking impossible. A lowly servant could not dispatch a man of Ichirō's station, but Daigoro knew he would have to honor the request, so he made sure never to approach within earshot while Ichirō could see him.

But he sat with Ichirō as soon as Ichirō fell asleep, or when he passed out from the pain or the heat. Sometimes Daigoro would creep up behind him, taking a servant's fan himself, and spend wordless hours cooling the back of Ichirō's head.

He did not know what else to do. Every day he knelt at the shrine to his father, asking for advice. All I have ever done, he thought, is adhere to your will, Father. All I have ever done is try to follow your path, and now that path has led to something you never would have willed. Your eldest son suffers worse than any animal under heaven. Would Glorious Victory have saved him? Its length, the strength of its steel—were they the advantages he needed? What should I have done differently? What am I to do now?

There was no answer to his questions within the family stronghold, so Daigoro took his thoughts, his *wakizashi*, and his father's *ōdachi* up into the mountains. He rode aimlessly for an hour, distantly hoping that some wind spirit would blow an answer past his ears. The mountains were lush and green, punctuated by the purple flowers of kudzu in full bloom. The flowers smelled of grapes, and their scent came to him on a warm zephyr that also carried tidings of an evening rain. Far below, the sea beat its susurrating rhythm against the stones of the shore. Izu was at its most beautiful, but it held no answers for Daigoro.

Looking up, he found himself suddenly at Kattō-ji, though he had no idea how he'd come there. He'd intended to ride in the opposite direction but then got lost in his ruminations. He wondered whether his mare preferred the temple. Perhaps some ancient buddha had been reborn into her. Daigoro did not care. A vine-covered hilltop was as good a place as any to fail to find the insight he sought.

"Young Master Okuma," called a voice near the temple's ash-gray surrounding wall, and Daigoro looked up to see the abbot standing there. "Are you still practicing your swordsmanship?"

"Every day."

"But not up here. Have you come to show me your masterpiece again?"

"No. I was just . . . wandering."

"Ah. Then perhaps your masterpiece has come to see ours. Come inside, won't you?"

Not knowing what else to do, Daigoro lowered himself off his horse, tethered her to a post beside the gate, and followed the abbot into the temple grounds. The old abbot was spry; he walked as quickly as a man half his age. "You presume a great deal," Daigoro said.

"Do I?"

"You do and you know it. You walk too fast for me to keep up. I could cut you down where you stand if I were to take offense to it."

"That you could," said the abbot. "But then, had I slowed to match your pace, you could have cut me down for taking note of your weakness and accommodating it. In truth, it's your prerogative to cut me down whenever you like. Better for me to go on as I'm accustomed, and for you to do the same."

They stood on the flagstones of a walkway surrounding a rock garden of gray pebbles. Large stones stood out among the pebbles like lichen-flecked islands, like turtles surfacing out of a pond. In the center of the garden stood a living contradiction: an enormous dwarf pine. Its gnarled branches twisted like plumes of smoke in a crosswind, and its moss-covered roots crawled through the rock garden like snakes. It was tall by any standards, colossal by the standards of its own species. Daigoro realized he must have seen it countless times before, for its crown would be easily visible even from the Okuma stronghold. Until now he'd mistaken it for an ordinary pine.

"Our masterpiece," the abbot said as Daigoro gaped at the tree. "This temple was built a hundred years ago, in celebration of the three hundredth birthday of this tree. On the day this tree first took root, that sword of yours was already an old man. Today the two old grandfathers finally meet, *neh*?"

Daigoro gave a slow nod. The sunlight hit the uppermost needles just so, shooting a white light through the treetop. The sight of it took his breath away. For the first time he understood how a man could give up everything he had to spend his life in a building like this one. If he were going to pursue enlightenment, this would be the perfect setting.

"Why is this place called Temple of the Twining Vines?" Daigoro asked. "Why not Temple of the Ancient Pine?"

"Everything is entwined by vines, young lord. This temple, this tree—to exist is to be entwined. The vines that entangle you are so heavy I can see the lines they leave on your face. You are too young to wear such lines, Okuma-san. What troubles you?"

Before he knew it, Daigoro was sharing everything. His frustrated desire to obey his father's will, his inability to find the path, his care for his brother, for their mother, for his family's honor: he laid it all bare. "I am so conflicted," he said, "that I no longer have any idea where to go. Maybe I should stay here and send this cursed sword back home with a messenger. Maybe I should shave my topknot and spend the rest of my life in your temple."

The abbot shrugged. "Why don't you?"

"I cannot. My sense of Bushido tells me I cannot. So does the ghost of my father."

"Then don't," said the abbot. "Just walk with me instead. Let the old grandfathers visit for a spell."

Daigoro followed the old abbot along the flagstones leading around the garden of the great tree. They climbed the shaded steps of the main meditation hall, a low, broad building of deep brown wood and red banners. Daigoro removed his gold silk overrobe, laid it on the floorboards of the porch surrounding the temple, then removed Glorious Victory from his belt and nestled it in the silk. He laid his *wakizashi* beside it. It was strange being unarmed in public.

He knew he should have felt vulnerable, but in truth he was strangely liberated.

Daigoro and the abbot ambled around the perimeter of the rock garden. An eastern breeze heavily laden with the smells of copper and steam made Daigoro guess the temple's bathhouse was nearby. "How do you know so much about me?" he asked.

"I was a young samurai myself once." The abbot turned and smiled at him. "Do you think your experience is so unique? All of us have turmoil. We are all entwined."

"But how do you know so much about my sword? The last time I saw you, you identified it as an Inazuma on sight."

"That is a very famous sword," the abbot said with a chuckle. "Those of us who dedicate ourselves to the sword as I once did . . . well, we make it our business to know such things, *neh*? Yours is known as Glorious Victory, I think."

That gave Daigoro pause. "How did you know that?"

"Have you ever dismantled that sword, boy?"

Daigoro didn't need to answer; he could tell the abbot already knew he hadn't. They wandered along the flagstone path, passing between the south end of the meditation hall and a small tea house behind a short fence of bamboo. Soon they reached what Daigoro guessed to be the abbey, judging from the many pairs of sandals arrayed along one wall of the entryway.

The abbot shed his own sandals, left Daigoro there for a moment, and when he returned, he carried a small oblong box of white oak. Daigoro immediately recognized it for what it was: a sword cleaning kit. The two of them returned to the meditation hall, where, as he'd expected, Daigoro found his swords lying just as he'd left them. At last he identified his earlier feeling of liberation. It wasn't that no one here would dare to steal the swords, though of course no one would. It was that no one here *wanted* a sword. Even an Inazuma blade was no temptation at all.

With precise, methodical movements, the abbot began to take apart the *ōdachi*'s grip. As he worked, Daigoro said, "Tell me the truth: is the sword cursed?"

"It is and it isn't. It depends on your perspective."

Looking up, the abbot saw the look of vexation Daigoro knew he'd been unable to wholly conceal. "You think I'm being evasive," said the abbot. "You think all Zen priests speak in riddles. Well, maybe we do, but not this time. Look here."

He'd removed the sword's grip entirely, exposing the metal tang at its heart. There was Inazuma's mark stamped into the steel below the etched name of the sword: Glorious Victory Unsought.

"I don't understand," said Daigoro. "My father didn't know the name of his own sword?"

"I suspect he knew it better than anyone. This sword has been called Glorious Victory for a long time, for that is what it brings—provided the wielder does not seek it himself. Not many understand this, but I think you will. It is a mixed blessing, *neh*, to bring victory only when it is unlooked for. Those who seek their fame through the blade will inevitably lose it, while those who do not seek it will gain it."

Daigoro frowned at the sword. "I still don't understand. Inazuma is said to be the greatest of all sword smiths. Why would he make a weapon so fickle?"

"Is it fickle? As I heard it told, the master's own glory was unsought. Think of it: to be remembered throughout the ages for creating instruments of death. As I heard it, Master Inazuma was sickened by the carnage his blades had wrought. Some were said to be cursed, others were said to be blessed, but in every case his blades were the best at shedding blood. It is not a reputation to help an old man sleep at night. Glorious Victory Unsought was the last sword he made, his final masterpiece. It would reward the best of warriors and punish the worst of them. You tell me if that's fickle."

Daigoro still frowned at the sword. The abbot laid a wrinkled hand on his forearm. "Have you studied the classics of warfare, young master?"

"Of course."

"Then you will know the line from Sun Tzu: 'Those skilled in war subdue the enemy without battle.' Your father had that skill. He fought only when he had to, and then fought to victory no matter the cost. His men knew their lives would never be spent rashly, and so they threw themselves headlong into any battle he chose. Such a man is terrible to face on the field. Against him there can be no victory."

Daigoro looked up, sudden understanding spreading through his mind like water soaked up by a cloth. "You fought against him, didn't you?"

"Fought?" The abbot chuckled. "No, he assured his victory before any of us had the chance to draw swords. We were outflanked, outnumbered, and outfoxed. I could not wear my topknot after that. He showed me what a samurai truly is, and I realized then that I could not both attain that status and fight against him. I could not betray my own lord, so I shaved my head and retired my swords. And now here I sit, giving counsel to the son of the man who bested my master."

He chuckled again, and Daigoro smiled with him. "Quite a reputation, your father," said the abbot. "So renowned in battle, yet such a peacemaker."

"That was why my grandfather made him head of the clan," Daigoro said, as much to himself as to anyone else. "That was why his brothers were bitter toward him. It had nothing to do with the sword."

"I expect so," said the abbot. "Many a skilled warrior would misunderstand that trait, and misunderstand the conquests that come with it. It was because he avoided combat where he could that his victories were so glorious."

"My brother would not like to hear you say it. You make it sound as if our father ran from combat."

"Ran? No. I said *avoided*. *Outmanuevered* might be closer to the truth. He fought when he had to, but only when he had to. That is the way your brother doesn't understand—though he may come to understand it now, given his injuries."

"Hm," Daigoro said. "You've been watching us very closely, haven't you?"

"Of course. When your father defeated my former lord, he became my teacher. I studied him carefully. How could I not study his sons?"

Daigoro could not help but grin. "Some would accuse you of spying," he said. "Some would say you bring warfare into what is supposed to be a house of peace."

The abbot inclined his head. "Peace is like everything else: a relative state. I just go on as I am accustomed. As you do. As your brother does."

The smile fell from Daigoro's face. "It's because I go on as I do that my brother is buried up to his neck. He may die, all because I did not give him the sword."

"He may live, all because you did not give him the sword."

Daigoro's mind lurched, then stopped. He hadn't thought of it that way. Could the sword have denied Ichirō victory just because he was seeking it? If so, how had their father survived so many battles? How could he fight without wanting to win?

He could not. It was impossible, at least for one who was not suicidal. To fight was to fight for survival. Daigoro was sure of it. But now, looking at the serene face of the abbot, he realized he'd asked the wrong question. It was not how to fight without wanting to win, but how to win without wanting to fight.

"Tell me what I must do," he said. "Help me find the path."

"No one can lead you to it," said the abbot. "Bushido is a path every warrior must find for himself. But I can tell you what to do with this sword. Remember what I told you before: your problem is the best kind of problem, because it contains its own solution. Go back to your Sun Tzu: 'All warfare is based on deception.' Find that passage; study what else he says there. You're a bright lad; the answer will not escape you."

Daigoro watched in silence as the abbot's sure fingers reconstructed Glorious Victory Unsought. He could neither speak nor move; he was totally engrossed in committing what the old man had said to memory. The *ōdachi* was back in its scabbard, whole and ready for battle, by the time Daigoro could utter words again.

"I think House Okuma would do well to call a warrior like you one of its own," he told the abbot. "I have half a mind to invite you back to the compound with me."

"I would respectfully decline," the abbot said with a bow. "It's too late for me; this old head of mine can't grow enough hair to make a topknot anymore."

Daigoro smiled. "Maybe not. All the same, in times of trial you'd be a good man to have."

The two of them walked past the great dwarf pine toward the temple gate, this time at Daigoro's pace. "This old tree has survived many an earthquake and weathered many a storm," the abbot said. "That sword of yours has too. It's all any of us can do."

"I suppose it is."

Daigoro bowed to him, thanked him, and took his leave.

# 48

"All warfare is based on deception," the book read. Daigoro's copy of the *Sun Tzu* was tattered along the edges. Like all samurai his age, he'd read it over a hundred times, committed whole chapters to memory, discussed it and the other classics innumerable times with his father and other martial instructors. The book was so worn that the edges of its wooden covers were soft in Daigoro's hands. He read on.

Even before he'd finished the page, he understood the old abbot's advice. At last he had a strategy. At last he could put Glorious Victory Unsought to good use.

Three months after the duel with Ōda Yoshitomo, Yagyū and his healers dug Ichirō out of the pit. His body had all but wasted away, and he stank worse than a corpse, worse than an outhouse. The stink alone was enough to earn Daigoro's pity; even if Ichirō were to reach his hundredth birthday, he would never outlive the shame of it. Not even the *eta* smelled so bad. Daigoro doubted even the southern barbarians could stink so, and the stories he'd heard of them almost made him retch.

It was another week before Ichirō could walk on his own under the red leaves of the maples in the compound, another month before he resumed daily sword practice. His skill with the bow, the healers said, would never return to him, for he could not turn his head far enough to sight down his left arm. But when he picked up his sword again, the men were astonished: it was as if he'd never been hurt. He trained with an intensity Daigoro associated with typhoons, with cornered animals. Ichirō had lost a good deal of stamina, but none of his speed and precision.

The Okuma samurai marveled at him, but Daigoro had anticipated as much. Every day Ichirō had been imprisoned in the rice, he had relived his last duel in his mind. Daigoro expected no less of him. He was samurai, after all; dedication ran through his veins. While he was healing in the rice, the itching had brought him to the brink of madness, but every time he returned from the brink, he meditated on combat.

"I've learned something of Ōda Yoshitomo," Daigoro told his brother after a practice session. Ichirō still eyed the Inazuma blade, but said nothing about it. "He's won over forty duels," Daigoro continued. "Most of them with steel blades, I hear."

Ichirō was panting, but he stopped upon hearing Daigoro's words. He sat next to Daigoro on the veranda, his toes brushing the sand, Daigoro's dangling in the air. "From whom?"

"I rode into Shimoda last week," said Daigoro. "A meeting with the other clans—you weren't riding yet. I overheard a pair of messengers eating on the roadside. One of them said Ōda is famous for what he calls his 'Hawk and Phoenix' style. They said he uses a trademark sidestepping cut—he calls it his 'Diving Hawk' cut. It seems you're the only one who ever survived it."

"What an honor," Ichirō grumbled.

"I think it is. Ōda claims to have killed horses with it. These messengers spoke of a Rising Phoenix and a Diving Hawk, and they said Ōda wins nearly all of his duels with his Diving Hawk."

"He won against me with it too."

"Yes," Daigoro said, "but don't you see? You survived the cut that fells horses. You survived the cut that's slain some three dozen men. What does that say of you?"

Ichirō nodded at that, and the grim hold on his face softened so that he almost smiled. Standing, he said, "Thank you, little brother. We Okumas are forged from fine steel, *neh*? And not just our swords."

Daigoro grinned at him as he walked slowly across the courtyard under the setting sun. *We Okumas*, he'd said. *We.*

# 49

A month later, snow was thick on the ground and Daigoro and Ichirō were finishing dinner in a mountainside inn near the Ashigara checkpoint. Ichirō had come as head of the clan, to hear a request for troops from another of General Toyotomi's emissaries. He'd invited Daigoro along for the company, and despite the wind and the chill, Daigoro had been more than happy to oblige him.

"Open this place up," Ichirō bade the serving girl. "That wall there—open it. Let us see the garden."

The serving girl obliged him immediately, despite the irregularity of his request. As she slid the shoji aside, a cold draft flowed over the low table; the steam off the rice took on a whiter, thicker hue.

"Think of it," Ichirō said. "Not fifty paces beyond this table, the Tokaidō Road is a mire of brown, trampled slush. Yet here, just outside our room, the snow on the rocks is pristine and white. The *sake* is warm in my belly, yet barely fifty paces before me, people are miserable, trudging through the cold."

Broad white flakes fell like cherry blossoms in spring, thickening the blanket on the rock garden outside. Steam rose from the hot spring pond in the garden, moistening the smell of the winter wind. The pond would never freeze, nor even grow cold. Beyond the garden wall, beyond the snow-laden branches of the spruce trees, Daigoro could hear the last of the evening travelers making their way down the Tokaidō. "It is a good night to be indoors," he said.

"It is a good night to be an Okuma."

A timid knock came at the hallway door behind them, which then slid open. The owner of the inn knelt beside it, his head bowed low enough for his chin to touch the brown kimono covering his chest. At first Daigoro thought the man had come to ask them to close off the cold wind. If he had, Daigoro would have been half-impressed, half-offended, by the impudence of the request. But instead the inn owner said, "A visitor for you, my lords."

"Who?" asked Ichirō.

"A master Ōda Yoshitomo. Begging your pardon eternally, my lords. He was most insistent."

Without a word, Ōda stepped into the room and knelt beside the doorway. He slid the door shut without dismissing the owner, and his bow to Ichirō and Daigoro was slight. "I am told you bested Katsushima Goemon," he said.

"That is a fact," said Ichirō.

"I fought Katsushima to a draw three years ago. I have trouble believing you beat him."

Daigoro could see Ichirō stiffen, but he was duly impressed by his brother's self-control. His brush with death had changed him.

"Three years is a long time," said Ichirō. "Perhaps Katsushima has grown slower with age."

"He is not an old man. I doubt it."

"Have some tea," said Daigoro. "Or *sake*, if you'd prefer."

"I am also told," said Ōda, "that you boast to be the only man who's survived my Diving Hawk."

Tension mounted in Ichirō's neck and shoulders, accumulating there as swiftly as the snow in the garden. Daigoro could see it, and he knew Ōda could too. But Ichirō's voice remained calm, if a bit cold. "It is a fact that I survived it," he said, "and as for boasting, that is something I try to avoid now."

"But you've spoken of it."

"People have spoken of it. I may have been one of them."

The muscles in Ōda's jaws flexed. "I will not have it. Especially not from someone who was so rude to me."

"You're one to talk of rudeness," said Daigoro. He struggled to get to his feet, to put himself between the other two, but the weakness of his right leg and the cramped quarters behind the table conspired to deny him. "You came in here without invitation," he went on, "and all you've done is hurl insults and insinuations." He touched Ichirō's shoulder. "Don't listen to him. This is only your karma, brother. Let it run its course."

"Yes, karma," said Ōda. "Karma to be insulted after insulting me. Karma to be sliced up like a huntsman's deer after carelessly slicing up those you duel. How is your neck feeling, Okuma? Strong enough to keep your head attached, I see, but for how long?"

Ichirō jumped to his feet, shrugging off Daigoro's restraining hand. Before he could say anything, Daigoro said, "Wait, Ichirō! He cannot challenge you to a duel—not and keep his honor, anyway. He won your last match; to call you out again would bring him total disgrace."

"Someone should cut out his flapping tongue," Ichirō said, his eyes fixed on Ōda instead of his brother.

"Yes," said Daigoro, "someone should, but let it not be you. You're walking a different path now; it's too soon to go back to your old one."

Ōda snorted. "That's right. Listen to your little brother—your little, crippled runt of a brother."

"Enough!" Ichirō bellowed. "I challenge you *now*, you son of a whore! We duel with steel, in the middle of the Tokaidō! When I'm finished with you, I'll send your arms east and your legs west, so everyone from Edo to Osaka can see what becomes of someone who speaks ill of an Okuma! Daigoro, give me the sword!"

"Brother, I can't—"

*"The sword!"* Ichirō stepped over Daigoro, whose traitorous right knee fought his every effort to stand up. Fuming, Ichirō picked their father's sword up from the floor beside his brother and strode right into the snowy garden. Ōda followed him, both men in stocking feet, heedless of the cold and the wet.

Daigoro yanked his leg straight, pushed himself to his feet, and rushed for the door. He paused to don his wooden sandals only because he had to: his feeble right foot might betray him if he stepped on a rock hidden beneath the snow, and a sandal would mitigate that risk. He hurried to the road as quickly as he could manage, all too conscious of the fact that the weight of Glorious Victory Unsought was not on his hip to slow him down.

By the time he reached the Tokaidō, a sizable crowd had gathered around Ichirō and Ōda. Wide snow-covered hats marked some as travelers; others, lightly dressed, stood in the doorways of nearby inns and eateries. Daigoro fought his way to the front of the crowd, which had cleared a wide egg-shaped arena around the two duelists.

The first exchange could easily have been Ichirō's last, had he not already seen Ōda's Diving Hawk. Ōda was fast, and there was scarcely enough moonlight to see by. But Ichirō parried the blow expertly, returning with a slash that cut Ōda's sleeve but not his arm. Daigoro wondered at that: the longer reach of the Inazuma should have drawn blood on that cut. But then he saw that Ichirō's feet were splayed too wide; the sword had unbalanced him, leaving him just barely out of range.

The next clash told much the same tale. Ichirō defended against a blindingly fast attack, then lost his balance just before cutting his opponent down.

And then came the Diving Hawk again. Ōda stabbed, sidestepped, chopped for Ichirō's neck. Ichirō anticipated the chop to the neck and parried as he did before. Ōda continued his swing, suddenly dropping to one knee. The fall surprised Ichirō, but only for an instant; then he moved in for the kill.

Ōda's sword ran him through from under the rib cage. It pierced the diaphragm first, then heart and lung, then emerged behind the shoulder blade. Bloodied steel glistened in the dim moonlight. Without so much as a cry of pain, Ichirō was dead.

The Inazuma blade fell with a dull thump in the slush. "That," Ōda said over the corpse, "was the Rising Phoenix." His voice carried strangely. At first Daigoro thought the night had grown unnaturally silent. Then he realized Ōda was speaking loudly enough to be heard by everyone in the crowd. "If ever I fail to kill with the Diving Hawk," Ōda said, "the Rising Phoenix claims the prey."

He's trying to restore his reputation, Daigoro thought. He's glad Ichirō fought him so publicly.

After a long moment, Ōda rose from his crouched position and lowered Ichirō's body to the ground. It was no small effort for him to reclaim his *katana*, for the corpse's innards seemed to be gripping the blade with inhuman strength. As Ōda struggled, Daigoro limped forward and bent to take up Glorious Victory Unsought.

"I challenge you, Ōda Yoshitomo." Daigoro tightened his fingers around the Inazuma's corded grip, still warm from his brother's hands.

Ōda looked up, surprise in his eyes but a smile on his lips. "You? You're nothing but a cub. You want to face *me*?"

"Want to? No. But you stand there gloating over the body of my fallen brother. You insult him, and thus you insult my family. What choice have you left me?"

Ōda looked at Daigoro's sword, then at his own, which was still stuck in Ichirō's body. "That sword's almost as tall as you are. Why don't you go home, little cub? Come back when you're older."

Daigoro stood his ground. "I won't fight you unarmed," he said.

"Then you're a fool. It won't go well for you if you let me retrieve my sword. You'd do better to kill me now."

Daigoro took two shuffling steps backward. "If you die tonight, at least you'll have a sword in your hands. Pick it up."

Ōda eyed Daigoro, then resumed his grip on his weapon. At last he broke the vacuum of the body and withdrew the bloody sword; foul steam rose from the wound and the blade.

Daigoro stepped into the middle of the road; the crowd widened around him. Ōda faced him, three or four paces distant.

"You shouldn't have begun this, boy."

"I didn't. My brother began it. You worsened it. I only walk the path already laid out for me."

Daigoro could feel the veins in his neck pumping hard. His skin was cold, more from the thrill of adrenaline than from the wintry air. As he and Ōda circled, he drew nearer to his brother's corpse. Ichirō's face had gone slack, now resembling the serenity their father's face had worn in death. Ah, Ichirō, he thought; you walked your own path too long to avoid its ending.

*All warfare is based on deception.* The phrase returned to Daigoro's mind as he limped to his right, taking two steps for Ōda's one. He was a canny fighter, Ōda; undoubtedly he knew the line from Sun Tzu as well. He'd been attempting to deceive Daigoro from the moment he'd heard Daigoro's challenge. For all his bravado, Ōda was scared, and Daigoro knew it. Ōda had two killing moves, his Hawk and his Phoenix, and Daigoro had seen them both. The Diving Hawk hadn't worked on Ichirō a second time; once was enough to know the trick of it. The Rising Phoenix would be no different. Ōda blustered and threatened because his best secrets were laid bare. He had relied on them too long, and without them he had nothing.

So Daigoro acted as if he was still scared of them. He breathed faster and shallower than he needed to. He let his shoulders slacken, admitted a subtle quake in his wrists. The best tactic was to point his sword at the enemy's throat, to prevent a sudden lunge; Daigoro let his long blade aim at Ōda's thigh.

All who looked upon him saw an undersized, crippled boy whose sword was too heavy for him. When Ōda made his first thrust, Daigoro parried at the hands.

The Inazuma blade took Ōda's right hand off at the wrist. Daigoro allowed the weight of the sword to carry him forward. Ōda stumbled past him, bleeding terribly. He whirled back around with a wild left-handed slash.

Daigoro parried; steel clashed. Ōda's sword passed just in front of Daigoro's nose. Daigoro's passed through Ōda's left collarbone.

Ōda dropped his weapon, his left arm hanging like a wet cloth. "Kneel," Daigoro said. "Quickly. You can no longer commit seppuku. Let me give you the honor of a proper beheading."

"How?" murmured Ōda. His face had gone as pale as the snow on the rooftops, and his bleeding was already slowing. "How could I lose to you?"

"'All warfare is based on deception,'" Daigoro said. He stepped behind Ōda, keeping him at sword's length. "'When capable, feign incapacity; when active, inactivity. When near, make it appear that you are far away; when far away, that you are near. Pretend inferiority and encourage his arrogance.' You know the passage?"

Ōda sunk to his knees. "I know it."

His head lolled heavily; Daigoro wondered whether he'd

knelt of his own volition or whether his body no longer had enough blood to supply the muscles of his legs. "It was your arrogance that killed you," Daigoro told him, quietly enough that only Ōda could hear. "I'm sorry to say the same is true of my brother. If either of you had had more self-control, we would have seen no bloodshed tonight. Now two braggarts will die here, all for want of the right path."

Daigoro's cut was neat and quick. Ōda's head fell in his lap.

# 50

Daigoro hired a palanquin to carry Ichirō's body home. Encumbered as they were by the snow, the palanquin bearers took three days to reach Shimoda, but mercifully the weather remained cold and the body did not ripen.

As the procession neared the Okuma compound, armored companies fell in behind as honor guards. The Nagatomos and Ushidas, the Soras and Inoues, all of them committed at least a dozen samurai to the growing file. At last, as Daigoro marched into Shimoda, the Yasudas contributed fifty men and twenty horses under green banners. Yasuda Jinbei rode among them, just as the lords of all the other houses rode at the heads of their own columns. Lord Yasuda had even dispatched a rider to summon more Okuma troops, so that Ichirō's own family would not be outdone by any of the attending clans. In all, some two hundred samurai and fifty cavalry accompanied Ichirō to the home of his birth.

The funeral was scheduled to take place the morning after Daigoro and the body reached the compound. A carrier pigeon from the Yasudas delivered the news in advance, so the Okuma fiefdom had fully prepared to receive its fallen son. As he rode through the front gate, Daigoro was met by the sight of a funeral pyre, and in that moment he felt something inside him release its grip on his grief. The stacked wood held the promise of finality, and the sight of it obliterated Daigoro's last attachment to his brother. During three days of riding he had been left more or less to himself, and in all that time he could not cry. Now, in the presence of his family and all its allies, the tears forced themselves upon him, and it was all he could do to maintain his composure long enough to limp into his quarters and slide the door shut.

He cried not just for Ichirō but for their father. That grief had waited a long, long time, and after being held back for so long, it burst from him like floodwaters through a collapsing dam. When at last he composed himself, Daigoro reflected on the nature of attachment. Detaching from his brother was not difficult; he'd been disentangling himself from Ichiro's problems for many months before Oda cut him down. Freeing himself from the vines his father had cast on him was a different matter. Ichiro's injury—and the trouble with the duels that had precipitated it—had distracted Daigoro from any concerted effort to come to grips with the loss of his father. But in dealing with Ichirō, Daigoro found he'd learned something about attachment and detachment. He had learned how to love and respect his family without becoming entangled, and now, grieving for his brother, he was finally able to grieve for his father.

As it happened, the morning of the funeral was also the morning of Daigoro's sixteenth birthday. In ordinary circumstances his coming-of-age would have warranted an elaborate celebration, but the funeral did not allow it. Even so, Ichirō's funeral amounted to a confirmation of Daigoro's coming-of-age, for now Daigoro was the only son left to lead the family. Daigoro had become the undisputed head of the Okuma clan, and thus, at all of sixteen years of age, the most powerful daimyo on the Izu peninsula.

Daigoro watched as Ichirō's body was committed to the flames. He saw the snow shrink away from the terrible heat of the pyre, watched the dark gray pillar billow up past the rooftops toward the white clouds. A sudden breeze cut the pillar in two, giving Daigoro a glimpse of a familiar figure he had not expected to see.

Katsushima Goemon still wore large, bushy sideburns, though today he did not have his sleeves and pant legs tied back for combat. Daigoro remembered him well—not six months had passed since Ichirō had bested him—and he and Katsushima circled the blistering heat of the funeral pyre to greet each other.

"I hope my attendance does not offend you," Katsushima said. "Your brother was a ferocious fighter, Okuma-sama. He deserves to be remembered for that."

"He will be, though I fear his ferocity may be the only thing he is remembered for."

"No. He will be remembered for his brother as well. The stories on the road say you stood over his body and defended him like a bear. The Bear Cub of Izu—that's what they call you now."

The wind off the pyre was hot enough to redden both of their faces. Daigoro feared his face would have flushed anyway. "I thank you for coming, Katsushima-san. I hope you will do us the honor of staying as our guest tonight."

"And I hope you will do the honor of facing me in a duel, Okuma-sama."

Daigoro was taken aback. "How can I face you, Katsushima-san? You are close to thrice my age, unless I miss my guess. What little wisdom I've managed to accumulate regarding swordsmanship cannot hope to rival yours."

Katsushima bowed. Snowflakes gathered in his bushy hair, highlighting the white and graying the black. "You have the advantage of youth. The years have slowed me."

"Even slowed, I daresay you outstrip me at my fastest. You must have walked a hundred *ri* to get here. It's an effort for me to limp from this courtyard to my own bed."

"In truth I borrowed a horse to come today." Katsushima allowed himself a small, embarrassed smile. "I dared not come late."

"Then I shall give you what you ask," said Daigoro, "but only on the condition that you will stay the night and share a meal or two. I want to discuss swordsmanship with you, and Bushido as well."

"I accept," said Katsushima. "I expect we have much to learn from each other."

It was as sincere a compliment as an older man could ever pay a boy of sixteen. In that moment Daigoro knew their duel would be but a formality, a conversation conducted with blades instead of words. Daigoro's bow to Katsushima was deeper than it should have been—the only way he could repay a compliment so profound. As they parted company, Daigoro was thankful for the gift Katsu-shima had given him: not just the compliment but the brief moment's respite from grief and pain.

With startling speed the body burned to nothing. Dai-goro watched side by side with his mother, her shoulder trembling under his hand as she wept. He could not be seen to cry in front of his bannermen and their samurai, so he squeezed her shoulder and meditated on impermanence. It seemed impossible that someone so vibrantly alive as Ichirō could simply cease to exist, but at the same time it seemed that in the blink of an eye there burned wood and nothing else.

When it was done, Ichirō's ashes were committed in the shrine built to honor their father a few short months before. Leaving the shrine, Daigoro saw Yasuda Jinbei waiting for him, his thin topknot the same color as the snow in the courtyard.

"Lord Yasuda," he said, bowing to the small man, "I noticed your grandnephew Eijun among your bodyguard. He honors my brother by coming."

"He honors you, Ōkuma-dono."

"He honors us both—as do you, Yasuda-san. Your family does a noble thing in forgiving my brother's rudeness in his duel with Eijun-san. I thank you for it."

Yasuda bowed his head. "There is nothing more to forgive, my lord. If I may say so, I fear your brother has paid the price for his rudeness. I do not ordinarily listen to rumormongers, but I have heard that his behavior in his duel with young Eijun was not unique."

"As direct as ever, Yasuda-san," Daigoro said.

"An old man cannot afford to waste time getting to the point." Yasuda bowed. "I have also heard that you fought with bravery and cunning to defend your family's honor. They say your father's skill lives on in you."

"I doubt it. He fought in many wars; I have only the one duel to my name."

"I had in mind his skill as a diplomat as well as his skill with the sword. If I may ask, what became of the one you killed, my lord?"

"I called for him to be cremated, and for his remains to be returned to House Ōda. I also ordered a small portion of his ashes to remain at the Ashigara checkpoint, to be interred where he fell. Tomorrow some of Ichirō's ashes will be sent there as well, to be laid to rest in the same grave."

Yasuda smiled. "A gesture worthy of your father," he said.

"It is more than a gesture. I had no time to compose a death poem for Ōda, and so he and my brother will have to share one. I will have it etched on the stupa marking where they lie."

"May I trouble you for the poem, my lord?"

Daigoro felt his cheeks warm. He'd spent more time than most as a scholar—his leg had never left him much choice—but even so he'd never considered himself a poet. Nevertheless, he withdrew the folded white rectangle from his overrobe and handed it to Lord Yasuda. It read,

> *Stones cannot climb up;*
> *A boar will never back down.*
> *Some can only fall.*

"I'm afraid I'm not much of a writer," said Daigoro.

Yasuda bowed deeply. "On the contrary, my lord. A testament to the folly of pride befits both men—yet as you've put it, they also have their merits. Boars are fearsome; stones are hard. You do them both honor, Okuma-dono."

Daigoro and Yasuda walked slowly across the courtyard, snow crunching under their feet. They walked in silence, away from the main hall where the other guests had gathered. Under the eaves of a storehouse, the two men, both lords of their houses, watched the snow gathering on the rooftops.

# BOOK SEVEN

## HEISEI ERA, THE YEAR 22

### (2010 CE)

On her way out of the station Mariko passed an orange-haired boy in snow-bunny boots passing out packets of tissues to everyone who passed him by, an ad for Mitsui Sumitomo Bank slipped into each plastic-wrapped packet. Mariko took one of the packets herself as she passed, not because she needed it but because she was cruising on autopilot, lost in thought.

*Kenjutsu* practice promised to be good for her tonight. She needed to take her mind off the rest of her life, every aspect of which was marred by failure. Picking up a sword was sure to bring her even more failures, but somehow those seemed small and transitory compared to everything else. There was still no sign of Saori, still no sign of Fuchida, still no hope of her calming her mother, still no hope that Ko would be anything other than an insufferable prick.

Mariko slipped through the shoppers milling about in front of all the little shops lining the sidewalk: booksellers, greengrocers, smartphone dealers, a rice shop, a punk used clothing store. Smells of fish and salt water assaulted her as she passed a little fishmonger's tank of live crabs. Red snapper were laid out like playing cards, gaping at her from their beds of crushed ice, their glossy eyes lifeless. The crabs skittered at the smooth glass panes in their black armor, trying to climb the walls and free themselves from their prison. Even in their tiny crustacean minds, surely they could see it was hopeless. Mariko sympathized. Hopelessness was all too familiar a feeling.

She wondered where Saori was, and whether she was sober, and why she herself would harbor even one second of hope that Saori might be sober during one of her disappearances. She wondered whether Fuchida felt the need to kill like Saori felt the need to use. Perversely, Mariko understood Fuchida's behavior better than Saori's. Getting mad enough to kill someone, or greedy enough, or jealous enough, or vengeful enough—that wasn't hard to imagine. Knowing a thing was poisonous, more poisonous to you than to most other people, and then needing to go find that thing and smoke it or snort it or inject it—that was beyond Mariko's ken.

But all such thoughts vanished once she got the huge Inazuma blade in her hands. All her hopelessness and self-doubt disappeared too. There was no room for them. Yamada faced her with a meter-long razor blade; she could not afford a moment's inattention.

Tonight's exercise was especially dangerous—a hell of a lot more dangerous than the TMPD's aikido course, and people broke wrists and elbows in there all the time. "Sensei," she said, nervously shifting her grip on her weapon, "are you sure we should be doing this?"

"Nothing sharpens the mind like live steel."

"I know, but . . . didn't you tell me once that only experts train with real swords? I'd feel a lot safer using one of those wooden *bokken* you told me about."

He clucked his tongue at her. "The purpose of the *bokken* is to simulate live steel. Nothing can simulate Glorious Victory Unsought. Never forget: this is a sword unlike any other. The only way to learn to fight with it is to train with it."

Mariko could appreciate that. The same went for the aikido and judo she'd learned at academy: practice was all fine and good, but the only way to know it worked was to do it for real. But risking a broken wrist was one thing; with Yamada's exercises she felt like she was risking death.

They started by exchanging overhead strikes, stopping each blow a hand's breadth from the other's scalp. Glorious Victory Unsought was too heavy for Mariko, so she pulled her strikes early, but more than once she felt Yamada's blade part her hair, stopping just millimeters from her skin.

This was only the warm-up, an attack drill to prepare her for learning a defense against it. Yamada had yet to teach her to block or sidestep; for him, defense meant chopping the opponent's hands off before he could land a blow. They practiced just that. One of them would strike to the head; the other would anticipate the blow and counter to the wrists. As before, she tried to stop her counterstrikes a good ten or fifteen centimeters away from her target, but still, Mariko found the exercise terrifying—terrifying, yet thrilling too. Mariko knew she was too easily bored—it was a major reason driving her to join the TMPD—but this time she wondered whether there was such a thing as too much excitement.

They started slow, but soon Yamada pushed her to attack and defend at close to full speed. She wondered how his eyes could find her. It was dark, and not much moonlight reached his backyard. If his accuracy was even slightly off, he would chop off both her hands, or else cleave her skull right down the middle. What must it be like, she thought, to have practiced something ten thousand times? That was the number Yamada used whenever Mariko complained of something being too hard: "Do it ten thousand times and it will not seem difficult." The Americans had a saying for someone like Yamada, someone whose skill had attained such a peak: *He could do it blindfolded.* In Yamada's case that might literally have been true. But the Japanese had a saying too: *Even monkeys fall from trees.*

Mariko found the exercises taxed her concentration every bit as much as they taxed her muscles. After two hours of drilling, her body and her mind were equally exhausted. She had enough energy to sheathe her weapon and lay it down respectfully; then she collapsed on the lawn. "That was a good one, Sensei."

"Yes. Your *shomen* strikes are coming along nicely."

He sat on his bench and Mariko pushed herself up to her knees. She found kneeling easiest on her ribs, whose pain had subsided to a persistent dull ache. She'd finally gotten around to getting X-rays the day before, and they showed two hairline fractures. The hospital had given her a rib brace to wear, but she found it interfered with her sword work, so it was sitting in the house rolled up next to her purse. So, ignoring that nagging ache in her side, Mariko cleaned flecks of grass from her weapon just as Yamada had showed her, then used the wrist stretches he'd taught her. A satisfying sort of pain ran in lines from palm to elbow.

"Will you tell me about Glorious Victory Unsought?"

"Hm. I was wondering when you would ask about that again."

"Well?"

Yamada set aside his own sword, then picked up Mariko's. "This is Master Inazuma's last weapon. His greatest, we are told. It is said that by the end he wished he had become a potter of teacups, not a sword smith. He could not bear the thought that his handiwork had ended so many lives. And yet he lived in an age when the world was carved into being by the sword. Battle was necessary, do you see? It was not like today, when average men and women can expect to go their whole lives without seeing warfare. You have seen violence, Oshiro-san, but you have not seen war. Believe me when I tell you your generation is the better for it."

His voice carried a somber note she had not heard from him before. His eyes seemed to look through her and into the past itself, and they were saddened by what they saw there.

Obviously he was old enough to have served in the Second World War. What had he done there? Mariko couldn't believe she'd never asked him. She thought of him as a friend now, a mentor, even a grandfather. She valued their training time so much that they never got around to talking about personal things, and of course personal talk was something Mariko was all too ready to avoid anyway, but with Yamada she felt safe to lower her guard. She resolved to take him to dinner one of these nights, maybe as soon as his case was over, so they could share the things that granddaughters and grandfathers shared.

Yamada was silent for a long moment before he continued. "Master Inazuma understood the inevitability of warfare, but he had no love of it. This blade was forged out of that contradiction. It brings glory and victory, yes, but only to the warrior who does not seek them. How many braggarts and warmongers have tried to carve out a place for themselves in history with this sword? We can never know. Every last one of them was laid low, betrayed by his own weapon."

"Just like Fuchida's Beautiful Singer," Mariko mused.

"Not *just* like it. Beautiful Singer is a jealous sword. She allows her wielder no love apart from her, and she will ruin any man who pretends to own her. Glorious Victory only threatens those who love combat more than peace."

Mariko frowned at that. She wasn't sure she was innocent on that count herself. Why choose police work if she wanted a life of peace? Why choose police work in Japan, knowing full well how much easier life was for female officers back in the States? And why the TMPD, the most elite department in the country, with the stiffest competition? Mariko had always told herself she'd done it to make her father proud, but there was an easier answer to all the questions: she was spoiling for a fight, plain and simple, and she always sought out the best place to get into one.

In that way she wasn't so different from Saori. Self-abuse took many forms. Joining the TMPD wasn't like smoking crystal meth, but both had their risks, and the Oshiro girls had each picked their poison.

Thoughts of poison and of Saori made a sudden connection with Fuchida in her mind. Saori poisoned herself knowing it was bad for her. Wasn't Fuchida doing the same thing?

"Sensei, did you ever tell Fuchida your stories about the swords?"

"Of course. He was my protégé."

"Does he believe in cursed swords?"

Yamada snorted. "Still such disdain, Inspector? You say it as if we were talking about ghosts or *kappa* or some such. Believing in the curse of Beautiful Singer requires no more faith than believing in stars. I cannot see them anymore, but there is more than enough written of them to make me a believer."

"It's not that I don't believe you, Sensei. . . ." Mariko said it to placate him, but as soon as she said it, she realized it was true: she was coming to believe in things she never thought she'd have a moment's patience for. But coming to grips with that was going to have to wait; for the moment, she was on to something with the Fuchida case. "What I want to know is, if he believes in the curse, why in the world would he want *two* Inazumas?"

A wry grin stretched across Yamada's lips. "Well, now. That is a good question. For myself, I have no doubt that Fuchida-san believes he can overcome the will of the swords. Indeed, he has proved his ability to do so. Beautiful Singer has destroyed countless families, yet Fuchida-san has owned her for twenty years. She has not destroyed him yet."

"But isn't he tempting fate by trying to get a second Inazuma?"

"Understand two things, Inspector. First, Glorious Victory Unsought is not cursed as such. It only harms those who seek glory. Second, in Fuchida-san we are dealing with a man of supreme self-control. What other sort of man tattoos his lips to test his pain tolerance? If he can bend even Beautiful Singer to his will, why should he not believe that Glorious Victory will bring him exactly what its name suggests?"

Mariko wasn't convinced. The Fuchida she knew was careful. His most recent killings were reckless, but still he eluded capture—hell, eluded so much as a sighting—and otherwise his track record described a man who accepted only calculated risks. And the risk posed by a second Inazuma was not easily calculated. How could it be? These were matters of magic, not of reason. Mariko would not let herself believe in magic per se, but she didn't need to; all that mattered was that Fuchida believed. And given that belief, why would he want a second blade?

The answer sprang out: he didn't. Not to keep, anyway. He intended to sell it, or trade it, or do something with it, anyhow. At last she had something to hope for. She no longer needed Fuchida to walk into her stakeout. As careful as he was, he'd never given her much hope in that. But she didn't need him anymore. She just needed to find his business partner.

"Sensei, please excuse me." She went in the house to find her purse and in it her cell phone. She had her team's hotline on speed dial, third only to her mom and her sister. "It's Oshiro," she said into the sweat-slicked phone. "I need you to research medieval swords. Expensive ones—nothing less than a hundred million yen. Find out who's got them and who's selling them. Then contact those people. Find out who's buying, who's bidding, who's inquiring but not buying. I need a list of all the players in the market."

The deputy on the other end was named Ibe. He was one of the precinct's newest recruits. Lieutenant Ko had outfitted her surveillance team fully, but not with his best.

"A hundred million?" said Ibe. "I wouldn't even know where to start."

"Auction houses. High-end antique dealers. Get on the web, figure out where the collectors are talking, get some names. See what other sites they're visiting. Don't limit this to Japan either; our buyer could be international."

Ibe protested again, but Mariko cut him off. "I'm going to put you on with a Dr. Yamada Yasuo," she said, jogging toward the open back door and talking fast. "Yeah, he's the house we're staking out. He's going to give you a list of names to start with. Don't take no for an answer, Ibe. Here's Dr. Yamada."

Yamada's memory was nearly photographic, encyclopedic in detail. Mariko was not surprised. A man had to have a good head for facts to write all those books. Ibe must have been writing furiously to record all the names—not just the names of the sword collectors themselves but also which sword smiths they favored, the names of the individual weapons, and the auction houses or galleries where they were stored. Yamada didn't know phone numbers, but his memory for addresses was uncanny. Not for the first time, Mariko's mind conjured the image of an island in the flow of time: the river of years flowing past Yamada yet unable to move him. He was a relic, the last gentleman warrior of ancient days.

However, he wasn't the only one with a good head for details. Mariko noticed there was one sword Yamada did not speak to Ibe about, and when their call was over, she asked him about it. "What about the third Inazuma? You said there were three: Beautiful Singer, Glorious Victory Unsought, and the one connected to those lone standing houses in the wakes of tsunamis and earthquakes. What was it called?"

Yamada shook his head, his face suddenly impassive. "Tiger on the Mountain."

"Right. If you don't tell Ibe who has it, it'll be harder to find out who might be trying to buy it."

"No one can buy that sword. Few even know it exists. Believe me, there are no leads there."

"I'd rather be the judge of that."

"I imagine so. It must remain out of reach—yours and everyone else's, save the owner and his family." Mariko frowned. She had heard this tone from him before. He'd probably get around to telling her the truth sooner or later, just as he'd done with everything he'd told her about Fuchida. Until then, however, he was going to clam up, and Mariko wasn't in the mood to wait. "Sensei, this is the first genuine lead I've had on this case. I need to pin down everything I can on the Inazumas and I need to do it right now. You of all people know what Fuchida's capable of if we sit back and wait."

"I do. But I also know there is no connection between Fuchida and the Tiger on the Mountain. You'd do better to simply put it out of your mind."

Mariko sighed. He was telling the truth—or most of it, anyway. She was certain he knew more, but equally certain that he wouldn't be sharing any of it no matter how hard she pushed him. A wry laugh escaped her mouth. "All right, I surrender. But you really would make my life a hell of a lot easier if you'd just tell me what you know."

Yamada cleared his throat, and with no attempt at subtlety he changed the subject. "Inspector, perhaps you would do me the honor of joining me tomorrow evening. How do you feel about Dvořák?"

Mariko pulled her black-and-white-striped blouse over her head. It stuck to her sweaty undershirt and made her feel wholly unsuited to talking about classical music. "Dvořák," she said. "Good, I guess."

"Dvořák is not one to guess about. Now you really must come with me. My wife and I, we were members of the symphony for the longest time. They still mail me tickets for two, even after all these years."

Yamada seemed softer for a moment, utterly harmless despite the long *katana* hanging from his rag doll right arm. This was the first Mariko had heard of his wife. She wondered what her name was, how they'd met, how long ago she'd passed. Were there children? Yamada had never mentioned any. Surely he would have by now. Realization dawned on Mariko's mind: she knew so little about this man. He knew about Saori, about Ko, and all she knew of Yamada was that he took his gardening as seriously as he took his swordsmanship.

No, she thought. That wasn't true. She knew a great deal about him personally. He was as prolific a writer as she was ever likely to meet. As voracious a reader as he was a writer. An anchor chain making sure the present never detached from the past. His home was an extension of himself, an island in the river of time, untouched by the last sixty years of progress. He appreciated the way a chrysanthemum blended its perfume with that of green tea. He was strong for his age, and spry, and never in his life had he tired easily. Mariko knew a good deal about him; what she didn't know, what she'd only first glimpsed here in the garden tonight, was his past.

"Dvořák," she said. "Tomorrow night?"

"Seven o'clock. Suntory Hall. Do you know where it is? Do young people still go there anymore?"

"I can find it."

Yamada smiled. "You'll enjoy it. They play Mahler as well as anyone, but . . . well, one can only listen to so much Mahler, *neh*?"

"I'm more of a White Stripes girl myself."

"Pah! You should listen to something Japanese."

Mariko laughed. "And what about you? The last time I looked, Dvořák wasn't a Japanese name."

"Hmph. That's what I get for associating with a police detective. Never misses a detail, this one."

Mariko laughed again, and Yamada chuckled with her. "You ought to be happy I don't miss much," said Mariko. "Otherwise I might not have a car ready to take you where you need to go."

"Oh, come now. I'm no invalid. I'll take the train."

"It's not safe," Mariko said with a cluck of her tongue. She walked with him into the house, where she found a pen and a sheet of paper. "Call this number," she said as she wrote. She paused, then flipped the page over and rewrote the telephone number in script large and dark enough for him to read if he held it close. "You'll reach one of the officers in the house across the street. He'll come in a taxicab and honk four times. Two quick beeps, twice."

Yamada raised a white eyebrow. "Clever. Your idea?"

"It was, as a matter of fact. Not that my lieutenant notices. Anyway, you need to go somewhere, anywhere at all, you call this number, *neh*?"

"I feel as safe as a baby in diapers." Yamada grunted, his tone a blend of annoyance and amusement. "You take good care of me, don't you, Inspector?"

"Of course. Who else do I have that can identify Fuchida on sight?"

Yamada laughed, his laugh lines deep and plentiful. "Too bad for you I can't see."

Mariko laughed back and patted him on the shoulder. "Call me if you need anything. And if not, I'll see you tomorrow at seven."

"Until then, Inspector."

# 5 2

This time, Fuchida promised himself, he would be more careful. He'd taken too much pleasure in the last three. They were sloppy kills. Perhaps the frustration had gotten to him. And now with the American breathing down his neck, he was feeling frustrated again. There was still one more to deal with, and a good killing would ease his mind. But no, he told himself. This time he would be more discreet.

But why? a part of him asked. Gruesome killings sent a message. Having heard it, dealers would be more likely to mind their tongues.

Fuchida had been hearing a lot from this voice lately. He even gave it physical characteristics: it was a high, singing voice, beautiful and hypnotic and therefore not to be trusted. In this case, however, it remained convincing. As he parked his car under the streetlights' glow, he wondered what to make of his dilemma.

Stepping out of the car, his beautiful singer in hand, he assayed the neighborhood. There was serious wealth here. Not the kind that would ever enable the people who lived here to buy a house, but the kind of wealth that would let them buy a parking spot within walking distance of home. In the neighborhood where Fuchida was hiding these days, renters paid sixty thousand yen a month for a parking spot and were happy to take an hour's train ride to reach it. Another sixty thousand would lease a flat three times the size of the bed those people slept on, a flat the size of the living rooms in this neighborhood.

Everything—asphalt, parked cars, concrete and glass—was lit in the sodium glow of the streetlights, colors washed out, the lights buzzing like cicadas. The smallest building here was twelve stories high. There might have been a thousand windows looking down on him as he tucked the sword within his overcoat.

Fuchida made up his mind. He would deal with Bumps more judiciously, but he would not regret killing the others. Kamaguchi Ryusuke said he wanted to hear no more rumors of Fuchida and narcotics. He would certainly hear nothing from those three.

But what if Kamaguchi heard of their deaths? It was the calmest, most rational part of Fuchida's mind that asked the question this time. Ordinarily an underboss in the Kamaguchi-gumi would not concern himself with anything some newspaper reporter might have to say in the police blotter, but there was a formal ban now on violent theatrics. If Kamaguchi Ryusuke caught wind of the dead dealers, he might be persuaded to give a shit. If the mood struck him, he might even be moved to investigate. Fuchida did not need the full weight of the Kamaguchi-gumi falling on him now, not when things with the American were so heated and yet so near to closure.

To hell with the Kamaguchis, that other part of his mind said. No one is so powerful that he can turn a deaf ear to the message you sent. Those pushers died like dogs. No—they died like dogs died a thousand years ago. There was something in a sword killing that recalled ancient fears. Underboss or not, even Kamaguchi Ryusuke would think twice about throwing his weight around if he saw Inazuma steel in Fuchida's hand.

Fuchida walked west along a street so narrow that car traffic could only pass one way. The sidewalk was narrow too, scarcely more than shoulder width. Fuchida thought of the old days when commoners would scramble into the lane rather than occupy the same walk as a samurai, lest they bump his scabbard with their filthy bodies and invite him to cut them down where they stood. He knew the name of Fuchida had no such lineage, but he wondered what it must have been like to be born into a caste where calling debts in blood was a birthright.

At the end of the narrow street he found a busy avenue six lanes wide. Headlights flashed by in both directions. The whole city was like this: quiet neighborhoods abutting screaming thoroughfares, miniature highways with computer-controlled lights intersecting tortuous, claustrophobic lanes whose names were already ancient when Tokyo was still an insignificant fishing village. Contradiction heaped upon contradiction. Zones, wards, subdivisions: they were all attempts at containment. Pathetic, Fuchida thought. These people thought that because their world was controlled, it was safe. But the illusion of control only helped the predators draw closer to the prey.

Fuchida turned, walked to the nearest crosswalk, and crossed to the other side. This was the shopping district. All the housewives on the far side of those six lanes would spend their time here, and their husbands' money, buying trinkets and kitchen gadgets and romance novels whose leading men could sweep them out of their lives and into a life that might mean something. It was just after six o'clock now. They had another three hours of shopping to do, another four or five hours before their *sarariman* husbands would come home, maybe smelling of cigarettes and whiskey, maybe expecting their obligatory weekly rut. Fuchida could not imagine enduring even a week of such a life before putting his sword through his belly.

He walked into Tokyu Hands and boarded the steep and slender escalator. He rose above picture frames and scrapbooks, calligraphy paper and flower arranging tools, colored pens and modeling clays, fully seven floors' worth of salvation in the form of distraction. As he neared the eighth floor he could smell coffee and stale pastry. The smooth glide of the escalator carried him up into view of the snack lounge, full of chattering women and the occasional table of schoolgirls. The crowd did nothing to improve Fuchida's general opinion of women. Not one in twenty of these would be worth even five minutes' conversation, and of those, fewer than half would be worth seeing naked.

The only men to be seen wore white cloth hats and white-buttoned jackets, and worked behind the food counters—with one exception. Shaggy peroxide hair and a rumpled gray suit jacket identified Bumps Ryota even from behind, even from across the cafeteria crowd.

Fuchida made his way over to Bumps, who was sitting with a frightfully skinny woman with cute hair but bad teeth. "Come on, one bump," she was saying to him. "Just one. Why not?"

"You see that panini grill back there?" Bumps pointed; the girl turned to look. "Your sister would fry my balls in it if I sold to you. Besides, I'm into E now. I don't even have what you're looking for."

"But you know someone who does," the girl said. She hadn't noticed Fuchida standing over Bumps's right shoulder. Neither had Bumps, for that matter, but the fact that the girl hadn't noticed him bespoke a focus only seen in jonesing addicts.

And swordsmen, Fuchida realized. With his beautiful singer in hand it was easy to lose himself. Even in the midst of a forest, he would be blind to every leaf; there was only the sword and its target.

"No," said Bumps. "I give you a name, I'll be in a world of shit. Not just with cops either. Your sister, she'll talk to *my* people too. I can't help you."

"You heard him," Fuchida said. "Get lost."

Bumps jumped. The skinny woman shot the kind of glare Fuchida would expect from a cornered rat, all anger and vulnerability. He gave her a look in return: the look of the eighty-kilo Akita that cornered the rat.

Strange, he thought as she got from her chair. He'd gone so long without police detection, and yet even ordinary people had instincts enough to know a killer on sight. "Good girl," he said, and fixed his glare on her until she made her way shakily to the down escalator.

"Bumps," Fuchida said, sitting in the chrome-and-pleather chair opposite him. The seat was still warm. The girl must have been nearly feverish for Fuchida to feel that through his clothing.

He laid the sheathed sword across his lap. Bumps eyed it nervously. A few other customers noted it too, but this was one of the few places in Yokohama where carrying a sword might be excusable. Stores like this still sold the cords and *washi* paper and wood lacquer needed for traditional sword displays. Police wouldn't allow the weapon, of course, but in neighborhoods like this the police didn't need to patrol much.

"H-hello," Bumps said at length.

"Surprised to see me?"

A nervous smile flickered across Bumps's lips. Fuchida found the man's graying teeth disgusting.

"Still selling to the housewife set, are you, Bumps?"

"It's good business. They got plenty of money, and nobody wants to lose face if they get caught. No risk of husbands pressing charges."

"Nice. Sell much E to these broads?"

Bumps swallowed. Fuchida wasn't supposed to know about that, and until this moment Bumps hadn't been sure how much Fuchida had overheard. He was certain now, though. Fuchida could see the color draining from his face.

"Some," Bumps stammered. "Their, uh, daughters. They buy too."

"Oh. Good." Fuchida smiled. "And cops? How much are they good for?"

Bumps's thin fingers gripped the tabletop. "Uh—I don't really know, Fuchida-san."

"Seems like you should. Seems like you talk to them an awful lot. *Neh?*"

"That girl," Bumps said, "the one who was here a second ago, she's a pain in the ass. I just told her that stuff to get her off my back."

"Really? Seemed to me maybe you said all that stuff because her sister's a cop. *Neh?* That's what I gathered from your riveting conversation. But I guess you must be playing the family angle just to get rid of her, huh?"

"Uh. Yeah."

"Their family named Oshiro by any chance?"

"I—" Bumps said. "I, uh, I don't know, Fuchida-san." The knuckles on the table grew pale.

"The reason I ask," Fuchida said, leaning forward to rest on his elbows, "is that there's a lady cop in Tokyo named Oshiro. Lady cops are pretty rare, *neh?*"

Bumps shrugged. He smelled like dirty laundry, even over the smells of the kitchen. "I don't know, Fuchida-san."

"Too bad. I was hoping you could help me out. See, I've got this lady cop on my ass. Oshiro. She went and crawled so far up my ass I find myself thinking about her every time

I have to take a shit. And when I think about her, you know what I think, Bumps?"

"N-no."

"I think, how in the hell did this lady cop get on to me in the first place? So I called my guy in the TMPD and I asked him. You know what he told me? He said this Oshiro that's up my ass is the same Oshiro that busted your ass for possession a couple of weeks back."

"Oh, yeah." Bumps gave him a nervous laugh and a meth-mouth smile. He couldn't seem to decide whether to look Fuchida in the eye or to look at the sword in his lap. "Uh, yeah, I remember her. Major bitch, *neh*?"

Fuchida laughed. Bumps said it like he was afraid of her. Fuchida couldn't imagine living a life like that, being afraid of people who weren't even in the room.

He toned his laughter down to a thin, polite smile, and even that caused Bumps to flinch in fear. Fuchida relished it. People knew what to do with a madman swinging a sword. No need to come to grips with fright; all they had to do was run screaming. A gentleman with a sword, though— that was an enigma. It was hard to know whether to placate him or to make a mad dash for the door. Fuchida enjoyed watching the indecision play on Bumps's sallow face.

At last Fuchida broke the silence. "Is she a bitch? I haven't had a chance to get to know her. But I suppose she'd have to be if she was going to fry your balls in a panini grill. This Oshiro, she *is* the one you were talking about a minute ago, *neh*? The tweaker's sister?"

Bumps shook his head. The stink of unwashed hair blended with his dirty laundry smell. "Fuchida-san, I got no idea—"

"That's all right. I can just go downstairs and ask your friend the tweaker. Hell, I can hook her up with some meth, since she's having trouble getting that from you. She'll probably be more than happy to talk to me then. But here's the thing, Bumps. I had my mind all made up that I was going to go easy on you. Dealers in this town, they're dropping like flies these days. It's some crazy fucker with a sword that's killing them. Maybe you heard about that."

"Uh. Yeah. I heard." Bumps's eyes flicked back to the sword in Fuchida's lap.

"Turns out they were talking too much, Bumps. The wrong ears were listening. Just like you, *neh*? But you were going to get lucky. I had my mind all made up that I wouldn't lose my temper with you. I was going to play it nice and discreet. And now I find out you've been talking to cops."

Bumps's eyes careened like *pachinko* balls. They gauged the width of the table, the distance to the escalator, maybe comparing these to the reach of Fuchida's blade. "Fuchida-san . . ."

"What's good to eat here, Bumps?" Fuchida leaned back in his chair. "All this talk of panini is making me hungry."

Bumps burst from his chair, sending it clattering to the linoleum floor. With a shriek he dashed for the escalator, colliding with every shopper between him and it. He careened off a trash bin, then fought his way onto the up escalator and scrambled madly downward.

Fuchida walked to the elevator and pressed the button with the curled knuckle of his forefinger. When diners looked at him, he shrugged, looking for all the world as if there wasn't a sword in his left hand. He lost sight of Bumps's wrinkled jacket as Bumps tumbled over the rubber handrail of the up escalator, landing gracelessly on the metal stairs gliding downward.

The elevator dinged and opened. Stupid, Fuchida thought. Bumps was considerably safer in public. But Bumps's judgment wasn't what it should have been. He suffered from that problem all too common among dealers: he partook of his own product. Stupid.

The button for the ground floor glowed under Fuchida's knuckle and the burnished steel doors glided shut. He slid his beautiful singer a few inches out of her sheath, then slid her home again, drew her out and slid her home, enjoying the sound of her steel. It was a song he felt more than heard, vibrations in his palm as steel moved across wood. He slid her out and home again, only a few inches, just enough to feel her song in the bones of his fingers.

The elevator opened on a crowd of undisturbed shoppers. Bumps hadn't made it down yet. Perhaps good judgment had finally caught up with him. Perhaps he'd scampered off to a fire escape. Or perhaps he was hiding between aisles somewhere upstairs, still gripped by amphetamine-amplified fears of his own making, not foreseeing the futility of hiding in a store that was soon to close. It hardly mattered. Bumps was no longer Fuchida's primary target.

Fuchida saw her half a block away, hugging herself, a cigarette glowing in her right hand. As he drew nearer, he could see her collarbones, the sharp corners of her hip bones. He'd seen her kind before. There was skinny, and then there was meth skinny. A lot of his girls went from the former to the latter, even though he always told them he wouldn't have meth skinny dancing at his club. It wasn't a moral principle. He just preferred a woman to have some jiggle to her, and besides, the meth made them jabber too much at the clientele.

"What's your name?" he said when he drew close enough.

"Piss off," she said, not bothering to look up from the sidewalk.

"You've got some fight in you. I like that."

That made her look up, and when she saw the one she'd just told to piss off, she blanched. "You," she said.

"Me." Fuchida bowed.

"What do you want?"

"I know some girls who like to party. They have what you're looking for."

"No." She took half a step back, her cigarette in front of her now, the world's feeblest weapon of self-defense. "I need to go home."

"Who are you kidding? You're a wreck, sweetheart. How long have you been wearing those clothes?"

"Shut up. Go away."

Fuchida smiled, then did as he was told. On his fourth step, without bothering to turn around, he said, "You've got the wrong idea about me. These girls I know, they've got a hot shower. Laundry. But you don't need any of that, right?"

He made it another four steps before she spoke. "Why should I trust you?"

"Don't," he said with a shrug. "I don't care." But he stopped where he stood. He pulled a small silver case from his pocket, and from the case he produced a business card. "My club," he said. "You want to talk to the girls I know, you come by. Any business you might want to do, they'll take care of you."

She came toward him with an air of feigned confidence, like she was ten years old and he was a dead animal her schoolgirl friends had dared her to touch. She took the card from his hand with a sassy snap of the wrist. "This is all the way in Akihabara."

"I'm going there right now," Fuchida said, pointing across the avenue. "My car is just across the street."

For three seconds she stood there thinking. Then she said, "All right. But don't try anything. My sister's a cop. She taught me how to do stuff you won't like."

"I'll keep my distance," Fuchida said with a smile. "What's your name?"

"Saori."

# 53

The cell rang in Mariko's purse while she was at her mother's. Her fingers fished past the Cheetah and the compact and her key chain before they found the chirping phone.

"Oshiro?"

"Yes," said Mariko, and then with her thumb over the receiver, "Just a second, Mom."

"Sorry to bother you off duty," said the voice on the other end. It was a deep male voice, vaguely familiar to Mariko, but she couldn't place it. "We got a fifty-two keeps mentioning your name."

Fifty-two. 10-52 was TMPD code for an ambulance request. Saori.

"How is she?" Mariko said. Her heart pounded so hard that the words shuddered in her throat. "Is she alive?"

"It's a male," the cop's voice said. It could only be a cop; no one else would use the term *fifty-two*. "Slender, average height. No ID, but he says his name's Kawamura Ryotarō. You know him?"

"No," said Mariko. Then, after a second, "Well, maybe. Which hospital?"

"Tokai. Better hurry, Oshiro. He's bleeding bad."

As soon as Mariko hung up, her mother was clinging to her arm, fingernails digging like a cat's claws. "Who was it?" she said. "Is it her? Is she all right?"

"I don't know, Mom. It wasn't Saori. Maybe someone who knows something, though. Mom, I need to go."

It took fully five minutes for Mariko to disengage herself from her mother, fifteen minutes more before she reached the hospital. She approached the desk attendant in a rush, and then for a moment she couldn't remember the name the cop on the phone had given her. At last she said, "Kawamura. Kawamura Ryotarō."

The desk attendant looked at Mariko's badge, then directed her to the waiting area of the emergency room. Just then the big white ER doors bumped open, tapped at first by the foot of a gurney, then pulled to the walls by the invisible hands of automated hinges. On the gurney lay Kawamura "Bumps" Ryota.

Bumps had one purple cheek, the eyebrow purple on that side too, and a fat pillow of ice packs was bound to his abdomen by what looked like half a kilometer of gauze. An IV drip hung from a tall chrome pole, its plastic vein snaking down until it entered Bumps's left forearm. He lay on clean white sheets, but blood spattered the blue jumpsuit of the paramedic wheeling the gurney. A uniformed cop followed him, sunglasses propped in his hair and reflecting the ceiling's rectangular lights.

"Officer Toyoda," Mariko said to the cop. She hadn't seen him since Toyoda let Bumps slip past him in the shopping mall sting. He looked at her with sullen eyes, his mouth expressionless, leaving it to Mariko to sort out whether he was still pissed at her for dressing him down or whether he was embarrassed that she found him at his new detail questioning ER patients. Mariko didn't have the energy for it. She told the paramedic, "I need to speak with your patient."

"He's lost a lot of blood," he said. "I'm taking him to surgery right now."

"Tried to help her," Bumps said weakly. An incoherent murmur followed, trailing into nothing.

Mariko walked alongside the gurney, which the paramedic was pushing toward polished steel elevator doors on the far side of the lobby. "You've seen better days, Bumps."

She saw Toyoda do a double take, then squint at Bumps, then groan. "That's the same Bumps we collared?"

"No, it's one of the hundred other guys around here named Bumps. Nice detective work."

Toyoda groaned again and rolled his eyes. Mariko tried not to enjoy it too much. In truth she could forgive him for not recognizing Bumps in his current condition. But pulped face or no, Mariko would never have forgotten a guy who out-juked her in front of a bunch of other cops.

She wished she had more time to relish the moment. "What happened, Bumps? Looks like someone kicked you in the face."

"I fell. After he stabbed me." Bumps slid his pale right hand up onto his bandaged belly.

She eyed the mountain of gauze that wrapped him like a cummerbund. She could see only one reason to have so much dressing on his back: his puncture wound must have gone clean through him. The biggest knife in Tokyo wasn't big enough to leave a hole like that. Either Bumps was attacked from the front and behind, or else . . . "You get stabbed by a sword, Bumps?"

Toyoda and the paramedic both stopped in their tracks. Mariko thought she could guess why. They both knew Bumps's wound was a through-and-through, but neither of them could imagine how Mariko could have known that. Toyoda, unable to restrain himself, blurted, "No wonder you made detective."

For his part, Bumps only said, "Uh-huh. Tried to help her."

"You know his name, don't you, Bumps? It's Fuchida?"

"Uh-huh. I tried—I tried—"

"Son of a bitch," Toyoda said. He gaped at her the way she remembered looking at twenty-year veterans when she was in her first month. There was awe there, and shame, and maybe a touch of dread that he'd never attain her status. But of course he didn't know what case she was working. He wouldn't know about the sword killings either. He certainly would have heard reports about the recent string of homicides, but Ko had slammed the lid on any talk of swords. As far as he was concerned, that aspect of the case was Mariko's private little flight of fancy. And as far as Officer Toyoda was concerned, Mariko had walked up to the victim, eyeballed him, and identified both the assailant and his weapon on the spot.

Mariko had no time to correct him. Her mind was racing. At last she had her connection between Fuchida and the rash of drug dealer murders. "Fuchida's the one you told me about, isn't he? The one who wants to blow the cocaine market wide open? What happened, Bumps? Did he come after you for talking to me?"

"Not you. Kamaguchis."

"I should have seen it before," Mariko said. "He needed to recruit people to sling for him, but someone started talking, *neh*? The Kamaguchi-gumi found out about his coke plans, and Fuchida had to silence everyone who could rat him out. Damn, I should have guessed it. Why else would he make dealers his targets . . . ?" Her racing mind doubled its speed. "That many dealers could move a lot of blow, *neh*? He must be getting one hell of a shipment. And *that* explains why he wants the second sword. . . ."

She snapped her phone from her purse and motioned the paramedic to take Bumps on his way. With the phone pressed to one ear and a finger pressed to the other, she walked quickly for the door. Her heels clacked against the marble and an ambulance wailed outside, but Mariko had no thought for anything but the ringing phone.

"It's Oshiro," she said as soon as someone picked up. "Run all the sword names you've got against narcotics convictions. Check with NPA, Interpol, everyone."

"Are you sure, Sergeant? Fuchida's *bōryokudan*. They're more likely to kill a coke dealer than to deal it themselves, *neh*?"

"Fuchida's looking to change the playbook. He's trading the sword for coke, I'm sure of it. I think he figured the bosses would've noticed if he paid in cash, so he tried an end run around them. It didn't work; the Kamaguchi-gumi's onto him now, and they'll be gunning for him soon if they aren't already. We need to catch him before they do, understand? They are *not* going to win this one."

"Yes, ma'am."

At last, Mariko thought. At last she had a clear vision of her enemy's plan. She even understood why he'd been so damned hard to find. Hiding from the police was one thing; hiding from yakuzas was a whole new level of complicated. At last the pieces were falling into place.

And as much as she hated to admit it, Yamada had been right from the very beginning. The forces of destiny were flowing, roaring in her ears as loud as a waterfall. Her cocaine tip, Yamada's case, the Kurihara murder—in the end they all proved to be facets of the same jewel. It was too much to call coincidence. Yamada-sensei would be delighted.

She looked at the screen on her phone. Seven oh two. She was late for Dvořák, late for meeting Yamada. Oh well, she thought. She'd find him at intermission. And now she had something interesting to talk about.

Three floors up, Bumps Ryota lay in an anesthetic fog. His last meth hit had long since worn off, a perfectly good high ruined by that maniac and his sword, but the oxycodone in his IV drip was kicking in nicely. A pillar of pain still stood firm in the left side of his belly—in his mind's eye it was a length of cloth, twisted and twisted so many times that its fibers were tearing—but the rest of his body was a thick gray cloud, cool and without substance.

He couldn't imagine what could possibly have possessed him to go after Fuchida and the girl. Trying to help was one thing, but Fuchida had a damn sword. It felt like the thing was still in him, stabbing through the fog.

After being stabbed he'd fallen on his face, and in falling he'd bitten his tongue. *Hard.* Between the oxycodone, his swollen cheek, and his handicapped tongue, he was afraid nobody could understand him. It was an elusive fear, one he had a hard time keeping track of in the fog, but it had real urgency whenever he found it, and so when he found it he spoke as best he could. "Forgot to tell her the most important part," he'd repeat. "Tried to help her. Her sister. He has her sister."

# 54

As she descended the shrub-lined stairs leading down to the Suntory Hall plaza, Mariko could tell it was intermission. It seemed much too early for an intermission—not even eight o'clock yet—but there were the lobby doors, black steel and glass, propped open despite the evening chill. All around them clustered a crowd of well-dressed people. But something was strange about this crowd. It took her a moment to sort it out, but at last she did: none of them were smoking. No gray puffs hovered above the crowd, nor did any smoke drift downwind of it.

Her stomach became a cold stone. She sprinted toward the crowd; the cold air ripped at her lungs, making her breath taste of blood. Something was terribly wrong.

She reached the crowd without slowing, punching through the first ranks of symphony patrons like a warhorse through helpless infantry. She muscled through the rest with sharp elbows and sharper words, men's words, words her grandmothers would blush to hear her say.

She fought her way into the lobby. At last, finding a ring of cold air in the center of the crowd, she saw the bleeding form of Yamada Yasuo. He lay on a gurney, a mask of clear blue plastic over his mouth and nose, layers of blood-sodden gauze heaped high on his belly. The paramedics weren't even keeping it compressed anymore. Yamada-sensei was—

No. She wouldn't accept that. She fell to her knees before his body, her fingers squelching in his blood as she pressed the gauze to his chest. There was no pulsing wound to compress, no bleeding to stop. She glanced at his face, hoping for some sign of response. The unseeing eyes made her wince and flinch away.

In some remote corner of her mind she asked herself why the paramedics hadn't stopped her from interfering. They should have pulled her from their patient by now. She looked up to see the two of them, their blue uniforms splashed with red, held back by three plainclothes cops from her unit. A fourth policeman, who like the others must have been working crowd control until Mariko had barged in, laid his long-fingered hand on her shoulder. "Sergeant," he said. That was all.

Later, when at last the ambulance men had their way, when Mariko abandoned their patient so they could do their job, when the crowd had dispersed, when the men in her unit commandeered a tower of napkins from the snack bar and a half-empty bottle of Sani-Kleen from the ambulance so she could wash the blood from her hands and clothes and face, Mariko regained the power of speech. Sitting cross-legged on the cold flagstones of the plaza, looking at the blood on her shoes, she said, "What happened?"

Ino—the one who had laid his hand on her shoulder, the tall one who had debriefed Yamada some days before— cleared his throat. "We never saw him coming. I was watching the lobby from the stairs. Mishima and Takeda had eyes on the front doors. We thought you were going to be side by side with Yamada. I spotted Yamada, and then I was looking over the crowd for you. Next thing I know, people are screaming."

Mishima, the chubby cop she'd worked with before in the mall sting, gave her a different story. "I'm watching Yamada from the moment he gets out of the taxicab," he said, his breath smelling like day-old coffee. "He's alone, which surprised me. But he's an easy guy to track in a crowd; just follow the silver hair. So I'm watching him, and all of a sudden that little head of silver hair drops out of sight. By the time I get to him, there's enough blood on the floor to fill a bathtub. No assailant in sight."

"I saw him," said Takeda, a short cop and the only other

detective on Mariko's team. "He walked right past me. Strange-looking guy: pale face but dark eyes, dark mouth. Long ponytail and long black jacket. He was walking fast, *neh*, and the crowd parted for him, but I figured they did that because he looks like a dead guy. I didn't know anything had happened yet, *neh*? Nobody's screaming yet, because so far nobody's seen any blood. Our perp, he must have killed him real fast, real quiet, *neh*, because he was a good ten paces from the body when he passed me, and still nobody was crying out."

All three of her men had more to say, but Mariko could only listen distractedly. They could not even agree on how tall Fuchida was, though now that Takeda mentioned the ponytail, all three of them recalled seeing him. She wanted to scream at them for their idiocy, their incompetence. Next time you stake out a lobby, a voice inside her yelled, you don't put the tall guy up on the stairs and the short guy on the ground outside. And maybe you should think to keep an eye on the man who looks like a corpse, the one wearing an overcoat long enough to conceal a sword. She wanted to bring back the crowd just so she could scream at them, a herd of sheep so wrapped up in their bleating conversations that they might just as well have walked past an atom bomb on the way to their seats.

But all of that was misdirected anger. Three cops and three hundred people did not notice a man walk up to Yamada and run him through with an enormous razor blade, but Mariko should have noticed because Mariko should have been standing right there. She should have seen Fuchida over her shoulder. She should have zapped him with the Cheetah and clapped her cuffs on him. Or trained her pistol on him before he ever got that close. At the very least she should have put herself between Yamada and the blade. She was young; she might have survived the stabbing. It should have been her in the ambulance now, bleeding but not dead, apologizing to Yamada for spoiling the concert. She'd had the opportunity to be the heroine and she hadn't shown up.

She went through the motions, trying to reconstruct the murder. Yamada had entered through the right-hand doors; Fuchida had exited through the left. According to the paramedics, the stab wound ran through the small intestine, the spleen, and the left lung. Yamada had turned to face him, then. Perhaps he'd heard the sword being drawn. He turned, and was face-to-face with Fuchida when the blade went in. At that distance Yamada might even have been able to make out his killer's face.

The footprints, bloody red on red carpet, suggested that Fuchida had walked Yamada to the wall of the ticket booth, then withdrawn the sword. "He was a tough old bastard," Ino said. "Managed a few steps before he fell."

What did it matter? Mariko wanted to say. He never had a chance. Eighty-seven years old, with a perforated spleen to spread its toxins through the wound, complicating any attempt at surgery. Yamada had trained his protégé too well.

Her phone rang. Mariko grabbed it reflexively, then thought better of it and almost let it fall back into her purse. There wasn't a single soul she wanted to talk to tonight. But that wasn't quite true. There was one, and her name was on the caller ID.

"Oh my God, Saori, please tell me you're okay." The words came tumbling out of her mouth. "Just . . . just say you're okay and tell me where I can find you. That's all I can handle right now."

"I have your sister," said a deep, masculine voice, "and I will give her back to you in exchange for the sword."

"The hell you will," Mariko said, and the haze of grief and shock burned away into nothing. Part of her wished she could say it was her training that did it, but it was hate and anger that cleared her mind. She snapped her fingers at Takeda and motioned for a pen. Her other hand was already in her purse, groping blindly for her notepad. "You're killing weekly these days. How do I know you haven't killed her already?"

A rattling sound followed: perhaps the phone being laid down on a hard surface. Footsteps. A thump, a squeal, and the man's voice again: "Say her name."

"Mariko!"

Another squeal, this one muffled, and a horrible chill in Mariko's gut doused her white-hot rage. As scared as she was for Saori, a tiny voice inside her was thankful to hear that squeal. Anger couldn't help Saori right now.

As footsteps drew closer to the phone, Mariko scribbled,

FUCHIDA. "The Inazuma," he said. "You will deliver it tomorrow."

CALL HQ, she wrote. LOCATE THE PHONE HE'S CALLING FROM. "I can't," Mariko said, jotting down Saori's phone number. "Thanks to you, nobody's getting anywhere near that weapon."

"There is no longer any need to stake out Yamada's house. Remove your officers from the area and get the sword."

"You just screwed any chance of that. That was your plan? To kill Yamada so we'd lift the surveillance?"

"There is no one there to protect. The house is meaningless except for the sword."

"Don't you see what you just did? Up until now we were looking for a high-end antiques thief. Now this is a homicide case. There's no way my CO lets me lift that surveillance. Not anymore."

Frustration seethed through the phone. "Find a way," Fuchida said. "Or I kill your sister."

"I'm telling you, it can't be done. Not by tomorrow, anyway. I'm a sergeant, Fuchida-san. A small fish. You want to make things happen quickly, go kidnap the prime minister's sister. Let mine go."

"No." Fuchida spoke now through gritted teeth. "I'll kill her. I'll leave her around the city in little pieces."

"All right, all right." Mariko's heart was pounding. She'd been toying with his emotions, hoping that in his agitation he might reveal some clue to his whereabouts. But she'd never trained to negotiate with a kidnapper, and now her temper had gotten the better of her. She'd rattled a man whose mind was already brittle and ready to crack. She wished she had Yamada to guide her. She wished she hadn't fucked up so bad that her sensei was dead.

But he was, and she was on her own, and now Saori was counting on her. "Please," she said, "settle down, Fuchida-san. It's just that I don't have a lot of room to maneuver. Look at it from my position. My lieutenant is going to want to know for a fact that we can get Saori back alive. And the fact is, you've killed before. We need to respect that. We need to be afraid you may do it again."

"You're damn right."

Good, Mariko thought. Keep placating him. "Give me

more time to talk to my LT. Please? Let me convince him you're not to be trifled with. And please, Fuchida-san, don't make any more threats about hurting Saori, or else I won't be able to convince him that this will end well."

Fuchida grunted. She could hear the breath coming fast and loud through his nose. "Fine," he said at last.

"Fine. Wonderful. Thank you, Fuchida-san." Her voice was all sweetness. "My LT's going to want me to be able to speak with you. I can call you later at this number, *neh*?"

"Fine." And the line went dead.

Mariko let out a sigh and slumped against the cold white wall of the concert hall. She wanted to cry. She wanted to throw her phone across the courtyard. Tension buzzed in her neck and shoulders; a piercing headache throbbed from the base of her skull. She closed her eyes and rolled her head back and forth against the cold, hard edges of the bricks.

"Oshiro," one of the other cops whispered. She didn't open her eyes to see which one. "You all right?"

It was the most idiotic question she'd ever heard. Her sister was kidnapped and her sensei was murdered. On top of that she was surrounded by cops too stupid to take any initiative of their own except to ask idiotic questions. Why the hell would she be all right?

But she couldn't say any of that, and even if she could have, she didn't mean it. They weren't stupid; they were looking to their sergeant for orders. She was the stupid one. She was the one who should have been on the scene. She was the one who could have kept Yamada-sensei alive. All she wanted to do was find a dark place and cry for him. All she wanted was solitude and silence enough to center herself. Right now her grief was enough to knock her over if she tried to stand.

"Get that phone triangulated," she said, eyes still closed, her pulse pounding in her ears like a *taiko* drum. "Call HRT. I want a team en route the second we have a fix on that phone. Then call our surveillance unit; tell them I want a tac team inside Yamada's house, armored up and armed in case Fuchida loses patience and decides to get ballsy. Have you contacted Dr. Yamada's next of kin?"

"Not yet."

"Do it. Let them know where they can find him. And one

of you, find me a bottle of Tylenol. And a bottle of Jack Daniel's while you're at it."

Ino, Mishima, and Takeda laughed, and Mariko forced herself to laugh along with them. In truth she wanted nothing more than to sleep for a week. To lose Yamada and then to botch negotiations with her own sister's kidnapper—it was too much for one night. Too much for one year, for that matter, and now she still had to stay sharp. They would find Fuchida soon. HRT would take point on it, but Mariko needed to be on the scene. This was Saori, after all.

Her three men on site each had phone calls to make. Mariko estimated she might have as long as two minutes of respite. Two minutes before one of them came back to ask a question. Two minutes before she would have to be made of stone again, so none of her men would see a moment of weakness and interpret it as feminine frailty.

# BOOK EIGHT

## SHŌWA ERA, THE YEAR 17

### (1942 CE)

# 55

Kiyama Keiji was running late.

With four arms he might have managed to don his boots, open the door, and hang his *tachi* from the belt of his smart tan uniform all at once. As it was, he could not even keep a firm grip on boots and sword, and when he dropped the weapon its handle punched a hole through the paper of the shoji door.

"Kei-kun," his father called from the back room. "Are you all right?"

Keiji could scarcely hear him over the clatter of boots falling to the ground. He tried in vain to scoop up the sword. It bounced noisily and ripped another panel in the shoji before it clattered to the floor.

"I'm fine," he called, falling to a seat and thrusting his left foot into his boot. This was no time for an extended discussion, and his father was famous for those.

His mother, of course, slept through the commotion just as if she were a corpse.

He put his second boot on, tied both of them, and hung his dusty scabbard from his belt at his left hip. "I'll fix the door when I get home," he yelled, then slid it shut behind him before any retort could follow.

It seemed he was not the only one in a hurry that morning. It was a gray morning, the fifth of April, and the narrow road overflowed with people and handcarts trying to reach their destinations between rain showers. Keiji wove his way between them, brushing the dirt from his scabbard as he ran.

It was two kilometers from the street the Kiyama house overlooked to the main thoroughfare defining the Tora-no-mon district, and another kilometer or so to the new duty station. As he rounded the corner into Tora-no-mon, Keiji was sweating hard. He was thankful the rain had started again; perhaps it might mask the sweat stains he knew were coming. Wondering how much time he'd made up in his great rush, he reached into his pocket only to discover he'd forgotten his watch at home.

The momentary distraction caused him to bump into another pedestrian, one whose head was down under her broad *sugegasa* and never saw him coming. Both of them landed hard, Keiji jarring his shoulder as he fell.

"I'm terribly sorry," he said, struggling to one knee in the press of the crowd.

"Watch where you're going," the woman said. Then, taking in his uniform, she said, "Don't we have enough enemies overseas? What's the idea, knocking down an old woman like me? You ought to be taking out your aggression on the Americans or the Chinese."

"Terribly, terribly sorry." He offered her his hand.

She was a rude old goat—and not much older than his mother, now that he got a better look at her. Keiji himself was only twenty-one; this woman couldn't be much past fifty. He helped her to her feet anyway, endured her abuses, and hurried on to his post.

He dodged a greengrocer's cart a block later—Keiji seemed to be the only one who was looking where he was going in this rain—and as he passed a watchmaker's shop, he saw it was ten minutes to eight. Barring further collisions he would just make it.

Within sight of the tall beige Intelligence building he slowed to a fast walk, hoping to cool off somewhat before entering. He nearly tripped over a street urchin, a little girl with dirty bandages over her eyes. She raised her head as if to look straight at him and she said, "I see the tiger! I see the tiger on the mountain!"

Keiji almost fell over, he stopped so fast.

"What did you say?"

"I can see the tiger on the mountain," the blind girl said. "There's a woman by the mountain, and the tiger is hunting her."

"How?" Keiji asked, so stunned he was hardly able to pronounce the word. He crouched before the girl, who turned a little bamboo *shakuhachi* over and over in her fingers. It was hard to guess her age, for half of her face was hidden behind the bandages that circumnavigated her head. A mop of unkempt hair hung down to her skinny shoulders, flopping over the bandages too. She was the size of an eight- or nine-year-old, but Keiji guessed she might well be older, for street children got little in the way of nutrition. How she knew the exact name of his *tachi* was beyond his ability to imagine.

"The tiger stays with you," she said. "That's so nice."

"Who takes care of you?"

"Mom."

"Where's your mom?"

"I don't know." A hopeful smile broadened under her brown-smeared bandage. "Do you know where she is?"

"No."

Her smile faded and her shoulders sank. Try again, he chided himself. "I mean, I'll help you find her."

The girl had stationed herself beneath the eaves of a butcher shop, and Keiji summoned the butcher with a wave of his hand. "Sir," Keiji said, "do you know where this girl's mother is?"

"No," the old man said. The way he frowned and shook his head told Keiji a lot more. The girl had been here often, and always alone.

"Watch her for the day, will you? I'm stationed right over there"—he pointed to the Intelligence building—"and I'll be back here between five and six o'clock to collect her. Make sure she gets something to eat, will you?"

"What am I supposed to feed her, raw meat? This isn't a restaurant."

Keiji reached into his pocket for his billfold. "Go buy her some—"

He cut himself short. His billfold was missing, and all his money with it. His identification too. Had he forgotten it along with the pocket watch? No. He'd felt the leather corner against his fingertips when he discovered the watch was missing.

The old woman.

"Son of a bitch," Keiji muttered. What a day to be pickpocketed. "Listen, sir, I'm Lieutenant Kiyama, with Military Intelligence. I work in that building right over there. I promise you, I'll come back this evening and reimburse you for whatever you buy her to eat. Please?"

Even at a dead run, Keiji was three minutes late for work.

# 56

Japanese military intelligence had its heyday after the defeat of the Russians, seventeen years before Keiji was born. Never before had such a tiny nation defeated one so vast. Never in the modern era had an Asian power bested a European one. And never before had a victor been treated with such international disdain. It had been military intelligence that defeated the Russians—or so Keiji had been taught in command school—and because of that victory, the intelligence division had enjoyed almost limitless favor with those who controlled the purse strings.

The Military Intelligence building in Shōwa-ku was one of the products of that favor. Western in every aspect of style, it was one of the first buildings in Tokyo whose original specifications included wiring for telephones. It stood out like an island, a Bauhaus atoll rising out of a sea of ceramic-tiled roofs.

On the fourth floor in a room of tall windows, General Matsumori paced back and forth. Hollow echoes resounded from his heels clopping against the concrete floor. "So this is the young lieutenant Kiyama," Matsumori said. "Late, damp, stinking of sweat. Is that mud on your boots, boy?"

Keiji's gaze did not waver from the far wall. He did not dare to move from his attention stance, not even his eyeballs.

He was surprised that Matsumori should be so concerned about the state of his uniform. The general wore neither his sidearm nor his sword. His jacket, blossoming with insignia of rank and battle honors, was draped over the back of his chair, and his cap lay flat on the desktop. He paced back and forth in his shirtsleeves, traces of white in his mustache, crow's-feet betraying a career spent poring over maps and peering through spyglasses. He had a big, round belly and forearms like hawsers.

"General Itō is an old friend of mine," said Matsumori. Keiji noticed the two of them were equal in height, though the general was stockier, rounder, more muscular. "A mentor, in fact. He recommends you highly, Kiyama. I cannot see why."

"Begging your pardon, General Matsumori. I will not be late again."

"Not to my station you won't. I'll have you toting a rifle in the East Indies and fighting off dysentery if you're ever less than ten minutes early. Is that clear?"

"Yes, sir."

Keiji spent the first day of his career in Military Intelligence cleaning toilets.

"She's fine," the old butcher said, smiling. "She has a *lot* of questions about how to cut up a pig. We ate *nigiri* together for lunch, and I was just going to take her for some skewered chicken when you happened by."

"Thank you," said Keiji. "Many thanks. I—I'm afraid I haven't any money with me. My billfold, it was stolen this— well, it went missing earlier. I wonder if I could repay you tomorrow for your kindness?"

The old man set his teeth for a fleeting moment. "If it weren't for that uniform, son, I'd say you were having me on."

"Understandable, sir. I'm terribly sorry."

"Go on home. Take her with you too, *neh*? I don't mind babysitting, but I've enough grandkids around the house already."

"Thank you, sir. Thank you very much."

Keiji crouched down and touched the little girl on the back of her hand. "How would you like to come home with me?"

"I was listening, you know. I'm not deaf."

"Oh. I know that. I just— Say, what's your name?"

"Shoji Hayano."

"Well, Hayano, how would it be if you had dinner at my house tonight?"

She crossed her arms and looked at the ground—or

would have looked at it, if only her eyes were healthy. It was the gesture a sighted child might have made; Keiji guessed she must have lost her vision later in life.

At length she asked, "Can we come back here tomorrow?"

"If you want to."

"All right, then. I don't want to miss my mom when she comes back."

They walked together hand in hand, the street mostly empty, the air wet with the scent of evaporating rain. "Hayano, can you tell me what you said this morning about the tiger?"

"Uh-huh. The tiger is hunting a woman. He needs to kill her. But his house will wash away if he leaves to find her."

"That's not what you said this morning."

Hayano pursed her lips. "Yes it is."

"No. You said . . . Never mind. Hayano-chan, where is the tiger?"

"With you, silly."

"No. This morning you said something about a mountain."

"Yes. The tiger lives on the mountain. But he has to leave it to get the woman, and if he does that, the mountain will go away."

Keiji stopped and knelt next to the girl. "What does that mean, Hayano?"

She giggled at him. "Silly! It means what it means."

He could hear her stomach growling. "Hayano, where is the tiger? Is it with me or is it in the mountains?"

"No!" She laughed again. "It *lives* on the mountain, but it *stays* with you."

He took her by the hand and set her tiny, dirty fingertips on the pommel of his *tachi*. "This is my most prized possession, Hayano. Its name is Tiger on the Mountain. Do you know what it is?"

"It's a sword, silly. Anyone can see that."

"How did you know the name of the sword this morning?"

She pursed her lips. "This game is boring. Can we go to your house now?"

"Please, Hayano. Please?"

"Bo-ring."

And that was the end of that.

"Kei-kun," his father said as Keiji slid open the shoji. "I'm glad you're home. I just finished making dinner this minute."

"I told you I'd be working until six," he called back to the dining room. "I also told you I'd fix this door when I got home. You didn't have to do it."

Keiji heard the clink of ceramic being set on the table, along with his father's long explanation of patching the shoji panels and how Keiji's mother certainly couldn't do it and of course Keiji was going to be at work all day. Keiji listened for as long as it took to wriggle out of his boots and socks, then interrupted him. "Dad, I wanted to talk to you about inviting a guest for dinner."

"Oh! How wonderful. A girl, I hope."

"Well, yes. Sort of."

He heard stockings rustling against the floor as his father bustled toward the entryway. "Excellent! It doesn't do for a man your age to go unmarried, especially not now that you've been promoted and— Oh."

"Dad, this is Shoji Hayano. She's lost her mother. She's obviously been injured too. I thought she might eat with us. And spend the night, maybe."

"Ah. Well, yes, of course. Hello, Hayano-chan. I'm Kiyama Ryoichi. Do come in."

Dinner was albacore over rice, accompanied by pumpkin and eggplant tempura. Hayano declared it delicious. "Where is your mom, Keiji-san? Doesn't she like eggplant?"

Ryoichi laughed. "Keiji's momma is very sick, sweetheart. She doesn't eat at the table; I'll bring her food after we've finished."

"Oh." She took another bite and chewed it slowly. "Why is she sick?"

"She has what's called an infection," said Ryoichi. "She had surgery, and the cut the doctor made got infected, and now she has to stay away from everything that could make it dirty. She's not even supposed to breathe anything that could be dirty. That's why she has to stay in her room; the smoke from the stove could make her sicker."

"Oh. I had surgery once. On my eyes." She took another bite of fish.

"Did you?" Keiji's father nodded thoughtfully. "And did you get an infection?"

"Nope."

"That's very good." He ate his last thin slice of pumpkin, then began assembling a plate for his wife. "Kei-kun, when she's finished, draw her a bath, *neh*? The poor dear's cheeks are dirty."

# 58

Keiji's parents' house was small, without a spare room, so he laid out Hayano's futon at the foot of his own. He shuddered to think what the neighbors might say—it wasn't as if he and Hayano were blood relatives—but as he saw it, impropriety had to give way to necessity.

The next morning he woke an hour early to prevent a repeat of the day before. He was out the door in record time, Hayano in tow with a band of fresh white cloth about her eyes. They made their way down the road under a bright sky, orange clouds on the eastern horizon suggesting late morning rain.

Hayano chattered as they walked, her discussion wandering as capriciously as a dog chasing squirrels. Keiji hoped he could steer the conversation toward Tiger on the Mountain, but when she latched her thoughts on to something, she was remarkably persistent about sticking to it until she latched on to something else.

At last, outside the butcher shop and within sight of his duty station, he said, "Hayano, can you tell me what you see when you see the tiger on the mountain?"

She smiled. "I told you already."

"Please?"

Suddenly her face grew grim. "Uh-oh," she said.

"What's the matter?"

"Earthquake. Coming soon. We better hide."

Keiji looked around. No one in the street was panicked. Even the butcher's caged chickens were calm. "Are you sure?"

"Mm-hm." She tugged on his hand, pulling him toward the butcher shop. "Come on! We have to hurry!"

"Hayano, that shop is much too small. Little buildings like that fall down in earthquakes. Let's go to the Intelligence building; it's big and it's made of—"

Her hand slipped from his, and she dashed headlong into the butcher shop.

Keiji ran after her, wincing as he saw her collide with the butcher's counter. She bounced off as only children can, barely missing a step. Just as Keiji entered the shop, the ground rumbled.

No matter how many earthquakes he lived through, he always found them disconcerting. They seemed both to drag on forever and to take no time at all. Ground was not supposed to make noise. Nor was it supposed to move. Nothing was as it should have been.

Now chickens squawked and knives rattled on the counters and people in the street shrieked and sought cover. A huge shock wave told Keiji the quake would be getting worse. "Hayano!" he shouted over the din. "Come on! Climb on my back! I'm going to try to get you to the Intelligence building! It's big and made of concrete. It'll—"

"This place is fine. Nothing bad will happen to us here."

"This place is hardly more than a shack! We need to get—"

"No. The tiger is here. We'll be okay."

A loud crack, and a light pole fell across the entryway to the Intelligence building. Roof tiles rained on the street, shattering. Then it was over.

Across the road, water sloshed back and forth in the big tanks of the fishmonger. His aquarium still stood but his shop was a ruin all around it. Next door, the greengrocer's building had fallen in on itself like a house of cards. Next door to that, a restaurant was on fire and people were already rushing to put it out.

Apart from a few upset chickens, the butcher shop was unharmed.

Keiji's mouth fell open. His heart hammered at his ribs, while Hayano's face was inexplicably serene. "How . . . ?" It took him a moment to put together anything more articulate than that. "You knew we'd be safe," he said at last. "How?"

"I told you. The tiger is here. Nothing bad can happen where the tiger is."

"Hayano, look around. The entire neighborhood is a ruin."

That got a frown out of her. She crossed her arms with a petulant flourish; wrinkles creased her nose and her lips pursed to a hair-thin slit. "I *can't* look around, Keiji-san. You're *mean*."

Keiji looked stupidly at his own hand, which pointed a useless finger at the burning restaurant. His head sagged and he smacked his forehead with his palm. "I'm sorry. That was stupid of me to say. I wasn't thinking. The earthquake has me all rattled up."

"Well, you should listen to me, then," she said, still cross. "I *told* you we'd be safe."

Keiji's head sagged again. "You're right. You told me. Can you tell me how you knew this building wouldn't fall? I'll listen this time."

"No. Ask me later. Right now I don't like you."

Shit, Keiji thought. He didn't know her all that well, but even a perfect stranger could see she wouldn't change her mind anytime soon. What do you know about parenting? he asked himself. It might have been smarter to just take her to the police and let them sort her out. Smarter, maybe, and certainly easier, but this little girl had just saved his life. He owed her better treatment than simply passing her off to some stranger to dump her off in an orphanage somewhere. Besides, if he let her go, the thousand questions he had for her would never find answers.

"Listen," he said, "I'm going to go to work, all right? But I'm going to come find you later, and I promise I'll be nice. You stay here with the butcher and make sure he gets you something to eat. Tell him I said you two should have dessert after lunch."

"Now you're just trying to bribe me," Hayano said.

I sure am, Keiji thought. Damned if I know what else to do. How do parents do this every day? "I'll come back later," he told her, squatting on his haunches so he could put his hands on her skinny shoulders. "We'll have some dinner together, and maybe later you can tell me what you want to tell me. I promise I'll listen."

"Maybe," said Hayano.

It was as big a chink in the armor as he could ask for. He trotted out of the shop, wondering whether he was quitting while he was ahead, or whether he was deep in a hole and had only stopped digging.

"Not bad," General Matsumori said as Keiji stepped over the fallen light pole. "Even with an earthquake you're forty-five minutes early."

The general was in his shirtsleeves again, standing with his hands folded behind his back to survey the damage. "You're early yourself, sir," Keiji said.

"I don't sleep. Come. Let's go to my office."

They climbed four flights of stairs in silence, Matsumori limping slightly as they walked. A whiff of dust lingered on the air, probably shaken loose from the rafters. The building was otherwise intact, though Keiji wondered how many thousands of pages had rattled loose from their shelves and scattered themselves over the floors. And even for being empty the building was strangely silent, a stunned, post-earthquake silence.

"You all right, Kiyama? Not the type to let a quake rattle you, are you?"

"No, sir. It's something else. A little blind girl . . . well, she told me the earthquake was going to happen before it did. She pulled me into the only shop that survived the tremors."

"Ah. Good luck, that. Good thing she was blind too. Probably heard it coming. I hear they've got ears like a dog."

"Maybe, sir. It didn't feel like that, though. It felt like she knew what was going to happen."

"Ha! Maybe we should conscript her into Intelligence."

They reached the general's office, with smoke from nearby fires rising along the skyline his windows overlooked. Matsumori shut the door. "General Itō tells me you have the makings of a good strategist, Kiyama. He says you're foresightful. Is that so?"

"The general is most generous, sir. I—"

"Prove it, then. What of the East Indies? If you were in my position, how would you proceed?"

"Your position, sir?"

"Yes. If you were charged with the logistics for the Pacific war, how would you handle the East Indies?"

Keiji swallowed. He felt his cheeks flush. "Sir, I haven't read your daily reports. Without those, I'm sure I couldn't—"

"Pah! Show some backbone, Lieutenant. Hazard a guess."

"Given what I know, sir, given only what I've read in the newspapers . . . well, with due respect, sir, I would abandon the East Indies."

Matsumori sat behind his desk, a bemused smile on his face. It was a Western-style desk, a blocky maple thing in keeping with the rest of the room. "Would you now? May I ask why?"

"Because the Dutch aren't our problem. We should be more concerned about the British and the Americans."

"Anyone with a map could tell you as much. The Netherlands are no bigger than a grain of rice. So? What, then? If not the East Indies, where?"

"Ceylon, sir. As soon as possible."

Matsumori's smile broadened. "Attack British interests directly? Is that wise, Lieutenant?"

"It is necessary, sir. That makes it wise."

"Very good, Kiyama. You do understand that nothing said here can ever leave this building, yes?"

"Yes, sir. Of course, sir."

"Good. The attack on Ceylon began yesterday morning. Where would you have me attack next?"

Keiji's tongue lay like a lump of lead behind his teeth. Three days earlier he had celebrated graduation from officers' school with his classmates. Now a general was confiding battle strategies to him. Was Matsumori reckless? Or worse yet, desperate? All the newspapers and film reels suggested the war was going well. Was it? Did men of Matsumori's stature need new officers so badly that they would share state secrets on the second day? Or was Matsumori simply indiscreet?

"Come on, Kiyama, I haven't got all day. We've been charged with planning the strategy and logistics of the Pacific theater. It is our duty to see the Empire to victory. Don't fall mute on me. Tell me what you would do to secure His Majesty's interests in the Pacific."

"Guadalcanal."

"Speak up, son. You're not in grammar school."

"Guadalcanal," Keiji repeated, willing his voice to sound stronger than his last reedy spluttering. "And Tulagi, and Florida. All the Solomons, in fact. If I were you, sir, I would be forming plans to take them."

General Matsumori shifted forward in his chair, rested his elbows on his knees. "Why there?"

"Supply lines, sir. After Hawai'i, Guadalcanal is the biggest island between California and Australia. What the Americans need is a port. We cannot let them have it, sir. If we take the Solomons—"

"We cut off the Brits in Australia as well," said Matsumori. "Hell, if we had an airstrip down there, we could harass every shipping lane in the south Pacific."

He stood and leaned back, hands at his waist, stretching his hips and back. Keiji wondered if the general had sustained a pelvic injury. Then Matsumori gave a sudden snort. "It's not bad, Lieutenant. Not bad at all. Give us a chance to show the *gaijin* what for." He rolled his shoulders and stretched his hips and back again. "Come on, then. Let's get cracking on it."

# 60

Keiji spent the rest of the day drawing up fallback plans for supply chains to the Philippines in the event of bad weather. General Matsumori knew his history; if a typhoon sunk all their rations, even the armies of Genghis Khan would have no choice but to watch victory turn to defeat.

After nine hours of poring over the deployments, patterns started to form in Keiji's mind. The Americans were damnably tenacious in their mountains on the Bataan peninsula. Estimates put their numbers in the neighborhood of sixty thousand, with another ten or twelve thousand Filipinos fighting beside them. Given the favorable terrain, their defenses would hold indefinitely against a direct assault.

What would defeat them in the end, Keiji realized, was hunger or disease. They were cut off. No friendly ship could reach them with food or medicine. And against disease their tens of thousands were only a liability; any contagion would spread like wildfire.

The connections in Keiji's mind were forming ever faster. If the American defense should collapse sooner than expected, then Japan's supply chains would need to deliver not only rations but additional personnel to manage POWs. There would be no long battle of attrition; those tens of thousands would give up all at once. Japanese troops could be expected to sell their lives to the last man, but the Americans were not reported to have that sort of discipline. They had no warrior code underpinning their culture. As soon as they perceived their predicament—as soon as beriberi set in, or something worse—they would capitulate.

Keiji wrote a memo specifying the particular need for additional officers and secretarial staff, and had it sent to General Matsumori. He found it satisfying to be stationed under a commanding officer who took his input seriously. Command school had led him to believe this would not happen often, but Keiji thought this was a station where the general might actually read a recommendation from a subordinate.

Walking home, he enjoyed the smell of rain not more than an hour old. He noted the milky rivulets running in the gutters, offspring from the union of raindrops and the plaster dust shaken free by the earthquake. Birds were singing cheerily, unusually audible because the quake had silenced so much of the evening's normal human activity. As he walked, Keiji caught a whiff of slaughtered yearling pigs hanging by their hocks in the butcher shop.

The thought of the butcher sent his mind racing back to the girl. His day had been so busy that he'd forgotten about Hayano completely. But there she was, sitting in the only building still standing within fifty meters, chattering to no one and everyone.

The two of them walked the three kilometers back to the house, learning as they went that they must have been at the very epicenter of the quake when it struck. Any number of obstacles forced Keiji to lift Hayano over them, but their frequency decreased as Keiji and Hayano increased their distance from the butcher's.

Keiji's father had done yeoman's work making the house presentable after the quake. The structure itself was undamaged, but every shelf and cabinet had vomited its contents, and tiny black-rimmed holes in the kitchen tatami suggested sparks from a fire only barely reined in.

"Isn't Keiji-san's mom going to eat with us tonight?" Hayano asked between mouthfuls of rice.

"No, she's still sick," Keiji's father said.

"Oh," said Hayano. "But what if she's hungry now?"

"What a thoughtful little girl," his father said. "Perhaps

we should bring her dinner right away. Would you like to help me?"

Ryoichi carried a platter with the food, Keiji brought the teapot, and Hayano was entrusted with a teacup and a pair of chopsticks. They walked down a narrow corridor, floorboards creaking underfoot, and Keiji slid aside the door to his mother's dark, antiseptic room.

His mother, Yasu, looked up from beneath her thick quilt, and Keiji's first thought was that she must have been getting worse if she was shivering in a room this warm. Her hair hung in limp strands and her face was flushed. "Hello, Keiji," she said. "Who's your friend?"

"This is Shoji Hayano," Keiji said. "Hayano, this is my mother."

"Hello," Hayano said, her high voice sweet as a bird's in the dark room. "Your tummy is sick, huh?"

"Yes, it is," Yasu said, nodding and smiling to her husband as he walked gingerly across the tatami floor and set the tray of food beside her. "I suppose my son told you that."

"I didn't," said Keiji. "Dad and I mentioned the surgery, but not . . . Hayano, how did you know about Mom's stomach?"

"I can see it," said Hayano. She pointed at the quilts. "There's something big in her tummy that's not supposed to be there. It looks like it hurts."

Ryoichi looked at his son. "What's going on here?"

"I don't know, Dad. I swear to you, I didn't say a thing about the cancer. Mom, I'm sorry."

He took Hayano by the shoulders and turned her to escort her from the room. Behind him, a word from his mother turned into a wet, hacking cough. Keiji had captured the word, though. It was "Wait."

"Mom? Are you all right?"

"No," she said between coughs. "I'm sick, son. And this little girl can see that. Are you a *goze*, dear?"

"No. I'm Hayano."

"You are, *neh*? You're a modern-day *goze*. Who would have thought?"

Keiji knelt on the floor between his mother and Hayano. "Mom, what are you talking about?"

"You should know," Ryoichi said, kneeling beside him.

"Have you forgotten your bedtime stories? Ah, but you always preferred your samurai stories, didn't you? Hayano-chan, have you ever heard of a *goze*?"

"No."

"The *goze* were blind women," Keiji's mother said, "from a long, long time ago. They played instruments and they walked the old highways, begging for alms."

"What's alms?"

"Money, sweetheart. Like monks ask for when they stand outside of temples with bowls."

"Oh."

"The *goze* were not beautiful women, and of course everyone thought them crippled, but they played the *shamisen* and the *shakuhachi* marvelously, and they saw what no one else could see."

"What was it?" Hayano hunched forward in anticipation.

"The future, little one."

From the way Hayano's hair shifted on her head, Keiji could tell her eyebrows must have risen halfway up her forehead. Her mouth made the shape of an egg, a black hole in her bright face in the dark room.

"Hayano-chan," Yasu said, "you should finish your dinner and have a bath. Your cheeks are dirty."


The moon was up, a caterwauling cat was crying out to it, and the Kiyamas had managed to get little Hayano cleaned up. Her bandages were fresh, and Keiji's father had taken a shot at trimming her hair. He'd done this for Yasu some weeks ago, and the effect on Hayano was more or less the same: not a bad job, all things considered, but since the only hairstyle Ryoichi knew how to cut was his wife's, Hayano wound up looking like an elegant dwarf. If only they'd had a fifty-year-old's clothes in nine-year-old sizes, she might have passed for a large and lifelike doll, albeit a sinister one given the white linen wrapped around her eyes.

The scars there were terrible. Keiji suspected an explosion, though he couldn't imagine where it might have happened. The war was in the Pacific and on Chinese soil, nowhere near the homeland. But then he chided himself. That's boot camp talking, he thought; explosions happened in civilian life too. In his mind he started to list the things that might explode, engines and boilers and the like, and soon found himself thinking about how quickly he'd shifted his frame of reference. He was a soldier now, no longer in the same category as his parents or this little girl. Civilian life was so far away from him it was like another country, one he could book passage to visit only after the war was over.

"Hayano-chan, you said you saw something growing in my mom's belly, *neh*?"

"Yes." Her voice creaked with sleepiness.

"How big was it?"

He saw her shrug under her covers. "Maybe like a yam."

Keiji swallowed. How long had it been since his mother had her surgery? Two weeks? Three? And back then the doctor had removed a tumor the size of an egg. "You can see the future, can't you?"

"Don't know."

"You can." He could not say the rest. The cancer coming back. Someday a tumor as big as a yam. Engulfing the organs around it. Killing her. Maybe before the end of the war. Maybe when Keiji was at his duty station. So close to home and yet not there. Not with his parents as a son should be. Not at her side to say good-bye.

He cried until he could not cry anymore; then he fell asleep.

## 61

The little brass hammer battered the bells atop Keiji's alarm clock and jarred him out of sleep. His father had always been able to wake at any time he chose, but Keiji hadn't inherited that gift, and getting up in the winter and spring was always the worst. Moving from the warm confines of his futon to the cold floor was the hardest thing he had to do in any given day—or so he felt, at least, in the moments after his hand fumbled blindly to silence the damnable clock.

It was set early this morning, as it was the morning before: Keiji knew he could not afford to be late for Matsumori ever again. He got himself dressed, got Hayano dressed and fed, and the two of them were out the door before Keiji's parents made it out of bed. As Keiji and Hayano walked toward Tora-no-mon, he said to her, "How about explaining the thing you were going to explain yesterday? About the tiger and how you knew the butcher shop wouldn't fall down, remember?"

"All right." She turned her head as if to look directly at the sword. "The tiger protects the mountain. He lives there. There's a beautiful lady, and when she comes by the tiger, the tiger has to kill her. But if the tiger leaves his house, his house might fall down. The forest spirit is going to wreck it if the tiger goes away."

"Who is the forest spirit?"

"The forest spirit is the defender of the trees. It has a great power: it can wreck things. It wrecks its enemies, but in some stories it wrecks its friends too."

None of it made any sense to Keiji, but the fact that she'd known the name of his sword and she'd seen his mother's cancer was enough to make him try to sort it out. As with the war effort, frustration would have to make way for necessity.

But by the time they reached the Intelligence building, he still hadn't been able to get a straight answer from her about the identity of the beautiful woman, nor about who this defender of the trees was supposed to be. Keiji had no choice but to leave Hayano under the watchful eye of the butcher, to whom he gave ten yen he'd borrowed from his father before leaving the house. "For yesterday and the day before," he told the old man, "and for today and the rest of the week too, if you're willing. I'll come back every day after six."

Keiji arrived at the Intelligence building thirty minutes early, set water boiling for tea even before the secretaries arrived, and started analyzing intelligence reports of the Solomon Islands. As near as he could tell, the islands were all but undefended. Once taken, keeping them from the Americans would be a trick, but seizing the islands would not be difficult. He wondered how many battle groups were already within striking distance of the islands, and how soon he could begin an analysis of the invasion.

"Kiyama," General Matsumori said. "You're early. Good. You can take a hint."

"Yes, sir."

"Well done with that report yesterday on the Philippines. I'm putting you in charge of rerouting personnel down there. You'll sort out where we'll keep POWs too, of course. Get to it."

"What of Guadalcanal, sir?"

Matsumori waved him off. "You'll get your share of the glory. We all will. But we'll take care of today before we worry about tomorrow. All right by you?"

"Yes, sir. Of course, sir."

"I'm ever so pleased."

The general went to his office, and Keiji exchanged his maps of the Solomons for maps of the Philippines. Gradually the other intelligence officers arrived and set about their tasks. The smells of coffee and tea and old paper filled the room, as did the slow whirring of the ceiling fan and the occasional cough or sniffle.

In its own way it was the optimal environment for intelligence work. Each man had his own assignment, and since there was no need for conversation, the only distractions came when someone else required Keiji's maps. He shared them when he had to, got them back as he could, and relied upon field reports for the rest of his data.

By six o'clock he'd drawn up a preliminary assessment. In eight pages he'd calculated how many officers ought to be sent per five thousand POWs, which officers were both suitable to the task and near at hand, what support personnel they would require, and which aircraft and naval vessels could accomplish the redeployments as efficiently as possible. Any one of a dozen hypotheses might have been ill founded—he had no idea how many POWs there would be, nor how many of the officers he'd selected were already KIA, nor how many of his chosen vessels were sunk or damaged—but as an initial assessment he thought it wasn't bad.

Again he had dinner with Hayano and his parents, and again he delivered the girl to the butcher shop the next morning on the way to work. She was a sweet child. She didn't deserve to have her mother run off on her. But it was wartime, and people were becoming unpredictable. Perhaps it was the rationing that made them that way, Keiji mused, but what could be done for that? Sugar, paper, gasoline—they were all in short supply, all vital for the war effort. Where had the samurai spirit gone? Where was the selflessness, the sacrifice for the emperor, the reliability in times of turmoil? If the newsreels showed Americans abandoning their daughters or letting their grown women become pickpockets in the streets, he might have understood, but how could it happen in Tokyo?

He arrived to find his preliminary assessment of the Philippine deployment missing from his desk. As he shuffled through his other papers in search of it, he heard the heels of General Matsumori's boots clip-clop into the room. Keiji snapped to attention.

"At ease. This is good, Kiyama. Itō wasn't wrong about

you." The general strode across the room and dropped his assessment—annotated—on Keiji's desk. "The *Oshima* is docked in Nagasaki for repairs, by the way. You'll have to find a different merchantman. And Colonel Arai is a libertine. Have you ever met the man?"

"No, sir."

"He should be fighting on the sumo circuit, if only he weren't so old. No good to send him down to the tropics; he'd just sweat to death."

"I'll replace him, sir."

Matsumori waved his hand. "Already done. I've got just the man for you. Iwasaki's his name. He did a good bit of fighting in Nanking and he understands how to make the enemy feel fear. Just the man to cow those Americans and Filipinos into submission."

"I'll track him down, sir."

"Good. Do you read English, Kiyama?"

"Only what they taught us in intelligence school."

"That's more than I can do. I've got a Californian newspaper being wired to me, and I want to know what's going through those people's minds from day to day. From now on, when you get here in the morning, come straight to my office and go over the headlines. If there's anything there that you think I need to know, give me a translation of the article. Don't spend all day at it; an hour should do."

"I'll do my best, sir."

"I expect nothing less." The general turned to leave, then paused. "Say, Kiyama, that's a fine sword you've got there."

"Sir?"

"Your sword. I recognize fine craftsmanship when I see it. May I?"

Keiji withdrew the blade from its sheath and handed it to the general with a bow. "Extraordinary," Matsumori said. "Almost floats on the air, doesn't it? And yet as sturdy as the heart of an oak tree. I'd say this is very old steel. Would I be right?"

"You would, sir. I'm told it's an Inazuma."

Matsumori's eyebrows arched at that. "Is it? Incredible. You know, today most people don't believe Inazuma ever existed. Even men like General Itō, men who have a passion for swords, doubt he was real. Hold a sword like this, though, and there's no doubt the creator was one of a kind."

Matsumori angled the blade to catch the light. "Believe it or not, Kiyama, this is the second Inazuma I've held in my own two hands. Quite a fortunate life, *neh*? Two Inazumas. The other happens to be my own. I shall have to let you see it sometime."

"I'd like that, sir."

"Good. Back to work."

## 62

Keiji came home in time to hear a fit of furious coughing from the back room. "You'll be all right," Hayano's little voice kept saying. "You'll be all right."

On any other day, he would have asked his father how his mother was doing. This time, hearing Hayano's words and knowing who had spoken them, he thought they were not mere consolation. If one who could see the future said, "You'll be all right," to Keiji there was no cause for alarm.

He found his father standing in the doorway to the kitchen, leaning and watching the door from which the coughs came. "Hi, Dad," Keiji said. "Let me help you with dinner."

The family ate together in the back room—the oncologist said it was best for Yasu to stay away from smoke, and therefore away from the kitchen and dining room—and afterward Hayano played her *shakuhachi*. Yasu clapped and otherwise tried not to exert herself; every time she laughed, she would lapse into paroxysms of coughing.

That night, as Keiji lay on his pillow looking at the ceiling, he heard sobbing from near his feet. Sitting up, he saw Hayano was crying.

"What's wrong?"

"Am I a *goze*, Keiji-san?"

"I don't know. I think so."

"I can't see my mom."

"I know, sweetheart."

"No, you don't!" Hayano pounded her little fist on the tatami floor. "If *you* can't see your mom, that just means she's not in here. If *I* can't see my mom, that means she's not coming. Because I can see the future, can't I?"

She broke down wailing. She cried into her pillow, then into her hands, then into Keiji's shoulder. He held her there, tight against his chest, rocked her until the tears soaked the fabric of his *yukata* and she stopped struggling to get free. At long last she stopped crying, and used the sleeve of his *yukata* to wipe her nose. He didn't care. He held her until she was asleep, and because he could not bear the thought of waking her, he lay down and nestled her beside him. He slept alongside her as if she were his own daughter, and both of them slept the sleep of the dead, peaceful and dreamless and warm.

# 63

The Californian newspaper was not at all like the intercepted memoranda he'd analyzed in intelligence school. The sentences were longer, many of the verbs unknown. Journalism did not admit much room for artistic flair, but compared to military memos, translating the articles was like interpreting poetry.

Keiji took on just one article, which pertained to something called Executive Order 9066 and had rather a lot to do with Japanese people in the western United States. It seemed they'd been rounded up for the last six weeks or so, not unlike the Jews under Hitler and Stalin. Keiji thought General Matsumori would be interested.

There was another article, one Keiji tried to piece together but did not bother to translate. It claimed new discoveries that Japanese troops had committed terrible atrocities in southern China, particularly in Nanking, including rapes, burning, torture, and wholesale slaughter.

Keiji would have written it off as propaganda were it not for the level of detail. Dates were given, body counts, locations, causes of death. Japanese bayonets were mentioned, and swords and rifles too. He could not doubt it: something awful had happened in that city. Could the Chinese have done it to their own kin? He could not be sure—but neither could he say with certainty that his own countrymen were not involved.

He translated as much of the 9066 article as he could manage in an hour—no more than a rough sketch of the highlights, which he hand-carried to Matsumori's office as soon as he finished. There he found the general in conversation with a lanky man wearing colonel's stripes. "Kiyama," Matsumori said with a smile, "here's someone for you to meet. Colonel Iwasaki, this is Lieutenant Kiyama. He's new in our division and already making waves. *Neh*, Kiyama? It's because of him that you have your new command in the Philippines, Colonel."

"Is that so?" said Iwasaki. He had a trim, close-cropped mustache like the general's and wore the decorations of a man who had seen long years in the service. "You have my thanks."

As was his wont, the general was in his shirtsleeves, the presence of a war hero notwithstanding. "Iwasaki here is going to corral those POWs in Mindanao," said Matsumori.

"Ah, good," said Keiji. "I understand you fought in China some years ago, sir? In Nanking?"

"That's right," Iwasaki said. "Showed those bastards a thing or two about who's running Asia."

He said it calmly enough, but there was something in his demeanor that made Keiji shiver. Indeed, it was the very serenity with which he spoke. This was a man who had seen the horrors of battle and was not troubled in the slightest. Even a schoolyard bully could appreciate the emotional turmoil in his violence. This was no bully. He was passionless, devoid of morality; a shark.

Matsumori slapped the two of them on the back. "What say we have a drink and a spot of lunch, gentlemen? I can trust both of you for a bit of *sake*, *neh*? Maybe a whiskey?"

Keiji balked. "On duty, sir?"

"Duty? Lieutenant, we're on the verge of taking the Philippines! The Solomons are next! If victory isn't cause enough for a drink, then this isn't an army worth fighting for."

The stairs of the Intelligence building were easily broad enough for three or four men to walk abreast, but General Matsumori lagged behind the other two because of his limp. With one hand on his considerable belly and the other on the handrail, the general said, "Say there, Iwasaki, that's a handsome sidearm you're wearing."

"My pistol, sir? It's standard-issue—"

"No, no, the *sword*, son. May I see it?"

Iwasaki's weapon cleared its scabbard in a flash. Keiji had never seen a draw so fast. It flashed again, and before he knew it the blade was at his throat.

"Beautiful, isn't she? Those Chinese bastards never saw her coming either."

Keiji stood very still and looked down at the gleaming steel. The temper patterns along the edge resembled those of his own sword, like little waves on a tiny sea.

"A fine weapon," said Matsumori. "Very old too, I should think."

"I wouldn't know, sir," said Iwasaki. He spun the sword once in the air and resheathed it. "Someone told my father it might be a Muramasa, but my father met a sword scholar at the Tokugawa Art Museum who was certain it's older."

"Does it have a name?" asked the general.

"It may have at one time. I don't know. I've named her Glorious Sun. For the empire, sir."

"Excellent!" Matsumori clapped. "My own blade is called Glorious Victory. We'll drink to both for the empire, *neh*? Come on, Kiyama. Don't lag behind."

Keiji followed the two of them out of the building and down the main thoroughfare bisecting the Tora-no-mon district. Matsumori was pointing out the finer places to eat and drink in the area—what was left of them, anyway; the earthquake had leveled most of them, and of the few survivors, more than half were ravaged by fire. A tavern with four standing walls and an able-bodied bartender wasn't ordinarily a rare find in Tokyo, but after walking a few blocks, General Matsumori joked that he should have sent an advance recon.

"Sir," Keiji ventured, "I think I know of a place."

"Speak up, Kiyama. Do you mean to tell me you can find us real live booze around here?"

"Do you know that butcher's shop just south of our post? I think the sushi restaurant behind it is up and running again."

"So long as they've got a few unbroken bottles, I'm game. Lead on, Lieutenant."

Keiji did as he was told, though he was careful to keep his distance; he had no wish to be within a sword's length of Colonel Iwasaki. Workmen and shop owners scurried about them, busy as ants. Teams of three and four erected new wall frames. Individual men and women replaced window-panes or reassembled broken furniture. There was no divi-sion of labor among the sexes, for every hand was needed. Even the children's hands were put to work, armed with little brushes to sweep the dust out of nooks and crannies. The air was heavy with smells of pulverized plaster and smoldering wood.

Those adults who had no more useful talents shoveled rubble into the street for collection. The collectors them-selves made slower progress, heaping the detritus into the back of a horse-drawn wagon. At first the sight of the horses took Keiji aback, but that was his soldier's thinking again. Before boot camp he would have understood immediately that gasoline was much too precious a resource for civilian uses such as this. Besides, in the aftermath of an earthquake, horses were more nimble than trucks.

"There she is!" he heard a voice cry, instantly snapping him out of his reverie. "There's the lady! Get her, tiger! Get her!"

It was Hayano, and despite the cloth over her eyes she was pointing right at Iwasaki.

"Shut your mouth," Iwasaki told her, "or I'll shut it for good."

"Kill her," Hayano said. "Kill her, Keiji-san!"

Matsumori and Iwasaki both looked over their shoul-ders. "Kiyama," the general said, "you know this girl?"

"No, sir. Just a coincidence, I'm sure. Perhaps if we just kept walking—"

"The hell I will," said Iwasaki. "This urchin keeps calling me a woman. Is this how you let civilians treat your officers, General?"

"Of course not." Matsumori turned on Hayano. "You shut it, little girl, or I'll have you lashed and your parents jailed."

"You can't," Hayano said, and she started to say more be-fore Keiji slipped behind her and picked her up. He put a hand over her mouth and she sank her teeth into his finger.

"Keep walking, sirs. I'm sure she's just sick in the head. I'll deal with her and catch up. Ow! Stop biting me."

"Keiji-san?" Hayano was crying, and said his name as soon as he uncovered her mouth.

"I'm sorry," he said, setting her down behind the half-rebuilt grocery across the road from the butcher shop. "Are you all right?"

"No! You said I'm sick in the head and you pretended you didn't even know me. I hate you."

"Well, you bit me and you yelled at a man who wouldn't think twice about cutting you in half in broad daylight. I was trying to save your life, Hayano-chan."

"You're still mean. I don't like you."

Keiji groaned and sucked on the tooth marks on his throbbing finger. "Listen, you can't be shouting for me to kill someone in the middle of the street. The one you were pointing at is dangerous."

"I *know*. That's why you have to kill her."

"Hayano, the person you were pointing at wasn't a woman. It was a man—and I think he's killed women and children before. Not here, not recently, but I wouldn't be surprised if he was willing to do it again."

"It's not him," Hayano said. "It's her. She makes him do it. And she'll make him do it again unless you kill them."

"Who?"

"The lady. Only the tiger or the forest spirit can stop her. And the forest spirit won't. I know he won't. You have to do it, Keiji-san."

"Hayano, I don't have the time to make sense of any of this."

"You *have* to. You have to kill her, and the man who carries her too. You just *have* to."

Forest spirit. An invisible lady haunting Colonel Iwasaki and making him attack children. Obviously the tiger was Keiji's own sword, but nothing else in her story made sense to him. "Hayano-chan, I'm really sorry I hurt your feelings, but I have to find those men before Iwasaki causes any more trouble. You hide back here for a while, all right? Don't go back to the butcher shop until it's safe."

"All right. But I'm still mad at you."

"You can be mad. Just do it back here and not out in the street."

Keiji left her in a rush, deep in thought as he tried to catch up with the general and the colonel. How anyone managed to raise children was totally beyond Keiji's comprehension. It was far easier to orchestrate a war than to get one little girl to behave.

## 64

"Lighten up, Lieutenant. We're winning the war."

"Yes, sir," Keiji told General Matsumori. "I've just never been a big drinker, that's all."

He had found the two officers not at the sushi restaurant he'd suggested, but rather at a pub across the lane. A rickety jumble of tables and chairs lay heaped like a haystack beside the front door, but despite the damage to his establishment the owner had managed to hang his lantern. Matsumori and Iwasaki had run up an impressive tab even before Keiji arrived. The general was drinking whiskey; Iwasaki, warm *sake*; and Keiji, water.

"Not a drinker? Pah!" Matsumori pounded the tabletop. "A boy your age ought to be swimming in it. Swimming in liquor and snatch. You married, Kiyama?"

"No, sir."

"Why not? Nothing better for a young officer. You get laid every week and you've got someone to iron your uniform."

"My mother is ill. I can't imagine a woman wanting to marry into a household with a sick mother-in-law."

"Just you wait until we take Guadalcanal." Matsumori punched Colonel Iwasaki on the arm. "Bright boy, this Kiyama. Big plans for giving it to the *gaijin*. There'll be medals in this for all of us by the time it's done. Put a couple of medals on that chest, you wait and see how the girls come running." Matsumori took a swallow of whiskey. "Sorry to hear about your mother, Kiyama."

"Yes, sir."

Lunch went on like that—short speeches from Matsumori, very little from Keiji, not a word from Iwasaki—until they'd downed half a dozen drinks apiece and eaten every last scrap of the proprietor's grilled chicken. General Matsumori fished in his pocket until he found his watch. "Damn. Nearly one o'clock. I've arranged a motorcar to take you to the air base, Iwasaki. Come on, one more drink and we'll go."

As they returned to the Intelligence building, Colonel Iwasaki wobbled a bit along the boulevard, but Matsumori's limping gait was as sure as ever. Keiji, having drunk nothing but water, trailed two paces behind the others, still wary of Iwasaki and his passionless eyes.

As they approached the butcher shop, Keiji froze. Hayano was there, and appeared for all the world to be looking right at Iwasaki. "There she is," he heard her cry. "Keiji, kill her!"

Iwasaki lunged forward. Keiji's body moved as if through water—too slow, too late. General Matsumori tried to grab the colonel's sleeve; he missed. Iwasaki's sword shot free of its scabbard. He slashed at Hayano's throat.

Keiji gaped as the little blind girl ducked under the stroke. Wisps of black hair hung in the air for a moment, whirling in the wake of the sword. Iwasaki stood frozen, his sword arm at full extension.

Only then did Keiji reclaim mastery of his body. He and Matsumori dove on Iwasaki's arms, grappling them to prevent a second attack. Women screamed in every storefront. Hayano took a step back, her bandaged eyes on the sword in Iwasaki's hand.

"Can you hear her?" asked Iwasaki. His black eyes were wide, locked on Keiji's, his right arm like an iron rod in Keiji's grasp. "Can you hear her singing?"

"Give me the sword, Colonel."

For the first time, a gleam of emotion touched Iwasaki's eyes. Rage. Pure, seething rage. And just like that, it was gone. "No one touches her but me," he said.

"Sir, put the sword back in your scabbard," said Keiji, and together he and Matsumori guided the weapon home, Matsumori still gripping Iwasaki's neck and left arm.

"Your Black Medal is here," General Matsumori said. "I think it's time for you to go."

A dusty T95 was indeed rolling toward them, its shocks squeaking as it bounced over a pothole. Keiji had always wondered how anyone got the nickname "Black Medal" out of "T95 Scout Car," and now he found himself oddly numb, wondering why he had attention to spare for such ruminations when he should have been wholly focused on restraining the sword-swinging madman.

"Can you hear her song?" Iwasaki said. Keiji could smell the *sake* on his breath. The T95 squeaked to a halt just in front of Matsumori's boots, but it seemed Iwasaki's glazed eyes couldn't even see it. The driver stepped out, walked around to open the passenger door, bowed, and said, "Sir."

Under a hundred guarded stares, Matsumori and Keiji pried Iwasaki's fingers off the hilt of his sword, then guided the colonel around the vehicle and into the passenger seat. Still numb, Keiji did not release him until he could put a hand on the door, which he slammed shut. Those hundred stares watched as the T95 belched a cloud of dark smoke and pulled away.

General Matsumori laughed a low belly laugh as his eyes followed the Black Medal. "Hot damn, you wouldn't want to face a man like that on the battlefield, would you? Those Philippine *gaijin* are going to have a hell of a time with that one."

Keiji shivered. "W-would you excuse me, sir? I'd like to make sure that little blind girl is all right before I, uh, report back to my post."

"Knock yourself out."

Keiji ran back to the butcher shop to find Hayano standing as if she, like the general, was watching Iwasaki's car depart. "The tiger should have killed her, Keiji-san."

"Who are you talking about?"

"The lady. The one who sings. People die when she sings, Keiji-san. Now I can't see how the tiger is going to get her."

It was all Keiji could do not to collapse beside her in the street. The adrenaline evaporated away seemingly all at once, leaving exhaustion in its place. Keiji wanted nothing more than to lie down and sleep. Propriety be damned, he thought; he sat right on the curb. "Hayano, what in the world are you—?"

A sudden flash of insight struck him, the sort that happens most often on the verge of total fatigue. "Are you talking about his sword?"

*"Yes,"* Hayano said. "You let her go, Keiji."

"I let her go." As if disarming a superior officer in the street was ever an option. As if that wouldn't have led to an old-fashioned duel with swords in the middle of the crossroads. As if that maniac Iwasaki would have had any compunction at all about chopping Keiji limb from limb. "I let her go," he said, "and now she's going to kill people?"

"Uh-huh."

"And you've seen this, have you?"

*"Yes.* Haven't you been listening?"

Keiji laid his tired head in his hands. "Hayano, she almost killed you. Are you sure that's not what you saw?"

"She's going to kill lots of people, Keiji-san. More than I can see. So, so many."

Oh no, Keiji thought. He looked at her. "Where, Hayano? Here?"

"Nuh-uh."

"Bataan? The Philippines?"

"I don't know. Somewhere far from here. On islands."

"Oh, no. Oh no no no. Stay here. I've got to go."

# 65

Two days later, a beaming General Matsumori entered the workroom of his intelligence analysts. Keiji and the others stood at attention until a nod from the general allowed them to stand at ease. "Gentlemen, it is a good morning. His Majesty's military has crushed all resistance in the Philippines."

"Banzai!" everyone shouted. "Banzai!"

Keiji chanted as loudly as anyone, but his stomach clenched like a fist as he did it. It was not the victory that sickened him—on the contrary, the news made him proud to wear his uniform, proud of himself and his country—but rather the swiftness of the victory. He'd been counting on at least another week to put his plan into effect.

"Gentlemen," the general said, "I must call particular attention to the efforts of our newest comrade, Lieutenant Kiyama. Young Kiyama foresaw the need for additional personnel in the event of an early surrender, and thanks to him I was able to deploy the best officers for the job. They started arriving yesterday and today—none too soon, *neh*?"

The rest of the intelligence men cheered Keiji, and he offered an abashed bow in return. "Two days ago," the general continued, "we had a visit from Colonel Iwasaki, a veteran from the Chinese front. He was slated to oversee POWs in Mindanao, in the southern Philippines. Two days ago our lieutenant Kiyama asked me to reroute Iwasaki to

Luzon in the north. And this morning, just as Colonel Iwa-saki's flight was touching down, the last resistance in the north collapsed. You've shown remarkable foresight, Lieu-tenant. I'll be recommending you for a medal."

Again cheers from the others; again a red-faced bow from Keiji. "Seventy-five thousand men," General Matsu-mori said, a bright smile on his face, "and not a true warrior among them! Do you know what they surrendered to? Dys-entery!" He laughed. "This is how these barbarians fight, gentlemen. They don't keep themselves clean, and they don't adequately feed their men. The empire's victory in this war is assured!"

"Banzai!"

Keiji cheered with them again, his face still flushed. He'd hoped the Americans would hold out for at least another week. He only needed a few days to see to it that Iwasaki was removed. Assaulting a crippled girl in broad daylight was enough to get even a colonel thrown in the brig, if only Keiji had time to push the paperwork through. General Matsumori could have signed off on it at once, of course, but Keiji knew Matsumori would never process it. Keiji had gone about it himself, stealing precious minutes from his work to send the proper requests and notifications to an-other general in Tokyo, and now it was all for naught. No one would remove Iwasaki now. He had been sent to man-age twenty-five thousand POWs and now had three times that number. Handling Bataan would require every last man and then some. Keiji could only hope little Hayano was wrong.

She wasn't. He was sure of it already. She'd protected him from the earthquake. She'd seen his mother's cancer. She'd even dodged that murderous slash from Iwasaki, and Keiji couldn't begin to explain how an ordinary blind girl could have managed that.

No, he was more than sure of it: there was going to be a massacre on the Bataan peninsula, and the blood was on his hands.

# 66

"It's not your fault," Hayano said on their walk home. "It's the lady's fault. She's the one who sings and kills them."

"You told me to stop her. I didn't."

A light drizzle left cold pinpricks on the back of Keiji's neck. He took no notice. His boots were getting muddy, and cleaning them was annoying and time-consuming. The damage was done. He stepped in another puddle. "I didn't stop her," he said.

What could he do? Fly to the Philippines? How? He had no orders there and no way to get there without being ordered. Could he call for Iwasaki to be jailed? On what basis? The speculation of a blind nine-year-old wouldn't go over well in a court-martial.

Keiji's mind raced in circles, the same ideas blurring by with less and less clarity. He was an intelligence officer. Theoretically a bomber could hit Iwasaki's location on bad intelligence. But plotting it amounted to treason, and even if Keiji weren't caught, knowing Iwasaki's exact whereabouts was impossible from Tokyo. He'd have to fly to Bataan and find the man personally.

That was it. He'd have fly there personally. He would remove Iwasaki. And errant intelligence would see it done.

"Hayano-chan," he said as they neared his parents' house, "I'm going to have to leave you here for a little while.

Tomorrow at work I'm going to see to it that I get sent to Bataan. Everyone will think it's an accident, and I'll be back right away, but I need to go find the lady you keep seeing, the singing one, and I need to make sure she doesn't kill all those people."

"No, you can't do that, Keiji-san."

"I have to. Those people can't die because of me."

"They're not going to die because of you, Keiji-san. They're going to die because of bad people doing bad things. And if you leave, the tiger won't stay in his home, and his home will get all smashed up."

Keiji slid open the door and he and Hayano ducked out of the rain. "What are you talking about?"

She sat to remove her shoes as she spoke. "That's the tiger's power. Wherever it is, that place can't get smashed up. Like the butcher shop during the earthquake, remember? But if you take the tiger somewhere else, then the place it's supposed to be will get all wrecked. It'll be real bad if that happens, Keiji-san. Bad for everyone."

Keiji sighed as he struggled out of his boots. "Hayano, sometimes I really wish I knew what you were talking about."

"Huh?"

"Nothing. Tell me again, would you, please? You're saying the reason the butcher shop didn't fall down is because my sword was in the building at the time?"

"Uh-huh."

"And that's true no matter where the sword is?"

"Of course. The tiger protects things. Nothing can make the mountain go away while the tiger is on it."

"All right. Let me get this last part right, too. You think there's a particular place I'm supposed to protect? A place the tiger is supposed to stay?"

"Uh-huh."

Keiji took a deep breath. His socks were wet. His uniform was damp; it would smell tomorrow. "Hayano-chan, what's the place I'm supposed to protect?"

Hayano giggled. "Where you *work*, silly."

"What, the Intelligence building?"

"*Yes*. Don't you know anything?" She giggled again.

"Sounds like someone's home for dinner," called a voice from the kitchen. Keiji's guts went cold. It was his mother's doctor.

"I'll be on my way, then," the doctor was telling Keiji's father. "Make sure Yasu-san gets plenty of rest, *neh*?" As he passed Keiji on the threshold, he said, "Your mother's doing quite well, son. Good evening."

Keiji led Hayano back to the kitchen, where he was surprised to find his mother sitting next to his father on one side of the table. "Welcome home," his mother said, her voice reedy. "How are you two today?"

"I don't like doctors," said Hayano. "Doctors lie. They tell you things to make you think you're going to get better when you're not."

"I've heard that too," Yasu said.

"I think it's dumb," Hayano said. "I think they should just tell you the truth. That way I would have known right away that my eyes would never get better."

"Well," said Yasu, "I suppose they don't want to make people feel afraid."

As she said it, she gave her husband's forearm a squeeze, and right then Keiji knew her situation had worsened. Hayano was right again. The doctor had lied. "Son of a bitch," Keiji muttered.

"That's no way to talk in front of our houseguest," Ryoichi said. "Come on, Kei-kun. Help me with dinner."

They ate in silence. Keiji had the feeling that his own thoughts were shared around the table—doctors lied all the time, the bastards; everyone knew it; the stories were all too common—but no one spoke them aloud. Five minutes after he'd finished, Keiji realized he hadn't tasted a morsel of food. He couldn't even recall what it was that he'd eaten. Rice and what? His mother was dying. What did it matter?

After his bath he went straight to bed. It was useless. He could not sleep. He listened to his father and Hayano chattering in the bathroom, heard his mother's snores in the next room. At least *she* was sleeping well.

After a while Hayano came in, walking on her little toes, with one hand on the wall for balance. She slipped under her covers as quietly as she could, so cute he could not help but smile. "Hayano."

"Oh! Sorry, Keiji-san."

"Don't worry; I wasn't asleep. Hayano, come here, please."

She crawled up next to him. "Hayano-chan, I want you

to tell me what happens if I take Tiger on the Mountain away from the Intelligence building."

"It falls down," she said. "It gets all wrecked. And someday Japan loses the war."

Keiji frowned at that. He hadn't even realized a child her age could understand the concept of war, especially not one fought thousands of kilometers away, one in which the motherland itself saw no fighting at all. It wasn't as if Hayano could read the newspapers.

She's a *goze*, he reminded himself. "Are you sure? Japan loses the war?"

"There are lots of endings to the war. But if your building falls down, all the winning endings go away."

How could that be? There were countless Intelligence offices, more than Keiji could count. How could the fall of one building result in losing the war? "You're certain?"

"Uh-huh."

"Hayano, I need to go after Colonel Iwasaki. He's the one with the sword that sings."

"I know who he is."

"I had it in mind to bring my sword with me," Keiji said. "I've got a hunch that Iwasaki may be willing to face me if I offer to fight him sword to sword. Can you see that, Hayano? Can you see a future where I fight him?"

"I don't think people fight with swords anymore, Keiji-san."

"I know. I just think he's crazy enough to do it. He thinks he's a modern-day samurai. Hell, maybe I'm the one who thinks that. I don't know who's crazy anymore." Keiji rubbed his eyes. "All I know is, I think you can see how things will go if I bring my sword and how they'll go if I don't. What should I do, Hayano? What can you see?"

Hayano wrinkled her face. "Only the tiger can kill the singing lady. But if the tiger leaves, its home will fall, and the tree spirit will make everything else fall down. The tiger has to fight the tree spirit or fight the lady; it can't do both anymore."

Keiji closed his eyes. *Can't do both anymore.* Not since Keiji ignored his little *goze*. Not since he let Iwasaki get away.

But in his mind the wheels were turning. He would not let Japan lose her honor, nor would he let her lose the war. There was a way he could save the POWs in Bataan and still use his Inazuma sword to protect his duty station. There was a way because there had to be one. He just had to see it.

# 67

The weather at the air base in Okinawa could not have been more beautiful. Tokyo's April had been a gray, dreary, drizzling mess, but the Okinawan skies were clear and blue, the sun warm, the ocean breeze crisp. Tall palms whisked and whispered in the wind, and the oily stink of hot aircraft engines was blown away and replaced with scents of salt and sea foam.

Keiji ambled back and forth along the long wall of the hangar, enjoying the sunshine. There were plenty of places he might sit, but he would be sitting soon enough, and for a long time, so he paced. Inside the hangar, technicians and crewmen were completing all the requisite preflight diagnostics. Outside, uniformed soldiers joshed with each other in groups of three and four. There were hundreds of them, all Keiji's age and younger. They wore heavy packs and rifles on their backs, playful smiles on most of their faces, and they chatted and joked and sparred to work off nervous energy. The flight to the Philippines would depart in half an hour's time and these young men were going to war.

"Lieutenant," a voice said behind him. Keiji turned, expecting to see one of the soldiers. Instead he came face-to-face with one of the air base personnel; the tan uniform was the same, but there was no pack on this one's back. The man was panting; a constellation of beaded sweat shone on his forehead.

"Yes?"

"Sir," the man said, breathless, "I'm so glad I found you. There's been a mistake. Your deployment orders. They're wrong."

Keiji withdrew a folded piece of paper from his jacket pocket and showed it to the man. "It says here I'm due to fly to Bataan. Colonel Iwasaki's orders."

"That's just it, sir. There was a clerical error. Colonel Iwasaki was deployed to Bataan; his orders were signed by a Lieutenant Kiyama in Intelligence. Obviously that couldn't have been you, sir, or you'd have seen the error. Here it says it was you, Kiyama, deployed by Iwasaki, and not the other way around. There must have been some sort of transcription error."

"Ah," said Keiji.

"In any case, sir, a General Matsumori in Tokyo caught the mistake and wired a message just now. You're to report back to Tokyo on the next available aircraft."

The man stood with an expectant smile on his face, still sweating from what must have been a desperate run. Keiji wondered what the odds were of this man finding him among the hundreds of uniforms milling about. On any other day Keiji might have been impressed by the meticulous efficiency of this feat. Today it was all he could do to suppress a groan. Another few minutes and the deception could not have been corrected. Men were lining up to board even now. A few minutes more and he would have been airborne.

"Good news, right, sir? You're not going to the front."

"Er," Keiji said, looking at that expectant smile, "perhaps I should fly anyhow? I'd hate for this to be another clerical error."

"No, sir. The general's message was most specific. You are Lieutenant Kiyama Keiji, Army Intelligence, aren't you?"

To lie was to invite a court-martial. "Yes," he said.

The next flight to Tokyo was two days later. Keiji was on it.

## 68

Keiji returned home to an alarming surprise. Hayano ran to the door to greet him, her little feet flapping against the tatami. Nothing unpredictable there; he'd asked his father to take care of her before he'd arranged for himself to be deployed to Bataan. The surprise came when he entered his mother's bedroom.

Tiger on the Mountain lay beside her. His mother lay still, her face sweating but serene, and he knelt down and stroked her forehead.

"Keiji," she said, her voice stronger than he'd expected. She smiled up at him. "Why didn't you tell me about this beautiful sword of yours?"

"It never came up." He found her hand and squeezed her thin fingers. "General Itō gave it to me when I graduated. He's a collector, I think. I'm told he gives one sword a year as a gift."

"My son." Her smile widened, her eyes disappearing into folds. "That was a wonderful honor. You should have told me."

"You were sick."

"Well, I'm still sick, and I'm still proud of you." She patted his cheek.

"Mom, how did the sword get here? I left it at my post."

"A man from your unit delivered it. Oh, Keiji, don't ever forget anything there again. Your father and I were worried sick when we saw a man in uniform coming to the house. We thought something terrible had happened."

"I'm all right, Mom."

"Well, I know that *now*, don't I? Oh, Kei-kun, we feared the worst."

"I'm sorry, Mom." He squeezed her hand again. "Do you mind if I take the sword back? I should go in to report."

"Of course, dear. It is a beautiful one, isn't it? Reminds me of my grandfather's."

Keiji kissed her forehead and took the sword.

In the next moment noise consumed the world.

An explosion shook the ground like an earthquake. Then came another, and another. Keiji's bones quaked in his chest. He crouched over his mother, certain the ceiling would collapse at any moment. There was the crackle of fire outside, and splintering wood, and the distant hum of propellers.

Air raid. But how? The thoughts whirled through Keiji's mind at typhoon speed. The American fleet was much too far to carry out a raid. His father and Hayano were somewhere in the house. No noise from them. Were they alive? Did the Americans have a new kind of bomber Army Intelligence hadn't discovered yet? It would have to have unthinkably long range to strike Tokyo. Screaming in the street mixed with dogs barking and the rushing, crumbling clamor of a house caving in. Why weren't his father and Hayano making any noise? China. An American fleet could land there after a raid and wouldn't need the long range for a return flight. Why weren't they making any noise?

The whir of the propellers faded. No more explosions came. Keiji got up, realized for the first time that his mother was crying, rushed to the shoji and slid it open.

The house was unscathed. His father sat beside the low dining table, Hayano clutched to him, she hugging him back. It was obvious from the way their hands gripped each other that she was comforting him, that he was clinging to her as a drowning man might cling to a floating spar. Her face was calm, her muscles relaxed, and she seemed to be looking at the sheathed sword in Keiji's hand.

The sword. It protected the house, just as it had done for the butcher's shop. Just as it was supposed to have done for the Intelligence building, which was why he'd left it there in the first place when he tried to follow Iwasaki. There was no point in hurrying now. He knew what he'd find when he arrived.

Keiji did what he could to fight the fires on his parents' street, and when those were doused he worked his way toward the Intelligence building. He joined in bucket brigades along the way, and pulled fallen roof timbers off of injured children, and clamped his palms down on bleeding wounds while those with lesser injuries limped away in search of clean cloth. By the time he reached his post the sun had long since set. Only the surrounding fires lit the bombed-out shell of the Intelligence building.

In truth the building was in far better shape than Keiji had expected. Fully half of it still stood. The eastern half—the half where his office had once been—was a gaping crater toothed with the jagged concrete edges of what used to be walls. The building was no longer burning, but vertical black stripes showed where the smoke had poured out. Keiji thought they looked like war paint.

The analogy made him laugh out loud. It was all so hopeless. The stars were shining as they always did, and nothing and everything was different. His hometown was a target. His hometown had been bombed. He couldn't grasp the enormity of that simple idea. Scores of people died in Tokyo today, he thought, and more died yesterday and more will die tomorrow. But today is different, because yesterday they died of old age and sickness and traffic accidents, and today they died under the bombs of the enemy. Old age and sickness and traffic would have taken their toll today as well, but yesterday there were no bombs.

And Hayano had said if the Intelligence building was destroyed, Japan would lose the war. Now it was half-gone. What did that mean? Would the empire half lose? Was half a building a destroyed building or only half-destroyed? How was he to read his latest failure?

Keiji couldn't answer any of those questions, so he reported for duty. He could not find General Matsumori, but a captain on the scene reprimanded Keiji for being late and sent him to help the fire brigade. Keiji considered saying he was late because he'd been doing that very thing, but then he thought better of it.

He spotted a chain of people passing sloshing buckets

toward a building wreathed in smoke, so he picked his way through the debris to join them.

"Kiyama," a gruff voice said behind him. "You're just in time."

Keiji turned to see Matsumori standing in the back of a puttering T95. "So, Lieutenant, did you enjoy Okinawa?"

Keiji started to answer but the general cut him off. "I've convened the Intelligence boys over there." Matsumori pointed to an inn across the rubble-strewn road. "Hurry up."

The recon car rumbled away. Keiji ran to the inn as quickly as he could.

General Matsumori had already begun his speech when Keiji slipped through the front door. "We already have men at work," he was saying, "making every effort to minimize the damage of this raid. The truth is, this was a desperate stroke. I expect it was aimed more at the hearts of our people than at the emperor's war effort.

"But the Americans got lucky. They can't have known our building housed His Majesty's plans for securing the Pacific. Their target was probably the factory district on the other side of the river. But they got lucky, damn them. We lost two good men today, but only two. The real loss was information."

Matsumori closed his eyes, breathed, opened them again. "Take a moment to remember our fallen. Lieutenants Okada and Sayakawa will be missed. But the mission comes first. You are soldiers; your duty is to forget them now, forget the losses to our city, and concentrate on your work. Our nation's success in this war hinges on success in the Pacific, gentlemen, and right now His Majesty's plans for securing the South Pacific light the street in a thousand scattered little fires. We move forward on Tulagi. We move forward on Guadalcanal. It is up to you to recall those plans as best you can, and to work quickly to fill in whatever gaps are left. Do you understand?"

"Sir, yes sir!" the intelligence men cried in unison.

"I have commandeered this inn for our use. Next door is a stationery store, not too badly burned in the raid. I have commandeered it as well. Take whatever dry paper you can find. Take pens and ink and whatever else you need. Then write down everything—*everything*—you can remember about your work these past days and weeks. Victory is still within reach, gentlemen. We will work through the night if we must."

"Sir, yes sir!" they said, Keiji with them.

At a nod from the general the intelligence officers scattered. Matsumori fixed Keiji with his gaze and said, "Not you, Lieutenant. Come here."

Keiji obeyed. "I won't work under a civilian roof when so much of our own remains standing," said the general. "You'll find me a room in our building and make it spotless. By morning I want a functional office. And you'll report there first thing."

# 69

"Not bad," General Matsumori said the following morning, his eyes roving the room. It was in the southwest corner overlooking the atrium, its tall windows blown out, a light breeze wafting through them. The lightbulbs were blown out too, of course, which hardly mattered since the electrical service had also been destroyed in the bombing. Keiji had swept all the broken glass into the corridor the night before, where for all he knew it still lay in a gray dusty heap, waiting for someone to brush it into a dustbin. He'd labored until oh four hundred hours, then reported back at oh six thirty bleary-eyed and seeing little of his immediate surroundings.

Two small oil lamps did what they could to light the room. They stood on the big steel table that served for the moment as Matsumori's desk. The general sat on the desk, legs dangling, his belly curving like a pregnant woman's over his belt. He was halfway toward his usual state of informal dress: his jacket and sword were already removed, but his cap still perched on his closely shaven head and his pistol was at his hip. "We could have used you last week, Kiyama. You're a man with attention to detail. What was all that nonsense about being deployed to the Philippines? You should have spoken up, son."

"Yes, sir."

"So? Why didn't you speak up for yourself? Stupid, fly-

ing all the way down to Okinawa just so you could fly back.
It was your idea, invading the Solomons, and then you disappear for over a week. What were you thinking?"

Keiji's eyes itched. He was sure they were red. He stifled
a yawn and pinched his fingernails into his palms to wake
himself. Should I tell him the truth, he wondered, or make
something up? You're too tired to lie, came the answer in
his mind. And another answer, too: The truth will get you a
court martial. Come up with something, you fool.

"I said, what were you thinking, Lieutenant?"

"Sorry, sir." Keiji looked at the empty window frames,
then back at the general. "Permission to speak frankly?"

"Permission? Hell, consider it an order."

"Sir, do you remember the little blind girl? The one Colonel Iwasaki attacked?" And he took the plunge.

By the time Keiji had finished his story, Matsumori was
sitting behind the steel table with his hands folded behind
his head. "Kiyama," the general said, "where were you when
the bombers hit?"

"At home, sir. That is, at my parents' house."

"How is the folks' house? Roof fall in? Anything like
that?"

"No, sir."

"And that's because of this sword of yours, is it?"

"I believe so, sir."

Kiyama lit a cigarette. "Too bad. I was hoping you'd tell
me a roof beam fell and hit you on the head. All this time
I've been waiting for some reason—any reason at all,
really—to believe I should have you thrown in the hospital
instead of the brig. You're telling me you deserted your
post—scratch that: you forged documents, *then* deserted
your post—to hunt down a decorated officer of this army
and murder him? All because a crippled street urchin told
you a fairy tale?"

Keiji swallowed and clenched his folded hands behind
his back.

"Well? Answer me, Lieutenant! You're telling me you
abandoned your post, what, ten days ago, because you believe this damned blind girl can see the future?"

"I . . . Well, that would be one way to put it, sir."

"Oh? Maybe you'd like to tell me another way to put it.
Maybe some way you'd put this in a positive light? Because

as I see it, you're either criminally negligent or criminally insane. I thought you had a bright future, Kiyama. Your mentor apparently thought so too—but then I don't imagine General Itō knew he was giving you a magic sword, did he?"

"No, sir."

"Shut up. You know what my favorite part of this story is? It's that you were going to try to kill Colonel Iwasaki because he's doing his job. He's on the front lines of this war, Kiyama, and you wanted to fly halfway around the world to challenge him to a duel—*a duel!*—so you could keep him from killing the enemy."

"Captured enemy, sir. There are rules in warfare."

"*You're* going to tell *me* about *rules*?" Matsumori's voice boomed. He threw his cigarette at Keiji; it bounced off his chest and smoked on the floor. "There are rules against forgery, you stupid son of a bitch, and rules against desertion too. You're lucky I don't have you hanged from what's left of this building. I'd leave you dangling from a rafter for all your friends and relatives to see. Hell, I'd even cart your little blind girl up there so she could get a good whiff of your rotting corpse, if only I didn't need every man I've got."

Matsumori was an inch from Keiji's nose now; Keiji could feel the spittle flecking from his lips. "You look like you've got something to say, Kiyama. Care to say it?"

"Sir," Keiji said, "I must protest my innocence. I did all that I did for the sake of the country. For duty, sir."

"Duty," Matsumori growled. "Oh, you're a genuine samurai, aren't you, Kiyama? Maybe you'd like to slit your belly open on my office floor, *neh*? That's how they protested their innocence in the old days. How about it?"

"They also protested by challenging their accusers to a duel, sir."

Matsumori jerked his pistol free and crammed it into the underside of Keiji's chin. "I'm a *general*, Kiyama. You don't threaten me lightly." His face was like a snarling dog's, furrowed and furious. "Give me one reason why I shouldn't spray your brains all over this room."

"Honor," said Keiji.

Matsumori's eyes widened ever so slightly. He returned the pistol to its holster. His face was still so close that Keiji could feel the heat of his breath. "You actually believe this samurai shit, don't you? You're living in a fairy tale. First you rescue the little blind girl, then you charge in on your warhorse and challenge big, bad Matsumori to a heroic duel. Was that it? Is that the future your cripple saw for you?"

No, Keiji was going to say, but then a puzzle piece fell into place. Matsumori. The name meant "pine grove," but "grove" was not the only meaning of *mori*; with a different kanji, it could mean "protect" or "defend." Matsumori would then mean "protector of the pines."

"You're the forest spirit," Keiji whispered, not even meaning to say it aloud. "She saw you from the beginning. You're the one who destroys everything."

"What?"

"Nothing, sir."

"No, do tell, Kiyama. I'm all ears."

"Hayano told me about you. She said the defender of the trees might destroy its friends as well as its enemies. You're the defender of the trees."

Matsumori didn't even dignify Keiji with a response. He turned his back and walked over to sit behind his desk. "I've given you every opportunity to save your career," he said. "Do you know what I'm going to do now? I'm going to fulfill your wish." The general removed his cap and slapped it flat on his desk. "You want to be a samurai? You want to fly around the world to some damn island far away from your little blind girl and your sick mom? Fine. Consider yourself demoted, Sergeant Kiyama. I'm making you a platoon leader. You're going to take Guadalcanal. Then you're going to jump to every island after that, and you're going to raise my flag on every last one of them. I'm going to teach you the meaning of the word 'duty,' Sergeant. I'm going to teach you 'honor' and 'glory' and 'victory' even if I need American bullets to drive the point home. Now get the hell out of my sight."

# 70

Dear Father,

Thank you for your last letter. I was so very sorry to hear about Mother's death and am sorrier still that I could not be home for you and for her. Lately I feel every decision I make leads me further astray, and this failure is the most painful of all.

It gladdens me to know that Hayano-chan is a buoy for you in these sad times. I would thank you for continuing to care for her, but it seems perhaps I should also thank her for continuing to care for you. Let me say instead that I am grateful that both of you can support each other, since I am so far away and cannot do my part as a filial son.

My lone success is one you will be happy to learn of: we have taken Guadalcanal. The nearby islands are expected to fall in the coming days, but my platoon has been reassigned to the construction of an airstrip, so I will see no more fighting. I will not write of combat this time; the brutality of it is still too near for me, and there is already too much death at home.

I have heard rumors that my former commanding officer, General Matsumori, will be promoted thanks to our victory here. I am told he will serve directly under General Tōjō. Obviously this is the highest honor for him, but I fear things will go poorly for our country because of it. Hayano-chan foresaw that Matsumori would either destroy his enemies or destroy his friends, and I now fear it will be the latter, for she also saw that Japan would not see victory in this war. It sickens me that I was so slow to decipher her message; I could have changed the future if only I had been quicker to see what she showed me.

Now I fear matters will become worse. Since my demotion I no longer receive all the intelligence I once did, but I would be very surprised if the Americans make no plans to oust us from these islands. I do not know how that will go. If we have time enough we may be able to fortify our positions, but their country is so large, and their people so many. Their factories will be producing weapons of war every day. While I still served under General Matsumori, I read terrible things about how they treat the Japanese within their own borders; it frightens me that I may become their prisoner.

More frightening still is the thought that the homeland should fall and the emperor be unseated. I left my sword at home so that you and Mother and Hayano would be protected. Now it seems the air raid that struck all around our home was indeed an act of desperation, not to be repeated anytime soon. (How long ago was it since we heard the bombs falling? Only a month? Is that possible? It seems so long ago—so much has happened since then!—but the calendar tells me it is so.) I am of two minds now, and since these days all of my choices go awry, I ask you to choose for me.

I should like my sword to remain at home, to protect you and Hayano-chan and anyone else who might take shelter there in the event of another air raid. I am quite convinced it will keep any building safe so long as it stays there.

But I should also like the sword to find a place in the imperial household. If Hayano-chan is right, and the empire is to lose this war, then at the very least I do not want the Americans and Russians and British to choose what government Japan shall take. This has been their habit all across Asia, and I do not want Japan to go the way of all the other European and American conquests. Our national spirit is the samurai spirit. If the enemy should depose our emperor, I fear that our homeland's spirit may be broken, and I believe the power of Tiger on the Mountain may protect against that dreadful day.

I have no inkling how to advise you. My duty as a son bids me to ask you to keep the sword for your own protection. My duty as a soldier would have me ask you to find some way to deliver the sword to the imperial palace. I feel as thin as a sheet of paper, and as frail; I feel I am being torn in two.

I can only suggest that you explain the decision to Hayano-chan and rely on her insight. My bitterest regret is that I did not put greater faith in her myself.

Please give my love to her. I think of her every day, and I miss her terribly. Of course I miss Mother too; whenever my thoughts go to her, I feel as though I am falling headlong down a well, and I need to pull my thoughts away before I fall too far. I miss you as well, Father, and I am so very sorry that I cannot be with you in your days of loss. I cannot imagine how I might make up for my mistakes, but I hope that I can survive this war and return home to do my best to try.

Yours,
Keiji

# BOOK NINE

◆◆◆◆◆◆◆◆◆◆◆◆◆◆◆◆◆◆◆◆◆◆◆◆◆◆◆◆◆◆◆◆◆◆◆

## HEISEI ERA, THE YEAR 22

### (2010 CE)

S aori's phone was a bust. Yamada had been right about his protégé: the sword's power was not yet so complete that he had lost all reason. Fuchida had wised up, and HRT found the phone dumped in the backseat of a taxi. "Keep it for prints," Mariko told the HRT commander over the phone. She rode shotgun in a squad car on its way to the morgue, screaming down a canyon of asphalt and steel and light. Headlights and taillights traced ghost lines in her bleary vision, streetlights flitted by overhead, huge LED displays flashed on every side, and the lights of the squad splashed stroboscopic red over everything. "We know Fuchida's our guy, but it won't hurt the prosecutor to have another piece of evidence. And interview the taxi driver. See if he remembers anything."

"Already on it, Sergeant. He says a long-haired guy stopped him and asked how much it would cost to get to Narita. We're guessing your suspect dropped the phone on the sly while he had the door open."

"Probably."

"I've spoken with Narita security already, and I'm sending men—"

"Don't bother. He's not flying anywhere. He's got his hostage; public places aren't on his agenda. Besides, he's in an awful hurry to get his ransom by tomorrow; no way he's leaving the country today."

"Good point."

"Find out where Fuchida hailed the cab. The bastard's got to be hiding somewhere nearby. It'll be a place a woman could scream without being heard. A good-sized room, I think; I heard him take three or four steps to get to the hostage after he set down the phone."

"Will do."

"One more thing. If Fuchida's in a hurry, maybe it's because he's keeping his supplier waiting. Or maybe his supplier's on his way here as we speak, and Fuchida needs to meet him. I take it back: go ahead and contact Narita. The port authorities too, here and in Yokohama. Tell them to tighten up all cargo checks. They're looking for cocaine. Focus on foreign carriers and ships out of foreign ports. But keep your team in the area; maybe we'll get lucky and find where Fuchida's holed up."

"We're on it, Sergeant."

The HRT commander hung up just as Mariko's squad pulled into the roundabout in front of the hospital. Mariko thanked the driver, then went inside and down to the morgue.

It was already late; it was likely the family would not come until morning. Mariko felt someone should be there for them, someone who could tell them what had happened to Dr. Yamada. And the morgue was as good a place to sit as any. She had no desire to go home; as badly as she wanted to sleep, dreams of Yamada's blood and Saori's squeals were not what she needed right now. Better to drift off in a strange place where she knew she could only sleep lightly. Dreamlessly.

Downstairs she found an old woman in white, wearing huge black Chanel sunglasses. She looked older than Mariko's grandmother, and she stood facing a window Mariko had seen before. There would be a body on the other side of it, and Mariko wondered whose it was. Yamada's would not be the only one here; in a city of thirteen million, any given hospital would have any number of corpses to deal with.

But the old woman turned to Mariko and said, "You're here for him too."

"What's that?"

"You'll have known him as Yamada Yasuo, I think," said the old woman. "How did you meet him?"

"He was my sensei . . ." Mariko said in a fog. "Wait—who are you? How did you get here? He's only been dead an hour. They can't have called the next of kin already."

Mariko was speaking as much to herself as to anyone, and much too quietly for most women this one's age to hear. But the old woman said, "I saw it. His death, I mean. It makes me so sad. And for his own student to kill him. Tragic."

Mariko wondered whether she'd fallen asleep. "This is surreal," she said. "You can't know any of this. No one here knows any of it yet, and I just got here."

The old woman looked at her. "My dear, you sound exhausted. You could use a good night's sleep, I think."

She was right. But even in its exhausted state Mariko's mind was still a detective's mind. Details still beckoned her attention, like the fact that this woman looked straight at her and yet said Mariko *sounded* tired. And the big black sunglasses, still on in a basement room at night.

This woman was blind. Mariko almost said so, but then remembered Yamada-sensei chiding her on his porch when she'd said the same to him. Instead she said, "Who are you?"

"My name is Shoji Hayano. Keiji-san and I have been friends for a long, long time. Since before your parents were born, I think."

"Why do you call him Keiji-san?"

"Why, that's his name. Kiyama Keiji. He only changed it to Yamada after the war. You couldn't get into graduate school with a dishonorable discharge. Not in those days. He had no choice but to change it. And oh, did he feel guilty for it! But I think leaving his name behind let him leave some of his other guilt behind."

Mariko still felt swamped by surreality. This woman spoke as anime characters spoke. She could have been a witch, or a dragon sitting on a giant mushroom, for that matter. She spoke as if Mariko had been in the anime all along, privy to the plot and therefore able to follow the bizarre conversation through all its twists and turns.

Mariko dropped herself in a nearby chair; her brain was working too hard for her to exert the effort to stand up as well. Still she collected the details. The chair's padding was clad in cracking green vinyl, and a metal leg missing its rubber foot scritched against the linoleum floor when her weight hit the seat. Shoji Hayano stood with two fingers resting lightly on the narrow metal ledge that framed the large plate glass window of the morgue's viewing room. Mariko herself had not yet walked as far as she'd need to in order to see her sensei's body through that window. She thought about that fact for a second, analyzing her motives—but only for a second.

"Guilt. You said Yamada-sensei felt a lot of guilt. For what?"

"Why, for not destroying the sword when he had the chance, of course. There were other things too. He was not there when his mother died, but I always told him not to feel guilty about that. We must not feel guilty for what we cannot control, dear. You need to learn that lesson too."

"Lady, you don't know anything about me."

Shoji smiled a cute little-old-lady smile. "Child, I see more than you think."

"Yeah, I'm getting that feeling," Mariko said. Mariko was good with details, but this woman was something else. She spoke with unnerving familiarity—the same kind that Yamada had so often spoken with, the kind magicians spoke with when they knew which card you'd picked while you were just certain there was no way anyone could know.

"If you don't mind," Mariko said, "I'm going to step way out of line and offer to buy you a cup of coffee. I know you and I just met, but I have this feeling there's a lot for us to talk about. There'll be a cafeteria someplace upstairs. Would you join me?"

"I'd love to, dear."

The café was nothing special. Old coffee and older muffins, and that antiseptic hospital smell. After a single cup of the stale, bitter coffee, Mariko switched over to green tea, which happened to be what Shoji was drinking.

"Keiji-san's student will call on you," Shoji said, her glasses fogging with steam from the tea. "You must offer him twice as much as he asks for."

"How do you—?" Mariko didn't even know how to finish the question. How do you know Fuchida will call? How do you know Fuchida will ask for a ransom? How do you suppose I'm going to give him double what he's asking for when he's not asking for money? His ransom demand is only a sword; how do you think I'm going to double that?

None of those questions were worth asking, for none of them could be answered. The old woman couldn't *know* any of the things she'd need to know to answer them. So instead Mariko asked, "Am I right in thinking you're blind?"

"Yes, dear."

"Is that how you met Yamada-sensei? You had the same doctor or something?"

Shoji laughed, a thousand crinkles deepening in her cheeks. "Oh, no. I lost my sight when I was a little girl. Keiji-san didn't lose his until both of us were old and gray."

Something in the way she said it made Mariko think

they'd been more than friends. And not lovers, that was certain; Shoji seemed to think of him like a brother, but one who was both many years older and many years younger. At times she spoke of him with reverence, the kind little children have for their adult siblings. Yet at other times her tone was protective, bordering on paternalistic, as if her vision extended far beyond his. She and Yamada had been close, but not so close that Shoji knew Fuchida's name; she referred to him only as "Keiji-san's student." Yet Yamada and Fuchida had been close too—Mariko was sure of that much; he'd always spoken of Fuchida with deep concern— and so once again Yamada-sensei proved to be an enigma. Who was Shoji to him? Was she as important to him as he so obviously was to her? And if so, why had Mariko never heard of her?

Yet another list of riddles Mariko had no time to solve. She could only address the most pressing question: "What makes you say Yamada's student will call me?"

"He must," Shoji said with a shrug. "You can give him what he needs. And he *will* take it from you before the end."

"This is crazy. You're talking about him as if all of this has already—"

A vibration from Mariko's purse cut her off. She unfolded the phone with her short, blunt thumbnail. "Detective Oshiro," the deep voice said. "You know who this is."

"Yes, I do."

"That wasn't nice of you, conning me into keeping your sister's phone. I barely got rid of it before all your officers arrived."

"Sorry about that."

"You're lucky your sister is still in one piece. I ought to kill her for what you did."

He was angry, dangerously so; his quivering voice suggested his body was shaking too. Shoji reached a wrinkled hand across the table and touched Mariko's fingers. "Offer him the sword," she whispered.

"You can have the sword," Mariko said, meaning it. "Just don't hurt her."

"Oh, quite the opposite," said Fuchida. "She's feeling as fine as can be right now."

At first Mariko thought Fuchida was insinuating rape. The fantasy of the victim thanking her perp for her earth-

shaking orgasms fueled the plots of a million *manga*; Mariko
saw the books on the trains every day, clutched in the sweating hands of vicarious rapists. But Mariko realized there
was nothing lascivious in his tone. Sinister, yes, but not
sexual. All at once she made the connection. "You got her
high?"

"Hole in one," Fuchida said. "In her less lucid moments
she rambles on and on about how disappointed you'd be. I
gather you've gone to great lengths to keep her sober."

Shut up, Mariko wanted to say, but she couldn't muster
the will. She felt as if her heart were plunging down a cold,
dark well.

"And your poor mother. What will she think?"

That cold, sinking feeling redoubled. In her ramblings
Saori must have spoken of home. Now their mother was a
target too. Fuchida had already proved his willingness to
send killers into the home of an isolated victim. Mariko's
mother might have been younger than Yamada, but she was
far less able to defend herself. Did Fuchida have people
outside her house already? The very thought of it left
Mariko paralyzed.

Shoji touched her fingers again. "The sword," she whispered. "Soothe his need for it."

"I'll give you the sword," Mariko said, struggling to
speak. "I swear."

"You'll do more than that," Fuchida said. "For starters,
you'll call off your dogs. If I catch even a glimpse of a police
officer, I cut your sister's throat."

"Okay."

"Next, you'll implicate someone else in Yamada's murder. I don't care who, just not me."

"I can't. I have three officers that place you at the scene
at the time of the murder."

"You'll do it or your mother's dead. Your sister says
you're good at your job, Miko-chan. I'm sure you'll find a
way."

"Okay."

"Last, you deliver the Inazuma to me by midnight, or
you get your sister back in tiny little pieces."

Shoji touched Mariko's hand once more. "Tell him you
have two Inazumas to offer."

"I don't," Mariko breathed, covering the receiver.

"Trust me," whispered Shoji.

Mariko took a deep breath. "I'll make you a deal. Let me get my mother to safety. In exchange, you get two Inazuma blades, not one."

Silence.

Mariko's heart froze solid. Did he think she was lying to him? If he felt Mariko betrayed him, Saori would pay a terrible price.

"Fuchida-san?"

No answer.

"Fuchida-san?

# 7 3

Two, Fuchida mused. The old man had always spoken of another, a third, but he'd never given so much as a whisper regarding its whereabouts. How did Oshiro know where it was?

"Fuchida-san?" Her voice was tiny and pleading over the phone.

"You're lying," he said.

"I'm not," Oshiro said after a sigh. "Its name is Tiger on the Mountain."

So she *did* know of the sword. The old man must have told her about it before he died. That bastard. Fuchida had trained under him for years, and in all that time he'd never given Fuchida more than the name.

The American was already en route. Fuchida was counting down the hours until their meeting. Even if he had Glorious Victory in his own two hands, at this point he could not claim even to himself to have owned two Inazumas; he was no more than a delivery boy, taking the blade from Yamada and passing it on to the American. But a third sword— now, that changed things. Fuchida could be the first in history to have held three Inazumas at once, and even after relinquishing Glorious Victory he could *still* be the first in history to own two Inazuma blades.

And yet letting the mother go was a risk. With her gone, his only asset would be the sister, and she was only valuable while she was still alive. Sooner or later he'd have to kill her. Not only had she seen his face, but she'd seen his strip club, and since he'd taken her she'd overheard things he couldn't allow her to repeat. The names of the dancers, of their dealer—people the police could track down and then use to hunt down Fuchida. No, the sister could not live long enough to talk. And without the sister, what leverage did he have?

Then again, he asked himself, what leverage did he need? Get Yamada's sword. Kill the sister. Disappear. That was all he needed to do. Or forget the other Inazumas. Just vanish.

No. These were the greatest swords ever forged. One did not simply forget them. And he still had to give Glorious Victory to the American. An Inazuma in his hand and two more within reach! Not even Yamada had ever been able to say that.

Some high, piercing voice keened in his mind. One was enough. His beautiful Singer. She outshone them all. The other two should be forgotten. Just disappear. Kill the girl and disappear.

No. Too risky. There was the American to deal with, and that meant acquiring Yamada's sword at the very least. And if he was to risk himself for one sword, why not two? Give up the mother. Get the Tiger on the Mountain. Then deal with the American and win your fortune.

You have fortune enough, the keening voice said. You have me.

Yes. You have her. But how much more could you have? Three Inazumas within reach. Only one man in history could say he had laid his own hands on three of them, and that was Master Inazuma himself. I must, Fuchida thought. I owe it to myself. I owe it to the swords.

The keening voice cried out: Not to me, you don't.

I owe it to my father. To my family name. To every Fuchida who spent his life following a Kamaguchi's orders.

Let your family burn, the keening voice cried.

I was going to secure my place in history. I still can. I only need the swords.

Forget your place in history. Your place is with me.

Fuchida balled his fists; the phone's plastic creaked in his hand. No, he thought. My destiny is mine to control. You must let me have this.

I will take care of you, cried the voice. Leave your destiny to me.

And there, right then and there, that high, singing voice crossed the line. "Your mother lives," Fuchida said into the phone. "You will deliver the swords to me by midnight."

A pause. Then, "Midnight tomorrow," said the Oshiro woman. "I need time to get them."

"Have them by tomorrow at noon. I will call you with the location. If I see a cop between now and then, your sister dies slow."

Fuchida hung up the phone, and Mariko released a sigh she'd been holding back for what felt like an hour. Her face was tingling and her breath came short. She wanted to cry but suppressed the urge: she feared she might collapse completely if she indulged herself in even a moment of weakness. Instead of crying, she nestled her tired, burning eyes into her palms and rested her elbows on the tabletop. "I can't deal with this," she said.

"Of course you can," said Shoji. "Whatever destiny saddles us with, that is what we must bear, but you're a strong one. You're doing fine, dear."

"Fine?" Mariko didn't bother looking up. "I talked a madman into promising not to kill my mother. His word's worth a lot, I'm sure. And my sister? If anything, I got her in deeper shit than ever. The only victory I can see here is that she's not dead yet—but in exchange for that, I promised two swords when I only have one. How is *this* 'doing fine'?"

Shoji said something, probably something encouraging, but Mariko wasn't listening. She hadn't opened her eyes yet, but she'd leaned back against the seat of her booth so her hands would be free to work. By the time she got the phone to her ear, one of her team at the precinct had already picked up. "Sergeant?"

Mariko didn't bother asking who it was. "Get two units to my mother's house right now. Take her and one suitcase and get them to Tokyo Station. Don't let her talk you into bringing more than one bag, or else she'll try and take the whole apartment with her."

"Sergeant, we can bring her to a safe house. Has Fuchida threatened her?"

"No safe house. Something doesn't feel right. I can't put my finger on it...." She trailed off, then chided herself: You're too tired. You haven't got the strength to see this through. "I don't know what it is," she said, "but something's not right. Fuchida shouldn't have known about the stakeout. He knows too much about what we're doing. Just drop her off at Tokyo Station, and don't let anyone talk to her about where she's going."

The next call was to her mom. It was equally terse: Pack one bag; go to Aunt Yumiko's. Please don't ask questions, Mom; just do it. Then she clapped her phone shut and rested her eyes back in her palms. The muscles above her eyeballs ached. Her throat felt like sandpaper, and her teeth felt filmy. She wanted a hot shower and a double dose of sleeping pills. Followed by a week in Hawai'i. Then maybe— *maybe*—she'd feel up to taking on the tasks ahead.

Getting her hands on Glorious Victory Unsought promised to be damned near impossible by itself. At the moment it was under her own team's surveillance, surveillance she could no longer call off now that Fuchida had introduced a fresh murder to the mix. The Inazuma blade was now the only bait TMPD had for the perpetrator of a public and gruesome homicide; no way in hell was Ko giving that up. Any requisition she filed to call off the surveillance would have to cross Ko's desk, and then he'd start asking questions, and Mariko didn't trust him. This went beyond his general misogyny; she was too exhausted to figure out what it was, but some niggling thing made her suspect his motives.

And even if she could lift her surveillance, there was still the matter of the Tiger on the Mountain. Yamada had spoken of that sword once before, but that seemed a hundred years ago, and in any case he never gave even a clue as to where the Tiger might be.

"How the hell am I going to get those swords?"

The words came so quietly that Mariko was hardly aware she'd spoken them aloud. She was certain Shoji-san couldn't have heard them, but then she remembered: Shoji had the ears of the blind. "It seems to me," Shoji said, "that you should ask for them."

"Oh, of course. I'm sure that'll—"

Mariko cut herself off. This woman had been right about too much to dismiss anything she had to say. So instead of completing her first thought, Mariko asked, "How did you know offering the swords would calm him down?"

Shoji shrugged. "It's in his nature. The forces of destiny are roaring now. One must only attune one's ear to hear them."

"Uh-huh." A sip of tepid tea did little to slake the dryness coating Mariko's throat. "I was planning to talk to Yamada-sensei about that. I never wanted to take his case, you know. I wanted to follow a lead on a cocaine deal. I wanted to drop everything and go look for my missing sister. Now I find out my coke dealer is Yamada's student, and also the sword killer, and now he's my own sister's kidnapper. It's too much to be coincidence, isn't it?"

"Yes, dear."

"And you—you talk like you know how all of it is going to play out. How? No, you know what? I don't even want to know how. Just tell me where this goes."

"I see forces coming together that haven't converged in many years. I see the tiger prowling on his mountain, and the singing woman returning to the mountain. There is a castle on the summit, and typhoon winds blow on the horizon. The typhoon is strong enough to destroy the castle and strong enough to kill the singing woman. Whether the tiger can protect against the wind, I do not know. So much depends now on which way the typhoon will blow."

Mariko looked at her, glad that the woman's blind eyes couldn't see the face Mariko was giving her. "I'm way too tired to make sense of any of that. I'm smart enough to see the Tiger on the Mountain has something to do with it, and Beautiful Singer too. I just don't see how I'm going to get my hands on the swords. Lieutenant Ko will have my ass if I confiscate Glorious Victory Unsought from the scene of a stakeout. And Yamada-sensei always told me the Tiger was in a safe place. He said no one could get to it. How am I supposed to bring it into the equation?"

"As I said," Shoji chirped, "we'll go and ask the owner if we can borrow it. But we can't do that until the morning, and you need sleep, I think. My apartment isn't far. It isn't much, but we can roll out a futon for you if you like."

Nearby. A strange place, so she'd sleep lightly. To Mariko it sounded like heaven.

# 74

Mariko was rinsing shampoo from her short, spiky hair when she struck upon a plan to steal Glorious Victory Unsought. That niggling feeling last night had taken shape. How had Fuchida known there was surveillance on Yamada's house? And how had he known Mariko was the lead on Yamada's case? Mariko wasn't the hardest cop in the world to track down, what with being both the only female detective in the city *and* the only female sergeant in the TMPD, but Fuchida had more on her than that. He'd known he couldn't strike Yamada at home, and he'd known to find Yamada at the concert hall. So either someone on Mariko's team was talking to Fuchida, or else Fuchida was monitoring Yamada's house with surveillance of his own — and if the latter was the case, Fuchida had known exactly where to lurk so that Mariko's team wouldn't spot him. That too suggested that someone in the force was talking.

But Mariko couldn't prove it was Ko. True, he'd ordered her not to investigate *bōryokudan* involvement in her case, and if Fuchida had an inside man in the department, that was *bōryokudan* involvement. That meant if Ko *was* Fuchida's insider, he would have immunized himself from investigation through his own direct order — an illegal order, as Mariko had been all too happy to point out at the time. All of it was suspicious, but none of it was solid proof.

A new realization struck, and it made Mariko laugh so

hard that it echoed in the shower. It wasn't even necessary to find out who Fuchida was talking to. Mariko had all the excuse she needed to move Glorious Victory to a new and secret location.

For once she was happy to give Lieutenant Ko a call. She didn't even wait to get dressed; she tarried only to place a quick call to her team, then—still wet and wearing a towel—punched in Ko's number. "Just calling to let you know I'm moving the sword, sir."

"Like hell," said Ko. "It's tied up in a major homicide and a kidnapping."

At least he was finally willing to use the word *major* in connection to her case. That had nothing to do with Mariko's leadership on the case, of course; it had rather more to do with the fact that bloody footage from Suntory Hall was all over every news network.

"Sir, I have reason to suspect someone in our precinct has been talking to the perp. I don't know who, but I'm sure you'll agree that moving the sword to an undisclosed location will make it more secure."

Ko had nothing to say to that.

"I'm sure you'll agree too, sir, that if anyone tries to interfere with moving the sword or tries to discover its new location, we ought to question that individual on any possible connection to the perpetrator."

"I'm sure that won't be necessary, Oshiro."

"Oh, it's no trouble, sir. I've already ordered a member of my team to prepare warrants to search phone records and such." She let him chew on that for a moment. Then she added, "Oh, but you ordered me not to investigate *bōryokudan* connections to this case, didn't you? If it turns out the perp's a yakuza, I'll have violated that order. Would you like me to call my guy back? Rescind the warrants?"

She had him trapped. If he said yes, he'd be ordering her to cancel not just yakuza-related warrants but all warrants, and only a guilty person would do that. If he said no, she'd get what she wanted *and* she'd get yakuza-related warrants too.

But like any other worm, Ko had a talent for wriggling out of tight spots. "Oshiro, I want you off this case. Your sister's kidnapping has compromised your judgment. I'll have HRT take command."

"They're way ahead of you, sir. HRT took command of

the kidnapping case last night." She didn't bother to mention that she'd taken the last call from Fuchida *after* the HRT lieutenant relieved her of command. Come to think of it, she hadn't even told HRT about Fuchida's call, or about the sword ransom. At the time she'd been too exhausted to think of it, and now gut instinct told her to continue on her present course. Or was it destiny? Mariko wasn't sure if she knew the difference anymore.

She wrapped things up with Ko, disappointed that he'd managed to slither out of her trap but happy that he couldn't object to her moving the Inazuma without implicating himself as Fuchida's inside man. By ten a.m. she had Shoji sitting beside her in a requisitioned squad car and Glorious Victory in the trunk, padded in a long sleeve of blue cotton fabric and resting in a rack meant for shotguns. "Okay," she said. "Job one, finished. Now how in the world do we get sword number two?"

"I told you already," said Shoji. She was wearing white today, Coco Chanel again, with a different pair of big black sunglasses. "We'll go to the owner's house and ask to borrow it."

"Uh-huh."

"We'll ask politely, of course."

"Uh-huh."


"You have to be kidding."

Mariko stopped the squad, lights running, beside the barrier surrounding the Imperial Palace. Heavy chain ran from one concrete pylon to the next, big steel links sagging. The whole series was utilitarian yet ornamental, decorative in a capable-of-stopping-a-speeding-armored-car sort of way. Behind this perimeter stretched a few hundred meters of white gravel, fenced in on the opposite side by a green metal fence and a moat. A castle's sloping foundation rose out of the water, ascending gracefully to a height overtopping the level of the street where Mariko had parked. On her left, traffic whizzed by; on her right was the sixteenth century.

"This?" Mariko made no effort to keep the acid from her voice. "*This* is where you wanted me to drive?"

"It doesn't sound right. There's a quieter entrance, where cars can—"

"Cars can what? Just drive in? So we can ask if the emperor's busy?"

"Well, yes."

"Well, shit." Mariko should have known better. This woman had been talking like a crazy person from the start. And now, lo and behold, it turned out she was crazy. "You know," Mariko said, "when you told me to drive to the Imperial Palace, I figured you were just getting us to the right neighborhood. You know, like, 'Go to the palace, then turn right onto whatever-the-hell.' I hate to admit it, but I really didn't see this coming."

"You could stand to learn a thing or two about speaking to your elders," Shoji said. "Most especially if we're going inside."

"Inside where? The palace? We're not going in. Not even in a squad car we're not. You need ten kinds of clearance to get in there. Even if I could get the clearance, it would take a month to get an appointment." Mariko hammered the steering wheel with her fists. "Why did I ever let myself think you were for real? Shit!"

"There is a quieter entrance. On the northwest side, as I recall, but as you say, you may have to drive around a bit before you find the right one. And you'd do better to mind your language."

"We're not getting in there."

"Do you have a better idea?"

She had Mariko there. So, after negotiating traffic and a series of mazelike roads, Mariko wended her way to a high wooden gate set in higher wooden walls with manicured trees visible through every window. "I am Shoji Hayano," the old woman said when the gate guards approached the vehicle. "Would you please let His Majesty know I'd like to speak with him?"

The guard gave her exactly the look Mariko had predicted. But instead of turning her away straight out, he said, "May I ask what it's concerning?"

"The death of a friend to the family," Shoji said. "And an old gift."

"Wait here."

Mariko wondered what kind of surprise they were waiting for. A bomb squad and half a dozen men with assault rifles seemed to be the minimum in store. Her patience grew thinner and thinner. Then, just like that, a man in a suit motioned her to pull forward.

Mariko idled over the threshold of the imperial family grounds. Her squad's wheels crunched tan gravel and threw reflections on a close-cropped lawn verdantly populated with trees. A black limousine pulled out in front of her, then drove slowly as Mariko tailed it. The road meandered under the green canopy until its terminus, an elegant brown building with wide roofs and rain chains descending from the gutters. No, not *building*. *Palace*. This was the emperor's home.

Mariko submitted to a weapons search and noted that Shoji-san was not required to do the same. Then, entering the warmly lit foyer, Mariko found herself sinking toe deep in the most luxuriant carpeting she'd ever felt.

"I feel *so* underdressed," she said.

Mariko took Shoji's elbow when a man in a black suit, a telltale bulge under his left arm, walked them down a white hallway. The accents were teak woodwork, the beige carpeting as soft as anything. They reached a sitting room of teak and white and that soft, lush carpet, all pale in comparison to the three walls of picture windows overlooking a serene and verdant water garden. Dwarf maples arched their boughs over a still pond, whose surface was disturbed only by the occasional red leaf floating on the surface. Something inside Mariko relaxed, while at the same time she dared not sit, lest she disturb the museum-like tranquillity.

And then they were there. Emperor Akihito wore a blue-gray suit, and his silver hair was immaculate. Empress Michiko wore a buttercream dress and a welcoming smile. They were shorter than Mariko had expected—no taller than she was, in fact—yet they carried themselves with an air Mariko could only describe as regal. And why not, she mused; their usual visitors included sheiks and kings and presidents, and even *they* would all feel unusually lucky to be here.

Both Mariko and Shoji bowed low, and of the thousands of bows Mariko had made in her life, she felt she really meant this one. Their Majesties received their guests with grace, ushering them to sit on the white couches overlooking the water garden. Steaming cups of tea already awaited them, arranged in perfect symmetry on a low teak coffee table. "My condolences, Shoji-san," the emperor said. "The news of Sergeant Kiyama's death reached us this morning."

"A terrible loss," said the empress. "How are you holding up, Hayano-chan?"

How did they know Yamada? They spoke with absolute sincerity—they *missed* him—but Mariko didn't dare ask why. And the empress—she spoke to Shoji as only a friend would, using the first name, the intimate -*chan*. How did those two know each other?

"I am . . . coping," Shoji said, sighing. "May I introduce Detective Sergeant Oshiro Mariko? She was Keiji-san's student. She is also investigating his murder."

"Ah," the emperor said. "You have our thanks. I daresay we have heard of you." He looked at his wife as if for guidance, just as might happen in any other house in Tokyo. Mariko found the intimacy endearing.

"Yes," said the empress. "There were stories about you in the newspaper, *neh*? A year or so ago. You are our first woman to be promoted to detective, isn't that right?"

"Yes," Mariko stammered. "Yes, ma'am."

"Wonderful," the empress said. "Our condolences to you too on the loss of your teacher. Sergeant Kiyama has been a friend to this house for . . . oh, who knows how long? Since before my time, certainly."

Mariko's mind staggered like a drunk. The emperor and empress had heard of her. They'd read about her in the paper. On top of that, they were old friends with Yamada-sensei. How?

Mariko tried to connect the dots. She put the emperor and empress at about the same age as her grandparents, so younger than Yamada by a good bit. Kiyama Keiji: that was how Shoji and Their Majesties knew him. And a sergeant, the same as Mariko. Had Yamada been a cop? In his youth, before his professorial days? No. The war. Yamada-sensei had fought in the war.

All of a sudden she remembered something Yamada once said: "There's an old soldier's saying: Commanders can always be relied upon to do the obvious, once all alternatives have been exhausted." It made her laugh now, just as it had made her laugh then. She contained her laughter to a small smile. Then she realized the empress would take that to be the retreating smile of a shy little mouse of a woman. Not the sort of woman to make sergeant and detective.

"May I ask," Mariko said, mustering every ounce of politeness she'd ever learned, "how Your Majesties came to know Yamada-sensei?"

The emperor regarded her with the smallest smile. The kind of grace that Mariko had to struggle to muster came to him like purple came to irises: naturally, beautifully, irremovably. "Your sensei once owned a sword," he said. "In the days of the war he served his country at Guadalcanal—a greater sacrifice for him than for most, as his mother was dying of stomach cancer at the time. Before his deployment, he left his father his sword. At Sergeant Kiyama's request, his father brought the sword to my father. Along with Shoji-san, by the way, who was only a little girl at the time."

He bent down, took up a teacup with two fingers, and raised it to his lips. Mariko wondered whether Yamada had ever had tea with him like this. She wished she'd known Yamada had lost a parent to cancer just like she had. She wished he could tell her stories about his parents, about the war, about what happened after and why he had to change his name.

But she had no time to think about that now: the emperor had set down his teacup, and his every word commanded her attention. "Detective Sergeant Oshiro, there are those who say our house survived the war because of the sword. I do not mean our palace. That was destroyed. Burned to the ground. No, I mean the Imperial House itself. Did your sensei ever speak to you about this sword?"

"He did, sir. The Tiger on the Mountain, isn't it? He said. . . . The legend says that if that sword was in a castle, that castle could not fall."

"Just so," said the emperor. Those pale eyes locked with Mariko's, and she found herself instinctively lowering her gaze. "And what do you know about more recent history? Did you know my father offered terms of surrender before the tragedy of Hiroshima? The Americans wanted unconditional surrender, and my father's generals offered surrender with one condition only: that the house of the emperor remain as the head of state. Then came Hiroshima, then Nagasaki. Afterward, the Americans accepted our country's surrender, unconditional but for one proviso: that the house of the emperor remain as the head of state."

"Your Highness," Mariko said, "are you suggesting that the Tiger on the Mountain preserved the Imperial House?

That the Allies would have unseated your father had Yamada not given him the sword?"

"We shall never know. The drama of history cannot be
replayed. We only know that my father did have the sword,
and he did retain his throne. If the sword had anything to
do with that, then Sergeant Kiyama gave to us as great a gift
as any emperor has ever received. He has been a friend to
our house ever since."

Mariko looked at the floor, gobsmacked. Was it possible? Could Yamada have saved Japan? *Gaijin* might never
understand it, but Japan without an emperor was not Japan.
Those sheiks and presidents were not emperors. Their
power came from wealth—or worse still, from the popular
vote. This man commanded reverence simply by sitting in
front of her on the couch.

And her sensei had known him—known him well
enough, in fact, that an old friend who wanted an audience
had only to knock on the door. Known him well enough,
Mariko realized suddenly, that if Yamada placed a phone
call, the Imperial House itself might be persuaded to make
an annoying police lieutenant stop putting obstacles in the
way of one of his detective sergeants. When Mariko had
asked Yamada who he'd called in the TMPD, she was thinking too small. Even her follow-up question about the may-
or's office wasn't nearly big enough. The idea that Yamada
had invoked the emperor's assistance on her behalf was
enough to take her breath away.

"It is the Tiger on the Mountain we've come to ask
about," Shoji-san said, and her words gave Mariko's
drunken, stumbling mind something to cling to. "Your
Highness, Keiji-san was killed for his Inazuma blade. It was
another Inazuma that took his life. The winds of destiny are
blowing like a typhoon now; Your Majesty's sword is a part
of that storm, I think."

"You think!" said the empress, smiling. "Hayano-chan,
you say, 'I think,' where anyone else could say, 'I am certain.'"

"Nothing is certain about the future," Shoji said.

"Ahh," Mariko blurted, knowing it was rude to interrupt
yet unable to contain herself. "Shoji-san, since the moment
we met, you've spoken as if you can see the future. Now Her
Majesty speaks to you as I do with my little sister, and she

seems to believe you can see the future too. Please, tell me what's going on."

Silence reigned for a long moment, and Mariko was afraid she'd given offense. Then, taking her eyes off of Shoji, she saw the emperor and empress were smiling, much as they might have with a toddler grandchild, as if they found her lack of refinement cute.

"Detective Sergeant Oshiro," the emperor said, "Shoji-san has been my family's seer ever since the war."

"Seer?"

"*Goze* was the old word. And as for my wife's calling her Hayano-chan, well, the two of them were fast friends from the moment they met. That was at our wedding, I daresay."

His gray eyes turned to the empress, who nodded her head ever so slightly. Her every movement was graceful. By comparison, Mariko thought she must have looked like an orangutan in a ball gown. Somehow it had never occurred to her that the empress might have personal friends. Now that Mariko had caught herself thinking it, she wondered how the idea had ever made sense, but somehow she'd always thought of royalty living a solitary existence. You didn't hear about them out playing golf, as the prime minister was wont to do.

"If I might be so rude," Shoji-san said, "I wonder if I can steer our conversation back to the sword. I think it plays a role in what is to come. If so, Oshiro-san must wield it."

*Wield.* Not carry. Not deliver as ransom. Wield. Just what did Shoji see in Mariko's future?

And how had Mariko come to believe that Shoji could foresee anything at all? *Goze* were the stuff of fairy tales.

Then again, so were magic swords.

So many strange things had happened, and in such quick succession, that Mariko found her thoughts came only in disjointed, stagger-stepped fashion. In hindsight she wasn't quite sure how she'd come to leave the Imperial Palace, nor how the long, heavy silken bag came to be in her hands. She remembered profuse good-byes and thank-yous, and a slow drive through the verdant grounds under a light rain. And then she was back in the world, stopped at a red light with the emperor's own sword lying on her lap.

It weighed little more than half as much as Glorious Victory Unsought, and was shorter by the length of her forearm. She could tell that much without unsheathing it—indeed, without even removing it from its black silken bag. The imperial seal, a round, stylized chrysanthemum blossom, was embroidered in gold on the bag, and the bag was tied shut with beautifully woven golden *kumihimo* cord.

A high-pitched digital chime gave her a start. Her cell phone. It was here somewhere. Even as she patted herself down in search of it, she realized her focus was slipping. Half a night's sleep, Yamada's murder, Saori's capture—they were adding up.

At last she found the phone and flicked it open. "Yeah?"

"You know who this is."

"Yeah."

"You have the swords."

"Yeah."

The car behind Mariko honked, startling her. She grunted and gave the guy the finger and a few choice words, which prompted a "Well!" from Shoji.

"Who's with you?"

"Nobody." Mariko had a lot of tasks before her, shifting into first while holding the phone to her ear while keeping the sword from slipping off her lap, but she managed them all. "I needed help getting your second sword. The one who helped me is in the car with me. She's old. No threat to you."

"Hmph!" said Shoji.

Fuchida grumbled. At length he said, "St. Luke's Hospital. Drive there now. Put your phone on speaker and leave it in your lap. If I hear you talk to anyone at all, your sister dies."

Mariko heard a yelp from Saori and she did as she was told. "I'll get there faster if I can run the lights and siren."

"Don't even think about it. Tell me the number of your squad car."

"Five-five-three."

"If you're lying, your sister dies. If I see any cop car other than number five-five-three, she dies."

"You're at a hospital, Fuchida-san. Cops are known to come there from time to time."

"Shut up. Do as you're told."

She could hear the tension building in him. There was a hard-bitten edge to his voice, and the grumbling continued just beyond her range of hearing. "I'm on my way," she said.

# 75

The twin towers of St. Luke's International Hospital were the tallest buildings within sight. Blue glass and sharp angles dominated, and the towers were connected three-quarters of the way up the shorter tower (halfway up the taller tower) by a walkway that gleamed with sunlight peeking through the thinning clouds. To Mariko the hospital looked like something built out of LEGO.

"I'm here," she said to her phone.

"There is a building across the street. The only one under construction. Park the car in front of the door."

Mariko did as she was told, finding the dust-brown building and bringing the squad to a halt in front of a makeshift front wall: two-meter-high plywood lashed to a scaffold skeleton with big fat zip ties looped through drill holes. The door was just a rectangle cut right into the plywood, affixed with hinges and locked by a chain and padlock. It bore signs reading HARD HAT AREA and DO NOT ENTER. Killing the ignition, she said, "You want me to turn the speaker off? So people don't hear you?"

"Yes. Do it. Get out alone."

Mariko clicked the speaker button with her thumbnail, then cupped the phone to her thigh. "Wait five minutes, then call the police." She spoke rapidly and softly, pulling her Sig Sauer P230 from the glove box as she did so. "The radio's in front of your right hand. You just push the button and talk, okay? Tell them where I am and that I'm with Fuchida and the hostage. Got it?"

Shoji nodded, and made a strange face when Mariko racked the slide to check her chambered round—an awkward motion with her right hand pressing a phone to her leg.

"Is that a pistol?" said Shoji.

"Of course," said Mariko. "You don't expect me to go up there and get in a sword fight with him, do you?"

In the next breath she was back on with Fuchida. "Sorry. Dropped the phone. Very sorry. Please don't be angry."

Had she put enough vulnerability in her voice to sell it? It seemed so. Fuchida said, "Stupid shit like that is going to get your sister killed. Don't do it again."

Angry, Mariko thought, but not unhinged.

She exited the car, sizing up the building as she did so. Big windows: lots of opportunity for snipers, if only she'd been able to call for one. Fuchida had listened in on her every move, and Shoji, one of the last dinosaurs in Tokyo, didn't have a cell phone, or else Mariko might have used it to text for backup. It hardly mattered. The windows were highly reflective, and the noon sun rendered everything behind them invisible.

She made sure Fuchida could see her hands if he was watching from inside, then ducked back in the car to retrieve Tiger on the Mountain. The Sig prodded uncomfortably against her floating ribs as she bent, but its weight was a comfort. She readjusted her jacket to cover it and made sure to keep her elbow close to her side to keep the pistol concealed.

Standing up, she felt the prodding of the Cheetah against the small of her back. It too was clipped to her belt, tucked into its little holster. She'd never actually used the holster in the field—she'd been wearing civvies for as long as she owned the Cheetah, and a big, black stun baton had no place in a civilian wardrobe—and now she hoped to hell it was as easy on the draw as she remembered it. Her jacket was already going to slow her draw, but there was no getting around that if she wanted to keep the weapon concealed. In truth her jacket wasn't long enough to hide it completely, but her squad would block any view of it from within the building—assuming Fuchida was actually in the building. If he was in the hospital across the street, she might have just revealed her backup weapon.

Damn. Nothing to do about it now. Keep walking. Keep focused.

Mariko popped the trunk, closed the driver's door, and went to the back of the squad for Glorious Victory Unsought. There was no good way to carry the swords, she realized. Not while keeping the cell to her ear. They deserved more respect than to be clumped together under her armpit. But what choice did she have? "Sorry," she said to them as she walked toward the door cut into the plywood.

"The padlock is open. Pull on it."

That was easier said than done, at least for someone who also had to manage two swords, two concealed weapons, a phone, and a rib cage that hurt like hell. But she got the door open and stepped into the cool dark behind it.

"Loop the chain through the door again. Lock it."

Mariko thought about the building layout. From the street-side windows there was no direct view of this door. Anyone in front of the door could still have been visible, but now that she was under the wooden slats of the scaffolding, she would be hidden from view. No one from the hospital's side of the street could have seen her either. She pinned the phone between her ear and shoulder, jingled the chain a bit, and clasped the lock through only one end of it. Backup wasn't likely to get here in time, but she wouldn't make their job any harder for them.

She wondered whether Shoji would be able to figure out how to work her squad's radio by touch. She wondered, too, whether Fuchida had thought to bring a police scanner with him to listen for the backup call. Was that the sort of thing a seer could foresee? I'd give anything, Mariko thought, to know the future of the next three minutes.

Fuchida had chosen his building well if he wanted a place backup would have a bitch of a time getting to. The roof might have been big enough to drop a tactical team by helicopter, but the high-rises all around would play hell with the wind patterns, and in any case the rotor noise would be a dead giveaway. There had to be another door to the ground floor—fire codes demanded it, even for half-gutted buildings undergoing rehab—but Fuchida wasn't telling where it was, and Mariko didn't have time to go looking. There would inevitably be a few cops in the hospital who could act as first responders, but none of them would be Special Assault Team operators, and even if they were, they wouldn't have any advance intelligence on the building's layout. Nor would they have the benefit of a psychopath on the phone guiding them in the right direction.

"Fifth floor," Fuchida said. "Stairs are straight ahead of you, in the back."

He'd covered everything. She'd be a bit winded when she reached him. If there was an elevator, it was probably stuck open on Fuchida's floor, and five stories were just enough to make it unlikely that she could beat the elevator in a race to the ground floor. He'd even thought to dust the stairs with gritty concrete mix; even if Mariko had somehow managed to contact SAT or HRT, they'd have a hell of a time getting upstairs without Fuchida hearing their approach.

When she reached the fifth floor, Mariko saw two figures silhouetted against the picture windows that comprised the far wall. One was well muscled, its right hand pointing a curving sword at the unfinished concrete floor. The other silhouette, reed thin, sat in the only chair—indeed, the only piece of furniture—on the whole floor. As she drew closer, Mariko could make out the long, fat zip ties pinning Saori's wrists and ankles to the square steel legs of the chair. The sight of her made Mariko's stomach sink.

Apart from the windows, the only source of light was a tall, lonely rectangle far off to the right: the elevator, waiting with its doors propped open. Stacked boxes of linoleum tiles stood guard at various points around the room, tall and wide enough for someone to hide behind. Sheets of drywall leaned against unfinished walls like huge books on a shelf. The gang box near the elevator blocked lines of sight to the whole back quarter of the floor. Even with a partner, this room would have been a nightmare to clear. Mariko could only hope Fuchida was here solo.

The drawn sword should have been enough to capture Mariko's attention. Her helpless sister should have been enough. But Mariko was a detective; her brain collected details whether she wanted it to or not. She took in everything about the room without breaking stride, and walked to the nearest stack of boxed floor tiles. Those things were heavy, maybe even heavy enough to stop a bullet, though

Mariko didn't figure Fuchida for a shooter. Even if he'd wanted to shoot her and have done with it, the sword had a hold on him now; if Yamada was right, Beautiful Singer wouldn't let him trade weapons.

Fuchida's sword was as long as his arm, and he stood close enough to Saori that Mariko didn't dare draw down and pipe him. The Sig was a 9-millimeter, too small to guarantee a kill on the first shot. Besides, Fuchida had chosen his ground well. The only thing behind him was a thin sheet of glass, and then St. Luke's Hospital. She couldn't shoot until her backdrop was clear.

"Here we are," Mariko said, laying the swords down on the stacked boxes. "Alone."

"Not all alone," Fuchida said. "We have your sister to keep us company."

Good, Mariko thought. Maybe he was lying, but she didn't think so. And assuming he was telling the truth, he'd just cleared the room for her.

"You can let her go now. Your swords are here."

"I'm not an idiot. Let me see them."

Mariko withdrew Glorious Victory Unsought from its cotton sleeve, then unsheathed the blade halfway and rammed it home. She did the same with the emperor's sword.

Fuchida took a step toward the Inazumas, then another. Still within sword's reach of Saori. Still a thousand patients behind him, with no more than dumb luck to protect them from stray rounds. Mariko tried to gauge his mental state, but she couldn't yet see his backlit face.

Two more steps toward the swords. He moved as though against a windstorm, as if he wore a fifty-kilo backpack. As he drew closer, laboriously closer, Mariko could see more of him, though still not his face. Until now she'd thought he was wearing a skintight shirt, perhaps a spandex runner's shirt elaborately decorated. Now she saw the pattern clinging to his right shoulder was a tattoo—an ornate spiderweb—and coiled around the other shoulder was either a serpent or a dragon. His hair was long and straight, pulled into a ponytail and capped by a *hachimaki*, the traditional bandana of the samurai. That wasn't a good sign. The kamikaze pilots had tied on *hachimaki* before they took flight, never to return.

Beautiful Singer gleamed in the sunlight. It was thinner than any sword Mariko had ever seen, calling images to mind of a panther's wicked, graceful claw, the slashing curve of a shark's tail.

Another step, and Fuchida stood almost within sword's reach of Mariko. His silhouette had eclipsed Saori's now, further frustrating any hope of a clear shot. But he seemed to have forgotten Mariko entirely. For him there seemed to be nothing else in the world except the swords—the swords, and that invisible force he fought against with every movement.

Very slowly, Mariko moved away from the Inazumas, angling her body so he could not see her right hand behind her hip.

Fuchida drew closer. One more step and he'd be in striking range. His body was angled too, right side pulling back toward the windows and his captive, as if Beautiful Singer were pulling him away from the other two swords. He took another step, close enough now to touch the swords. Mariko tensed. Beautiful Singer pulled him back, just out of Mariko's reach. But Fuchida's will proved stronger than the sword's. He reached out and laid his left hand on Glorious Victory's scabbard.

The Cheetah crashed down on Fuchida's forearm, crackling with its 850,000 volts. He roared and pulled away. Mariko darted forward, stabbing Fuchida in the chest with the Cheetah's head. He grabbed it with his bare left hand. Mariko pulled the trigger. The pain meant nothing to him; he ripped the Cheetah from her grasp.

It clattered across the floor as he rounded on her. She retreated around the boxed linoleum tiles, her only cover. Now his face was fully lit and terrifying. His lips were dark, as were the rims of his wild eyes. His flesh was a quilt of tattoos, rippling as he raised Beautiful Singer overhead. In the center of his chest a buddha wreathed in flame slashed with a sword of its own.

Mariko's hand dove for the Sig. She drew it, found her two-handed grip, put her front sight on the fiery buddha.

The sword flashed down.

The gun didn't fire.

All at once the blood in Mariko's arm turned to gasoline. Even with her eyes locked on his red-splashed sword, her mind found time to note the burning pain. He'd rushed her too hard and now he stumbled past her. She tried to shoot him again, and again pain flooded her arm.

Fuchida had chopped off her trigger finger.

The sight of her maimed hand terrified her. Even in a rage, he struck deftly enough to take her finger and only her finger. Yamada had been right from the beginning: Fuchida was a master.

Fuchida turned on her and Mariko retreated. Something hit her in the butt: the stack of tiles. Mariko groped blindly for a sword, found one with her left hand, and tried to circle around the stack. Fuchida was faster, circling with her.

Only blind luck allowed Mariko to duck Fuchida's next attack. She instinctively raised her arms to fend off the third, and again blind luck saw her parry his blade with her Sig Sauer. The clash knocked her pistol across the room. She would have been dead a second later if only Fuchida had been in position to strike. But his slashes were wild, overpowered. He lost his footing, giving Mariko time enough to draw her sword.

She nearly dropped it, blood-slick as it was. Only when her left hand found the hilt did she establish a firm grip. Fuchida was on her again, and this time Yamada's training paid off. She sidestepped and counterstruck.

But Fuchida was the better swordsman. He shrank back a hand's breadth out of reach, then squared off against her.

Her attack should have cut him. But, then, her sword should have weighed double what it did. Mariko looked down to see the Tiger on the Mountain in her hands.

She was lost. She'd never trained with a sword this size. It was light, tiny, fast as hell, but everything she'd learned about staying at range was useless now. Glorious Victory's greater reach had been her sole advantage. The Tiger seemed even shorter than Beautiful Singer, and certainly Mariko's arms were shorter than Fuchida's. He was the stronger fighter too, and the more experienced, and she was already bleeding and scared.

Fuchida inched closer. Mariko stepped back. He lashed out with a stab to the throat. Mariko batted down at his hands. She missed, but she made him miss too.

"Yamada wasn't idle in his last days, was he?" Fuchida sneered at her. "You fancy yourself a swordswoman?"

Mariko didn't fancy herself anything. The only part of herself she could think of was her butchered hand. Her heart beat against her ribs the way a boxer beat a punching bag. "Just take your sword and go," she said.

"You're a meek little thing, aren't you? You talked tough on the phone. And I'll give you this: it took balls to come in here on your own. But now we get to see the real you. When the cards are down, you're just a whimpering little school-girl."

He feinted a stab at her. She tried to parry it and missed. He stabbed for real, capitalizing on her overreaction, and this time her blade was just able to knock his aside. His mouth curled into a snarl. He was angry now. Was it just that she'd stood too long against him? Did he want the quick kill, and had she—miraculously—denied it?

Still snarling, he pounced at her, his sword flashing. She sidestepped. Fuchida tripped over her foot. It was the same sweep Yamada had done to her, she realized. Fuchida hit the floor in a heap, and too late Mariko saw she could have closed and finished him. By the time she'd noticed, Fuchida was up into a crouch, sword in hand.

Mariko glanced at Glorious Victory Unsought. It was right next to him, resting in its scabbard atop the stack of boxes. "Take the sword and go," she repeated, trying this time to keep the desperation out of her voice.

"Oh, I'll take it," Fuchida said. He rose to his feet, switched Beautiful Singer to his left hand, and wrapped the fingers of his right hand around Glorious Victory's long grip. "I'll kill you with it. Then I'll kill your sister with it."

Lines of ink rippled across the muscles of his arms. Then, suddenly, he lunged at her, chopping with Beautiful Singer. His swing was well short of her, and for half a second Mariko thought he was feinting, setting up a second attack. Then she realized the truth: it wasn't Fuchida who attacked her.

It was Beautiful Singer.

It was drawing him away from the other weapon. But even in his demented state, Fuchida had incredible strength of will. With stomping steps he returned to Glorious Victory Unsought, and in one smooth motion he drew the massive blade.

It took impossible strength to wield Glorious Victory in

one hand, but Fuchida was impossibly strong. His eyes were wide, crazed, his head shifting side to side as if looking for the best angle of attack. At last he came at her, both blades whirling, a manic scream bursting from his spit-flecked mouth. Mariko threw herself sideways, lashing out with the Tiger on the Mountain.

Glorious Victory clattered to the floor, half an arm still attached to it.

Fuchida didn't even register the blow. He whirled on her, and before Mariko could regain her footing, she felt Beautiful Singer plunge through her belly. Fuchida drove the sword all the way to the hilt. The pain made the whole world disappear.

No. Not the whole world. She still had a sword and a target. With her last breath Mariko ran the Tiger on the Mountain sidelong into Fuchida's rib cage. She caught him through both lungs, her bloody blade lancing out from the opposite side of his body.

They fell together. Mariko did not register her head hitting the concrete floor. Her shrewd detective's mind did not notice when she puked, nor when she pissed herself, nor when her body entered a violent fit of agonal spasms. She couldn't even feel the pain from the stump of her severed finger anymore. The world disappeared into a haze of white, and the only thing left to her was Saori.

Saori screamed and cried and begged Mariko not to die. But Mariko died anyway.

## 76

Two bolts of lightning hit her in the chest.

Smells came to her: blood, ozone, urine, vomit, dust, sweat. Sounds came next. Saori was still crying. Someone said, "We've got her back. Keep pressure on that." A wet gurgling sound came now and again, weak underneath all the other noises but close enough that Mariko could make it out. It took several repetitions before she recognized it as her own breathing.

Mercifully, her tactile sense was dead to her, muted by hypovolemic shock. Nor was there much for her to see; just vague shapes drifting in the white haze. She could taste blood and vomit. Gusts forced cold air down her throat at regular intervals, each breath tasting like the inside of a plastic water bottle.

She had no sense of time, no sense of continuity. Saori would be wailing, and then all consciousness would lapse, and when it returned none of the old background noises were there anymore. There was a beeping, and the ingress and egress of air pushed mechanically through some narrow hose nearby. Then those things would vanish and she would regain consciousness drowning in a sea of pain. Then haziness and light. Then nothing at all.

And then, after a thousand such episodes—or was it only a dozen?—Mariko opened her eyes. Blurs of various shades resolved themselves into ceiling tiles, a sliding aluminum rail for a curtain, the top edge of a wooden door. "She's awake," Mariko heard Saori say, and then a new set of blurs resolved themselves into the crying, smiling faces of her sister and mother.

"I thought I'd lost you," Saori said, at the same instant their mother said, "I knew you'd make it." But Saori went on, the words tumbling from her mouth like snowflakes in a blizzard. "I was stuck there. I couldn't do anything. I couldn't move. All I could do was watch you die. I'm so, so sorry, Miko-chan."

Mariko tried to speak but found something had been taped into her mouth. She could not move her jaw, and even if she could, there was the thing in her mouth to gag her. She grunted, and then Saori and Mom disappeared for a while, pushed out by a sudden influx of nurses.

It was another twenty-odd hours before Mariko could keep a hold on consciousness for more than a few seconds, and in those hours each waking moment seemed to blend into the next. One moment she would be talking to her sister; then she would blink, and opening her eyes she'd find it was her doctor she was talking to, and it was not sunlight but streetlights streaming through the window.

"I'm so, so sorry," her sister said.

Her doctor said, "You're a very lucky woman, Oshiro."

"Not your fault you got kidnapped," Mariko told Saori.

"We couldn't save your finger," said her doctor. "By the time we had you stabilized, it had been on ice too long. I'm sorry."

"I'm sorry," said Saori.

"What happened to the emperor's sword?" asked Mariko.

"In the ER," the doctor said. Mariko couldn't sort out which question he was answering.

"I'll never do it again," Saori said, and hugged her tight.

Mariko fell asleep in her arms, and when she woke, she was lucid.

# 77

I t was light in the room, probably early morning, and someone was standing at the foot of Mariko's bed. "Hi," Mariko said.

Her doctor, who wore glasses and a Moe Howard haircut, looked up at her over the top of the manila folder whose contents he'd been reading. "Oh!" he said, smiling. "You're awake. And looking much better than yesterday, I must say."

He was thirtyish, cultivating the beginnings of a potbelly, and because she was lying down Mariko had a hard time guessing how tall he was. "What happened to the emperor's sword?" she asked.

"Do you mean the one you had sticking out of you when you came into the ER? They're still talking about you down there, you know."

"No," Mariko said.

"Oh, yes they are. You made quite an impression, Oshiro. You're a very lucky woman. First, whoever stuck that sword in you didn't pull it back out. Second, when you fell, you landed on your side, not on the sword. Third, your friend called backup for you just in the nick of time."

"Friend?"

"Yes, the blind woman. Just in the nick of time. Did you know you arrived at the hospital DOA? That was another piece of luck for you: you got your fatal stabbing right across the street from a hospital. You were dead for almost four minutes. Uncanny, that luck of yours. By all rights you shouldn't be here."

"The sword, the emperor's sword," Mariko said, horrified by the memory that's she'd bled all over it. "And the other one. Where are they?"

"I don't know if it's the emperor's or not," the doctor said with a laugh, "but your coworkers claimed the sword you had in your small intestine as evidence."

"Not that one. There were two others. Where are they?"

Mariko attempted to sit up, but spikes of pain stabbed her in the gut and the back. Teeth clenched, she slumped back into her pillows.

"Easy, now," the doctor said. "Don't go ripping out your stitches. There was another sword the police claimed from the ER. It used to be stuck in the fellow they brought in with you. Not so lucky, that one. He probably would have bled out from what was left of his arm, but the sword that stuck him went through both lungs and nicked his descending aorta. Never had a chance."

"Is Shoji-san here? The blind woman? I need to talk to her."

"Easy, Oshiro. You need to stay calm."

"Sorry." Mariko took a deep breath. "Doctor . . . sorry. I don't really remember your name."

"Anesthesia will do that to you. My name's Hayakawa."

"Dr. Hayakawa, there was a sword—"

"Don't worry about that," said a familiar voice, and Mariko saw Shoji standing in the doorway and flanked by Saori and Mariko's mother. The two of them rushed to Mariko's side, abandoning Shoji and all but shoving Dr. Hayakawa out of the way.

"You're awake!" Saori said.

"Hi," Mariko said. She could muster little else, crushed as she was under her family's embrace. Those spikes stabbed her in the gut again when she tried to hug them back.

"I guess I'll be moving along," Hayakawa said, and after a few moments Shoji-san took his place in Mariko's field of vision.

"Don't worry about the Tiger," she said. "I've seen it safely home for you."

Mariko couldn't bring herself to ask whether the em-

peror would forgive her for bloodying his family's heirloom.
That would have to wait.

Her mother, looking as weary as if she'd just delivered a
child, sat in one of the room's padded chairs. Saori released
her hug only to clasp Mariko's hand in both of hers. It was
a sensation Mariko had never felt before, and after a moment she realized why: she had no index finger on that
hand, and so she felt Saori holding a stump as well as the
three remaining fingers. Some instinct bade Mariko to feel
embarrassed by her deformity, but Mariko had no inclination to oblige it. She was happy to be alive, nine fingers or
ten, and the idea of shame seemed, for the first time in her
life, a trivial concern.

Saori's wrists were bound in broad bandages the color of
white people's skin. The bandages were puffy, and through
the haze of delirium-addled memory Mariko recalled that
similar bandages circled Saori's ankles. In straining at her
bonds, Saori had pulled *hard*.

"I'm so, so sorry, Miko." Saori was on the edge of crying.

"Don't be," Mariko said. "You didn't do anything wrong
to get kidnapped. That's all on Fuchida, not on you."

"Not that," said Saori. "I was an idiot. I talked myself
into thinking I didn't have a drug problem. But I do, and
you knew it, and I didn't listen. I'm so sorry."

Mariko opened her mouth to speak, but Saori shushed
her. "Don't say it's okay. It's not. But I couldn't see that. I
thought it was *my* problem. I didn't know what it was like
for you, or for Mom, watching me kill myself and knowing
there wasn't anything you could do to stop me. But then,
when I was strapped to that chair, when I saw him kill you
and there was nothing I could do . . . I'm sorry, Miko. I'm so,
so sorry. I didn't know."

Mariko swallowed, and pursed her lips in an attempt
not to cry. It failed. Saori was crying too, and they hugged
as tightly as their mutual injuries would allow. "I'll never
do it again," Saori said. "I swear to you, I'm never using
again."

"I know," said Mariko, and though she'd heard Saori
make the same promise a hundred times before, she could
tell this time was different.

And just like that, the moment was over. They were the
fabulous Oshiro sisters again, wiping their tears away and

laughing out of embarrassment. "That Dr. Hayakawa," Saori said, "he's cute, *neh*?"

"Yeah, I guess. I hadn't really noticed."

"Then you don't mind if I . . . ?"

Mariko laughed so hard, she nearly tore her stitches. "Saori, is that all you think about?"

"Well, it's not like I'm going to be getting high anymore. A girl's got to get her kicks somewhere."

A blushing Shoji-san cleared her throat in a matronly way. "We've brought something for you," she said, holding up a copy of the *Yomiuri Shimbun* in her wrinkled, ring-bedecked hand. "Obviously I haven't read it myself, but I'm told you're in two of the headlines."

"Oh, give it here," said Saori, her hand darting out for the paper. Her lunge caused her to lean far over Mariko, the motion crushing her slightly and causing the incision in her stomach to bite back in protest. Mariko restrained a grunt of pain.

"Yeah, this is the one," Saori said. "It's a few days old, now. Sorry. But listen: 'Policewoman's "Samurai Showdown" Ends in Two Fatalities, One Wondrous Recovery.' And this one too: 'Drug Ring and Kidnapping Ring Busted.' Cool, huh?"

Mariko felt something inside her wince. She'd always been better at taking criticism than praise. But that was in her past life; now she doubted she could find time to feel ashamed even if she were hailed as a hero.

Saori read on. " 'Tokyo police officers and NPA agents arrested twelve men and seized about fifty-five kilos of cocaine in a midnight raid in Tokyo Harbor. It was "by far the biggest cocaine bust Japan has ever seen," said Lt. Ko Takeo, forty-nine, of the TMPD.' "

Mariko groaned. "Don't say anything about that man."

"Yeah, we saw him on TV. Seems like kind of an asshole, *neh*? Anyway, blah blah blah, street value of the cocaine is five hundred million yen, bail set at blah blah blah. . . . Here we go: 'The arrests took place between midnight and one forty-five a.m. in Harumi 5-chōme, aboard the Bahamian-flagged M/V *South Sea Nova*, a freighter out of Los Angeles. An investigation headed by Det. Sgt. Oshiro Mariko, twenty-seven, led to the discovery of the incoming cocaine shipment. Detective Oshiro was hospitalized at the time of the arrests, so command duties fell to Lieutenant Ko.' Sorry, Miko. Let me get back to the good stuff."

"It's all right. Keep reading."

"'kay. 'According to authorities, the twelve men arrested were part of a ring headed by Fuchida Shūzō, who allegedly planned to finance the cocaine deal using profits from ransoming kidnap victims for Heian period antiques.'"

It took a moment for Mariko to register that one. The *Yomiuri* had it wrong; Saori's kidnapping was a last-minute gambit, not a plan. Then again, Mariko was the only one who could correct the error, and she hadn't been conscious long enough for anyone to interview her. As soon as that thought struck her, she was a little surprised that hordes of reporters hadn't already forced their way into the room. She wasn't sure why that was. Perhaps the TMPD had cordoned off the ward—or for that matter, maybe Shoji had asked Their Majesties to intervene—but whatever the explanation, Mariko was thankful to be left alone with people who loved her.

She returned her attention to Saori, who read on excitedly. "'NPA authorities say they are working with the American Federal Bureau of Investigation in apprehending Fuchida's American supplier.' No, wait, here's the good part: 'Fuchida was killed in a face-off with Oshiro, who is listed in critical condition as of press time. No other injuries resulted from the raid. Blah blah blah. A TMPD official said Oshiro should be "praised for her heroic actions," adding that "her quick thinking and immediate response saved innocent lives."' You want me to read the other article?"

"The one where I get killed and come back from the dead? No, thanks."

"Oh, come on. I'm in that one."

"Does Ko get to take the credit for everything in that one too?"

"So glad you asked. Let's find out."

Saori read on, smiling, and Mariko marveled at her resilience. All of two days ago, she'd been a kidnap victim—and half a second away from being a murder victim to boot. Now she was back to being just a little sister.

Mariko remembered Yamada telling her how food tasted better after a near-death experience. She'd heard similar stories about how sunsets were prettier and all that sort of thing. Mariko hadn't seen a sunset yet—her only window faced east—and she'd be taking food intravenously until the length of intestine the surgeons sewed back together had fully healed, but she did find that simple things revealed new beauty to her. The yellow tulips on her bedside stand, their scent, the way their petals glowed like they did right now with the sun at just the right angle: such things really were special. And Saori's capture was itself a near-death experience. Perhaps she was seeing the world in the same way.

Mariko listened as Saori finished the article, and noted that although the reporter made mention of the sword fight and the resulting injuries, nothing was said about the fate of the swords themselves. Confined to bed rest until her doctor said otherwise, Mariko knew there was nothing she could do to pursue the matter, but still the question burned in her: Where was Beautiful Singer?

## 78

Yamada's funeral had been rearranged for Tuesday afternoon. It was first scheduled for Sunday, two days after Mariko had awoken from her long meandering in the anesthetic mists, but Dr. Hayakawa insisted that Mariko was not to leave her bed for another three days at a minimum. The risk of sepsis was gravely real; Mariko needed round-the-clock supervision.

Hayakawa was a kind and decent man, despite his habit of referring to Mariko as "Oshiro" all the time. (She did not expect him to grasp the subtleties distinguishing *sergeant* from *detective sergeant*, but basic politeness dictated at least an Oshiro-*san*.) Unlike many men his age, and unlike most of the men Mariko had met in his profession, Hayakawa never made any attempt to grope her. Many physicians believed this was their prerogative, one of the perks of the job, but Hayakawa seemed to have had stricter scruples than that. Or maybe, knowing she'd come back from the dead after taking down a sword-wielding sociopath, he simply allowed wisdom to overrule lust.

Scruples, wisdom, and libido aside, he was sincerely concerned for his patient, but Shoji-san could argue most forcefully when pressed. She bullied Hayakawa into releasing Mariko a day early, only for the morning and bound by her own promise not to attempt to leave her wheelchair. Shoji had also persuaded the funeral director to delay Yamada's service by two days so Mariko could attend.

Some of the flowers had already arrived on Saturday afternoon and were beginning to wilt, but the service was beautiful nonetheless. The largest, most elaborate of the floral wreaths had come from the emperor himself, the accompanying card signed by Their Imperial Highnesses and stamped with the golden chrysanthemum seal. The music was Dvořák's Eighth Symphony, a fact Mariko learned only when Shoji-san whispered it in her ear, and one that caused Mariko to cry. She dabbed at the first tear with a bent knuckle, wondering whether this was what she was to have heard with Yamada on the night he was killed.

Mariko was by far the youngest person in attendance. Silver-haired professors from Tōdai and shuffling veterans of the Great War all paid their respects. Mariko overheard whispers that the emperor and empress themselves might come later for a private gathering before Yamada's urn.

When everyone took their seats and the eulogy began, Mariko took it like a push from a rooftop. She felt as if her wheelchair had plunged through the floor and was falling down a bottomless pit. Her sensei would be buried as Kiyama Keiji, a name that filled her with pangs of regret. It wasn't any defamation of the name Yamada that troubled her; it was only that she'd never pressed him to tell her about his past. And what a storied past it was: a lieutenant in Army Intelligence; a survivor of the first American strike against the motherland in the Great War; a combatant and later a prisoner of war in the Battle of Guadalcanal. Demoted to sergeant for reasons untold, and yet honored with the star of the Supreme Order of the Chrysanthemum, something Mariko had never heard of until the eulogy. Mariko could not keep from thinking about the story the eulogist left out, the one that explained why her sensei had earned Japan's highest honor, a medal ordinarily bestowed only on emperors and foreign royalty.

Mariko wondered how her sensei had garnered such prestige while even his own neighbors had probably never heard of him. To them he was only the old man up the block with the beautiful garden. His academic work was so specialized that no one outside of a graduate program in Japanese history was ever likely to read it. Yet he'd been decorated by the emperor himself, and in his modest bed-room he'd kept a sword worth millions.

But stranger things had happened, Mariko supposed. After all, the same sword was hers now, or would be once the Fuchida case was closed. She expected it would sit in a locker as seized evidence for a while, but in time Glorious Victory Unsought would come back to her. Yamada-sensei had bequeathed everything to Shoji-san, who accepted the house but had passed along the sword and the hundreds of history books. Mariko had eagerly accepted the offer of the books, even though she couldn't imagine where she'd keep them. Glorious Victory was different, though, and she'd tried to turn it down. "Oh, shush," Shoji had said. "I haven't got any use for swords."

"But it's worth a fortune," Mariko had said.

Shoji had only smiled. "I haven't got any use for one of those either," she'd said. "When you get to be my age, you stop worrying about such things."

As the eulogy came to a close, Mariko drifted out of her reverie. Her gaze fell on the framed black-and-white photo on the altar beside the urn. It was Yamada, perhaps in his sixties, his eyes glittering and full of kindness. He wore an understated smile in the picture, and his stubbly hair had been considerably thicker back then. Predictably, he was dressed in the traditional kimono of the old days. Mariko was able to keep a stiff upper lip until she looked at that photo and whispered to herself, "Good-bye, Sensei." The finality of that good-bye made her cry hard and silently, hugging herself in her wheelchair and squeezing her eyes tight.

She noticed Shoji-san did no crying of her own. "I've shed all my tears already, dear," Shoji said later. "It's harder when you can see it coming, but it's easier on days like to-day."

"You saw his death in advance?"

"Mm-hm."

"So you could have stopped it."

"What makes you think that?"

Mariko turned her chair to face Shoji's, taking her time wheeling it about so that more of the crowd could leave the room. Groups of twos and threes gathered here and there, wrapped up in their own conversations, but still Mariko kept her voice low. "You can see my future too?"

"I would say I see some of your futures."

"Before we visited the palace, before I went in to face Fuchida, how many of these futures had me dying in them?"

Shoji shrugged. "Death is in everyone's future."

"You're dodging the question. How many of these futures showed me dying on Fuchida's sword?"

"All of them."

Mariko nodded. "And how many of them showed me coming back?"

"None of them. You surprised me."

"So you let me walk into a fight, knowing it was going to kill me?"

"No. Destiny did. And destiny gave you a sword renowned for its ability to protect. It also gave your opponent a sword that compelled him to fight to prove his love for her, as well as a sword that punishes a wielder who seeks to prove himself in battle. There was only one way that battle could go."

Mariko could not hold back a rueful little laugh. "It sure didn't feel that way at the time."

"Of course not, dear. How can a leaf on the wind see what propels it? It's the same for those swept up by the forces of destiny. You, Keiji-san, that awful student of his—you're simply carried along."

"Keiji-san. You mean Yamada-sensei."

Mariko looked at Shoji the same way she'd have studied signs of struggle at a crime scene: the evidence was there, just waiting for her to put the right story together. At last she said, "You knew him back then. *Neh?* You know why he was honored with that star from the emperor too, don't you? That Supreme Chrysanthemum thing."

Shoji shrugged, reached into her big black Chanel purse, and produced an envelope of the faintest blue. Inside it was a folded sheet of paper as thin as onion skin. She handed it delicately to Mariko, who felt as soon as she touched it that this was something very old and very precious. Without unfolding the brittle page, she saw a spidery scrawl:

Hayano-chan foresaw that Matsumori would either destroy his enemies or destroy his friends, and I now fear it will be the latter, for she also saw that Ja-

pan would not see victory in this war. It sickens me
that I was so slow to decipher her message; I could
have changed the future if only I had been quicker to
see what she showed me.

"It's a letter from Yamada," Mariko whispered. Inspect-
ing it further, she said, "It's to his father. Shōwa 17. That's
during the war."

"1942," said Shoji. "I was just a little girl."

Mariko's re-read the same paragraph. In her mind it was
Yamada's voice reading the words, and felt good to have a
new connection with him. "Some of this is sensitive information," she said. "Weren't they censoring soldiers' letters
back then? How did this letter get through?"

"Who can say? Destiny follows strange paths where the
Inazumas are concerned."

"Is it true that you foresaw Japan losing?"

"Yes."

Once again Mariko directed her attention back to the
letter, unfolding it as carefully as she could. Her clumsy
four-fingered right hand made her afraid she'd tear the paper. She read from the beginning this time, her eyes skim-
ming over the faded, spidery lines. "'More frightening still
is the thought that the homeland should fall and the emperor be unseated,'" she read. "'I should like the sword to
find a place in the imperial household. At the very least I do
not want the Americans and Russians and British to choose
what government Japan shall take.' I can't believe it. But it's
true, isn't it? Yamada saved Japan."

"He may have," Shoji said with a shrug. "It's hard to say.
But for all these years he's also carried the fear that it was
his fault we lost the war. He had a chance to destroy Beautiful Singer once before. I'm not sure how much would have
changed if he'd done it, but who can say? The Inazuma
blades had the forces of destiny forged into their steel. They
certainly commanded the fate of families and clans; why not
a whole country?"

"Why not?" Mariko echoed. "But it sounds grandiose,
doesn't it? *One man* lost the war for us, and the same man
saved us from becoming a colony?"

"Better to say that one man stood where those two
threads of destiny intertwined. Many followed the paths of

those threads and took their part in weaving them. Keiji-san was one of the few that followed both paths."

"And you saw that? In advance?"

"After a fashion, yes."

"Just like you saw me dying on Fuchida's sword?"

"Yes."

Mariko swallowed. "And still you let me walk into a fight you knew would kill me? Why didn't you tell me?"

"Suppose I had. Suppose I told you Saori would escape with her life but you would not. Would it have made a difference?"

"No."

"Of course not. One way or another, destiny will find its path. Its roar still echoes in my ears, Detective Oshiro. Our work is not yet done."

## 79

Tokyo Prefecture maintained a high-security evidence storage facility on the north side of the harbor. It was the only place that made sense to keep two seized Inazuma blades. If Yamada's appraisals were correct, at auction each of the swords could easily fetch five hundred million yen. Storing such treasures in a cardboard box in Lieutenant Ko's precinct simply would not do.

The storage unit by the harbor was also the most likely place to hold fifty-five kilograms of seized cocaine. Only two government facilities had the capacity to dispose of cocaine in such quantities. One was the incinerator at the National Police Agency headquarters. The other was the incinerator at the storage building north of the harbor. Fifty-five kilos of ecstasy pills might have been divided among Tokyo's precincts for use in officer instruction and narcotics stings, but cocaine was useless in that regard. Thanks to the long-standing agreement between the *bōryokudan* and the police, no sensible dealer in Japan would touch the stuff. Because of the recent seizure, yakuzas would tread carefully around the cops for months to come, but the safe prediction was that sooner or later things would return to status quo.

Since the swords and the coke were connected to the same suspect, both would likely be held in the same evidence locker. Mariko, navigating the harborside facility in search of that locker, found that she and Shoji made a good team. Dr. Hayakawa had forbidden Mariko from using her arms to wheel herself around—too much upper-body movement might rupture her stitches—so Shoji used Mariko as part walking stick, part Seeing Eye dog.

A flash of Mariko's badge was enough to gain them entry. Judging by the raised eyebrows she got from the officer maintaining the security checkpoint, Mariko guessed the stories of her encounter with Fuchida had already spread through every precinct in greater Tokyo. Even among cops, who were supposed to have an eye for detail, rumors spread like a virus, mutating with each new infection. In all likelihood, whatever the officers at this facility had heard bore little resemblance to what had actually transpired, but Mariko didn't mind the celebrity if it gained her access to a locker that would have been denied to her under ordinary circumstances.

If it weren't for all the big steel lockers, someone could have landed a helicopter in the main space of the storage facility. The immense roll-up door facing the water was big enough to run a highway through it. The propane smell of forklift exhaust was inescapable in the dusty, cavernous room, and the lights hanging by long wires from the ceiling were scarcely bright enough to see by. If Mariko had to guess, she would have said there were a thousand lockers here, a little over a meter high and stacked double, their mesh faces painted institutional gray.

The swords, the security officer had said, were in locker 409. As Shoji wheeled Mariko into the 400s, Mariko let out a little gasp. Locker 409 was hanging open. It was empty.

"What's wrong?" said Shoji-san.

"We need to get back to the security desk right away."

They spun about and headed back the way they came. Shoji's quickest pace wasn't all that quick, and Mariko had to stick one hand in her purse and sit on the other one to keep from trying to wheel herself faster.

As they went, Mariko thought she heard a swishing sound. "Shoji-san," she said. "Stop for a second."

"Stop, *please*," said Shoji, but she stopped anyway.

There it was: that sound again, like a swooping bird. It came from the far side of the bank of lockers. Had Mariko been able to walk, she might well not have heard it; it was faint and would have been lost under the sound of the air passing by her ears were she moving any faster.

As faint as it was, Mariko knew that sound. What surprised her more was that she had a good guess who was making it.

"Turn right," Mariko said. "A little more. Now straight, please, quietly as you can, and mind the big crack in the floor right under my front wheels."

They progressed silently toward the end of the aisle, and, reaching it, Mariko peeked around the corner to see Lieutenant Ko with Beautiful Singer in his hands. He stood between two long columns of lockers, his suit jacket lying on the floor nearby, Beautiful Singer's scabbard resting on top of it. Glorious Victory Unsought was nowhere to be seen.

Ko's back was to her, and he raised the sword high and slashed down diagonally. The blade hissed as it cut the cold air. Now a chest-high cut, parallel to the floor. The movement turned him on his heel, bringing him face-to-face with Mariko.

"You!" Ko stuttered, his face red. "What are you doing here, Oshiro?"

"Funny. That's what I was going to ask you."

"Be careful with this one," Shoji whispered. "I see two futures for him. He stands on the razor's edge between them."

"Shut up," Ko barked. "Get out of here, Oshiro, or I'll have you—"

Suddenly his face broke into his winningest shit-eating grin. "I've got you," he said. "At last I've got you. You're breaking protocol being here. You're still on medical leave. Thank you, Oshiro. You've finally given me the excuse I need to strip your rank."

"No, sir," said Mariko. "You've given me all I need to crash your career into the ground. You're tampering with evidence."

"You'll never make that stick. It's my word against yours."

"I don't need to make it stick. You told me yourself so many times: all I need is the allegation. And I'll allege more than tampering with evidence. Do you remember the very first case I worked under you? Bumps Ryota? That sting went down so bad, I told myself it's like the new LT and this

Bumps are on the same side. I never guessed how close to the truth I was. You weren't in bed with Bumps, but I'll bet a month's pay you were in bed with Fuchida."

Ko scoffed. "Don't be ridiculous. I never even laid eyes on the man before seeing his dead body."

"Maybe. Maybe not. But Fuchida sure knew a lot about me—too much, in fact. He knew I was the lead officer on the Yamada case and he knew I'd staked out Yamada's house. Only an insider from our precinct could give him that information. Fuchida was talking to a cop."

"Right. Obviously. Tell me, Oshiro, what kind of pain medication do they have you on? Because when Internal Affairs hears about your insubordination, I might be lenient and tell them this bullshit is just the drugs talking, not another one of your asinine conspiracy theories."

Mariko shrugged. "If it's any consolation, I really didn't think you were corrupt at first. I thought you were just a sexist prick understaffing my operations to set me up for failure. Then I saw you talking to that great big *rikishi* I took down at Dr. Yamada's. Too bad for you he's the fattest guy ever arrested in our precinct. If he were a normal-sized perp, fewer people would have noticed him, but at his size I'm sure everyone who was there that night will remember you two had a nice long chat."

"So what? You *saw* a talk; you *heard* nothing. We might have been talking about baseball for all you know."

"I don't care if you were talking about how many times a day you stop to check out my ass. The fact is, you were talking to Fuchida's hit man, and the next time I walked into your office, you ordered me not to investigate *bōryokudan* connections to my case. Fuchida was a yakuza, and that means you gave me a direct order—an *illegal* direct order—not to investigate my lead suspect."

Ko flinched as if she'd slapped him. Right then Mariko knew he was guilty of everything she suspected. "That's enough," he said, squeezing the sword's grip so tight that Mariko could hear the wrapping shift under his fingers. "Conspiracy theories are one thing, but I'll be damned if I'll sit back and listen to you accuse me of breaking the law. Do you know how easy you're making it for me to bust you down to patrolman? I'll have you directing traffic for the rest of your career."

"No, sir. Everyone in the precinct knows you've got it out for me, and now I've got you on record in my case file trying to protect a serial killer. Who knows, sir? If you had let me run my investigation the right way, maybe I wouldn't be in this wheelchair right now. Maybe Fuchida wouldn't have kidnapped my sister. Maybe he wouldn't have murdered my friend."

"That's nothing but speculation. You'll never prove a word of it."

"I don't need to prove it to ruin your career. Like you said, all I need is the allegation."

Mariko could hear him grinding his teeth. "Shut your damn mouth," he said.

"The only thing I don't get is the why. Did Fuchida offer you something if the cocaine deal went through? Or are you really so threatened by me that you'd get in bed with a yakuza just to see me fail?"

"I said shut up."

"Why risk your career just to prove women can't be cops?"

"God damn you—"

"That's not it, is it? You're not worried that I'm good at this. You're worried that I'm better at it than you are. Now *that's* something you'd risk your career to disprove."

Ko advanced on her, Beautiful Singer quavering in his right hand. "This is beyond insubordination! I'll have your head for this."

"You'll want to put that sword down, sir. You just threatened an officer with a deadly weapon. Don't make things worse."

He stepped back, but now his other hand tightened down on the sword. Sweat stains emanated from the armpits of his white shirt. "I'm not going down without a fight."

"I didn't come to fight. I'm here to save your life."

Ko scoffed again. "Right. Of course you are."

"I can hardly believe it myself, but it's true. That sword has a hold on you. It had a hold on Fuchida too. That's why I'm here: it needs to be destroyed."

"And you accuse *me* of tampering with evidence? Ha!" He stabbed a fat finger at her. In his other hand, the sword pointed right at her chest. "Traffic control is too good for you. I'll have you cuffed to the station coffeemaker by the end of the week."

Mariko smiled. "You're going to bust the woman in the wheelchair? The hero cop from the headlines? No, you've been playing the political game too long for that. You're going to put that sword down. Then you're going to forget I was ever here, in the hopes that I'll extend you the same courtesy."

"No." He marched straight at her, sword in hand, and at the last instant he turned the blade aside so as not to run her through. He loomed over her, close enough that Mariko's toes brushed his pant legs. "The sword is mine," he said.

"Have it your way," said Mariko. Her hand emerged from her purse holding the Cheetah. She jabbed it hard into his groin and pulled the trigger.

Ko shrieked and crumpled, balled in a fetal position. The Cheetah's voltage left him conscious enough that he could still groan, so Mariko touched the silver studs to him again, this time on the cheek. Ko twitched once and fell still.

"What was that?" asked Shoji. "You hit him with something. It smells like ozone."

"Can we roll about two steps to the left? Back up a bit so we don't run him over."

"You didn't tell me you were armed."

"I'm a cop. I'm always armed."

Mariko's front right wheel touched Beautiful Singer's hilt. "Feel that?" she asked.

"Yes," said Shoji. "It's the sword?"

"Yeah. Hand it to me, will you?"

*"Please,"* said Shoji. But again she obliged.

The sword was so light it seemed to float. Of all Master Inazuma's creations, surely this was his masterpiece. It was easy to see why men had died for it.

Mariko talked Shoji through the various aisles and corridors they needed to navigate to reach the incinerator, but all the while her mind was on the sword. What would it mean to destroy it? Beautiful Singer was a cultural icon: the finest sword by the finest master, and the master himself the greatest of a land whose sword smithing exceeded all others. It was worth more money than Mariko would ever make in her lifetime. But more important than that, it was a piece of history.

At last they reached the incinerator. Mariko had envisioned a great potbellied thing, cast iron, with a gaping maw opening onto glowing red-orange hellfire. What she saw was a door in the wall, not so different from the door she'd find on the front of a microwave. It was unguarded—but then, what was the use in guarding it? It had no value; its only function was to destroy things of value. And after all, the building itself was secure.

"Straight ahead, six paces," Mariko said, and soon rolled to a stop in front of the little door. She tested Beautiful Singer's weight in her hands. The edge of the blade was so fine that were she to drop a single hair on it, she was certain the hair would be cut in two.

"This is the third Inazuma blade I've held in my own two hands," she said. "How many people in history do you suppose could say that?"

"Master Inazuma himself," said Shoji. "Not many others."

A little voice in Mariko's mind cried out in protest. She couldn't destroy the sword. It was evidence. Destroying it would ruin her career. And besides, the sword was worth more than all the pay she'd draw from the Tokyo Metropolitan Police Department in her entire lifetime. It wouldn't be hard to keep it for herself. She could say Ko stole it. Or incinerated it. He was lying helpless. It wouldn't be a hard thing to kill him.

For the first time Mariko could understand Beautiful Singer's power. It *was* worth killing for. But no more so than a Mercedes-Benz. People committed homicide over expensive property in every corner of the world. They killed for jealousy too, but Mariko wasn't feeling any of that. As elegant as it was, Beautiful Singer inspired no thoughts of possessiveness in her. For the first time Mariko understood the full weight of what Yamada had told her so many weeks before: *I don't believe there's ever been a man alive who could overcome the sword.* No *man* alive. And from the beginning Yamada said he'd been waiting for a student like Mariko.

The dots connected so fast that Mariko could hardly follow them. Beautiful Singer was possessed by a geisha, a samurai's jealous lover. It wasn't so long ago that Mariko would have scoffed at herself for thinking such a thing. But now she was sure of it: the *kami* that lived in this sword was female, and it had a unique power to infect men's minds. But not Mariko's. Yamada had told her once that the old guard would have stripped him of his rank for teaching swordsmanship to a woman, but now Mariko saw it couldn't have gone any other way. Only a woman could accomplish what she was contemplating now: extinguishing the spirit within Beautiful Singer.

And incinerating Beautiful Singer with it. The rarest, most conspicuous, most expensive piece of evidence in the whole facility.

"I wish I could be sure I'm doing the right thing," Mariko said. Then she opened the incinerator door, thrust Beautiful Singer into the chamber within, and closed it quickly.

"Now we just have to figure out how this thing works," she said.

## 80

"**C**ome on," said Saori. "You just know you're going to get a hero's welcome."

Mariko shook her head. "I've just spent a week in the hospital. I look like hell."

"You look like a war hero. Besides, some of those guys you work with are cute. You gotta love that uniform."

"Not when I have to wear it, I don't." Mariko sighed. She'd lost the battle already and she knew it. As a last ploy she said, "Besides, I thought you were hitting on Dr. Hayakawa."

"Nothing says a girl can't work on two guys at once." Saori winked and smiled. "Come on, Miko, put your face on. Let's go."

Six nights and seven days: that's how long Mariko had been cooped up in her bed until Hayakawa pronounced her free from the risk of sepsis. And now she didn't want to leave the apartment. She knew it didn't make sense, and she knew she'd have to go to her precinct sooner or later if she was going to get HQ to sign off on her six weeks of recuperation. Mariko still couldn't sit up without pain, two hot stripes of it, one in her belly and the other in her back. Fuchida's sword had done far worse to her on its way through her body, but it was the muscle punctures that kept her immobile. If she was going to be paid while she sweated through rehab, she'd have to go through the paperwork.

So as much as she hated Saori for pushing her into it, Mariko got ready to go back to post. "I have no idea what to wear," she told Saori. "What the hell goes with a wheelchair?"

It was the thought of being seen in the chair that daunted her. She'd worked long and hard to be seen as an equal—or, if not an equal, then at least as a strong, independent woman who didn't need to be mollycoddled or rescued. Letting the department see her in a wheelchair would destroy that image, and Mariko feared it would take another four years to rebuild it.

It was seeing Glorious Victory that cinched it. It hadn't been in the evidence locker because it wasn't evidence; no one would be pressing assault charges against a dead man, and without a case against Fuchida it was just Dr. Yamada's private property. Yamada had bequeathed everything to Shoji-san, and Shoji didn't have much need for ancient cavalry swords. When Mariko returned to her apartment, she found Saori had bought her a sword stand as a welcome-home present, and for lack of a better place to put it in her minuscule apartment, Glorious Victory Unsought was sitting on Mariko's kitchen table.

It was far and away the most expensive, most beautiful, most daunting gift she'd ever received. The sword overhung both ends of the little table, larger than life. Mariko thought of the Bushido tradition it symbolized; she thought of her fallen sensei; she thought of what both of them would have to say about trying to avoid her fears.

So she rummaged around for some blush and lip gloss. Makeup was hardly her usual style, but she couldn't show up at the precinct looking like the pallid zombie she'd become after lying flat on her back for a week and surviving on an intravenous diet. In the end she settled on wearing her police uniform. Again, hardly her usual style, but at least she'd be seen as a sergeant in a wheelchair instead of a poor *girl* in a wheelchair.

As they approached the station, Saori said, "Don't look so nervous. It'll be fine."

"They're *guys*, Saori. They're going to pity me."

Saori spun her about, pushed the glass door open with her butt, and pulled Mariko inside. The second set of double doors was also made of glass, crosshatched by steel wires within, and Mariko looked over her shoulder to see Ino rushing up to open them for her. It begins before I even get inside, she thought, and Ino's long arms pulled back the door.

"Well, aren't you a tall drink of water?" Saori said. Without even looking, Mariko knew what smile she was giving him.

But Ino ignored her entirely. "Hey, guys!" he said. "Oshiro's back!"

The last thing in the world Mariko expected was applause. Everyone in the precinct was on his feet, cheering and shouting. Ino was the first to clap his hand on her shoulder, just as he might have done for a teammate who drove in the winning run at the interprecinct baseball tournament. As Saori ushered her into the station, one cop after another congratulated her, their smiles genuinely collegial. One gave her a punch to the upper arm and did not pull it. There would be a bruise later. She would treasure it. Sergeant Takeda, not much taller than Mariko even in her wheelchair, took one look at her missing finger and joked that she'd have to learn how to shoot left-handed. It was the kind of joke he should have made only with another man. She adored him for it.

"You got rid of the old man!" said a cop she didn't even recognize.

"Yeah, pled guilty this morning," said someone else behind her, someone she couldn't see through the crowd.

Whoever he was, his comment generated almost as much stir as Mariko's appearance had. "A guy I know at the courthouse just sent me the e-mail," the rumormonger said. Mariko still couldn't tell who it was; all she could see were backs and belts. "They nailed him on obstruction of justice and tampering with evidence. My guy says the prosecutor decided not to push for destruction of evidence. Better to take the easy conviction, I guess."

"How long will he get?"

"Who cares? Just so they put him away long enough for me to retire."

"Oshiro, is it true you nailed him in the 'nads with a Taser?"

"Yeah, Oshiro, is it true when they found him, he pissed himself?"

Mariko couldn't keep track of all the chatter. It was enough for her that Ko hadn't been convicted of turning Beautiful Singer into ferrous ash. Mariko was guilty on that count, and it wasn't right to let another cop stand punishment for her crime, not even a cop so noxious as Lieutenant Ko. Ex-lieutenant Ko, she thought, who had left his fingerprints all over Beautiful Singer's sheath, which had probably been sitting right on his jacket when the police arrived to examine the scene. It was his only gentlemanly act: to remove himself from her life permanently.

"Who do you think burned the sword if it wasn't him?" someone was saying.

"It *was* him. They just couldn't pin it on him, because they couldn't find prints on the incinerator."

Mariko smiled. She knew why that was: she'd wiped her own prints clean. Even after destroying the sword that had ruined so many lives, she had to watch her ass. Guilt made her face flush, despite the fact that she was the only one who could turn the boys' gossiping in the right direction.

And then, all of a sudden, she smiled. It was a broad, beaming smile, accompanied by the beautiful realization that had just leapt into her mind. She was gossiping with the boys. More to the point, the boys were gossiping with her. She was *in*. One of them. A member of the club.

And to join, all she'd had to do was die and come back.

She shuddered at the thought of what it would take to make lieutenant.

**anime:** cartoon

**banzai:** traditional military cheer

**bokken:** solid wooden training sword, usually made of oak

**bōryokudan:** literally, "violent crime organization"; the term used by police, and in the media at the behest of the police, for organized crime syndicates in Japan

**bushi:** warrior; soldier

**Bushido:** the way of the warrior

**daimyo:** feudal lord with large land holdings

**dan:** an enumerating suffix for ranks of black belt (e.g., "fourth *dan*" means "fourth-degree black belt")

**eta:** outcast; untouchable

**gaijin:** literally, "outsider"; foreigner

**gakubatsu:** a strong and lasting bond, originating from a shared alma mater, entailing the exchange of favors

**geisha:** a skilled artist paid to wait on, entertain, and in some cases provide sexual services for clientele

**goze:** blind itinerant female, usually a musician, said to have the gift of second sight

**gyoza:** Japanese pot sticker, usually filled with ground pork and shredded cabbage, onion, and other vegetables

**hachimaki:** the bandana traditionally worn under an armored warrior's helmet; also used by kamikaze pilots to signify their willingness to die

**hakama:** wide, pleated pants bound tightly around the waist and hanging to the ankle

**iaidō:** the art of drawing and resheathing the sword, and of attacking off the draw

**kappa:** a water-dwelling mythological being, humanoid with reptilian features, with a topless head and a water-filled bowl in place of a brain

**karōshi:** death from overwork; also known clinically as "occupational sudden death"

**katana:** a curved long sword worn with the cutting edge facing upward

**kendō:** the sporting art of the sword

**kenjutsu:** the lethal art of the sword

**koku:** the amount of rice required to feed one person for one year; also, a unit for measuring the size of a fiefdom or estate, corresponding to the amount of rice its land can produce

**kumihimo:** woven cord, sometimes used to bind swords

**manga:** Japanese-style comic books

**naginata:** pole arm with a very long blade

**ninkyō dantai:** literally, "chivalrous group"; the term used by criminals for organized crime syndicates in Japan

**NPA:** National Police Agency

**ōdachi:** a curved great sword

**onsen:** hot spring bath

**okonomiyaki:** literally, "grilled whatever-you-like"; an omelette-like dish consisting of various meats and vegetables, shredded and bound together by batter, often cooked by the customer (*okonomiyaki* restaurants usually feature griddles on each table)

**OL:** office lady; general term for any woman in pink-collar work

**oyabun:** head of an organized crime syndicate

**pachinko:** a machine used for gambling, akin to a vertical pinball machine

**punch perm:** a hairstyle of short, tight curls, often dyed, which for many years was a trademark style among yakuzas

**ri:** a unit of measurement equal to about two and a half miles

**rikishi:** sumo wrestler

**romaji:** the roman alphabet when used to write Japanese words

**rōnin:** literally, "wave-person"; a masterless samurai

**sarariman:** salaryman; a typical large-office employee

**sashiko:** a traditional Japanese quilting art

**sensei:** literally, "born-before"; a teacher, professor, or doctor, depending on the context

**seppuku:** ritual suicide by disembowelment; also called hara-kiri

**shakuhachi:** traditional Japanese flute

**shamisen:** traditional Japanese lute

**shinobi:** literally, "magic person" or "secret person"; a ninja

**shinogi-ji:** the flat of a *katana* or *tachi*

**shinogi-zukuri:** a style of sword featuring a flat of the blade, so that the blade looks roughly bullet-shaped in cross section

**shōchū:** rice liquor

**shodan:** literally, "beginner's rank"; first-degree black belt

**shogun:** commander in chief; historically, the true ruler of

Japan (the emperor being merely the shogun's most important hostage)

**shoji:** sliding divider with rice paper windows, usable as both door and wall

**shomen:** an overhead strike

**shoyu:** soy sauce

**southern barbarian:** white person (considered "southern" because European sailors were first allowed to dock only in Kyushu, the southernmost of Japan's major islands)

**sugegasa:** broad-brimmed, umbrella-like hat

**tachi:** a curved long sword worn with the blade facing downward

**taiko:** a Japanese-style (and often enormous) drum; alternatively, the art of drumming with said drums

**tsuba:** a hand protector, usually round or square, where the hilt of a sword meets its blade; the Japanese analogue to a crossguard

**wakaru:** to understand

**wakashū:** a low-ranking yakuza

**wakizashi:** a curved short sword, typically paired with a *katana*, worn with the blade facing upward

**washi:** traditional Japanese handmade paper

**yakuza:** member of an organized crime syndicate

**zabuton:** a broad cushion used for sitting on the floor

# AUTHOR'S NOTE

There is a scene in the film adaptation of *The Fellowship of the Ring* that got the attention of some vociferous critics with a lot of time on their hands. The four hobbits sit around their campfire on Amon Sûl cooking a dinner of tomatoes, sausages, and nice, crispy bacon. The critics complained that tomatoes are a New World food, and that it is therefore unrealistic for hobbits to be eating them. This sort of complaint tickles me. Four hobbits travel in the company of a ranger still in the prime of life at eighty-seven years old, they search for a wizard on a hill with an Elvish name, they are soon to be attacked by deathless wraiths, and what's unrealistic about this scene is that they're *eating tomatoes*.

Some readers may find errors in this book that are more substantial than hobbit tomatoes. My background is primarily in philosophy, not history, and so I take certain risks in writing historical fiction. I've never been a police officer either, so I take further risks in choosing Mariko as a protagonist. That's all right with me; to crib from Socrates, the risk-free life is not worth living. If readers do find anachronisms and inaccuracies in this book, I expect I'll be seeing some e-mail. Please send it. I look forward to learning from experts about police procedures and Japanese history, and if I build a collection of hobbit tomatoes in the process, so much the better. I promise to do something fun with them.

My editor tells me that the rest of my readers—those

who aren't police officers, Japanese historians, or the sort to go looking for hobbit tomatoes to sling—may be curious to know which parts of the book are historically accurate and which are my own invention. Master Inazuma himself is fictitious, but the other details regarding the forging of swords are as accurate as I know how to make them: Muramasa and Masamune are real historical figures; the sword smiths of Seki were (and are) Shinto priests, and Seki was (and is) the sword smithing capital of Japan; virtually identical swords were classified as *tachi* in one era and *katana* in another, and were classified differently based on how they were worn.

Perhaps most important for purposes of this book, it was not uncommon to give a sword a name, especially if something remarkable was accomplished with that weapon, and neither was it uncommon to describe a sword as having a certain personality. Japanese culture is at bottom a culture thoroughly infused by Shinto, and central to Shinto beliefs is the idea that *kami*—mistranslated as "gods," poorly translated as "spirits," and best left untranslated at all—reside in living and unliving things alike. Waterfalls have *kami* as surely as foxes do, and on this view there is no reason a sword should not be able to have its *kami*.

All of the historical periods in this book are accurately named and dated, and though the names of the characters and their families are invented, the details surrounding their lives are again as historically accurate as I know how to make them. Samurai boys like Daigoro did come of age at sixteen (though some families chose other birthdays to celebrate coming-of-age). Women like Hisami were samurai, and they did have their own schools of weapon training, including training with hairpin blades. The transfer of Saito's loyalty from Lord Kanayama to Lord Ashikaga was possible, and the alternatives—seppuku or becoming *rōnin*—were grim.

I also sought to make regional politics faithfully mirror historical fact. The Owari territory of Book Two was hotly contested throughout the most turbulent parts of Japan's history. The Izu peninsula in Books Four and Six had five dominant clans, the heads of which were called *Izu-no-kami* (Lord Protectors of Izu). I have renamed the Izu families, but a clan like House Okuma would have commanded the fealty of smaller clans like House Yasuda. Toyotomi Hideyoshi is a real historical figure, and his power was such that not even a regionally dominant clan like the Okumas could afford to ignore his wishes.

Incidentally, Okuma Ichirō's neck wound is also true to life, as is Ashikaga Jinzaemon's. Lord Ashikaga's was inspired by an acquaintance of my grandfather's who was shot in the throat; his gravelly voice stands out in my memory, as does his scar like a satellite view of a hurricane. Ichirō's wound is borrowed from an account in the *Hagakure*, as is his treatment. Despite the seeming impossibility of surviving such a grievous wound given such limited knowledge of medicine, the victim in the *Hagakure* lived to fight another day. That someone in that era could survive being nearly beheaded was too tempting for me to pass up.

As soon as I discovered that part of the story of the Inazuma blades would have to take place in World War II, I scoured the histories looking for the ideal moment. Two events stood out to frame that moment. The first was the unexpected American surrender near Luzon on April 9, 1942. The second came just nine days later: the only American air raid to strike Japan in 1942, known today as the Doolittle Raid (named for the architect of the attack, not for the fact that the attack didn't do much).

Colonel Iwasaki is fictitious, but the crimes I have him commit in the Rape of Nanjing and the Bataan Death March are all too real. Keiji Kiyama and General Matsumori are invented, but the events of World War II in which they are involved are actual events. Disease did cause seventy-five thousand Americans and Filipinos to surrender much earlier than anticipated; that the Japanese were caught unprepared almost certainly contributed to the atrocities that followed in Bataan. Japanese soldiers did take Tulagi, the Solomons, and Guadalcanal, and after the American counterinvasion the fighting on Guadalcanal was as bloody and vicious as any you can imagine. Whether or not all the island-hopping was orchestrated from a single building in Tokyo, and whether or not any intelligence officers from that building were demoted and shipped off to fight in Guadalcanal, are questions I took liberties in answering.

Executive Order 9066 is not a fiction; Japanese Americans were rounded up and concentrated in internment camps, and if comparing those to the concentration camps of Hitler and Stalin seems unfair to you, I hope you will grant that it might not have seemed that way from the perspective of a young Japanese officer of that era. In the course of Tiger on the Mountain's story I make brief mention of anti-American propaganda; this too was real and would no doubt fuel the fears of someone in Kiyama Keiji's position.

Yamada Yasuo is based in part on my sensei and mentor, Dr. Yuasa Yasuo. Yuasa-sensei was a philosophical mentor for me, not a martial one, but like Yamada, he did fight in World War II. (Yuasa-sensei's career in the war was worthy of Vonnegut and reminiscent of Heller: he was a combat engineer, and he told me that by the end of the war he was rebuilding the same bridge every night, which American bombers would blow up again the following day.) Like Yamada, Yuasa-sensei was nearly blind. Like Yamada, he published voluminously. On that note I will confess to stealing one of Yamada's wisecracks directly from Yuasa-sensei, who once told me his publisher might at least have the good graces to wait until he was dead before calling his complete works *complete*. Like Yamada, he exhibited extraordinary generosity, always willing to share his wisdom. The one respect in which they are not at all alike is that, to the best of my knowledge, Yuasa-sensei was never a total badass with a sword.

Some aspects of Mariko's life may strike non-Japanese readers as odd because police work is so different in Japan than elsewhere. Most noticeable is the fact that Japanese cops almost never use their guns. By this I don't mean merely that they don't fire their guns; most never even draw them. In the U.S., very few police officers ever fire at a human being, but even in rural areas many officers will find it hard to imagine getting through a summer without ever drawing and aiming at a suspect. (One officer I interviewed for this book told me he draws his service weapon weekly and has to take aim at a suspect at least once a month—and he serves a fairly sparse population.) By contrast, you can find cops in Japan who not only haven't drawn their weapon in years but who don't even know of anyone in their police station who has. Japanese cops pride themselves on their marksmanship, but the idea of using a pistol in the field is anathema.

This is hardly the only discrepancy between the Japanese and American legal systems. Japanese medical examiners almost never perform autopsies. (Confucian taboos still prohibit tampering with corpses.) Defendants in criminal courts are almost never acquitted; by the time a case gets to trial, a conviction is all but secured. The Tokyo Metropolitan Police Department occupies an especially strange conceptual space, for Japan is without an equivalent of the American FBI. There is a National Police Agency, which is like an FBI with all of the bureaucrats but none of the agents or law enforcement power. The NPA commandeers local police officers as necessary, often from the TMPD, and the TMPD has the power to involve its own officers in crimes outside of its jurisdiction. Smaller police departments may also request personnel from the TMPD, which is how Mariko becomes involved in Dr. Yamada's life.

Organized crime syndicates go by many names in Japan. "The yakuza" is not one of them, despite the fact that in English "the yakuza" is almost invariably used to mean "the Japanese Mafia" rather than "the Japanese mafioso." The terms I use most often here are *bōryokudan* ("violent crime organization"), which is used by police, and *ninkyō dantai* (literally "chivalrous group," though it is not such a stretch to translate it as "Order of Knights"), used by yakuzas themselves. The difference between these two should tell you something about the difference between how police think of yakuzas and how yakuzas think of themselves. The word yakuza literally means "eight-nine-three," but better translations would be "mafioso" or, oddly enough, "useless guy" or "good-for-nothing." (The cards eight, nine, and three form an utterly worthless hand in a traditional card game that yakuzas used to run.) Yakuzas are yakuzas because they were deemed to be unfit for any other occupation. Revenge must have been sweet when society's most useless members carved out a new and supremely influential place for themselves.

The role of organized crime is misunderstood by virtually everyone, and in Japan that role is particularly bizarre. It is even difficult to apply the word "crime," because in Japan such shadowy activities are often conducted in broad daylight with no legal reprisals. It is common knowledge, for example, that yakuzas own almost all the vending machines in the country, and the price of a bottle of soda is therefore defined by yakuzas. (Convenience stores dare not undercut it, for obvious reasons.) Yakuzas routinely carry business cards and maintain office buildings. The name of the criminal organization is displayed prominently above the front door, just like any ordinary business. When police raid such buildings, they phone in advance to make an appointment for the raid. I swear to you I am not making this up.

There is no Kamaguchi-gumi, and neither Fuchida Shūzō, his father, nor Kamaguchi Ryusuke is based on any actual person. I repeat: *no yakuza in this book is based on a real person*. It may well be that the risk-free life is not worth living, but even so, I want to make it clear to all the gangsters out there that I am sure you are all perfectly nice fellows and you are just misunderstood. Please do not make me sleep with the fishes.

—Steve Bein
Undisclosed Location
August 2011

# ACKNOWLEDGMENTS

My heartfelt thanks go out to all of the people who assisted me in researching this book: to Alex Embry, my primary resource on all cop questions; to all the other police officers I interviewed but who preferred to remain nameless; to D. P. Lyle for all of his guidance on getting the medical and forensic details right; to the members of Codex for their collective resourcefulness in answering just about any question a writer can imagine; and to Luc Reid for getting Codex started in the first place.

I am also indebted to all the people who helped to make this book a reality, especially Cameron McClure, my wonderful agent, and Kat Sherbo, my attentive and insightful editor. Cameron and Kat proved invaluable in polishing and tightening the manuscript. My thanks also go to Charlie Bee and Luc Reid, both of whom provided important insights on the structure of the story itself, and to my Mom, who also volunteers as my proofreader.

Thanks as always to Michele, who puts up with me when I'm having trouble with my computer, and who doesn't put up with me when my computer drives me beyond the brink of sanity. I am eternally grateful on both counts.

# ABOUT THE AUTHOR

STEVE BEIN teaches Asian philosophy and Asian history at the State University of New York at Geneseo. He holds a PhD in philosophy, and his graduate work took him to Nanzan University and Ōbirin University in Japan, where he translated a seminal work in the study of Japanese Buddhism. He holds a third-degree black belt and a first-degree black belt in two American forms of combative martial arts, and has trained in about two dozen other martial arts over the past twenty years. His short fiction has been published in *Asimov's Science Fiction*, *Interzone*, and *Writers of the Future*. Please visit Steve on the Web at www.philosofiction.com, and like him on Facebook at www.facebook.com/philosofiction.

Read on for a thrilling excerpt from
the next novel of the Fated Blades,

## YEAR OF THE DEMON

by Steve Bein
Available in October 2013 from Roc.

D etective Sergeant Oshiro Mariko adjusted the straps on her vest, twisting her body side to side to snug the fit tighter. The thing was uncomfortable, and not just physically. Mariko hadn't had to wear a bulletproof vest since academy. Even then it had been for training purposes only; she'd never strapped one on in anticipation of being shot at.

"Boys and girls, listen up," Lieutenant Sakakibara said, his voice deep and sharp. He was a good twenty centimeters taller than Mariko, with a high forehead and a Sonny Chiba haircut that sat on his head like a helmet. He looked perfectly at ease in his body armor, and despite the heavy SWAT team presence, there was no doubt that the staging area was his to command. "Our stash house belongs to the Kamaguchi-gumi, and that means armed and dangerous. Our CI confirms at least two automatic weapons on site."

That sent a wave of murmurs through the sea of cops surrounding him. CIs were renowned for their lousy intelligence. Narcs with holstered pistols, SWAT guys with their M4 rifles pointed casually at the ground, all of them were shaking their heads. They all spoke fluent covert-informantese, and in that surreal language "at least two" meant "somewhere between zero and ten."

Mariko was the shortest one in the crowd, and if she looked a little taller with her helmet on, everyone else looked taller still. Police work attracted the cowboys, and the boys really got their six-guns on when they got to armor up and kick down doors. Being the only woman on the team was alienating at the best of times, and now, surrounded by unruly giants, Mariko felt like she was a teenager again, awkward, softspoken, trapped in the midst of raucous, rowdy adults and just old enough to understand how out of place she was.

It was no good dwelling on how she felt like a *gaijin*, so she returned her attention to Lieutenant Sakakibara. "There's going to be a lot of strange equipment in there," he said, though he hardly needed to. SWAT had downloaded images of all the machines they were likely to encounter. The target was a packing and shipping company, an excellent front for running dope, guns—damn near anything, really—and the machinery they'd have on site would offer cover and concealment galore. Everyone knew that, but Sakakibara was good police: he looked out for his team. "Weird shadows," he said, "lots of little nooks and crannies, lots of corners to clear. You make sure you clear every last one of them. Execute the fundamentals, people."

Again, everyone knew it, and again, everyone needed the reminder. Mariko marveled at how some of the most specialized training in the world boiled down to just getting the basics right. In that respect SWAT operations were no different from basketball or playing piano.

"B-team, D-team," Sakakibara said, "you need to hit the ground running. I want to own the whole damn structure in the first five seconds. Understand?"

"Yes, sir," said twelve cops in unison.

"C-team, same goes for you, but don't you forget"—Sakakibara pointed straight at Mariko as he spoke—"Detective Sergeant New Guy is a part of your element. The Kamaguchi-gumi has put out a contract on her. I won't have her getting shot on my watch, got it?"

"Yes, sir," Mariko said with the rest of C-team.

The first of the vans started up with a roar, and the sound made Mariko's heart jump. She chided herself; she was thinking too much about those automatic weapons, and now even the rumble of a diesel engine sounded like machine-gun fire. She unholstered her Sig one more time, taking yet another look down the pipe of the pistol she already knew she'd charged.

"The seven-oh-three gets here in"—Sakakibara checked his huge black diver's watch—"six minutes. That gives you five and a half to get where you need to be. Now mount up."

"Yes, sir," the whole team said, and Mariko started jogging toward the B and C van. The rest of her element fell in behind her.

When she reached the dark back corner of the van her heart was racing, and she knew it wasn't because of a ten-meter jog. Her hand drifted to the holster on her hip, satisfying an irrational need to confirm that her Sig was even there. Running her left thumb over the ridges of her pistol's hammer, she absently wondered why the movement should still feel strange to her. It wasn't as if she hadn't logged the hours retraining herself to shoot as a lefty; at last count she'd expended about two thousand rounds on the pistol range. She hadn't yet hit the same scores she'd been shooting right-handed, and that idea weighed on her, heavier than the ceramic plating of the body armor that now made her shoulders ache. Despite all the training, somehow her brain couldn't even get used to the fact that when she held something in her right hand, she held it with four fingers, not five.

Thinking about her missing finger made her think about the last time she'd had to point a pistol at a human being. Fuchida Shūzō had cost her more than her trigger finger. She'd actually flatlined after he rammed his katana through her gut, and she had matching scars on her belly and back to prove it. But more than this, he'd scarred her self-confidence. Everyone on the force knew they could die in this line of work, but Mariko *had* died, if only for a few minutes, and ever since then she wondered how things might have gone if she'd pulled that trigger even a tenth of a second earlier—if she'd put a nine-millimeter hole right in his breastbone, if she'd spared herself the weeks of rehab, if she'd earned herself a bit of detached soul-searching about the ethics of killing in the line of duty rather than ruminations on everything she'd done wrong to let things get that far.

Those ruminations plagued her day and night, and images of Fuchida and his sword flashed in her mind every time she visited the pistol range. Sometimes it got so bad that she couldn't even pull the trigger. The more she *needed* to hit the target dead center, the more she got mired in the fear of failure, and once she fell that deep into her own head, she couldn't even put the next shot on the paper.

Her former *sensei*, Yamada Yasuo, had a term for that: paralysis through analysis. Swordsmanship and marksmanship were exactly the same: the more you thought about what you were doing, the less likely you were to do it right. So long as Mariko trapped herself in doubting her marksmanship, she was a danger to herself and others.

Now, listening to her pulse hammer against her eardrums, she worried she might freeze up when those van doors opened and her team had to move. Two thousand rounds she'd slung down range, trying to train her left hand to do its job, and two thousand times she'd failed. Now other cops were counting on her, and if she failed tonight the way she did with Fuchida, it might be one of *their* lives on the line. She drew back the slide on her Sig again, knowing it wasn't necessary, needing to do it anyway.

She felt a tap on her shoulder pad and looked up. "Hey," Han said, "you think you checked that weapon enough yet?"

It was a little embarrassing being caught in the act, but the fact that he'd noticed was reassuring. Han and Mariko were partners now, and his attention to detail might save her ass someday. She'd already made a habit of noting the details about him. He always put his helmet on at the last minute. He tended to bounce a little on the balls of his feet when he was nervous. He had an app on his phone that gave him inning-by-inning updates on his Yomiuri Giants. The TMPD patch velcroed to the front of his bulletproof vest was old, curling at the corners. Hers was curling a bit too — the vests usually sat in storage, sometimes for years, and who would ever bother to peel the patches off? — but Han's patch had a weaker hold on his chest, probably because he brushed the curled-up corner of it with his thumb every time he reached up to brush his floppy hair away from his ear. He wore his hair longer than regulations allowed, and his sideburns — longer and bushier than Mariko had ever seen in a Japanese man — were against regs too. But violating the personal grooming protocol was one of the perks when you worked undercover, and Han made the most of it. He'd have worn a beard and mustache too, if only he could grow them, but his boyish face didn't allow him that luxury.

"I'm pretty sure that chambered round hasn't gone anywhere," he said. "Then again, I haven't checked it myself. You mind checking it for me?"

"Smartass."

Han grinned. "Guilty as charged."

She noticed he was bouncing a little on the balls of his feet, and since he didn't make any noise Mariko knew he'd strapped everything down tight. The SWAT guys that filled the rest of the van were equally silent—no mean feat given the close quarters and the sheer numbers of magazines, flashbangs, gas masks, and radios they'd affixed to their armor.

The floor rumbled, someone pulled the door shut, and they were off. The lone red light bulb cast weird shadows. There was an electric tension in the air, a palpable enthusiasm silenced of necessity but champing at the bit. "Han," Mariko whispered. "You ever had to wear a vest before?"

"Sure. At my brother's wedding."

"You know what I mean."

"Not since academy."

"Me neither," said Mariko. She lowered her voice even more and said, "Does it make you scared, knowing they have submachine guns in there?"

"Well, *yeah*."

Mariko took a deep breath through her nose and held it a while before blowing it out. It felt good to have someone on the team she didn't have to be defensive with. With everyone else she was always on her guard, because everyone else was all too willing to see her as a girly-girl if she ever showed a moment's weakness. But she and Han could tell each other the truth—even if only in private—and while she wouldn't be caught dead whining to him, just being able to admit she was scared lessened her fear somehow.

"Jump off point in one minute," the driver said.

That palpable, silenced excitement mounted. It was strange, feeling that much nervous energy restrained by cops who were otherwise as rowdy as hormone-addled teenagers. She couldn't see them well in the red light, but somehow Mariko knew even the SWAT guys were tensing up. "Han," Mariko said, "you put your lid on yet?"

"Nope."

"Well, put it on, dammit. I don't want to tell the LT C-team didn't hit their door on time because my partner bobbled his helmet while he was getting out of the van."

"Jump off in twenty," said the driver. The doors opened up and suddenly the cabin filled with light and industrial stink. Acrid paint smells told Mariko there had to be an auto body shop nearby, and a wind out of the west carried all the smog that Tokyo and Yokohama should have been marinating in. Or maybe that was the exhaust from teams A and D, which pulled away faster and faster as Mariko's van slowed to a halt.

Then she was following Han, her heart pounding just as hard as her heels pounded the pavement. She wished her gear wasn't so heavy, wished her goggles weren't fogging up so soon, wished she'd spent a little less time on the pistol range and a little more time training for her next triathlon.

But just like running a tri, this too proved to be a case of pre-race jitters. She overtook Han as they turned the corner into a narrow alley. She could have passed the SWAT operators too, but she reminded herself that it was their job to breach the target, her job to seize the dope once the target was secure.

As they passed a shabby, weather-beaten, wood plank fence, Mariko got her first look at their target, a two-story slab of beige bricks nearly identical to the buildings beside it. It was one of six, lined up like the pips of a die on a dirty, seldom used lot. Apart from being a tenth as high as most of the buildings in the neighborhood, the target and its little siblings were utterly without character. Light shone through most of the windows, which was good; it was easy to see perps behind them. Mariko kept the darkened windows in her peripheral vision as she ran. Her focus was on the back door, and on the empty expanse of concrete between her and it. It was the only exposed stretch of their approach, but there was no getting to the C-side of the target, the back side, except to cross it. If the buildings on this dirty lot were the six pips on a die, the target building was the lower right pip and C-team was just rounding the lower left. Running right past the two were the twin tracks of the Chūō-Sobu line, where the *clackety-clack, clackety-clack* of the 7:03 was getting louder and louder by the second. There was no crossing the train tracks—they were fenced, and the chief of police had nixed SWAT's plan to just cut through the fences and approach the C-side directly—and so the only way to the back door was to cross that shooting gallery of a parking lot.

Mariko's team tucked themselves into a corner to catch their breath. They waited for the train for the same reason they'd been so careful in strapping their gear down tight: speed and surprise were their only sure defense against automatic fire. The helmet and vest were half armor, half security blanket; every cop knew there was no protection against a lucky shot. Submachine guns could spit out a *lot* of potentially lucky shots.

Mariko heard a little *snik* behind her and turned around to see Han adjusting the straps of the helmet he'd just put on. He shot her a wink and a grin. "Go time."

The train was upon them before she knew it, and then they were running again. Off to Mariko's left, A-team's big black van roared through parking lot side door and B-team was almost to the B-side windows. As Mariko's element reached the C-side door, the SWAT guy with the ram—a damned heavy thing by the look of it; Mariko couldn't believe he'd kept pace with the rest of the team—charged the door and laid into it.

The ram bounced back.

He hammered the door again, but the ram bounced off like it was made of rubber. "Shit," Mariko said. So much for owning the building in the first five seconds.

Now that the train had gone she could hear shouting, shattering windows, the explosion of flashbangs. Now two SWAT guys were on the ram, beating the holy hell out of the door. They were supposed to have made their breach by now. A-team would already have punched right through the front door, and if Mariko's team couldn't punch their door, their suspects would only have A-team to shoot at.

Mariko didn't like the thought of volunteering to draw some of that fire, but the whole point of converging on the target at once was to overwhelm and confuse the opposition. Besides, the longer her suspects had to think, the more time they had to find weapons or flush product down the toilet.

She pulled a flashbang grenade from her belt and set it

on the windowsill behind her. "Get down," she said, and she tried to hide her whole body under her helmet.

White light consumed the world. The concussion was enough to buckle her knees. It sounded like Armageddon but it sure blew the hell out of the window. Mariko hopped through the gap, Han following like her own shadow.

For Mariko the world narrowed to whatever her pistol could see. She put her front sight on the empty doorway, then this corner, then that one, not checking the other two because that was Han's area and she knew he'd do it right. The furniture didn't even register to her except as cover.

With the room cleared she and Han made for the hall, looking for the bathroom. When they raided residences, that was where perps disposed of product, and there was no reason a commercial storefront's toilets couldn't be used for the same purpose. Mariko reached the hallway just in time to see the C-side door exploding inward, finally succumbing to the ram. Two of her SWAT guys breached and held. The other two followed Mariko and Han.

Footsteps thundered on a flight of stairs somewhere nearby. So many voices were shouting through Mariko's earpiece that she couldn't keep them straight. She rounded a corner and saw a balding man in a maroon tracksuit closing a door behind him. She only got a glimpse of the room on the other side of the door, but she thought she saw some kind of heavy machinery back there.

In an instant Han had a pistol on the suspect too, shouting at him to get down, and both SWAT guys had him in the wavering glow of the flashlights under-mounted on the barrels of their M4s. The man in the tracksuit gave all four cops a cocky smile, held his hands up near his head, and let something small and shiny fall from his right hand.

Keys.

That arrogant smile told Mariko all she needed to know. Her suspect didn't care about being arrested. All he had to do was stand there getting handcuffed long enough for some machine on the other side of that door to destroy all of her precious evidence.

She rushed the perp. Still wearing that cocksure smile, he stood with his hands in front of him, as if to offer his wrists. It was the sort of pose she'd only seen in people who had been handcuffed before. Mariko took the tiniest bit of delight in seeing his eyes widen a bit as she drew near. Apparently he assumed she'd slow down before she reached him. But body armor wasn't just for stopping bullets.

She hit him like a wrecking ball. They crashed through the locked door, which, unlike the reinforced door that had repelled the battering ram, was just an interior door like the ones she'd expect to find in the average apartment. She let her shoulder pad sink into her suspect's solar plexus, rolling right over it and up to her feet. Han would be on the guy; Mariko didn't need to look back and check. She didn't recognize any of the weird machines standing in front of her—and there were a *lot* of them—but she didn't need to. She just hit the stop button on the one that was mixing a bunch of white powder.

She learned afterward that the machine was for making those biodegradable packing peanuts, and that doing so involved turning cornstarch into tiny little pellets, which were then subjected to extremely high heat to expand them to their peanutty volume. She also learned that mixing highly combustible amphetamines into the cornstarch wasn't exactly a foolproof method to make a whole lot of speed disappear, but if you let the laced cornstarch hit the pellet processor, it was a great way to flood the building with noxious gases and make the whole neighborhood smell like ammonia for a week. In the moment, though, Mariko stood with her hands on her hips, panting a bit and smiling down at the guy she'd just blasted through the door.

Frowning at the splintered doorframe, Han said, "You know, Mariko, I thought we worked pretty well as a team, but I have to tell you I didn't see that one coming."

Mariko grinned at him, enjoying her adrenaline high. "Opened the door, didn't it?"

"Yeah. But you know, these do that too." He jingled the perp's keys at her. "And these don't give the SWAT guys heart attacks and make them hope they can clear the big room full of weird-ass machines before someone puts a bullet in the chick they're supposed to protect."

SWAT had indeed cleared the rest of the factory floor, and judging by the chatter coming over the wire, the operation was over. It seemed impossible. "Han, how long did this thing take?"

"What, the op?"

"Yeah."

He shrugged. "Starting from when we first hit the back door? I don't know. A minute, maybe? No, less than that, I think."

"Me too. Call it forty-five seconds."

"Okay. So what?"

"So," Mariko said, "was that the best forty-five seconds or what? Damn, I love this job."